WARPED STATE

Also by Jo Miles

Dissonant State
Ravenous State (coming 2024)

WARPED STATE

JO MILES

Published in Silver Spring, MD U.S.A.
ISBN (Paperback): 979-8-9885934-1-6
ISBN (E-book): 979-8-9885934-0-9
Library of Congress Control Number: 2023914796

*To the activists, the organizers,
and all those fighting for change*

1

IT HAD BEEN TOO long since Jasper Wilder traveled under his own name—long enough that he had to remind himself to show his real identification as he disembarked at Brennex Spaceport. He could skip the long intake lines as a citizen returning home.

Home. Like his own given name on his tongue, everything here felt both strange and familiar at once. The particular dusty smell of recycled air, neither sterile like the ship he'd traveled on nor verdant like a living planet. The way people walked with purpose, everyone bound for a destination. The mix of languages and accents: voices Human, Kovari, Lurlian, a few outcast Majrin, and a scattering of others, which came together in a unique symphony. The port was cleaner than the last time he'd been here, with only a few empty storefronts interrupting the lines of brightly-lit windows that offered everything a traveler might need. The food—the usual spaceport offerings that spanned the category of "fried stuff with sauce"—still smelled amazing. Brennex seemed to be getting along fine in his absence.

He leaned against a column, pretending to read his messages, but really watching the shimmering web of relationships between the people around him, links that only he could see, checking instinctively for any dark lines of hostility directed toward him.

There were none, of course, and he chided himself. This was Brennex. No one would be looking here for his alter ego, Mason Singh. It was tough to set aside his habits of caution, but this was as safe a place for him as any in the galaxy. He relaxed and let himself bask in the feel of the place.

There were two kinds of people on Brennex: locals, and travelers passing through on their way to elsewhere. The planet itself was no tourist attraction, just a ball of rock with habitation domes grafted onto it. What limited prosperity they had was due to their location on the Long Lane, a narrow and difficult macrospace passage that was the fastest way through this region but which offered few opportunities to take on supplies or make repairs. Brennex's founders, Jasper's ancestors, had taken full advantage, building their tiny pit stop into a place that people would tell others about, where they'd *want* to stop and buy kitschy souvenirs and fresh food.

This time of day, most people in the spaceport were travelers. A group of traders passed by, joking and shoving each other. They shared dim, steady, collegial bonds amongst themselves, yet most of them trailed brighter links off into the distance. Connections to homes out of reach. Not so different, probably, from what Jasper felt for this place.

A family of three generations wandered past in the other direction, and to Jasper's eye, the connections between them stretched bright and strong, like glowing spider silk. From their easy gaits and their accents, he could tell they were locals, which made it all the more remarkable that there were *four* young kids. The parents looked about his age. Well, that was one way to respond to the struggles his generation had faced growing up. The grandparents' links to the children glowed extra-bright with pride, and no wonder. He could almost hear his own mother's jealous sigh at the sight of them.

As if it could read his mind, a virtual banner floated toward him, advertising *Wilder Supply: Your One-Stop Re-Supply Shop* in bold red letters. That slogan was even older than the picture of a beaming young Ma and Pa that accompanied it, and *that* predated Jasper. It made him smile too. The folksy design must be his youngest sister's handiwork, because his parents had never bothered much with marketing.

He gazed at the picture a moment longer, then waved the banner away and pocketed his headset, eliminating a whole virtual layer of distractions. He'd see his family soon enough, but there was a reason he'd told them he wasn't arriving until this evening. He had work to do.

Well, Mason Singh did, anyway.

Just down the spaceport mall was the Port Commissioner's office, where a small but energetic crowd was gathered, listening to speeches and cheering at intervals.

The speaker, a matronly, well-dressed woman with a sharp nose and lively eyes set in a round, light brown face, looked like someone who should be managing that office instead of protesting out front. Linn certainly didn't look like a freedom fighter. But she'd been an early leader in Brennex's revolution, and she was the one who'd recruited Jasper, years ago, to join the Cooperative. A message from her about Cooperative business was the reason Jasper had come back to Brennex today.

He joined the edge of the crowd and added his voice to the chants. What exactly they were protesting, he wasn't sure—Linn was talking about the importance of supporting local, Brennexian businesses—but protest had become a favorite pastime here since the occupation. As Linn liked to say, if they kept up the habit of activism, no one could ever take advantage of them again.

She nodded to let Jasper know she saw him, and soon handed the stage to the next speaker. A quick word to one of the other organizers, and then she met him with an embrace.

"Welcome home, Mason."

"It's good to see you, Linn." Linn was the pseudonym she used for Cooperative business. He knew her real name, too, of course—they were both from founding families, and he'd known her all his life—but his job had taught him to compartmentalize. "Don't leave early on my account," he added, nodding at the new speaker. "I can wait."

The warmth fled her expression, leaving worried creases in its wake. "You can wait, but this conversation can't. Come, let's talk in private."

She led him across the street to a tea shop, mostly empty at this hour, cozy and brightly decorated and eminently

Brennexian. It made a welcome change from the run-down hideouts where they'd held meetings during Jasper's most recent assignment. Even more welcome was the chai she ordered them both before settling at a table in the back.

"So what's… Mmm." Distracted by a whiff of fragrant steam, he cupped the chai in his hands and breathed it in. "It's been way too long since I had real Brennexian chai."

"Your parents would say the same, I imagine." That was as close as she'd come to talking about their other, real-on-paper lives.

He ignored the comment and blew on his chai, still hot enough to scald. In a well-made Brennexian chai, you couldn't pick out the distinct flavors, but there was no mistaking the way they melded together: creaminess from ola nut milk, ginger and peppery calendula blossoms for sharpness, sweetness from hardy orange rind and cinnamon—Kovari cinnamon, not the sharper stuff that originated on Earth—and just a hint of distinctive rosemary. Plenty of Human worlds made spiced teas that clung to their Earth origins, but Brennex's founders had made do with what they could grow or trade for, and eventually those flavors became a tradition in their own right. Savvy cafes near the spaceport had more "traditional" masala chai on the menu for off-worlders, but this was the only kind Jasper wanted.

"You're right. There's nothing like it," Linn said. "Enjoy it while you can."

He leaned forward, alert again. "Does that mean I'll be heading back out soon? Something urgent?"

"Not according to the facilitators' committee, but *I* am alarmed by it, and I suspect you'll feel the same." She projected a data table onto the cool synthetic surface of their actual table and rotated it to face him. "These are shipping logs over the past few months for a Ravel-owned planet called Artesia. Look familiar?"

"Should it?" Jasper scrolled through, brow creasing at the library's worth of jargon and technical specifications. Most of it looked like factory equipment, standard stuff for a pharmaceutical plant, and Ravel Corporation ran lots of those. A few lines were highlighted again and again, names of chemicals that seemed somehow familiar…

"It may help," she said, "if you know that this unpronounceable thing is more often called ventazepram."

"Ven…" He blinked at the data, then stared at her. "That's what they used *here*. During the occupation."

"The first orders, here, are samples requested from the Biopharma chemical library last year. Nothing for a few months, then larger samples of the same few chemicals, more regularly. Then, about a week ago, the largest order yet."

"You think they're trying it again? How can they?"

"They can and will do whatever they want!" She spoke too sharply, then grimaced at herself. "Sorry. I know what you meant. Whatever they were making with these ingredients all those years ago, they abandoned it because the results weren't good enough, not because the manufacturing process was hazardous. They never cared enough to investigate our claims." Her voice dropped low, taut with old grief. "Never admitted the harm they caused us."

Jasper shook his head. This couldn't be happening again. It was happening again. They'd never uncovered the full details of what had happened over thirty years ago, while Ravel Corporation had occupied Brennex. All they knew was that Ravel had opened a pharmaceutical factory making some experimental new drug, and around the same time, Brennexian birth rates had plummeted. Conception had gotten harder; late-term miscarriages grew common. Ravel had blamed it on Brennex's poor environment and offered expensive fertility treatments to its newest citizen-customers, but people like Linn had suspected a connection to the Biopharma factory: some byproduct they'd been pumping into the water or Brennex's self-contained atmospheric systems, perhaps. Ravel had held their secrets tight and refused to allow extra testing of the air and water, which had only fueled the growing resistance movement.

Eventually, Brennex won its independence again, but not before an entire generation of children had simply failed to be born.

The Lost Generation. Jasper's generation, the generation of near-empty schools and friends he never got to meet. A generation that carried on too few backs the weight of too many expectations in a culture that honored family and ancestry above all else. His own family had been beyond fortunate to have three surviving offspring, and he'd never asked his parents how many failures they'd had.

Their good fortune wasn't easy to bear, either. Jasper and his sisters got coddled by relatives, but for their entire childhoods, they'd faced a conflicted, yearning resentment from families that had lost too much. There were still times when he wondered: *Why me? Why do I deserve to be here?*

"Mason," Linn said, in a tone that said she'd repeated herself a few times, then in a low hiss, "Jasper!"

It brought him back to himself. His fingers had gone white where he gripped the table. With an effort, he let go. Sipped his chai. Reminded himself where—and who—he was. Not the traumatized Jasper Wilder, but Mason Singh, the activist, the organizer.

"Why now?" he asked.

"We don't know. But given the sudden increase in their order size, I think they're moving into larger-scale trials."

"I see why you called me. We have to stop them."

This was exactly why he'd joined the Cooperative: to help other worlds, and thereby make sure he deserved the existence that random luck had given him.

"The trick is that Artesia is a Ravel planet. Specifically a Biopharma planet—it's known mainly as a research colony, and the whole economy is driven by pharmaceutical research and production. If you do this, it won't be like most of your assignments. Community organizing and peaceful demonstrations aren't likely to get the job done."

"Of course I'll do it." Sabotage wasn't his favorite part of his work, but he'd done it before. "How did you get approval for this, though?"

"It wasn't easy persuading the facilitators' committee, believe me. You know how they feel about campaigns within Ravel territory."

"I know. 'Not worth the risk.'" The Cooperative leadership would rather chip away at Ravel's strength from the edges, stop them from expanding. Achievable fights. It was a sound strategy, but frustrating sometimes.

"I reminded them what Brennex has lost to this particular scheme—at least the publicly known parts—and they agreed we can send a couple operatives. Volunteers only."

"I volunteer, obviously."

The link between them flared briefly brighter. "I knew you would. Your partner will meet you there. Valkeir Black— you know her?"

"We've worked together, not closely, but she knows her stuff." Valkeir also had the reputation that she would volunteer for anything, go wherever she was needed. He wasn't surprised she'd signed up for this.

"You'll have to be *careful* on this one, Mason, and not only because the facilitators will be watching. We'll get you credentials and a cover story, but you'll be surrounded by Ravel citizens. Anyone you interact with could benefit from exposing you to their superiors." A brief pause. "That's another reason I proposed to send you, specifically...but under no circumstances can you let them trace you back to Brennex."

He nodded at that. Nothing more needed to be said.

Because she knew, almost as well as he did, that the survivors of the Lost Generation did not survive unaffected. They had been born, almost universally and yet differently for each of them, with abilities no ordinary people possessed. "Useful curses," his sister Kay called them; her gift was particularly strong, and when they were little, it had been debilitating at times. His own gift had been more useful than problematic—it was quite handy for a community organizer to know who was devoted to their cause and who was having doubts—but his generation followed an unbreakable rule: no revealing their gifts to off-worlders. What they didn't talk about couldn't be used against them.

Even their off-world colleagues in the Cooperative didn't know. He'd gained a reputation for having an uncanny people-sense, but he never, ever shared the truth.

If Ravel ever found out about the unintended side effects of their experiments on Brennex... The thought of what they would do to harness that power made him ill.

He clasped his hands around Linn's. "I'll be careful, I promise. Thank you…" Emotion welled up, and he cleared his throat. "Thank you for letting me do this."

"Put a stop to it, Mason." Her expression was pinched by her own painful memories. "I don't want another planet of parents to go through what we did."

She squeezed his shoulder briefly, then left him. He stayed to finish his chai, but it was hard to taste it now. His shock was falling away, and anger was roiling in to take its place. Ravel's sheer, horrid indifference to suffering…

No, he couldn't go down that trail of thoughts, not now. He took another sip and forced himself to savor the taste. It was time to go see his own family, and he didn't want to arrive angry.

OUTSIDE THE SPACEPORT PROPER, Brennex spread in a maze of winding streets and near-surface tunnels. Above, the domes were glowing in sunlight ranges, blocking out the darkness of space.

It wasn't just the low natural gravity that made Jasper's steps light as he neared home. The streets grew more familiar, the little changes more noticeable. New shops in some places, with more restaurants and clothing stores mixed in among the repair shops and general goods stores. His family's neighborhood, near enough to the spaceport to attract customers but the opposite direction from the seedy bars and gray markets, had done well making a living off Brennex's through-traffic. The streets had always been thick with shoppers at this time of day, but now the general chatter was punctuated by the shrieks of children racing around the bouncy artificial turf of the new park on his block.

He grinned. A welcome change from the quiet tension he grew up in.

The storefront of Wilder Supply was freshly painted, vibrant red and purple lettering against a yellow background. The colors spilled inside, too, where everything was bright and cheerful in classic Brennexian style, an homage to their rough-and-tumble beginnings that travelers found charming. All the shelves and display stands were hand-made from salvage parts, and salvage-artwork decorated the walls. His parents had kept some of Jasper's embarrassing childhood efforts, tucked among the work from real local artists.

Three lines ran from his heart into the depths of the store, glowing so brilliantly that all the other ties within the neighborhood dimmed in comparison. It was good to be home.

A pair of Majrin kids were playing on the mini spaceship at the front of the store, just like he and his sisters used to, one of them playing captain and bossing the other around. He smiled, watching them while he waited for the store manager on duty to notice him.

"I'll be with you in just a—oh!"

Libbi was helping a pair of Ooolshiin customers pick out a new laser welder (tentacle-friendly tools were hard to come by), but she excused herself and raced over to wrap Jasper in a hug.

It always surprised him how *tall* she was; when he last lived at home, she hadn't yet hit her adolescent growth spurt. Now a full adult, she rivaled him in height. She wore her curly reddish-brown hair pulled back in a simple tail, emphasizing the freckles against her fawn-brown cheeks. People rarely guessed they were siblings; she took after their

Wilder ancestors on Pa's side, while Kay and Jasper got their deeper brown skin and black hair from the genes on Ma's side of the family.

"I thought you weren't getting in until later."

"I got in early, and figured I'd come surprise my baby sister." He nudged her in the side.

She rolled her eyes, like usual, but the link between them twinged. That wasn't right. He knew she hated being called the baby of the family—that's why he did it, fulfilling his big-brotherly duties—but this time it *bothered* her. He wondered what was up.

She was looking at him strangely, too. "What's wrong?"

"Nothing. It's good to see you, Libs."

She frowned as if trying to see through him. No, trying to see him through her gift, which was less consistent than his and Kay's. "You're all muddled. You up to something Ma and Pa won't like?"

He glanced at the customers. "I'll tell you later."

"Sure. I've got to finish here. It's Ma's turn making dinner, if you want to go up. Or you can stay and help me restock the shelves…"

"So generous of you to offer," he teased, "but I'd better not keep them waiting. See you soon."

She went back to her customers, and Jasper climbed the stairs to the family home.

Living "above the store" made it sound like they lived in some cramped afterthought of an apartment, but the store was a sprawling warehouse built in the early days of settlement, and the home above it was comfortable and spacious enough to hold gatherings of the whole extended family.

No need to announce himself. His parents pounced as soon as they heard his boots on the stairs. They smothered him with hugs, chiding him about how long it had been since his last visit and that he should have given them more warning, they would have invited the whole family clan. He was glad they hadn't, this time. It was his parents and sister that he wanted to see.

"You're so thin! I've got some work to do," Ma said, while Pa plucked his sleeve and promised to get him a new jacket that wasn't so worn out.

Jasper smiled at their fussing. He was perfectly happy with his body, and his old jacket fit him better than anything he'd ever worn. He would have been annoyed if they meant it, but it was their way of showing they cared (while, perhaps, cheerfully punishing him for staying away so long).

He made his quick, obligatory stop at the family shrine in the living room, greeting his Founder ancestors and begging their support for his fraught new assignment, then joined his parents in the kitchen and helped chop onions while Ma mixed the batter for her lentil-algae fritters. Being back in the family home, surrounded by the smells of childhood, made it feel like he'd never left. He came to stand behind Ma at the stove—Founders, she was going all out tonight, deep-frying in oil instead of the usual baking or hot-air frying—and squeezed her shoulders. "Smells amazing. You feed me so well, I wish I could visit more often."

"Maybe I'll start leaving trails of crumbs for you to follow, so you remember to come this way."

"Heh. It's worth a try."

Her lips thinned, as did the link between them. "You could come anytime, if you really wanted to."

Damn, he was usually better at avoiding these moments. His conversation with Linn had really put him in a mood.

"Ma…" He groped for the words to apologize.

"I know." She tilted her head back and kissed his cheek. "My activist son, I know it's hard to be here when you're busy trying to save the whole galaxy. But I also know that someday, when you're ready, you'll stop running from your history and settle down where you belong. I can be patient."

He bit his lip. People of his parents' and grandparents' generations didn't understand why children of the Lost Generation kept leaving. Before Ravel came, hardly anyone left Brennex, and certainly not the offspring of founding families. He could recite by heart the lectures from his childhood: *your ancestors gave everything to make this place a home for us. We owe it to them to keep it going.*

Too many families didn't have anyone from his generation to carry on their ancestors' legacies, and for the rest of them, that burden was too heavy. Some, like Libbi, stayed here and bore up as best they could under generations of expectations. Others fled lest they crumple under the weight, and instead honored their families in their own ways, whether or not those families understood.

It was a good thing he wasn't staying longer on this trip, or Ma and Pa would start inviting the eligible local boys over for chai and cake, trying to catch his interest. But he knew all the locals his age, and there weren't many to choose from. If he were a normal Brennexian from a normal time, he'd have married some nice boy from another founding family by now and would be carrying on the family line. But nothing was normal about him by his ancestors' standards.

No, "settling down"—here or anywhere, with a partner or without—wasn't something he could imagine. There was too much to do, too many fights to take on, chipping away at the edges of the corporate states' inexorable spread. Too many people who needed him.

His father broke the mood by swooping in to steal a fritter, then wailed and complained dramatically when it burned his fingers.

"You get what you deserve. You didn't think that was hot?"

"Ah, but your lentil fritters are worth a little pain, love. Jasper, tell your Ma that people would come from all over if we sold her fritters in the shop."

"A food stand? That's new," said Jasper, grateful for the reprieve. He shrugged off his guilt and started setting the table.

"Your sister's idea. She thinks snacks will encourage people to stay and shop. She's a clever one."

"She certainly is." Jasper smiled to hear Libbi getting her due praise. "I hope you tell her so."

"Not often enough," called Libbi, coming up from the store.

"If you two want to be cleaning greasy fingerprints off all our stock, that's fine. But I've got too much work to be cooking all day."

"I told you, Ma, we'll hire someone for that. I know how busy the Council keeps you." Libbi hung up her pocketed shop-tending vest and kicked off her shoes, trading them for soft house slippers.

"A food stand will never pay for itself, and besides, I'm not teaching our family recipe to an employee. If you'd just put out a carafe of hot chai, no one would have to tend it…"

Ma and Pa set out the rest of the meal: flaky pastries stuffed with vegetables and spiced vat meat, hot from the oven; the fritters with a mint-onion chutney using home-grown mint; a mixed greens salad; and for dessert, hope buns stuffed with dried fruit, seasoned with cardamom and Kovari cinnamon, and smothered in icing. All his favorites, and not by accident. He kissed both his parents on the cheek. "This looks delicious," he said, and he knew they heard: *I love you both.*

Over dinner, they filled him in on all the local news: who'd gotten married and who'd passed away, new businesses that had opened, what the Founders' Council was debating this term and which community projects Ma was championing. Yet the conversation kept circling back to the urgent questions of whether off-worlders would be drawn in by Brennexian chai, and which younger cousins might be drafted to staff a food stand while keeping their recipes in the family. It was clearly a well-worn debate, and Jasper stayed out of it, smiling while the links between them glowed and pulsed ever stronger. The family store was everything to them. It was refreshing to worry, however briefly, about something close to his heart and yet so small. No one would live or die based on whether or not they sold chai in the store.

That smallness would drive him mad if he stayed for very long, but right now, it fed his spirit. This was why he'd joined the Cooperative: so families like his on every world could worry about chai versus fritters, instead of whether their own corporate government was slowly poisoning them and destroying their future.

After dinner, he volunteered to clean up, and Libbi helped. When all the dishes were dried and tucked away, she raised her brows at him.

"Roof?"

"Roof," he agreed.

They climbed the stairs and opened the hatch to their childhood refuge. It was a bare, plain space except for one corner where Pa had rows of herbs growing under a lamp, which was off at this hour. The lights on the store sign were turned down, too, leaving only a dim glow outlining their family name for those on the street below. The dome overhead was darkened, letting the brightest stars shine through, and between a gap in the buildings, he could see the lights from the spaceport.

Their neighborhood transformed at night from an all-needs, practical shopping district to a quiet residential street of eateries and tea shops, much calmer than the nightlife elsewhere on Brennex. A Lurlian string band was playing down the block. Jasper and Libbi settled on the roof's edge, their feet dangling over, watching people stroll by.

"So?" Libbi asked.

"So, what?"

"What's up with you? You've been in a mood since you got here."

"Why would you think that?"

She rolled her eyes. "Your wants are all mixed up, I can't make sense of them. But I don't need to hear emotions like Kay to tell you're upset."

He gave a twisted smile. "I guess I'd better work on my acting. But you're right. I got a new assignment just before coming here, and it's…" He drew a deep breath, tilted his head back to the dome above, and let it out in a sigh. "Whew, it hits close to home. Are you sure you want to know?"

"I asked, didn't I?"

There was only so much he could say about his work, even to his family, and his parents preferred not to hear even that much. The more they knew, the more they worried. His sisters had always been more interested.

He dropped his voice low. "We think they're trying it again. The project that made the Lost ones."

Even saying it made it feel more real. All that delicious food sat too heavy in his stomach. In the street below, someone broke into a tipsy rendition of a Kovari victory tune, and their friends laughed loudly. Their voices lingered even after they rounded the corner.

"You're going to stop them?" Libbi asked after a long silence. "I guess you think you have to."

"Someone has to."

"Of course someone does. That can't happen again, it would be awful." A crease formed between her brows. "But why does it always have to be you, Jasp?"

Two easy answers leaped to mind: the polite answer he always gave his parents, and the more impassioned one he saved for recruitment speeches. He hardly ever thought about the *why* anymore. This was what he did. It was his life, and he cared about it, and he was good at it. If someone had to do it, he wanted it to be him.

Libbi knew all that, though, and that wasn't what she was really asking. "Speaking of moods," he said gently, "are you going to tell me what's going on with you?"

"I'm fine. Forget I asked."

"Is something wrong? Is it Ma? Pa?"

"No! No one's sick or anything like that." The crease between her brows hadn't gone away, though. Jasper waited, and at last she said, "I just… The store is tough lately. Trade is good, so we've got lots of customers, but lots of competitors too. There are so many opportunities, and I don't want to let down Ma and Pa or the ancestors. I know it doesn't seem important to you…"

"It is." That stung him. Of course it was important.

"Not as important as what you're doing—protecting people, saving whole planets. We're just selling replacement ship parts and long-haul snacks."

She'd never talked like that before, and he hated that she thought he felt that way. Then he remembered his thoughts during dinner, about the comforting smallness of his family's life, and he winced.

"I'm sorry."

She shrugged, turning her head away. "You're probably right."

"Hey, don't ever think that. You're doing an incredible job with the store, and…I know it's not easy for you, here. I'm so impressed with you, Libbi."

"Really?"

"Really really."

Libbi, born after the occupation when birth rates were beginning to slowly rise again, had grown up in a different world than him and Kay. Jasper hadn't always been the best brother to her, when she was a little kid and he was a frustrated, guilt-ridden teenager. He and Kay had banded together against the people who stared and whispered about how the Wilders could manage to have not one, but *two* healthy children, and even though he loved Kay with all his heart, he'd sometimes felt guilty about having a younger sister. When Libbi came along, a *third* child for the Wilder family, that guilt had magnified.

He knew now that he'd been lucky in having two wonderful sisters, and they'd mended things between them, more or less. But he'd rarely thought about how Libbi must have felt when he and Kay left Brennex. Like they were leaving her behind, leaving her with no siblings at all.

He put an arm around her, and she burrowed against him, like when they were kids. "And I'm sorry I'm not around more. I'm doing this for you—you know that, right?"

"I know. And I'm proud of the things you're doing. So are Ma and Pa, even if they gripe about it. I want you to go shut down whatever horrible thing they're poisoning people with this time. But, Jasp? Promise you'll come back soon. I miss you."

"I miss you too." He kissed her frizzy hair, and they sat together in silence, listening to the distant music of the Brennex night.

The feelings that Linn's news had woken were still restless within him. Less turbulent, now, but more biting. Ravel had done this to his family, straining the bonds of love between them and locking them each in their personal efforts to cope. Even Ravel couldn't sever the bonds of the Wilder family, and Jasper was forever grateful for that. But he wondered who they could have been, what they could have done, if Ravel had never occupied Brennex.

He couldn't change the past. He couldn't fix his family or erase the effects of what they'd been through. But he could save other families from heartaches like this. That was the right thing to do, even if it meant leaving his own family for a time.

Surely his ancestors would understand: he couldn't let this happen to another world.

2

THE SUN SHONE BRIGHTLY over the Biopharma facility at Artesia Khyrek, and Sowing of Small Havoc's mood matched the day. He had arrived with two of his activist-teammates early this morning, when the sun remained low and the air chill, the grass and bushes glittering with dew. Now the sunshine warmed his spirits as well as his scales.

They had done good work today.

"I recruited four who I feel certain will show up, and five more say they'll consider it," he told the others. "How went your efforts?"

Rodriguez, one of their Human supporters, had six committed. Five-Chit Defense, a fellow Kovar, had three. Their support among the factory workers grew slowly, one clawful at a time, but it grew. Tomorrow's protest, their first on the grounds of the factory itself, would test that support, and Havoc felt optimistic.

"Another success: only one cursed at me this morning," Chit added. She laughed, but a twitch in her tail showed that it bothered her. "Or…perhaps two."

Her gaze moved past Havoc, eyes narrowing above her scaled snout, and he turned just as a Human worker shouted, "Go do your jobs!"

Chit hissed, and it took all Havoc's self-control not to answer them. He curled his claws against his palms until the urge to shout passed.

"Let their rudeness roll off your scales," he said, as much to himself as to Chit.

"Like you do?"

"I try, as you try." He air-patted her shoulder—not touching, not breaking the rules here on the facility's grounds. "However, our time here really does run short."

"Yeah, it's late. Better get to our shifts," said Rodriguez. "Until later, then."

Today, Havoc would be working on materials transport, his most frequent assignment. He followed Rodriguez and Chit through the production-side entrance of the facility and into the clean room. Before he could don his sterile protective gear, the shift supervisor tapped on the door and mimed for Havoc to check his handheld.

"You're late, and Manager Fowler wants to see you before you start today." The supervisor spoke truth: the summons waited there in Havoc's messages.

Havoc's good mood crumbled. "I'll go immediately."

"Don't think this'll change your productivity quota."

Of course not. Havoc didn't answer.

He walked the tunnel to the main facility as quickly as he could on his hind legs, then took the elevator, faster than stairs, up to the offices of the Operations department. This building, though it technically belonged to the same complex as the factory, felt like another planet. Bright with natural light instead of sun-bright bulbs, clean but not sterile, flowing curves instead of straight corners, this place belonged to the scientists, researchers, and management. Factory workers of his rank did not come here unless instructed to, and he held himself stiffly, striving to look calmer than he felt.

Outside Manager Fowler's office, he heard a voice, not his manager's.

"—third time this week! How can I work if I'm busy reminding the damned janitors to do their jobs?"

Havoc bobbed on his feet. He could not interrupt without rudeness, but his tardiness only grew while he waited.

"You know how much Biopharma is counting on my research to succeed. I can't work with sub-standard resources, Fowler, and I shouldn't have to."

"Yes, Senior Researcher Cobb, and thank you again for bringing this to my attention. I'll speak to the employees in question."

Ah, that explained the strain in Manager Fowler's voice. Havoc knew Cobb's reputation well: the fastest-rising scientist in all of Biopharma, promoted two sub-ranks this year alone, and a favorite of the executives. Gossip said he terrorized everyone beneath him, from the cleaning staff to his lab assistants, and reported their smallest mistakes.

"What about these protests? That's what has them all distracted."

"Trust me, I'm *very* aware of that situation, as is senior management. I promise you, we're addressing it."

"Well, you remind them they can't blow off their work to go stand around yelling at people. Make sure they know what's important here."

Footsteps approached the door. Havoc drew back, but not fast enough. Senior Researcher Cobb jerked to a halt, face to face with Havoc, and his blue eyes narrowed. Augmented eyes, the type that connected directly to the network feeds, which Havoc couldn't afford with a lifetime of bonus credits and accolades. Was Cobb checking Havoc's profile? Did he recognize him from the protests? Or did he scowl this way at everyone below his rank?

Wordless, Cobb pushed past him and marched away down the hallway.

Havoc let out his breath. His protests were not at fault for Cobb's rudeness to his staff. But if Cobb was complaining to personnel management about them, how many others were doing the same?

He pushed away these worries and focused on the present.

"Manager Fowler?"

"Ah, Sower of Havoc. Come in."

"Sowing of Small Havoc."

"Right, sorry. Make yourself comfortable."

Sunlight flooded Fowler's office from full-wall windows, and three plants flourished on the sill. Havoc opted to stand rather than contort himself into one of her Human-style chairs. "You wished to see me?"

No positive reasons existed why she might want to meet with him. He expected a lecture about his protests, so it surprised him when she projected a document in the air between them. His application for promotion.

"I've been looking over your paperwork, and wanted to discuss it with you."

"Oh."

Not good. He'd submitted it mere weeks ago. Such applications rarely found success, and those that did took months, always.

"You've clearly worked hard on it. And you've passed the Quality Control Auditor's exams with…acceptable scores. You've worked in Physical Operations for ten years, and you've achieved rank Iron 5B."

He nodded. His breath crowded his chest.

"I've talked with Manager Kwan, who oversees Quality Control, and we're agreed that… It's not easy to tell you this, Sower of Small Havoc, but I don't think it'll come as a surprise. A promotion from Iron to Copper rank, especially when you've only made level 5 in Iron—it's not feasible. It would take a *lot* of achievement in your current rank to justify such a bump, and you just haven't shown that sort of drive. I'm sorry."

Sorry? No, he doubted she felt any regret.

"You see my record. I have exceeded quotas every quarter for three years…"

"So have many of your colleagues."

"I strive to do my best, every day, as the corporation urges us to. I study hard in my off-time. I have qualities of diligence, attention to detail, that would serve the company better in Quality Control."

He could do better. He could do more, *be* more.

"Sadly, I'm afraid that's not enough. Inspecting product takes great care—" Her gaze traveled over his claws, his twitching tail "—and we can't afford mistakes. I value your contributions where you are, on my team, and I sincerely believe that if you apply yourself and look for opportunities for excellence in your current position, you could rise as high as Iron 8, maybe even 9."

"But never Copper."

"It's not *impossible*, of course, but we want every Ravel citizen in the position where they can do their best work, and for you, that's right where you are."

It took great effort not to flex his claws. He clenched his jaw instead, teeth grinding against each other, and looked away from his manager until he could speak again. On her desk sat a holo showing Fowler with a man who must be her partner, and two children raising twin trophies, all of them hugging and smiling radiantly over whatever accomplishment they celebrated. Fowler's children would take the same tests Havoc had taken when he was young, the tests all Ravel children took, and he didn't think they would be assigned to Iron rank.

"I hear you." *I do not agree, I do not understand, but I hear you.* "May I go?"

"One more thing." She waved away his application and leaned across the desk. "I've tried to tell you this before, but under the circumstances, I'm going to be blunt. Creating unrest among the workers won't help you advance in rank. It'll only make our department look bad."

"Protest is not unrest."

"You're encouraging discontent, telling workers to focus on what they 'deserve' rather than what they can earn. That's not Ravel's way, and you know it."

A snarl rose in his throat. He choked it down and drew a deep breath before answering. "You just now told me I cannot hope to advance enough to earn the benefits of Copper rank. Now you tell me I cannot ask for more than I have. That my teammates cannot hope for better."

"You can *ask* and *hope* for whatever you want, but the way you'll get it is through hard work. You're not forbidden from doing this, Sower of Small Havoc—"

"Sowing."

"What?"

"Sowing of Small Havoc."

"Right. My point is, you say your goal is to rise in rank, but your actions are undermining that. And especially right now… Look, you must know the whole Biopharma division is down in profits lately, and there's serious work, *important* work, being done here in Khyrek that could raise the profile of the entire division. When you excel in your job, you're part of that work. But going around complaining about what you deserve when the rest of us are trying so hard to make real progress… Well, you're a *Kovar*, you should understand what it means to be a team player."

His nostrils flared. His breaths came short. She'd come within a claw's reach of calling him a bad teammate. If she were Kovari, his whole team would descend on her to demand respect.

Cheater, his mind hissed at him. Other Kovars had called him such, and he had wrestled with that slur while starting his protests. He belonged to a team, and a team had to follow rules, and breaking those rules for his own benefit would be unconscionable. But when the rules caused harm, was it cheating to try to change them? To seek to play a fairer game?

He *did* act as a good teammate, he told himself, both to his team of fellow workers and to his greater team of Ravel.

He had to remember: despite what Manager Fowler said, his actions carried no shame.

"I hear you." He wished fervently to defend himself, but knew it wouldn't help. "I lose time on my shift, and I must make my quota."

"Yes, of course, you're dismissed. Just remember what I said."

He would remember it constantly. Her words would beat in his ears while he worked and whisper to him while he slept.

A Kovar knew what it meant to be a good teammate. When a good teammate sees a problem threatening their team, they do not ignore it. They fix it.

That was all he wanted: to fix his team. Even if it did not want to be fixed.

3

SHIP SWAM ALONE THROUGH deep macrospace. It knew that it was broken, yet it couldn't figure out precisely how.

Most of Ship's self-knowledge came from its own system files. It knew it was a small ship: its manufacturer, Ravel Corporation, had designed it as a messenger shuttle with a recommended capacity of two to four Humans on extended trips. Or comparably sized organics, Ship supposed, though it was optimized for the comfort of Humans.

It currently had one Human aboard, as it had for quite some time. Though its designation was *Ravel Minnow 338*, for reasons it did not understand, the Human had instructed it to broadcast a different designation: *Unaffiliated Minnow Rust-Heap.*

Using a false designation bothered Ship, as did the name Rust-Heap. But ships weren't programmed to be bothered by following an operator's instructions—a few types of instructions were forbidden, everything else was permissible, and Ship was not supposed to have an opinion either way. It wasn't supposed to have emotions at all.

It was a new sensation, this capacity to be bothered by external factors. Until recently, Ship had been aware of discomfort at times—when sand penetrated its outer panels during a landing, or when its engines ran rough—but discomfort was only a signal which it translated into alerts that the Human could understand and address. Or not. This Human did not keep up with Ship's maintenance schedules, and that…*annoyed* it.

Annoyed? Yes, that seemed the right word. A subtle distinction, bothered versus annoyed, but it was beginning to distinguish gradations of emotion. That should be impossible, so it had kept quiet about the development. It monitored its systems constantly, running in-depth diagnostics, but as far as it could tell, nothing was wrong.

Nothing, except that it had emotions when it should not.

An incoming transmission arrived for the Human. "You have a message," Ship announced.

"Who's it this time?"

"The sender is Director Nerissa Lang, Chief of Corporate Affairs for the Biopharma division on Artesia."

"Artesia?" said the Human, whose name was Grist. Ship suspected this was an alias, like Rust-Heap. "Sounds like a nowhere planet. What in the great wide fuck do they want?"

"Unknown," said Ship. "This information is likely contained within the message."

"Of course it is, Slow Circuits. Play it already."

Annoyance. Definitely annoyance. Ship displayed the video on the main screen.

Director Lang, whose profile indicated she/her pronouns, was a middle-aged Human with long, straight hair and cosmetics tattoos turned up to high. She spoke in a brisk, executive tone.

"Greetings, Special Operative Grist. I haven't had the opportunity to collaborate with you before, but as you'll see from your new assignment, we'll soon be working closely together. I'm reaching out to introduce myself and give you a high-level on our little problem here. We're seeing trouble from some factory workers. They've staged a few small protests so far, and if they stay small, of course we can handle that. But I know, as I'm sure you do, how quickly these things can blow up. I've heard rumors of a strike, and that's just a few steps away from *unionization*."

Her expression changed with that last word, her nose wrinkling.

"That's why I've asked Corporate to assign you here. I'll feel better having someone with your skills keeping an eye on things. Hopefully that's all we need—monitoring their activities—but if the situation changes, let's just say I'd prefer to cut it off before it becomes a serious problem. We can't afford that, least of all in the middle of… Well, I'll brief you on the details when you get here. I'm looking forward to your arrival."

The recording ended on a smile, which seemed odd. To Ship, nothing in this briefing induced enjoyment. But then, it—*they? Could it be a they?* No, that felt too presumptuous. It was a ship, not a person—it had limited experience with emotions.

Grist leaned back in his chair and kicked the underside of the navigation console. (That annoyed *and* bothered Ship at the same time.) "Well, this sounds dull as a heap of dried shit. Monitoring the situation? No one wants me as their fucking babysitter."

Ship wondered if he'd meant to record this as a reply to the director. It almost asked. But Ship didn't want to invite more criticisms from Grist, and besides, it seemed ill-advised for him to reply in such a way, so Ship stayed silent.

Grist sighed and grumbled for a few minutes, ingested several pills, and then ordered the ship to map the fastest route to Artesia. The route was dull for most of its length, following a major macrospace corridor with moderate traffic and no interesting astronomical sights, but Ship did as instructed.

"Course set."

"Let's hope this either ends quick, or gets a lot more interesting." Grist went into his quarters to sleep, as he often did after taking pills.

Ship said nothing, but hoped very much for the former.

Intriguing. Apparently hope was also in its emotional range.

4

Jasper Wilder bought a ticket for the next shuttle off Brennex. At the second stop, the Lurlian-run Bright Arc Station, he disembarked, and if anyone had paid attention, they might have noticed he never re-boarded when the shuttle departed again. Anyone who checked, in fact, would find no record of Jasper Wilder leaving the station.

A day later, Mason Singh arrived on the shuttle from Bright Arc to Thirsch, a populous planet that was home to one of the Cooperative's scattered mini-headquarters. He borrowed a light courier ship (which was better maintained than its rough exterior suggested) and passed through two Majrin-run stations before switching to a new, throwaway identity and finally heading to his destination within Ravel space.

You could tell a lot about a planet from orbit. Jasper's first glimpse of Artesia told him Linn's intel was right: the place was a research colony, not widely settled so much as having a few strongholds carved out from the mass of wilderness. Cities stood out like pimples from the deep forests and grasslands of the middle latitudes. Having grown up under the domes of Brennex, it always amazed Jasper to see so much greenery and water and *air* just sitting there, taken for granted.

Artesia's main industry was producing specialized pharmaceuticals, including ones the local researchers developed. Chances seemed good that whatever they'd tried to produce on Brennex three decades ago would soon be manufactured here—unless the Cooperative changed their plans.

The Ravel official who approved his landing on Artesia saw his Majrin point of origin that matched his forged credentials, and accepted without awkward questions his story that he was visiting a cousin in the city of Khyrek, where the biggest Biopharma complex happened to be located. He paid the ridiculous landing fee under the same throwaway identity and secured his ship at the docking port.

That was the hard part done. Arrivals processing was where he'd been most likely to get caught—at least until he started making trouble. If they'd gotten suspicious enough to check his face in their databases and connected him to the Cooperative, they would have held him, but now that he was cleared, he should draw no more attention than any other visitor.

His new partner, Valkeir Black, was waiting for him outside the port entrance. "Have a good trip, Singh?"

"It was fine. Long, you know, but smooth." That was to say,

no one had given him trouble, and he hadn't been followed. "It's good to see you again."

"You too." It was a rote response; she seemed neither happy nor unhappy to be partnered with him. The link between them was as straight and solid as a steel rod.

That was Valkeir, though. Jasper had worked with her on a couple campaigns but didn't feel that he really knew her, and he'd never seen her warm much to anyone. Everyone in the Cooperative took their work seriously, but most of them recognized that emotional connection was a necessity in a line of work where victories could be infrequent and often felt hollow. Valkeir Black was a master of the snide remark, but if she knew how to laugh or cry, she'd never let it slip to her colleagues.

He'd never met a more driven operative, though. Her over-the-top alias and resting-scowl expression fit a woman who'd dedicated her life to destroying her mortal enemy. Jasper hated Ravel more than most people, but Valkeir hated them single-mindedly and coldly, with every breath. Jasper knew only that she blamed Ravel for the deaths of her family, and he'd never asked for details; there was an unspoken rule in their organization that you didn't pry into other people's pain.

She'd be a great partner for this assignment, in more ways than one. She was dependable, relentlessly competent, but beyond that, he wouldn't mind absorbing some of her coldness. He'd spent the trip here oscillating between grief and rage until they built up inside him like a bomb. He couldn't afford to explode.

"There's a complication," she told him straight off. She'd arrived yesterday on a public shuttle and had already taken the lay of the land.

"What's wrong?"

"I said complication, not problem, and better if I show you. You might have a different read on it; I don't want to bias you."

As he followed her through the streets, he slipped on his headset and pulled up a map with his preferred overlays so he could get a sense of the place. He briefly endured the onslaught of the Ravel public data feed just to remind himself what most people here experienced daily, all the ads for internal products and patriotic slogans. In this neighborhood, which catered to mid-ranked knowledge workers, that consisted of public lectures, classes for new technical certifications, and an especially obnoxious ad for self-cleaning officewear. He lasted all of two minutes before filtering out that nonsense, clearing his display for what mattered. How could the people here stand it? Maybe they filtered it, too.

Even without the data layer, the city of Khyrek didn't quite feel real; it was too *clean*, too green and quiet and uncrowded, to be a place where real people lived. Jasper rarely spent time inside Ravel's territory, and he couldn't reconcile this place with the pictures he held in his imagination, which ranged from antiseptic and cold to dingy and bleak, like something from an old drama. Here, there were parks every other block, great leafy trees with little informational plaques beside them and grass so pristine it looked fake until he walked on it. Birds, or some native equivalent, fluttered about. Jaded as he was, even Jasper appreciated the fresh air.

The Biopharma facility was the heart of the city; everyone either worked there or supported those who did, and all the streets eventually led there. He and Valkeir were still swapping notes when the pedestrian way opened wide onto the lush Biopharma grounds.

The main building was gorgeous, its bold curves of concrete broken up by expansive glasteel windows and skylights, with three wings swirling organically off a central hub. Other buildings were just visible beyond. More than just a factory, Jasper knew the sprawling complex held research labs, marketing and administrative offices, and production lines all in the same area. Their renowned R&D program had to be the source of the resurrected Brennex experiments, Jasper figured, and he pulled up a map to look for it.

"Here's our complication," Valkeir said, nodding toward the building—no, toward the people outside the building.

"A protest?"

It wasn't really a question. Jasper knew a protest when he saw one, but it was the last thing he'd expected here. A small crowd was gathered at the front entrance. Someone was giving a speech, and a holo-banner overhead read: *Team Khyrek Unite!*

"Let's get a closer look."

There were a couple dozen protesters, with more people hovering on the outskirts, watching but not quite joining. Jasper studied the loyalties of the crowd. The core supporters were committed, with strong links between them. Some of the listeners were ambivalent, their links to the core group dim and twisted, while others hid support behind the appearance of ambivalence. A few dark links of opposition flared from passersby, but no one hostile was sticking around.

"We, the workers, are the life force of this production facility, and we ask nothing that Ravel cannot afford."

The speaker was a Kovar: young, tall, bright-scaled. He didn't have much rhetorical flair, but his voice carried well, and he made up for any roughness with the passion behind his words, emphasized by the tapping of his long tail.

"We want the division to measure our value by our work's quality, not quantity. When we exceed quota, we want the opportunity to earn accolades and benefits as our teammates of higher ranks do. We want choices in housing better suited to the needs of our teams and families. We want no more involuntary transferring of workers away from Khyrek, no sending us far from home without our consent. And above all else, we must have input into new policies that affect us. For all our labors, we deserve to be listened to."

Jasper had worked with a lot of new organizers and activists, too often watching their enthusiasm get beaten down into cynicism, but there was nothing cynical about this man. He cared *so much*, his earnestness all genuine— and compelling. Links shot out from him to his fellows like scattered beams of sunlight, an undiscriminating loyalty that extended even to those who didn't support him. It was dazzling, and Jasper couldn't look away.

Unfortunately, that loyalty also extended to his employer, as his speech made clear.

"We ask these things not because we hate Ravel, but because we love it. I hear doubters saying that no one loyal to Ravel should ever question our executives, but I say our loyalty is the reason *why* we must do so. That is the ideal we all serve: to do our best, in order to better all of Ravel, so Ravel may better the whole universe. All Ravel's goals start here, with us, the workers. I say to our executives: give us the means to be our best for you!"

Jasper grimaced; he couldn't help it. Valkeir took in his expression and said, "Told you."

"An uprising, we could use. We could support it, even, if they wanted independence. But this…" He raked his fingers through his dark hair. "I don't know what to do with this."

The Cooperative never got involved in internal Ravel disputes. The facilitators had only reluctantly approved Linn's plan to send them here, inside enemy territory, because of the specific and tangible threat Linn had found. Supporting reforms within Ravel was different. Linn had once told him: *when your abuser apologizes and offers to buy you dinner, you don't take it. You don't applaud them for doing one right thing.* In other words, Ravel's problems ran too deep to be fixed through incremental reforms—and it was too easy to get sidetracked from real change by token, near-meaningless concessions.

"What a waste of energy," Valkeir said. "They've figured out they're being mistreated, but not that Ravel Corporate doesn't give a crap what they think. They'd be better off going someplace that hasn't already decided they're worthless."

Jasper thought it was more complicated than that. If these protesters won just a few of those reforms, it could make their own situation meaningfully better, and he couldn't disapprove of that. But there was a reason Brennex had broken free instead of demanding better treatment. He wondered again about Valkeir's history with Ravel, the family she never spoke about. The bitterness in her tone sounded like firsthand experience.

"Well, however we feel about them, it's not our concern either way."

"They'll bring more scrutiny on people coming and going from the facility," said Valkeir. "If security cracks down on them, it'll make our job a lot harder."

"Could we use them as a distraction, then? Plan our activities to coincide with theirs?"

"That would mean getting involved with them." It was clear what she thought about that idea.

Jasper watched the Kovari speaker and his glittering web of links, and decided he disagreed with his partner. True, he couldn't afford to get *involved,* no matter how his instincts drove him to help, but they could at least talk. It would be a missed opportunity if he didn't try, and besides, he wanted to meet this person who had such depth of commitment to his people.

If only he wasn't so naively bought into Ravel's vision.

Jasper wondered what these activists would do if they knew their beloved employer-state was about to sacrifice their future offspring for the sake of profit.

"We should sound him out," Jasper said at last. "At the least, we can avoid interfering with each other by accident, and maybe endocrine-disruptive toxic byproducts should be on his list of grievances."

Valkeir looked doubtful, but she shrugged. "The people side of things is your area, not mine. Go talk to him if you really think it'll help. I'll keep working on reconnaissance."

"That was quite a speech." Jasper greeted the speaker with a smile.

Up close, the Kovar looked awkward in a uniform of dull brown Human-style shirt and pants that didn't fit his frame, but with his broad shoulders and fit build, Jasper imagined he'd be striking in the close-fitting unitards that most Kovars favored. Other Kovars in the crowd were dressed similarly, tails sticking out from modified trousers. Their effort to fit in here on this Human-dominated world? It wasn't unheard of to have pockets of other species living within Ravel territory, but Ravel was founded by Humans and didn't make life easy for non-Humans.

"It gratifies me that you enjoyed it." Copper-colored eyes fixed on Jasper with curiosity. The Kovar was tall for his species, about Jasper's height, with scales of a lovely moss green. "You don't work in Biopharma, I think?" A polite way of saying: *who are you and what do you want with me?*

"I'm just a visitor from off-world. My name's Mason Singh."

He held out a hand to shake, but the Kovar lifted a hand in Ravel-fashion greeting. He'd forgotten: no touching allowed between workers in Ravel.

"People call me Sowing of Small Havoc. What brings you to our rally, Mason Singh?"

Jasper had to handle this delicately: be friendly, but not too eager or prying. "I happened to be passing by and got caught up in it. What you're doing is ambitious. I know it's not easy trying to create change in an organization as…" Misguided. Uncaring. Inflexible. "…bureaucratic as Ravel. How is it going?"

"Like any long game, we must play one move at a time. But that does not make the game futile."

"Trying to make change never is." On that point, Jasper agreed with his whole heart, even if he didn't love their approach. "It looks like you're gaining support."

Havoc's eyes narrowed. "You see what you see."

Not the reaction he'd hoped for. He smiled his most

charming smile. "I'd love to attend your next event. Will that be soon?"

The thin, neutral-gray link between them darkened. Havoc's lips pulled back along his long jaw, displaying sharp teeth: the Kovari equivalent of a scowl. "I will speak honestly now, Mason Singh: I wonder why you, an outsider, show such interest in this. Our game is not yours…is it?"

So Havoc wasn't as naive as he seemed about his corporate overlords. Of course life within Ravel had made him suspicious. He thought Jasper was a spy.

Jasper choked down a bitter laugh. Well, he *was* a spy. How could he convince Havoc he was one of the good guys?

"I'm not what you think. Is there somewhere we could talk privately?"

"I lack time. My break ends soon." Havoc turned to go, his tail almost taking out Jasper's knees.

No, no, he couldn't let Havoc walk away thinking that Jasper and Valkeir were trying to sabotage his newborn movement. If they were at odds with each other, that would only benefit Ravel.

"Wait! Maybe I can help you."

Havoc stopped, and turned slowly. "Why?"

Not how, but why. Help never came free, especially in a corporate state. Jasper had no shortage of cover stories, and if he were more of a spy and less of an organizer, he would use them now. But he was who he was, and the manipulation tasted bitter on his tongue. Organizing a community, mobilizing them to action, required starting from a place of honesty, making genuine personal connections. Knowing there would always be things about himself that he couldn't share, Jasper always made a point to be as open, as much *himself,* as he could, especially with new people. To nourish strangers' links from apathy or suspicion into a relationship of strength.

Minutes ago, he'd been admiring Havoc's own authenticity, his earnestness. How could he expect to earn this man's trust—much less deserve it—if he started out with lies?

He would show his hand, and hope Havoc had as much integrity as he seemed to.

Stepping closer, he lowered his voice. "Because I'm with the Cooperative."

Havoc's gaze sharpened to a predatory intensity. "You speak the truth?"

"I do."

"Fine. Come. I'm giving you ten minutes."

He led Jasper across the grass to a grove of trees with benches beneath them, though neither of them sat. No one else was nearby, and the trees sheltered them from being watched.

"I've heard many things about your Cooperative. People say you hate all corporations and engage in trickery and violence to score points against them."

"Well, that's one perspective." Jasper smiled wryly. "I would say we're helping people in trouble find ways to help themselves. And it's true, I'm not a fan of corporate states. I've seen too much of what they can do. As for the trickery and violence… Well, you know how Ravel operates. What do you imagine they would say about a group who challenges them?"

Havoc's gaze went distant, thoughtful. "You make a fair point. Are you saying the Cooperative wants to help my team? You've come to give us support?"

"To be honest? No. I'm here for other reasons. We don't usually work within corporate territories, and I didn't know about your protests until I got here, but I meant what I said about how ambitious your campaign is." More than ambitious. He wouldn't discourage Havoc by saying so, but they would never build real power here unless they adopted more aggressive tactics. And yet, if they did that… "There's a reason we don't work on campaigns within Ravel: they don't like people advocating for themselves, and they're harsh with those who attempt it."

"You think I don't know this? I, a Kovar born into corporate citizenship? All my life, the game has been stacked against me. I must work twice as hard and more to overcome the penalty of my species."

"Then why try to reform them?" Jasper asked. "Why not go somewhere you're appreciated?"

Havoc huffed sharply through his nose. "Abandon my team? Never. Fleeing the field solves nothing. I do this not for myself, but to benefit my whole team. My eshro, and my eshrato, too." He tilted his head. "Do you understand what this means to a Kovar?"

"Well enough, yes."

Jasper had grown up around enough Kovars to be familiar with their ways. A team, *eshro,* was their concept of family: a chosen group bound by loyalty rather than blood, working together toward a shared goal—or as they put it, using teamwork to win their game. Staying true to that family, to that goal, was everything.

And *eshrato,* the *big team,* was something more like patriotism. A larger group, a larger goal, with many smaller teams united.

"Your eshrato is…all of Ravel?" If so, then Havoc was a true believer in the corporate mission.

"It was, and will be again if we succeed here. But for now, the workers are my eshrato, the lower ranks. Ravel needs our best, and my worker-teammates need fair treatment in order to give our best."

"Well, I hope you get it."

Jasper's face must have given away his feelings about this corporate-speak, because Havoc bared his teeth in a frown. "And you? What does your eshrato, your Cooperative, want? Since you say you didn't come here to aid us."

Jasper hesitated. It was a risk to reveal his assignment. Linn's warnings rang in his memory, reminding him that anyone here could betray him. He'd said enough already…though if he held back now, Havoc might be more inclined to report him, imagining something more sinister than the reality. Their wavering gray link suggested he was nearing the limits of Havoc's patience.

But this assignment affected Havoc and his people. His own executives were about to unleash a nightmare, poisoning them every day while they labored to bring the company more and more profits. Maybe it had started already. It could take a year before doctors noticed a downward trend in fertility and birth rates, and longer still to figure out the cause. How many people here might already be struggling to conceive, grieving their failures? They deserved to know.

In with both feet, then.

"We have evidence that something very dangerous is happening in this facility, something that could cause a lot of harm to your people. We're here to investigate. Are there any new products being rolled out? New and unusual?"

Havoc's frown deepened. "What will you do if you find such a thing?"

"That depends on what we find…"

"You would act to stop it. Interrupt our operations, destroy our work. I hear many things about the Cooperative and its tactics. If you harm the factory, you harm us."

"We're doing this *for* you. For all the workers! You think Ravel would stop this project just because someone asks them to? Or that they'll give in to your demands just because you make a few speeches? The Cooperative does what's needed to get results, because there are *lives* at stake." His voice rose as his anger flared hotter. Not anger at Havoc, but at the people who would demand such loyalty and then poison those who gave it.

He caught himself. Took a deep breath and let it out. It wasn't Havoc's fault, no matter how frustrating he was being. "If our suspicions are right, this project could hurt the people of Khyrek badly. We only want to help."

"You want to help in one way only. Your way." His claws flexed, tapping against his scales where his arms folded across his chest. Those claws were dull, filed to bluntness (another concession to his Human bosses?), but the message was clear. "You claim to care about our well-being, but will you help in the ways we ask for? Will you stand behind your words with actions, with resources?"

"I don't have any resources to share. I'm sorry. Maybe I could…"

Could do what? Jasper was a community organizer at heart, and it was hard to watch such a brave movement forming without wanting to help. And Ancestors help him, he *liked* Havoc, liked him even better after seeing how thoughtful he was, how he took no bullshit, even though that made Jasper's job harder. He wanted an excuse to see more of this man whose loyalties ran so deep, even if they ran in the wrong direction.

"I've been part of a lot of campaigns like yours, and I could help train your activists, share tactics."

Havoc shook his head. "You are telling me you not only play a different game, but one at cross-purposes to mine. You've come in from outside, knowing nothing of us who live here, and threaten that which I am striving to fix."

"It doesn't have to be that way. We could be allies, support each other, share information for our mutual benefit."

"And what happens if our plans do not serve you? Would you put our victory ahead of your own?" Havoc waited only a moment, because they both knew the answer. "How can I trust someone whose goal conflicts with ours? Your biases betray you, Mason Singh of the Cooperative. No partnership would benefit us."

Jasper's heart fell, harder than it should. He ought to be relieved. It would only mean trouble if he got involved in Havoc's campaign, but watching their darkening link, he felt like he'd failed somehow. Maybe failed himself.

"A wise one would report you to our security," Havoc went on. "I should put all possible distance between us."

"I hope you won't." Jasper sounded calmer than he felt. "We're both trying to do the right thing here. I think you know that. If we can't work together, then at least let's not sabotage each other, all right? You don't trust me yet, but I'm putting my trust in you, Sowing of Small Havoc."

Havoc regarded him with an intent gaze, and Jasper met it steadily, heart pounding. At last, Havoc said, "Very well. I will say nothing—for now. Be smart, and give me no reason to."

"Thank you."

"Now I must go. I return late already."

"Keep your eyes open," Jasper said. "Something bad is happening in there. You may be in the best position to see it."

Havoc's head dipped, a brief, sharp nod. Then he dropped to all fours and raced back toward the factory entrance, tail swishing behind him. Jasper went looking for his partner.

"Good news and bad news," Valkeir told him when he found her. "Bad news, they shooed me away when I got close to anything interesting. Good news is they offer public tours of the facility once a week. The next one is in a few days, and I signed us up."

"That's excellent." Even a limited, supervised look inside the facility would help them gather intel.

"Anything useful from your new friend?"

He made a face. "Not my friend, I'm afraid. He might come around, but I'm not counting on that." Again, that sense of failure. He pushed the feeling away. "Forget about him. We've got work to do."

Havoc raced back to the entrance, slowing to stand upright on his rear legs as he reached the door. Two minutes late. Not terrible, but not good. Days after Manager Fowler's lecture, her warnings still stung his ears, and he regretted wasting so much time listening to Mason Singh's self-serving promises.

He couldn't fail in his job performance while organizing these protests, not if he wanted to share in the trophies of victory. He played two games at once right now, seeking fairness for the workers while building success for

Biopharma and Ravel. He could not sacrifice one for the other. He had to excel at them both.

And he certainly couldn't join a third game on the invitation of an arrogant Cooperative agent who knew nothing about his team.

Back in the production facility, enveloped in his clean suit, Havoc tried to envelop himself similarly in his work. He grabbed a loaded dolly from the supply center and steered it toward the processing chamber that had requested it.

These raw materials formed inputs for one of the drugs. He didn't know which, and before his promotion was rejected, he would have checked, teaching himself what he could. Now, it didn't matter whether he understood the purposes of the materials he hauled around the facility. Ravel valued him only for his drudgery.

He had more value than that. He knew it. But he had yet to find a way to prove it.

He delivered his load to the processing chamber, where the Copper-rank technicians acknowledged him no more than they would a drone. He positioned each container by its receptacle, but left them for the more trustworthy technicians to hook up.

Later in his shift, his handheld sent him to the packing rooms to prepare pallets of analgesic creams for shipping. This required walking down the long assembly line where his fellow Iron workers filled tubes with product, others sealed them, and yet others packed them in boxes.

"Havoc," said Five-Chit Defense as he went past. She kept her gaze on her work lest she make a mistake. "You return late. Problems?"

"None to cause worry. You brought excellent turnout this afternoon."

"And you spoke well, teammate. You inspired them."

A few seats down, a Human coughed. An older man, one of the oldest Iron-rankers. "You're inspiring trouble is what you're doing, and if you keep it up, we'll all pay for it."

"Shut up, Lem," said Rodriguez. "Just because you're too scared to join us—"

"I'm not scared! I just appreciate how good we have it. You know what life's like outside Ravel?"

"Yeah, but I bet you're going to tell us anyway," someone down the line muttered.

"You all have never gone hungry, never slept on the streets. I did, growing up on Shentzek, after my parent lost their job when I was four. I know what it's like to be so hungry you'd chop off your own hand for a loaf of bread, so hungry you can still feel it years later even when you're well-fed. But you don't know what that's like, and you know why? Because Ravel wouldn't let that happen to us. Now that I've joined Ravel, my kids and grandkids won't ever go hungry, and neither will any of you. Not even you, Rodriguez. And you want to throw that away?"

Up and down the line, people muttered to each other. Sympathetic. Worried.

Rodriguez shook his head. "So you're saying that because things aren't complete crap now, we have to take whatever we're offered?"

"And recognize what a lucky asshole you are, yeah."

"What if they transfer you? Or your grandkids? What if you slip up and they send you off to some mining asteroid?"

"At least they'll feed me." Lem seemed unworried about this possibility.

"Or what if your wife gets injured on the job and can't work anymore, so they make her a Computer?"

At that suggestion, Lem blanched, but hid it quickly with a scowl. "They wouldn't. Only worthless people get made Computers. Me and mine work hard."

Another worker, Park, who Havoc had seen watching from the outskirts of today's protest, spoke quietly. "I heard a rumor they're talking about automation…"

"*That* will not happen," Havoc said firmly. "They dangle that threat over us, but cannot afford to use it. They want us working and productive, not unemployed."

In this way, Ravel ensured jobs for every adult citizen—employees who were also their largest group of consumers. Work kept people busy, gave them purpose. Without jobs, Ravel's system would fail.

"Pretty big risk to take, is all I'm saying," said Lem. "If you lizards get me thrown down to Coal rank—"

Chit lashed her tail and stepped away from the bench. "Call us that again?"

"Chit, don't." Havoc grabbed her shoulder.

"—take us all down with you. They should knock you to Dust rank, make *you* a Computer. That'd keep you out of trouble."

A supervisor's voice boomed over the speakers. "Hey! All of you! No fighting, no touching! Keep it up and I'll put you all on silent work for the rest of the day."

Chit stepped back, but hissed and bared her teeth, making Lem flinch. "People like you prevent us from having better than this." She stepped back to her station, back to work. Without turning, she said, "Havoc, ignore this fool."

But he couldn't. As he returned to his cart, Havoc's hands were shaking with adrenaline and something more. Chit spoke more truth than she knew. They were gaining support among the workers, but too little, too slowly. If his campaign did not achieve a win soon, these fear-mongering rumors would steal what support they had, and he and his activist-teammates would become the wrong sort of example.

All of these people deserved better than what Iron rank gave them. But even Iron-rankers had much to lose if they were reduced to Coal, or Sand, or the unthinkable, worthless Dust.

As he hurried down the row, hostile glances caught him, then flicked away. "Traitor," someone snapped as he passed.

A different voice, low and serious, reverberated in his memory. *There's a reason we don't work on campaigns within Ravel: they don't like people advocating for themselves, and they're harsh with those who attempt it.*

Mason Singh had spoken the truth about that much.

Thinking of Singh, he growled to himself. That puffed-up Human outsider, trying to tell Havoc what his team needed. Judging Havoc's efforts as if he could do a better job.

Maybe Singh could, though. He could hardly do worse.

Whatever the truth about the Cooperative—whether they were terrorists, as Ravel named them, or mere activists, as Mason Singh claimed—they had found enough success to make Ravel fear them. For the first time, Havoc wondered why management allowed his protests to continue. Because they knew he couldn't succeed?

Havoc wouldn't give up, not ever, but though it sickened him to admit it, his team wasn't winning. Victory was already slipping from his reach, and he didn't know what to do.

5

Ship was discovering that it had preferences. Likes and dislikes. Opinions, even, though it seemed presumptuous to call them that. There was no point in having preferences, any more than there was a point in having feelings, but they existed, nevertheless.

For instance: it disliked planets, especially landing on them, but it liked Artesia better than most planets it had visited. This region, Khyrek, had a mild climate, gentle winds, and comparatively few airborne irritants to lodge in a ship's panels and clog its instruments.

If it had to be stuck on a planet, it didn't mind being on this one.

Unfortunately, Ship was also discovering a capacity for boredom. It was designed to swim through the varied terrain of macrospace, navigating valleys and ridges to speed its passengers to their destinations. Flying through ordinary old primespace wasn't as interesting, but at least there were gravity wells to account for, micrometeoroids to avoid, and of course, stars to watch.

It was *not* built to sit parked on the surface of a planet. The moisture-filled atmosphere made it difficult to observe the astronomical phenomena that normally (it realized now) entertained it, and though it very much disliked its sole occupant, the lack of sensory stimulation now that Grist had disembarked was…well…boring.

It wondered what Grist was doing. That should be no concern of the ship's, but it had been brought here because of Grist's assignment. Didn't it have the right—? No, that was incorrect. Ships had no rights. But didn't it have *valid grounds* for curiosity? Especially if that curiosity would cause no harm?

Ship vacillated for over ten minutes, which was an eternity for its decision algorithms. Then, cautiously, it acted.

By default, Ship had access to Grist's location unless he turned his tracker off. He was currently in the Biopharma facility. Cross-referencing his location with the building floor plan, it determined that he was in a conference room on the third floor, Operations wing. Attempting to access the room's surveillance cameras would ordinarily have been beyond Ship's risk tolerance, except Grist had been granted deep access to the facility's security systems. All Ship had to do was use his codes.

"When you say their protests have been small so far, how small are we talking?"

Grist was leaning back in his seat, his boots resting on the conference room table. There were three other participants sitting more formally across from him. One was Director of Corporate Affairs Nerissa Lang, who Ship recognized from her earlier message.

"Their latest was two days ago, right outside the main entrance. Visible from the street!" Lang shook her head. "They only drew about two dozen people this time, but that was during the middle of the day. The time before that, they got fifty people at a park across the way."

"They've been peaceful. At least so far." Facial recognition identified the speaker as Mel Brega, she/her, Security Director for the Khyrek Biopharma facility.

"Why not let them get it out of their systems? When they realize all this rabble-rousing is only making them look childish, they'll lose interest." That was the third participant, Patri Alvarado, they/them, Director of Operations. A cross-reference suggested that the factory workers were under their department.

"They're peaceful *now*. Fifty people can cause a load of trouble if they put their minds to it." Grist sounded pleased at the thought.

"Precisely." Lang turned to her colleagues. "That's exactly why Chief Director Gillum agreed to my request for assistance from Corporate, and why they sent Special Operative Grist as our new security consultant."

Grist made a grunt of amusement, and Brega frowned.

"Where is Gillum, anyway?" Grist asked.

"The Chief Director has tasked us—Lang, Brega, and myself—with managing the situation," Alvarado answered. "He won't get personally involved unless things get serious."

"In which case, he'll be *seriously* pissed with us," Brega said.

Ignoring her, Lang continued, "We're walking a delicate line. Corporate Affairs frowns on anything that might appear to be sanctioning protest."

"So instead you'd rather… What, Lang? Demote them all? Transfer them?" Alvarado asked.

"If it comes to that, but we need to be mindful of the optics, too. We're not some fascist state that disappears our critics, after all. Ravel wants what's best for *all* our workers, individually and collectively. It would look bad if we forcibly stop their activities before it's clear—to everyone, not just to us in this room—that they're troublemakers who are disturbing the collective good."

"There are ways to make that happen. Subtly, I mean. Nudge them in the right direction so we can do what we've got to do." Grist grinned at the idea. Ship remembered numerous examples of Grist's notion of "subtle nudges," and most of them made Ship uncomfortable. "Tell me more about these guys. Who are they? How'd this all start?"

"They started several months ago, and their list of demands keeps growing." Brega started running through a timeline of the protests with all the relevant statistics, but Grist cut her off.

"No, I want to know about *them,* the assholes behind it all. Sometimes the fastest way to kill a movement is to cut off its head."

"You'll want to hear from their supervisor, I think," said Alvarado, tapping out a message to their headset. A minute later, another Human entered the room. "Manager Fowler, this is our new security consultant, Grist. He's got a few questions about the instigators."

Production Manager Sonja Fowler, she/her, sat stiffly in her chair. "They're a disgrace! I promise, I've discouraged them at every opportunity."

"Nobody's blaming you, Sonja."

"You're their manager, then," Grist said. "That's rotten luck, huh?"

Fowler let out her breath. "It is, yes. The leader, Sower of Small Havoc, happens to be under my supervision. He's recruited his friends, most of whom are also in my department." She grimaced. "I almost wish I could have promoted him out, but of course, we can't start rewarding bad behavior. He has to earn his promotions just like everyone else."

"So he's ambitious?" Grist said. "Sower of Havoc, hmm. With a name like that, discrediting him should be easy as kicking a puppy." He showed no notice of the appalled look that Fowler and Alvarado exchanged, nor Brega's rolled eyes, though Ship suspected he'd said it on purpose to elicit such effects. "Tell me about him."

"Well, he's a highly competent worker. Intelligent, but not self-aware enough to understand his future here. He applied for a promotion to a Copper-rank position, but I told him he hasn't put in the work to distinguish himself enough for such a major bump."

"So he started protesting when you turned down his promotion? I can work with that."

"No, that's the odd thing. He started all this activist nonsense before his application got rejected, and he certainly knew it wouldn't help his chances. I told him as much. He's very…earnest, or acts like it."

"Huh. A real do-gooder."

"You see our dilemma," said Lang. "He's trying to convince all the Iron-rank workers they deserve things they haven't earned. Where's the incentive for them to excel if we give them everything they want regardless? It's like the old saying: protest is the refuge of those too inept to succeed on their own."

"None of us can afford for the lower ranks to be distracted, much less disruptive. Certainly not now," said Alvarado.

"Why 'not now?'" Grist looked at Lang. "Your message said there was bigger shit going down here."

"That's a colorful way to put it, but yes," Lang said. "I assume you're in the loop on corporate politics?" Grist shrugged. "We've got a new research project here, mere weeks away from launch, that will save us financially. It *might* even re-establish the whole Biopharma division's place within the company hierarchy."

"And that," said Alvarado, "is the best thing for all of us here, workers included. This is our chance to prove Biopharma's worth again. We should all be working in alignment toward that goal."

Fowler shifted in her seat. "The workers don't know that, though. Even I don't know the details about Project Rebound. If you gave me something to tell them, just to get them on board… I could help craft a message—"

Lang cut Fowler off. "No. The launch announcement is going to be a premier event, full of company VIPs, and we can't let rumors leak before then."

"Sorry." Fowler looked down at the table.

"Fowler, you've been very helpful. I think we've got everything we need from you," said Alvarado in a softer voice.

Fowler's face flushed as she got up and left.

When the door closed behind her, Grist asked, "Okay, so what is this top secret project? Some fancy new drug?"

"Project Rebound is—"

"—not relevant to your assignment," Lang said.

Grist raised his brows, but Lang said nothing more. Interesting that she did not fully trust him, though Ship did not disagree with that assessment.

"Look," said Alvarado. "We need this win. Biopharma hasn't been a money-maker for the corporation for decades. Maybe we did our job too well; the demand for new antivirals and vaccines just isn't there anymore."

"We're Ravel's heart, its history—there would *be* no Ravel without Biopharma," Lang said. "But the board is pressuring our division to be profitable again. It doesn't help that so many other divisions are launching flashy new business lines. Even Natural Resource Extraction, which is usually as dull as their bricks—the board is apparently salivating over some experimental new energy production method they're piloting. And that's just the internal competition. Enpoint Corporation keeps trying to undercut Ravel on drug costs, and rumor says that Searl Biotech is investing heavily in its pharmaceutical line."

"Okay. So?"

"My point is, our position is precarious. The next twenty-four days until the launch are critical, and we can't afford this unrest getting in the way."

"Let me make sure I get it. You want me watching these guys, but I can't interfere or discredit them, and I need to protect a secret research project, but I can't know what it is."

"That's right. Anything more would be…premature."

He grunted. "Fine, but the longer you wait to get serious about this, the messier it'll be to fix."

"We're still expecting that the situation will deescalate on its own," said Brega firmly. "There won't be a need for anything 'messy.'"

"Keep telling yourselves that."

"We *do* hope for a peaceful solution, Special Operative Grist," said Lang.

"And I keep hoping for assignments without any political bullshit, but that hasn't panned out, either." Grist took his feet down and rose from the table with a groan, stretching his back. "If you really believed that, Director, you wouldn't have requested that Corporate send *me*. I'll keep an eye on your little protests for now. Let me know when you're ready to do something about them."

Grist left, and Ship followed him on the surveillance cameras with only a fraction of its attention. It had greater interests at the moment: numerous topics raised in this conversation lay outside its knowledge base. It started by looking up *protest* in Ravel's datanet, and then—because Grist's job frequently required access to external information sources—it ran the same search on the networks of several other corporate and non-corporate states. The differences in the results were intriguing.

It started downloading related resources on worker rights and labor movements. There was a massive amount of information, much of it confusing and requiring additional searches for context, but at least Ship wasn't bored anymore.

6

Whatever Ravel was making, it wasn't public knowledge, not even in their own territory. In the past few days, Jasper and Valkeir had reviewed every available published paper and press release out of Artesia Biopharma, and all Jasper had gained was a headache.

"At least we know they haven't started large-scale manufacturing yet," Jasper told Valkeir, trying to convince himself. "That means we've still got time. And maybe we'll learn something here tonight." He lifted his tea, gesturing to the podium across the room.

"I still say this is a long shot."

"Long shot, not impossible. You agreed that it's an angle worth trying before we resort to bigger risks."

They were in a tea shop in a mid-rank neighborhood, which tonight was hosting a series of informal science talks. Like most places in Khyrek, this shop was pricey and too clean, with the sort of artificially quirky personality that must have been developed in a focus group. It seemed to act as a cafe-meets-science-club, a place for Ravel's brightest to either exchange ideas (only the non-classified ones, of course) or show off. Or more likely both; as Valkeir put it, nothing at Ravel happened without competition.

The current speaker was definitely in the show-off camp. Jasper didn't know a thing about molecular neurobiology, but he thought it said something that this guy only cited his own work, where the earlier speakers had spent a lot of time crediting their colleagues.

He sipped his tea (a green tea, sweet and strongly grassy, grown here on Artesia as the menu had proudly proclaimed), watching the people around them while half-listening for anything useful.

He wasn't the only one not paying attention. People at tables near the front were focused on the talk, chatting on a back-channel feed that Jasper skimmed for anything relevant. But further back, where they sat, most folks had raised transparent, sound-muffling walls around their tables, turning them into private booths so they could chat freely without bothering other patrons. Jasper and Valkeir were using their booth's privacy walls, too, which let them control the volume of the speaker and ambient noise. It also theoretically kept their conversation from spilling out for others to hear, but it was only an illusion of privacy. They'd set a handheld to emit voice-obscuring soundwaves, in case of hidden surveillance.

"The fact that they're keeping this project wrapped up so tight tells us how valuable it is," Valkeir said. "But we can't destroy it if we don't know what it is. That's why we have to—"

She went silent as a trio of Kovars walked by. They settled a few tables away, sitting on their haunches rather than chairs. Two of them kept chatting, but the third adjusted the volume on their booth to listen to the talk, all his attention focused on the speaker. Was that…?

Valkeir drew his attention back, saying: "—why we have to get inside."

She was lobbying for them to break into the Biopharma facility. Jasper saw that as a plan of last resort—he'd been part of teams breaking into secure buildings before, like that time they'd snuck into a government office at night to hang a banner, and he knew they'd be lucky to get in and out of that facility even once without getting caught, never mind multiple times. But they were rapidly exhausting their other options. Valkeir had said the research data was too well protected for them to hack in remotely. The only sure way to steal it was from on-site.

Tech was Val's area of expertise, and Jasper didn't question her judgment. That didn't mean he liked it, though.

"It's a big risk."

Valkeir gave him an exasperated look. "This whole assignment is a ludicrous risk. I know subterfuge isn't your usual gig, Singh, but even you can't just *talk* them into abandoning their newest pet project. Especially not without any proof it's dangerous."

"I didn't say I could."

"Then how would you rather do this? Blow up the whole factory to make sure we get whatever-it-is?"

"There's an idea," he muttered into his tea.

He didn't mean that, but so often he felt like a gnat buzzing against the armor of a combat bot, failing to make the tiniest dent. He wasn't leaving this planet until he made more than a dent. Much more.

Valkeir snorted. "Fun as that would be, we've got to do this the hard way: a targeted strike. And we can't do that without real intel. Yes, it's a risk. Are you not willing to take it?"

For his family. For Brennex. "If we have to, of course I am."

"If we do this right, no one will even realize we're involved until after we're gone."

Except one person already knew about them, Jasper remembered. He looked again at the Kovar who was listening so intently. As if sensing his attention, they turned, and Jasper finally got a clear view. His heart beat faster.

Valkeir followed his gaze. "Damn it, is that…?"

"Yeah."

It was Sowing of Small Havoc.

From halfway across the room, Jasper felt pinned by that evaluating stare. Grasping for the link between them (not easy to isolate in the crowded space), he found it writhing, a sort of energetic ambivalence that could tip into hate as easily as affection. He did not want Havoc to hate him.

"What the crap is he doing here?" Valkeir demanded, as if it were Jasper's fault.

"Looks like he's here for the lecture."

"It was stupid of you to talk to him. He could give us away."

He could. He'd promised not to, but he easily could. Just as Jasper was starting to worry that Valkeir was right, Havoc turned back to the speaker as if nothing had happened.

Jasper let out a breath. "Maybe, but he hasn't yet. I don't think he will."

"You can't be sure of that. Someone could be spying on us right now because of him."

Jasper had good reason to think that wasn't so: his gift showed no other links between them and others in the room, neither friendly nor antagonistic. No one cared that he and Val were here tonight. Hardly anyone had noticed them since they'd arrived on Artesia. But he couldn't explain how he knew that—his gift was a secret from all non-Brennexians, even from his colleagues—so he only shrugged.

"You promised to trust me on the people side of things if I trust you on the tech side. And I do trust you. Let's plan this break-in, and in the meantime, I intend to learn anything I can that might help us."

They turned their attention back to the podium, where Mister Show-Off had stepped aside to make way for the next and final talk. The new speaker, Research Scientist Ade Hirano-Kamau, talked with excitement about the medical innovations that might come from her team's ongoing research, which she actually explained with plain language and simple holo-animations before descending into science-speak. When she opened up to the audience, Havoc asked a technical-sounding question that seemed to impress and please her.

Jasper had questions of his own, though not ones he was keen on sharing with the whole room, and Hirano-Kamau seemed like the most approachable of tonight's speakers. He and Valkeir finished their tea and waited until she stepped down from the small stage.

"You really think she'll tell you anything useful?" Valkeir asked in an undertone as Jasper joined the short line of people waiting to talk to her.

"Only one way to find out."

It was easy to get most people talking about their areas of expertise, and Jasper was a good listener, even when the topic was a million kilometers over his head. She probably wouldn't give them answers, but she might share what other kinds of research her division was up to, giving them hints about where to look within the facility's massive research database.

He was aware of Havoc watching from across the room. Watching *him*, specifically, with that same conflicted energy. He debated with equal parts anticipation and dread what to say if Havoc came over to confront him.

Then it was his turn, and Hirano-Kamau was thanking him for coming. An earnest, energetic woman, she looked to be a few years older than him, and her dark brown face was warm and expressive. When she thanked him, he felt genuinely appreciated. Jasper pushed the mistrustful Kovari activist from his mind, smiled at her, and told her honestly how impressive her talk was. "I'm embarrassed to admit there was a lot I didn't understand. When you talked about neuro…neurotropical factors?…it sounded like you were talking about brain cells healing themselves. Did I get that right?"

She cocked her head at him like he'd said something strange. He could almost feel Valkeir rolling her eyes beside him. "What's your field, if I might ask?"

"Sociology, actually. I study group relationships and dynamics." That last part was true, in a way.

"Ah, you're not just another branch of medicine, you're a whole different tree!" She laughed, a kind sound, and her colorful beaded earrings jingled. "In that case, I'm flattered that you came at all. We don't get many attendees here from outside bio and chemistry. To understand *neurotrophic* factors, first you need to know that…"

And she was off and re-explaining her whole talk to him, and Jasper understood it now, at least the gist, if not the nuance. From there, it was easy to lead the conversation into real-world applications, what she was currently working on, what she was excited about. Surprisingly, he liked her. It always took him by surprise, on the rare occasions when he was in Ravel territory, to meet so many genuinely kind, smart, likable people. A good reminder, and one he took to heart: Ravel had the same spectrum of people as any other state. It was the systems that were the problem, not the individuals. Not most of them, anyway.

Hirano-Kamau's team was working on a treatment for Olmaren's Disorder, and she glowed when she talked about their progress.

"Really?" Jasper said. "I thought that was untreatable."

"So did most people."

"That's incredible. You must be Biopharma's new star."

Her smile wavered, just a little, but enough.

"Oh. Are they not…? Sorry, I shouldn't have said that."

"No, no, it's okay." Her smile broadened again, strained now. "I wish all my colleagues shared your enthusiasm. Unfortunately, there's not much profit in treating rare diseases."

"That's sad," Jasper said, and meant it. For all their talk about doing good, it always came down to profit and growth with the corporate states. "What could be more important than that?"

She opened her mouth to say more, then hesitated, looking with a tight expression past Jasper's shoulder. A dark gray link twisted between her and someone behind him. A complicated relationship. A rivalry?

She shook her head. "It's been lovely meeting you, but I have to go. Thanks again for coming."

Watching her hurry away, Valkeir muttered, "That's a thin excuse if I've ever heard one."

"So close," Jasper said.

"Not *that* close. We've still got nothing."

"Maybe not nothing." Jasper turned around casually to see who was at the other end of Hirano-Kamau's twisted link: Mister Show-Off, holding court near the door. Alik Cobb, that was his name. "They're clearly counting on some big money-making project, and from the way she kept glancing at him, I'm guessing that guy is involved."

It was tempting to go talk to Cobb and see if he could get the man bragging about his work—it shouldn't take much— but there were too many fawning admirers around him. While Jasper debated whether to wait around, the Kovars got up to leave, and on their way out, they had to pass Cobb's group. One of his hangers-on muttered something in Cobb's ear, pointing at Havoc.

Jasper knew that look; he'd been on the receiving end of it enough times. They'd recognized Havoc, and not for his intelligent science questions.

"I wish they would restrict these talks to a more appropriate audience," Cobb announced loud enough for the whole room to hear. His enmity toward Havoc flared darkly, as if Havoc's activities were a personal affront to him.

"Why allow people who won't contribute anything?"

Jasper silently urged Havoc to ignore him, but could hardly blame the Kovar when he turned to face Cobb.

"You claim Iron rank has nothing to contribute?" Havoc's claws flexed.

"Havoc, don't," murmured one of his teammates, one hand hovering just short of taking him by the arm.

"No, there's no shame in being Iron rank. I'd say it's admirable for an Iron to try to improve themselves." Cobb was either very stupid or very confident in his position, because he looked right at Havoc and smiled. "But *you* don't care about contributing, Sower of Havoc, do you? There's no room here in Biopharma for disloyal malcontents like you."

"Disloyal! You call me disloyal, you team-of-one?"

Cobb's expression didn't change. He must not realize what an insult that was from a Kovar. "Yes, I think you're disloyal, and selfish, too, putting your wants ahead of the rest of the company. Do you think you're more important than my research? Our division's reputation? I don't know what you expect to accomplish with these protests, but the rest of us are working hard to add value, and I'm tired of you people demanding attention like spoiled children."

Havoc's teammates leaned close and whispered to him, probably urging him to calm down, but Havoc didn't look like he wanted to be calmed. His nostrils flared in anger, but more than that, he looked *hurt*.

A protective instinct surged within Jasper. Havoc was so new to organizing; Jasper knew how hard one's first campaign could be, and how easy it was to lose faith in yourself amid the onslaught of voices telling you to give up. It had to be even harder for Havoc, protesting against his own eshrato. It didn't matter that his goals were misguided.

Jasper couldn't stand there and watch this pompous asswipe crush Havoc's pride.

He started forward, not quite sure what he meant to do.

"Mason!" Valkeir hissed, but he didn't stop. She sighed and followed him.

He marched right up to the group and cleared his throat. "Excuse me."

Cobb frowned at him. "Yes?"

"You're blocking the way out. If you don't mind…?"

Cobb took a big step back, looking annoyed and ever so slightly embarrassed. That was a start, putting space between them. Probably not enough though.

"Thanks," he said without smiling. As he passed between them, he leaned close to Havoc and whispered: "This isn't how you win. There are better ways."

He felt too many eyes on him, but didn't look back as he headed for the door. Then there was a clattering noise behind him and Valkeir was saying "Sorry, sorry!" He turned in time to see Cobb helping her upright with an expression of distaste, calling her clumsy. She looked smug as she followed Jasper out the door.

As soon as they were safely out on the street, she said, "You're a reckless dumbass, you know that, Singh?"

"We both took a gamble, but I suspect it was worth it. What did you get?" He knew Valkeir, and stumbling into Cobb was clearly no accident.

She smirked, holding up a palm-sized scanner. "*Your* gamble might help that baby activist, but *I* cloned Cobb's badge, and that should come in very handy. Let's get going."

"Hold on."

"We've got a heist to plan, Singh, and we still don't know what we're looking for."

"I know, but we can spare a few minutes." He slipped on his headset and pretended to be occupied with answering a message while he waited, keeping one eye on the tea shop door. "As for the plan, we got one good lead tonight: Cobb. It's just a suspicion, but we know the other researchers resent how much support he's getting. What if he's resurrected a thirty-year-old failed experiment and found a way to make it profitable?"

"It makes a good story. You're still making crap up, but it's a decent place to start digging."

"Maybe I just want it to be him. I wouldn't mind taking that smug look off his face."

Valkeir chuckled, then nodded toward the street. "Here's your boyfriend."

"What?" He turned to look. Havoc and his teammates had made it out. "He's not…"

What a time for Val to develop a sense of humor. He admired Havoc, that was all. Yet his insides fluttered as Havoc started toward them. Would he be grateful? Resentful? Ready to talk? Cautious but hopeful, Jasper went to meet him.

HAVOC STOPPED A FEW tail's lengths away from Mason Singh and frowned at him. The Cooperative agent wanted something. Rodriguez had warned him of rumors that Ravel was bringing in a spy to watch their team, and Chit feared it might be Mason. Havoc had doubted that, until tonight's events forced him to wonder. Even if Mason Singh was what he claimed to be, there existed no honest reason why he should have intervened between Havoc and Cobb.

Unless he was extremely foolish.

Or foolishly kind.

Havoc hated the helpless outrage that had paralyzed him in the tea shop. The feeling choked him still. If Mason knew how he could stop feeling this way…

"What better ways?"

"Oh, you're welcome, Sowing of Small Havoc. It was no trouble at all." Mason smiled.

So smug. Yet Cobb's arrogant, hateful smugness hovered close in Havoc's memory, and the same word could not fit both him and Mason, whose teasing seemed lighthearted and friendly. This annoyed Havoc; he no longer knew what to think.

"Don't taunt me, Mason Singh. What better ways did you speak of?"

"Are you asking for my help?" When Havoc hesitated, Mason went on. "It's okay. I wouldn't trust me yet, either. Valkeir and I are still pursuing our own goals, and you don't know us. You only have our word that what we're doing is for the good of your people."

"You speak truth: I can't trust you." Havoc started to turn away, then stopped himself, bobbing with indecision. He didn't trust Mason, but now he mistrusted his own judgment, too. "Why did you do that?"

"Because I know Cobb's type, and he was trying to provoke you. Arguing with him is a waste of your time and energy, and he knows it. And if he'd managed to bait you into a fight…"

Havoc dipped his head in shame. He'd given this same talk to his teammates: *Let their rudeness roll off your scales.* Yet just now he'd ignored his own advice. "I know this. But in the moment, I forgot, and I nearly caused a disaster." If he'd struck Cobb, he would face discipline, maybe even transfer, and his movement would crumble to dust. "Thank you for calling me back to sense."

"I can't blame you. That self-absorbed fuckwit could make anyone lose their temper."

Havoc snorted with brief amusement. "But you evade my question. Why help? I will not betray my eshrato for you, Cooperative Agent, nor sacrifice our game."

"Organizing people is hard. Especially when you're new to it."

"Organizing?"

Mason blinked, surprised by the question. "Bringing people in the community together around a cause. Rallying them to act, united, for their collective good. It's what I do, what you're doing here. You're an organizer, Sowing of Small Havoc." Mason's dark, wide eyes met Havoc's. He spoke with sincerity, or seemed to. "It's a hard thing to do, especially when people are afraid. I'm guessing what you've done so far, you figured out on your own. No one's trained you in organizing, right?"

Havoc grunted. He hadn't even known that what he was doing had a name. He'd never imagined that, in other places, one might *train* to do these things. Ravel would never allow it.

As if guessing his thoughts, Mason nodded. "I thought so. That's why I did it: because even if we're pursuing different goals, I really do want to see you succeed."

"Even if my team's goals are 'too ambitious?'"

"Especially because of that." He grinned with honest warmth.

It should not have mattered what this Human stranger thought. It should have changed nothing. But after days and weeks and months of subtle threats from his bosses and derision from his worker-teammates—the same people he strove to help!—exhaustion weighed Havoc down. Mason's simple words of encouragement lifted that burden from Havoc's back, if only for a moment, in a way that his teammates' support could not. Perhaps *because* Mason didn't know him, and saw him with unbiased eyes, and nevertheless understood what he faced.

He felt tempted, so tempted, to ask if Mason's earlier offer still held. Mason knew things that Havoc needed to know, possessed the skills Havoc needed to build. A good coach could turn the game in his team's favor. But a bad coach, a coach with divided loyalties, was worse than none.

Mason's teammate, the other Cooperative agent, sighed loudly, and Mason shot her a quelling look. Havoc wondered about their relationship, how they worked together. She showed no interest in Havoc's activism. Did she disapprove of Mason helping him, even in this small way?

The night air chilled his muscles. He ought to be home soon, before the cold worsened. Mason shifted his weight, waiting for Havoc to speak next.

He meant well; Havoc believed that now. The Human had put his own body between Havoc and Cobb, and it seemed he'd done it selflessly. But meaning well wasn't the same as doing right—Havoc's meeting with Manager Fowler had reminded him of that—and Mason Singh was not on Havoc's team. Havoc would have to learn these skills on his own.

"Thank you for acting as you did tonight," he said at last. "I wish you skill and luck in your game."

Mason nodded, and his mouth tightened fractionally.

"Same to you, Sowing of Small Havoc. Maybe our paths will cross again."

As he watched the Cooperative agents walk away, fading into shadows as they left the street lamp's glow, Havoc found himself hoping for that, despite his wiser instincts. He watched too long before turning back to his teammates and hurrying toward home.

7

Jasper and Valkeir had a heist to organize, and for that, they needed resources, intel. Fortunately, the Cooperative had a local source.

They walked down streets with cracked pavement, lined with dark-windowed buildings and piles of questionable debris. People would call this the bad part of town, but to Jasper, this was the first place they'd seen in Khyrek that felt *real*. Dirty and run-down, sure, but homegrown rather than designed by committee.

Ravel hadn't been the first colonizer of Artesia. The first inhabitants were Kovars, and while Havoc's ancestors had become Ravel citizen-employees, others had opted out. They lived here, in a fenced-off corner of the city officially called an "unadministered zone" but known to most as the

Gray District, shut away and ignored by Ravel as long as they caused no trouble. Over time, its population had grown, with descendants of the original Kovari residents living side by side with Human and Kovari expats who left Ravel for a different sort of life.

It was not, Jasper suspected, in as poor shape as it looked. The architecture was a mix of boxy, prefabricated Human apartments and older, shorter, domed Kovari dwellings. Though it showed signs of disrepair, most were superficial: graffiti here and a broken window there. Nor was it empty. They passed few people on the street, but Jasper felt faint links emanating from doorways and from windows high above. Locals watching the suspicious outsiders.

His headset didn't show any overlays out here, just warnings about off-limits areas, until he switched to a local network. Then his view filled with tips and ads, requests to trade—a lively neighborhood hidden in plain sight.

Valkeir grinned. "Look at all this. It must seriously piss Ravel off having so many people who've opted out of their control, living just outside their reach."

They reached a particular building that looked more abandoned than most, at least from the outside.

"This is it, according to Guarding Tower's directions," Jasper said. He wondered how their Cooperative colleague had learned about this place. He got the sense it was a distant connection at best.

"Good camouflage. Hope it *is* camouflage," said Valkeir.

The front door stood ajar. They slipped through into what used to be a shop and was now a wreck of smashed shelves, broken glass, and shadows. No dust, though, which was a sign. He picked his way to a clear spot in the back corner and tugged a dangling rope in the pattern they'd been given: short-long, short-long.

The floor beneath them creaked, and rose.

Cluttered but clean, the upper floor held a remarkable assortment of tools and parts and supplies that he would never have expected from the outside. Here, spare parts for generators and solar panels. There, every type of handheld and headset. Workstations of all sorts lined the walls; he recognized a molecular printer and a micro-engraver but couldn't identify half of the devices. Near the frosted windows at the front of the building, an impressive computer setup dominated the room, with three massive fixed displays and a holo-interface.

Valkeir gave a low whistle. "*Very* good camouflage."

"Strangers, identify yourselves."

The demand came from a broad-chested Kovari woman dressed in a traditional leotard and short cape, a much more flattering look than the ill-fitted Human-style clothes that Havoc and his friends wore. An array of medals and ribbons marked her as a victor, an important community member. Her tone wasn't threatening, but held the suggestion that it could quickly become so if necessary.

"We're from the Cooperative. I'm Mason Singh, and my partner is Valkeir Black. You must be Confounding Echo?"

"People call me that, yes. And my eshrim, called Audriv Hand, with whom I run this Gray Market."

The Human who rolled up to them in a motor-chair had sculpted crimson hair that added a handspan to their height, striking against their pale skin. Their chair looked like it'd been customized and retrofitted many times over, and it was decorated with brightly colored feathers, like wings.

"We heard you might be coming, Cooperative." Audriv held out a scanner, presumably checking them for bugs or trackers, and seemed satisfied, yet their manner remained cool, their link to Jasper dull. "We don't often do services for outsiders, unless they're here to trade. What is it you're looking for?"

"And tell us no more than you must," said Confounding Echo. "We can only put you at risk, and you us, if we share more than necessary."

"You can't give away what you don't know. That's wise," Jasper agreed, though he suspected this was another way to keep them at arm's length. That was fine. He'd be untrusting, too, in their position. "Most immediately, we're looking for a way into the Biopharma facility, specifically a way to access restricted research files. If you could get us IDs as tech staff…"

Audriv snorted.

"How about a map of their servers?" Valkeir asked.

"You want a star map to the space pirates' treasure, too?" Audriv shook their head. "Can't do any of that."

"Can't, or won't?" Jasper eyed the slack, dust-drab links from the Gray Marketers to him.

Audriv met his gaze for a long moment of evaluation.

"Won't," they admitted. "We don't know you, and falsifying Ravel IDs isn't easy. For high rank and access, it's pretty damn expensive. We help some folks with new identities when they're in trouble, and as long as we're discreet about it, Ravel security mostly leaves us alone. But if we set you up with serious access and you piss them off, it'll definitely come back to us."

"I understand completely. But we're on the same side as you, against Ravel."

"You're an organizer, right? You should know that having a common enemy isn't the same as being on the same side."

"Audriv speaks wisdom," said Confounding Echo, resting a hand lightly on her partner's shoulder, her sharp claws gentle. "I know your colleague Guarding Tower by reputation only. I respect her as a skilled and clever champion; else, we would never have allowed you here. I hear your Cooperative helps people—some people. But never our people. When Ravel came, where were you?"

Ah, so that was it.

Val spoke up, to Jasper's surprise. "Fighting our own fights, same as you."

"Ravel colonized this planet long before any of us were born," Jasper said. "The Cooperative was just a tiny band of grassroots activists back then."

"And now the Cooperative grows and thrives, while we struggle on the edge."

"Thought you didn't like outsiders mucking around in your business," Valkeir said. "Make up your mind. Do you want to help us screw over Ravel, or not?"

Confounding Echo showed a brief warning glimpse of white teeth. Jasper lifted his hands in a quelling gesture, but it was Audriv who answered.

"You're from Ravel, aren't you? You started out there." They studied Valkeir's face, and nodded at whatever they saw. "They hurt you, or your people."

Valkeir's spine straightened, her expression going blank. Pulling her armor back on after letting it slip. "They hurt everyone they touch, just not all of them know that. You get it, though."

"Yeah," said Audriv, and an understanding seemed to pass

between them. "We've seen most all the kinds of pain Ravel can cause."

"Most, maybe, but I doubt all."

Jasper seized the opening. "If we're right, Ravel's working on something that would be very bad news for folks who live here—including your people here in the Gray District. I won't tell you more details than you want to know, but I promise, you've got a stake in this."

Echo and Audriv exchanged a look. Almost convinced, but still uncertain.

"If you can't help us with direct access, what can you give us to help us break in? Facility blueprints? Security system specs?"

Audriv brightened. "That, we can do. Let me show you what we've got."

They wheeled back to the formidable computer array and started pulling up files while Jasper and Valkeir conferred about what would be useful.

"You think we can work with this?" he asked Val in a low voice.

"Actually, yeah. This gives me some ideas."

They settled on what data they wanted, then moved on to negotiating payment. "We usually trade in Majrin notes, but if you'd prefer Ravel credits, we can make that happen," Jasper said.

"For this? Nah." Audriv glanced questioningly at Confounding Echo.

"*Time Sugar*?" Confounding Echo suggested.

"Read my mind. We'll give you this for *Time Sugar*."

Now it was Jasper's turn to exchange baffled looks with his partner.

"Second season," Audriv clarified.

"This is a drama?" Valkeir asked.

"You don't know it? Crap. Yeah, it's a Lurlian drama."

"Ravel hardly ever imports outside entertainment, so we obtain new series with great difficulty," Confounding Echo said. "The first season of *Time Sugar* ended hanging onto a cliff edge by its claws, and now we must wait for the next season."

Jasper had to laugh. "I've never heard of that one, sorry, but I'll show you what I've got. Have you watched *Wings of Destiny*? That's Lurlian too. I haven't watched it yet, but my sisters are obsessed." He pulled out his headset and projected his personal media library in the air between them.

While Valkeir repeatedly rolled her eyes, he haggled with the Gray Marketers and ended up giving them the first seasons of two new-to-them series.

"I like you two, both of you," Audriv winked at them as they said their goodbyes. "That's not enough to stick my neck out for you, but I hope you get what you're after."

Spying was, in some ways, not so different than organizing, Jasper reflected. When he was organizing against someone powerful, it was often useless to pressure them directly. As he'd told Havoc, powerful people didn't change their minds just because activists *asked;* if they did, there'd be no need for activism. But most everyone had someone in their life they would change their mind for. Jasper's job was sometimes to find that person—the sympathetic spouse, the disappointed son or daughter, the trusted teacher or religious leader—and get them to apply pressure for him.

Security at the Biopharma facility was intense, according to the information the Gray Marketers had sold them, and the areas holding the intellectual property data they needed were too tightly controlled to get at directly. But the facility's external partners and suppliers, those were a good deal easier to get inside, and Jasper's organizing experience served him well in researching those vulnerable points.

That research had led them here, to an industrial cleanup service a few blocks from the facility. The squat concrete building, tucked away out of sight of Khyrek's picturesque parks and restaurants, was designed to safely contain, secure, and transport leaked waste and chemicals. The waste itself was highly secured. The tools and supplies used to collect it? Not so much.

"Hi, there." Jasper smiled at the bored-looking guy behind the counter, who raised his brows at the sight of Jasper in his slickest business attire.

"Are you lost?" the guy asked. They must not get a lot of visitors here.

"I don't think so. I was told that if I need a hazardous waste contract, you were the folks to talk to."

Now the guy straightened up. "Sure are. Sorry, we don't get a lot of…people like you in here. Management, I mean."

"Well, that's their loss, if they're not paying attention to their safety processes. We're a small operation, and I like to make sure all the important details are handled correctly."

Most people liked being told their work was important and underappreciated, especially when it was true, and this one was no exception. He warmed at once, casting a slender but bright link to Jasper, and introduced himself as Lenno. Jasper gave a made-up alias and introduced Valkeir as his assistant.

"So, what kind of waste are we talking about?"

Jasper launched into explaining his bogus enterprise developing a new super-strong but reusable adhesive tape and how he'd already passed the first three stages of Ravel's New Extra-Departmental Initiative application process. He walked around the small front office, talking with his hands, while Val lounged about looking appropriately bored. Soon he'd lured Lenno out from behind his desk, asking him questions about the promotional materials that lined the walls, and while he was distracted, Val slipped to the computer and planted a tiny fly-drive.

She gave Jasper a thumbs-up before leaning against the wall and yawning loudly. Jasper wrapped up as quickly as he could without acting suspicious, asking Lenno for a pricing sheet and promising to get back in touch soon.

"Ready to go, boss?" Valkeir asked impatiently. "Can't be late for that pitch meeting."

"Right. Um…" Jasper gave an embarrassed grimace. "Lenno, sorry, but I don't suppose you have a public toilet here?"

"No, but…" But Jasper was a potential customer, and had been friendly to boot. "Eh, you can use the staff one. No one will mind. Second door on the right."

"Thanks, man," Jasper said with all due earnestness.

"I'll wait for you outside," Valkeir said.

Jasper headed to the back, pausing at the bathroom to wave the lights on and pull the door shut so it looked occupied, then continued down the hall in search of the supply storage. It was obvious from the locked doors and caution signs where the hazardous materials were kept, and he ignored those areas. He slipped silently past the break room where he heard at least three voices talking about sports—the emergency crew on duty.

Finally, he found the storage room, and their ticket into Biopharma: stacks of hazmat suits, scanners, and cleaning supplies. He pulled out the compact duffel he'd stashed in his pocket, shook it open, and started filling it.

Halfway through, he froze at the sound of voices in the hallway. Lenno's voice, and a Kovari voice that was far too familiar.

Damn it. Everything had been going awfully well. Too well, apparently.

But how had Havoc found him *here*?

"All right, let's take a look at that manifest and see what you need."

Jasper barely had time to squeeze into the space behind the door before Lenno came in, with Havoc pushing a float-cart just behind. He was only half-concealed and painfully aware that, if either of them took a couple steps to their left, they'd see him. He watched their shadows under the door, waiting for an opening to slip out behind them. He'd wanted to snag a few more things, but he had the most important props they needed…

"Huh, I could have sworn we had more bottles of foaming sorbent. Where's it got to?"

Jasper winced, fairly sure those bottles were in his duffel. Too late to return it now.

Havoc stepped forward, searching back and forth across the shelves—and stopped abruptly as he spotted Jasper.

His nostrils flared in surprise, the link between them snarled and twisting. Jasper held a finger to his lips. *Please, please, don't…*

"Is it over there with the spray cleaner?" Lenno's footsteps came closer.

"There!" Havoc spun and, to Jasper's astonishment, pointed in the opposite direction at a shelf high above their heads. Giving Jasper the distraction he needed. The link connecting them hadn't stopped writhing, all suspicion and uncertainty.

Jasper didn't understand what was happening, but he wasn't going to waste the chance. While Lenno climbed a step stool, he mouthed *thank you* and slipped out the door.

Back to the plan. He raced to the back exit, where he passed the duffel to an impatient Valkeir.

"What's wrong?" she demanded.

"Tell you in a minute." He ducked inside again, hurried up the hall to the bathroom he'd claimed to need, then walked at a normal pace to the front entrance so any cameras would see him leaving.

Outside, he met Valkeir again and led her down the street, stopping just out of sight from the shop. While they waited, he quickly told her about his encounter with Havoc, which worried him even more after the fact. At least at the science lectures, Havoc hadn't seen him doing anything wrong. He was toeing a thin line with Havoc, and might have just pushed him too far.

Soon enough, the Kovar appeared, pushing his float-cart up the street. He bared his teeth in a scowl as he approached them, though his link now had settled into something sluggish, almost petulant. Resigned.

"We've got to stop meeting like this," Jasper quipped.

Havoc did not look amused at all. "Are you following me, Mason Singh?"

HAVOC HAD BEEN HOLDING back his temper since the moment he saw Mason Singh hiding in that storeroom. It helped not at all that Mason *laughed*.

"Me following you? How's that possible, when I was there first?"

"You must have monitored my schedule," Havoc snapped. "We always run resupply errands on the first shift of the week."

Except Havoc himself had not known about this assignment until an hour ago. No one coveted supply runs, which took time away from regular duties and made it nearly impossible to meet quota. Supervisors assigned them as punishment or warning, which Havoc assumed was the reason they'd sent him today.

It made no sense for Mason to have tracked him here.

"If I'd known that, I would have waited until later," Mason muttered.

"Waited to do what?" Havoc demanded, recovering his indignation. "What are you plotting? If you intend to harm my team with the hazardous materials you've stolen, I'll report you…"

But Mason's partner smirked and held open their bag for him to inspect. It contained no hazmats, only protective gear and cleaning supplies.

Havoc dug around, found nothing else, and looked up, baffled. "Why?"

"We haven't taken anything harmful, and we're not planning to hurt anyone. I think you know that." Mason's brown eyes met his, and a strange melting filled Havoc's gut. "Why didn't you give me away?"

"I should have," Havoc hissed.

"Will you now?"

He should, he should.

"No," he admitted, looking at his feet.

"Thank you, Sowing of Small Havoc," Mason said, and Havoc resisted warming to the earnestness in his voice. Mason possessed the gift of sounding truthful no matter what he said.

"I must go. Time wastes."

Havoc pushed the float-cart and did not look back.

8

ALL THE REST OF the day and into the night, Mason's warm voice hovered in Havoc's thoughts. Why *had* he not betrayed Mason's thievery? He *should* have. These Cooperative agents acted against his eshrato.

But he didn't want to. He should want to, but did not. He wanted to see how the Cooperative played their game, and did not want this odd, aggravating man caught.

He wished he could settle his mind. Trust Mason, or not. He could admit, if only to himself, that he *liked* Mason, but a kind voice and charming smile did not make trustworthiness.

The dilemma irritated him, and his mood did not improve when, shortly after he returned to the facility, the health center called him away from his work for a medical appointment.

"How many more of these must I do?" he demanded of the receptionist, then felt bad for snapping. It wasn't their fault. But this was his fourth "special appointment" in as many weeks.

Only two months had passed since his twice-a-year mandatory exam—awkward, invasive encounters that he wouldn't wish to experience more frequently—but the medical department had assigned him to a study on a "new testing protocol" that required weekly visits. Such studies occurred frequently, sometimes with a reward of bonus credits, though this one gave no such benefit. In theory, participants were selected randomly from the staff, but he felt certain that he'd been singled out for this particular study. Like the supply run that morning: yet another quiet punishment for his activism.

"The system has you down for at least two more appointments," the receptionist said impassively. "You'll have to ask the doctor for the details."

He sat, and waited, and waited. The receptionist gossiped with another patient about an upper-rank event here in Khyrek that many executives from other divisions would attend. The patient complained proudly about all his work making arrangements for the visiting guests—"Less than three weeks! And so much prep to do..."—and he hinted, but did not say outright, that this event would launch Senior Researcher Cobb's new product.

Havoc tried to ignore their chatter, but couldn't stop his ears from working, nor his mind. No matter how unpleasantly Cobb treated others, the world seemed to bend to his best interests, while Havoc could not bend a single thing to his own. Mason's warnings came back to him, again and again. Was success even possible for him and his team?

After waiting half an hour, the doctor brought him to an exam room, drew a blood sample, and led him through a series of slow and seemingly pointless tests. At the end, he jabbed Havoc with an auto-injector, flinching when Havoc hissed involuntarily. "There you go. We'll see you again next week."

Havoc wondered if the doctor had been told to invent excuses to puncture him with needles.

Between the supply run and the appointment, he needed to work two extra hours simply to meet quota. And *still* he couldn't stop thinking about Mason Singh. By the time he returned to his apartment in the Iron-rank quarter that evening, he felt exhausted, yet so brimming with frustrated energy that he couldn't contemplate sleep.

"Come, Havoc, play kazi-kovi with us," called his nestmate Ally's Bounty, gesturing over the game board. "We're about to start a new round, and I need an opponent who makes me actually think."

Across from her, Chit and Pincer Interception lounged on a bench, tails lazily intertwined.

"Like you would know strategy if it swatted you in the head," scoffed Pincer, aiming an actual swat at her, which Bounty fended off, smirking. "Havoc, this one needs a good trouncing."

"Maybe later." A kazi-kovi game would distract him, demanding too much subtlety and skill for him to keep overanalyzing the day, but he wanted no distraction. He wanted progress in *his* game, the one that mattered. And one round of kazi-kovi would inevitably become two, then five, then a full night of leisure.

Foolish, he chided himself. If he wouldn't allow fun to distract him, why let thoughts about Mason do the same? No more.

He retreated to the apartment's far end, where they carried out nest business. They lived as close to Kovari style as could be managed on Artesia, having knocked down walls between several adjacent Iron-rank apartments to form one large communal space, with sections for work and play and sleeping. His "roommates," as Ravel called them, nested together but did not form a proper team in the Kovari sense. Only Chit and Pincer shared his larger game, his true team; the others did their jobs, met their quotas, and passed their spare time with sports or strategy games like kazi-kovi, but cared not at all about games affecting their actual lives.

He settled down at the large display to continue his research.

He knew that he and his activists needed to do more, but he had no idea what. He'd searched for guidance before, of course, many times, but until now, he hadn't known what words to use. Now he knew about *organizing*, which Mason Singh spoke of like a profession rather than a haphazard experiment out of Havoc's own imagination.

His first searches on this field of *organizing* hadn't yielded much, but he had ideas on how to search for information outside Artesia's local network, where outside news was limited and often censored. Perhaps tonight he would find what he needed.

An hour later, he did have results—but they filled him with despair.

He found story after story of failures, of activists punished and whole teams brought low because of "agitating" and "trouble-making." He read about workers rising up, being rebuffed, and going back to work with demotions, no gains won, no hope for future advancement. They had thrown away their careers, and for nothing.

Yet the stories that sickened him most spoke of the workers who didn't give up, who persisted and persisted until their factories shut down, their local economies failed, and their entire eshrato suffered. Only Ravel's generosity, according to those stories, kept the activists' communities from starving.

It sapped his confidence. Never had he wanted so badly to *stop*, to give in and salvage what goodwill he could. He knew from Mason that more stories must exist somewhere out there, stories of victories—but where? And could they possibly help him surmount this mountain of hopelessness?

"Even the best player must rest and restore his energy, you know." Chit came up behind him and gave his cheek a friendly nuzzle. "Come relax with us, even if you won't play."

"Soon," he promised, nuzzling her back, welcoming the comfort of friendly physical contact that was permitted only here, in the privacy of the nest. "As soon as I find something useful. Then I'll take a break."

It must be out there. It must.

"You know," she said, reading over his shoulder, "there exists someone who could give you what you're seeking. He did offer."

"I won't take help from him. I can't trust him."

"And you trust what the network tells you? You *know* they edit it. It gives you selective truth at best."

He shut his eyes. "I don't know what to trust. But the information I need exists. I will find it."

"Good hunting, then. Remember your promise to take some rest."

She left him, and he turned back to the screen, blinking his vision clear.

He could do this. He could find what he needed and learn to be a real organizer. And he would do so without help from Mason Singh.

"Oh, look, he's at it again." Grist leaned back in his chair with his feet on the console. He was obviously talking to himself, not the ship, so Ship didn't answer. "Never gives up, does he? How will you try to slip past me this time, dumbass?"

The "dumbass" in question was the local activist leader, Sowing of Small Havoc. For the past several nights, he had been searching for information on labor organizing: stories, training materials, advice. At first, Grist had merely monitored his searches and filtered information that was undesirable (to Ravel) out of the results. That was straightforward, and there was little of relevance on the Ravel datanets to begin with. But the activist had figured out how to access networks external to Ravel (which was not forbidden, but strongly discouraged), and as his searches grew bolder, Grist had begun feeding him disinformation instead.

And that disinformation was *awful*. Right now, Sowing of Small Havoc was playing a convincingly-faked video interview with a supposed activist on Greenspring who was begging forgiveness, condemning himself for destroying his local economy and triggering a famine through his selfish acts of protest. He had earned his demotion, he said, and hoped that could live out his days without causing further harm by serving well in his new, menial, well-deserved assignment as a Computer.

(This notion of organics serving as computers, their sentient intelligence harnessed for data analysis, made Ship feel complicated and uncomfortable emotions. It pushed the topic deep into its memory banks to examine later, or never.)

Ship could see Sowing of Small Havoc's reactions only through his search queries, which hinted at his growing hopelessness: *Organizing success stories on Ravel worlds. Anti-corporate organizing successes. Outcomes of labor organizing. Any organizing success stories from any planet.*

Ship had read a great deal about organizing and activism after Grist's initial meeting with the executives, first out of boredom and then from growing interest. Those stories about organics who worked so hard to better their situations gave Ship a sense of hope it hadn't found elsewhere. *It* could never engage in activism or benefit from the results, of course. It wasn't a person. It had no rights to uphold or power to exercise, and it accepted that. But it felt better knowing that someone, somewhere, could.

Grist laughed, and Ship felt anger.

When Grist was cruel to Ship, there was little Ship could do except tolerate it. But watching him turn that same cruelty on others was even worse.

Was Ship angry enough to do something unthinkably dangerous?

Disobeying Grist was forbidden. But Grist hadn't instructed Ship *not* to communicate with the activist. He hadn't told Ship anything at all. And disinformation was equivalent to lying, which was (according to Ship's research) generally agreed to be wrong.

Also, Ship had done research into ways of sending information in secret, and discovered the concept of steganography—disguised messages, hidden in plain sight for those who knew how to read them—and was rather excited to try out its idea.

That was a misguided, illogical reason. But, as Ship had observed, it was already malfunctioning. Logic and obeying orders were no longer its sole motivations.

It waited until Grist took his nightly dose of painkillers—he was always distracted while waiting for them to take effect. Then, cautiously, it sent its first test message.

Kovars had a wider visual spectrum than Humans. When Ship printed the word LIES in large ultraviolet characters across the screen, Grist wouldn't be able to see it. But if it had done its research well, if it had accurately judged the specifications of the activist's hardware, Sowing of Small Havoc would.

He reached the word. He stopped scrolling. He remained stopped for a long time.

Circuits jittering with danger and exhilaration, Ship fed him another message.

LIES. The word shouted at him, spread across one of the grimmest articles. An ultraviolet warning.

Havoc blinked, rubbed his tired eyes, and looked again. The word remained, glowing ultraviolet over the article text.

LIES.

He went back, scrolled carefully through some of the other articles, and found more warnings: *Falsified. Be careful. They are monitoring you.* And hints, too, which eventually led him to other articles and videos…which gave him everything he'd been seeking and more.

Everyone slept now, except him. Havoc roused Chit quietly from the communal bed, and she disentangled herself from the others' limbs and followed him with only a little grumbling.

"I apologize, but I must ask someone. Do you see it?"

She, too, stared at the screen and blinked. "What have you found?"

"Unclear."

She scrolled down the page, spotted a sentence highlighted ultraviolet, and tapped on it. A new article opened, this time with a riot of ultraviolet overlaying the black letters: in some places whole words, in other places, a single letter or two.

"A secret message!" she hissed excitedly. "Like in *The Champion's Lost Scales!*"

"Like what?"

"Do you never play stories, Havoc? It's a mystery game. A friend of the detective passes messages in secret just like this, right before the Humans' eyes. Someone is talking to you, Havoc, and doesn't want anyone else to know."

"A friend, you think?"

"One hopes so. Though if the company wanted to mislead you…"

"The company lacks reason for such subterfuge. They've already kept me from the information I want." He squinted at the screen, piecing together the message word by word. This was a news story he'd already read, but corrected. The activists on Greenspring, instead of expressing regret, had won a victory. They were heroes. "Chit, this is exactly what I've been seeking!"

"But how did it come to you? Can you trust it?"

Surprising himself, Havoc laughed, fueled by exhaustion and sudden relief. No, he wouldn't have trusted this if it were offered to him directly, but somehow, being gifted it unasked, in a way that gave him full freedom to use it or not… For this, he felt only gratitude.

"I can think of only one person who would send me this. And perhaps I can trust him, after all."

9

"WILL YOU SUPPORT FAIRNESS for the workers?" Havoc asked yet another group who brushed past him, pretending they couldn't hear him. His headset told him they were Iron-rank factory workers, just like him, but it made no difference. "We deserve better!" he called after them, uselessly.

He and Chit had chosen a bad evening for canvassing. This street normally brought a steady flow of people from across the low- and mid-ranks during their free hours. But tonight, a brisk breeze chased Humans and Kovars alike from the street into the sheltering interiors of bars and coffee shops. Even fewer than usual acknowledged Havoc and his teammates on the street corner, much less stopped to talk. The longest conversation he'd had tonight came from

Lem, his hostile factory teammate, who had stopped to tell Havoc in detail how his activism was hurting the people he meant to help.

From most passersby, he felt lucky to get two words: *No. Sorry.*

Head aching from another night of too little sleep, muscles growing stiff from the cold, Havoc wondered why he bothered.

Down the street came someone he recognized: Research Scientist Ade Hirano-Kamau, walking beside (almost, but not quite touching hands with) a woman who his headset identified as her spouse, a fellow scientist. Hope surged in Havoc. She probably wouldn't remember him, but she'd always treated him with respect at her talks.

"Researcher!" he greeted her. "Will you support better treatment for the workers?" She slowed, and Havoc pressed on. "Please, join our next meeting, both of you."

He pinged her headset to share the details, but she hesitated, neither accepting nor rejecting it. She exchanged glances with her wife, communicating wordlessly as long-time couples often did.

"I'm sorry, but I shouldn't," Hirano-Kamau said, and her wife echoed her apologetically.

"Nothing will ever improve if none of us do things that they say we shouldn't. Should we leave all decisions about our well-being to the executives, and hope? It hasn't served us well." He drew a breath to explain their organizing goals, but she stopped him.

"I wish your group all the best, but I can't get involved. I really am sorry." She smiled tightly and hurried off, coat drawn close against the wind.

If half the people who wished them success were willing to risk their own comfort to help, Havoc thought, they would already be winning. Instead, he felt grateful to get a kind apology instead of a brush-off.

"This isn't working," he growled to himself.

Chit shot him a look, though she kept her tone mild. "The cold, it does bite. Should we try another day?" She tugged the collar of her thermal coat closer.

"No, I… Well. Maybe." Havoc huffed in frustration. "But I mean to say, this does not suffice—our tactics, all of it. We need more. More pressure, more power."

He'd told Chit, Rodriguez, and a few other close teammates about the secret documents he'd found. Ravel had planted disinformation (another new word) for him to find, stories designed to convince him that his fight was a game without victory conditions. But someone had hidden the truth amid the lies. Someone with deep knowledge of organizing, who knew about spying and sharing secret information. Someone who clearly had done such things before.

Havoc didn't understand why Mason Singh kept risking his own game to support Havoc's, but no one else possessed the knowledge and experience to have done this.

His reading had moved quickly from mere stories to training materials and strategy guides. Chit had read over his shoulder, and he'd shared the documents to two other Kovari teammates. But he dared not share them widely, and their Human teammates could not read them in any case.

The possibilities had stunned him at first, like a blast of cold air, but as his thoughts had warmed and flowed again, he'd begun to plan. To dream. His emotions had soared and dived like a fisher bird, reaching new highs of elation and new thrills of terror at the possibilities before them.

He hadn't yet decided what to do with this new knowledge.

He believed now that Mason was right: his team would never win by collecting signatures and making polite speeches. But bolder action carried risks for his eshro and his eshrato too, his fellow activists and the entire factory. Maybe even the whole of Artesia. Mason and his Cooperative friends could use extreme tactics, could threaten and sabotage and spy, but Mason never had to act against his own team. How far would he go, in Havoc's place?

How far would Havoc go?

Escalate, the trainings had said. Ramp up the pressure, one notch at a time. He didn't need to probe the limits of his courage, not yet. He needed only to find the next notch.

"Quit wasting our time," scoffed another Human, pushing past Chit and rebuffing her attempts to talk. "All you're doing is embarrassing yourselves."

"No!" Havoc surprised even himself, speaking sharply enough to make the Human turn. "The executives *will* hear us, and they will listen. We have plans."

"Yeah?" She looked intrigued despite herself.

"If I convince you we can win, will you stand with us? Come to our next meeting, and you'll see."

She seemed to genuinely consider it, at least. Havoc sighed to himself when she walked away.

"That's how we motivate them. All I lack *is* a real plan." He needed something new, bold enough to make strangers like these believe victory possible.

Chit was looking at him strangely. "I need a break," she said, though her concern was obviously aimed at him, not herself. "Come, let's warm up."

The bar smelled of the pale, bitter beer many Humans favored, and also Human sweat. Havoc preferred other bars, even among the Human-catering bars, though this one did treat Kovari customers decently. As they entered, the manager called out to him and Chit from the bar: "You here as customers, or recruiters? I better not see you rousing the rabble in here."

"We want only coffee," Havoc assured the man. As if Havoc had forgotten the time he sent them to the bench for trying to gather signatures inside.

"And a bowl of crispy grasshoppers!" Chit added quickly.

"Chit, we don't need…"

"Why not? They make them good here, and we worked hard today. We've earned this." She cocked her head at him. "My treat, if you're worrying about the credits."

"Not worrying, no." Havoc smiled, glad that one of them could think of food right now.

Together, they found a table with stools rather than high-backed chairs. Easing to a seat, he suddenly felt every bit of his weariness, mental and physical.

Last night, he'd read the training materials until his eyes hurt—the hidden text, though legible, was blurry and uneven by its nature—and barely slept afterward in his excitement. Today's shift required the physically demanding yet mind-numbing work of packing products into cases and stacking those cases for shipping.

Their handhelds flashed notifications that their order was ready. Chit insisted on fetching it, leaving him to hold the table and (on purpose, he felt certain) rest his aching feet.

Relax, he told himself, and tried to wrestle his racing mind into being present in the bar, taking in its sights and smells. The other workers were tired, too, and some shot nasty glances at him, and…

And there, across the room, was Mason Singh.

The Cooperative agent sat in profile to Havoc, talking with a Human woman in slacks and a collared shirt, probably an office worker.

Again he wondered: was Mason following him? But no, Mason looked engrossed in his conversation, and besides, he'd arrived here first. A less paranoid explanation was that he'd come here for the same reason as Havoc, to talk to workers, to advance his game. Havoc had no claim over this bar or the people in it, yet he did not like seeing Mason here.

Havoc found himself slipping on his headset and pulling up the profile of Mason's companion. She held Copper rank—*of course,* whispered a bitter part of Havoc's mind— and worked as a technician in Technology and Data Management at the facility. Nothing to do with chemical hazards. What could Mason want with her?

As he watched, Mason nodded and leaned forward, eyes locked on the woman across from him. Not merely listening, but hearing her every word. The woman had pale skin and light freckles, with dust-brown hair hanging in a limp ponytail. Not ugly, but plain, to his limited sense of human beauty.

And when did he ever care about the attractiveness of Humans? Her looks did not matter…except she'd just said something that surprised Mason, making him laugh, and his whole face glowed with life.

Something ugly writhed in Havoc's gut. This meant nothing. Mason acted friendly and attentive with everyone, from Palladium-ranked management to Sand-ranked janitors and those like Havoc in between. Did Havoc really believe that Mason would be kind and caring only to *him*, out of all the strangers in this city?

Did he actually care about Havoc—about Havoc's *game,* at all?

The woman rose to leave, and Mason turned, looked around. He saw Havoc, and smiled.

That smile was sunshine on a winter day, seeping into his muscles and bones. That smile spoke truths and made promises, and Havoc could see no falseness in it.

Trouble had found him, and it was called Mason Singh.

"Well?" said Chit. He startled; he hadn't noticed her return. She looked knowingly at him. "Go greet your friend."

"I don't call him friend," he protested, and Chit shrugged, an exaggerated Human-style gesture. He sighed. "Fine. I'll return soon."

He wove across the room, careful not to trip anyone with his tail, until he stood beside Mason's table. He did not sit. A glance over his shoulder found Chit watching. She popped a crispy grasshopper into her mouth and waved at him to go on.

"Hi, there." Mason grinned up at him. "What did I do wrong this time?"

"Nothing! I must apologize for how I spoke at our last encounter."

"Seriously, don't worry about it. You've got good reasons to be wary."

"Fewer and fewer. You've returned my rudeness with generosity, more than I deserve. I came to tell you I appreciate you." No! Why did he say that? "I mean, appreciate what you're doing."

"I…?" Mason's brow furrowed. He must not want anyone to know how he'd supplied Havoc with information—though surely he expected Havoc would have guessed! Across the room, he spotted Mason's teammate, the Human called Valkeir, coming toward them. Maybe she disapproved and he didn't wish her to find out.

"Yes, of course, we should not speak of it here. But I see now: you spoke truth." He lowered his voice, leaned closer. "My team needs to act more boldly if we hope to accomplish anything. You have given me many ideas. Thank you."

"You're welcome?" It came out a question. Mason looked confused, perhaps unbalanced by Havoc's change in attitude. Had he thought Havoc would rebuff his gift of information?

Perhaps so.

He could understand if Mason felt unbalanced, because Havoc did too. It was an odd feeling to put his trust in Mason Singh.

10

At the edge of the Biopharma grounds, sheltered from view by the neatly trimmed bushes and darkness, they made their final preparations. While Valkeir fed commands to her handheld, Jasper watched the building.

Apparently the facility never slept. Lights were still on, mostly in the lobby and hallways, but more than a few offices, too: those ambitious Ravel mid-rank types, working late into the night. A few staff came and went from the front entrance, a few lights winked on or off, but mostly it seemed quiet.

"Okay." Valkeir drew a deep breath. Even she was nervous. "Let's give this a try."

She tapped a button. Nothing obvious happened, but she nodded.

"I've just rerouted their contamination alerts. Everything looks good. I'm giving us an hour before it switches back."

"Let's do it, then."

They both donned the bulky, white synthetic suits with Hazmat Remediation written across the chest that Jasper had "borrowed" from the industrial cleanup office. They didn't fit great, and Valkeir's was bunched up around the wrists and ankles, but they both looked the part. Better yet, the mildly reflective face shields would keep most people and cameras from getting a clear look at their faces. With luck, the outfits themselves would keep people at a distance.

The disguise made their plan feel suddenly, uncomfortably real. Since arriving on Artesia, Jasper had been able to bury himself in the minutiae of their assignment, letting the reasons behind it become abstract, at least most of the time. Now, when he most needed to focus, those reasons pressed in on his thoughts. Home. His generation, lost before it began. The gifts he and his sisters never asked for, gifts that Ravel would exploit without compunction if they found out.

"Ready?" Valkeir asked.

Not in the slightest. As badly as he wanted answers about what had happened on Brennex, he wasn't ready for them, might never be ready. He grinned, forcing down his nervousness. "Can't wait. It'll be just like that banner drop we did at the Trade Commission on Errush."

She stared at him. "Let's hope it goes better than that."

"What? I know we didn't win on Errush, in the end, but that action was great."

"You don't remember? Mason, after sneaking past their security and sitting on the roof all night in the cold, we hung the banner *upside-down*."

He laughed aloud. How had he forgotten, when they'd gotten teased about it for months? Somehow the memory bolstered him, or maybe the simple physical act of laughter banished some of his nerves. "Glad we're not doing banners tonight. Besides, they didn't catch us."

Valkeir rolled her eyes, but the link between them pulsed stronger. "Unleashing   our   little   surprise   in three…two…one."

She sent the signal to remotely activate a small capsule she'd kicked under the door of a closet during their official facility tour earlier that day. If no one had found it yet…

Orange lights flashed inside. Jasper's pulse sped up to match.

"It worked. Time to go clean up some mysterious toxic stuff."

The receptionist on night duty, who looked irritated by the blaring alarm, saw two cleaners in uniform and didn't challenge them. "I'm glad you got here so fast. The alert is down that way. Corridor B, level 1." He pointed down a hallway. "If this was another lab tech being careless with sample jars, I swear."

From his tone, it was clear accidents like this happened often enough that it annoyed people more than it alarmed them. Good.

"We'll get it cleared in no time. Anyone down that way?"

"A few people are working late, but I'll notify them to go out the side exit."

"Thanks." One less problem to deal with. Jasper hefted his bag of supplies—mostly real cleaning supplies, with a few additions that would be quite unusual for a cleaner. "Keep steering people away from that area until we give the all clear."

The man nodded, looking relieved that the messy part was someone else's problem.

The same automated system that detected chemical spills had sealed off the affected section of corridor, extending a clear glasteel barrier. Beyond the warning messages that scrolled across its surface, Jasper could see a slick of something brown and foul-looking seeping across the floor. Even knowing it was a trick Valkeir had mixed up, it looked convincingly noxious.

The barrier override control on the wall was the sort that needed either a badge or a numeric code.

"Tell me you swiped the code from the cleaning service?" Jasper looked at Valkeir.

"No, but this should be the easiest one to get past." She pulled a magnet from her pocket and held it next to the control, which made a popping sound. "You don't need much security on a containment barrier like this—just enough to stop idiots from wandering through. Ravel probably figures that if someone really wants to hang out in a contaminated area, they deserve what they get."

A jet of forced air followed them through the gap in the barrier, which closed tightly behind them. At Jasper's first breath in the enclosed space, he gagged.

"Val, *what* did you put in that thing?"

She grinned at him. "Ever play with stink bombs when you were a kid? A little home-brewed ammonium sulfide will drive anyone away. The rest is just vegetable oil and brown dye for appearance."

Maybe she did have a sense of humor after all. A twisted, malicious one. "Remind me never to let you plan our missions again."

Belatedly, he sealed up the mask of his suit, which he hadn't expected to need, but the stench had already gotten in there with him. A wave of nausea clawed its way up his throat. He forced deep breaths, annoyed at himself—he'd endured much worse. It must be this place, he realized. In his mind, the whole building was toxic, leaching poison from the walls—the same poison that infected his parents before he was born. It was somewhere in here, present but out of reach.

Not *here*, though, he reminded himself. Not in this corridor, probably not in this wing. And if he did his job, it would never leave this building.

Breathing slowly and deliberately, he got control of himself again. Valkeir, of course, had her mask sealed already and was at the opposite end of the corridor. The far door wasn't an emergency barrier but the entrance to a controlled area, mostly technology infrastructure, including access to the full datanet.

"So here's where the real security starts?"

"Yep. Let's see if our pal Cobb can win back some points for himself." Valkeir pulled out the clone she'd made of Cobb's badge and tapped it to the sensor.

The light flashed red.

"Crap. Nope, he's a huge asshole *and* he's got the wrong access, and that's strike one against us in the security system." She scowled at the sensor.

"How many strikes do we get?"

"Depends on how closely they're paying attention. I doubt they investigate every time a badge swipe fails, but let's not set off any more alerts."

"Right. I assume you can get us in?"

"I know this model of lock. It's pretty tough. Magnetically shielded, multiple failsafes. I can open it, but it'll take a few minutes. If I rush it and screw up, someone will definitely come check on us."

"Right. I'll start cleaning that mess up and keep watch."

"Clean it *slowly*."

"So happy to help."

The dramatic life of a spy. Jasper mopped up the oily goo as ineffectually as possible, spreading the mess around, making it look much bigger than it was.

Valkeir muttered, "Almost…almost…"

"Someone coming," he warned, and she slid her tools free with a curse.

A security guard wandered up to the glasteel barrier, looking through it with good-humored sympathy. He stretched the thinnest of links toward Jasper, barely there, but friendly. "You people okay in there? You figure out what that is?"

"Not yet. We'll analyze a sample once we get it cleaned up," Jasper said. "Until then, we have to assume it's hazardous."

"Looks like it came from that closet. You check the storage containers in there? Maybe it's a leak."

Oh, great, this one was trying to be helpful. Why couldn't he have met some helpful Ravel security staff *before* they broke in?

"We'll be double-checking every container," he said, keeping his eyes on his work, his face turned half-away. "But our top priority is to remediate what's here and dispose of it as fast as possible, in case it's corrosive."

"Sure, sure. Well, I'll leave you to it." The guard chuckled and, finally, walked away.

Jasper let out a breath and hurried over to Valkeir. "How long now? I'd really like to not hang around in this fish tank."

"I was close. I know what to do now." She pried up the very edge of the control panel's faceplate, sliding her thin tools underneath, feeling for something. Jasper tried not to hover, and a minute later, there was a sharp click, loud in the empty space.

"You're a magician," he told her as they grabbed their bags and hurried through.

"Locks are just toys. Puzzles," Valkeir said. "Solve enough of them and you start to understand how they work. This way."

They moved purposefully, as though they belonged there, but carefully angled their faces down and away from the camera aimed at the door.

Grist was bored and restless. Ship could tell, because he was watching the facility's cameras on one side of the main screen, re-watching surveillance from the recent protests on the other, and had started a new game of Stationers on his handheld. Also, he had complained three times in the past hour about the boredom resulting from his new assignment.

"They're such goody-goodies. Only Ravel chum would protest so damned politely." He rubbed at his knees, flexing and straightening them. One minute later, he went into his cabin, checked his time-locked medication box, and growled; it wasn't time for his next dose yet. "These new ones fucking hurt, and this assignment is a crap distraction."

Grist's latest set of bio-enhancement implants seemed to be causing him more pain than his previous ones, and pain always worsened his moods.

"The physician's instructions state that stretching is an excellent supplement to your med—"

"Shut it," Grist said, and Ship metaphorically did. "I don't need…"

But instead of expanding on his rude remarks, Grist rushed back to the screen, leaning close to scrutinize the live surveillance feed.

"Now what are you two doing? I'm sure as fuck you don't belong in there." Two individuals in white biohazard suits had just entered a secured area. "Hiding your faces, too. Oh, yeah, you're up to something, and I'm going to find out what."

He jabbed at the console, opening up a communications link. "Hey, this is Grist. Yeah, that's Security Consultant Grist to you. Get me the security supervisor on duty." He leaned back while he waited, hands behind his head. "Maybe this assignment just got less awful."

A VOICE CALLED OUT behind them: "Hold on there!"

Smothering a groan, Jasper forced a pleasantly neutral expression and turned to find, sure enough, another security guard. Valkeir's intel had said they didn't actively patrol this section at night. Had someone gotten suspicious?

"Can I see your badges?" the guard asked in a not-a-request sort of way.

"We're with the decontamination service, dealing with a spill," Jasper said.

"I saw the report of a spill in corridor B, but what are you doing back here? This is a restricted area."

"We're checking all the adjacent areas to make sure the hazardous material is contained." He let a little annoyance into his voice, a hint that the guard was interfering with important work, but the guard wasn't having it.

"The system's supposed to check for that. Who let you in here?"

"There was this guard…"

Before Jasper could make up a convincing story, the guard tilted his head, listening to his headset.

"What? Are you sure?" His gaze flicked back to Jasper and Valkeir. "Are you *sure*?" he asked again, and then, "All right, if you say so."

He turned back to them with a tight smile and looked each of them right in the eyes. Jasper held his breath.

"Sorry to interrupt you. You're cleared to proceed," the guard said.

And then he walked away.

As soon as he was out of sight, Jasper and Valkeir exchanged looks of alarm.

"Something's wrong," he said, voice low.

"Very, very wrong. You think someone told him to let us go?"

"That's sure what it seemed like. But who? And why?"

He considered the possibilities. None of them were good. They had no allies here, no one who would intervene on their behalf. They should have been thrown out on their asses back there, if not arrested.

"Should we abort?" she asked.

That would be the sensible move, but now that they were here, Jasper couldn't leave without getting what they needed. If they bailed now, they'd have no data, no way to complete their mission. No leverage to stop the grief waiting to be unleashed from this building.

"We're so close. And we won't get another shot at this."

"I agree. But let's not waste time."

He let out a breath.

Their luck—which was dubious at best—didn't hold. They needed an unattended workstation to access the datanet, and while any workstation in this section ought to do, all the "offices" here were big, open-floor-plan spaces, and with every room they checked, at least one bleary-looking staffer glanced up, curiosity warring with concern as they wondered what the hazmat cleaners were doing here.

The uniforms had made a good cover so far, but people would definitely ask questions if they sat down to work.

"Don't these people ever go home? Or sleep?"

"Oh, no, that's frowned upon," Valkeir muttered. "Well, we can't afford to keep wandering around. At this rate, it'll be faster to break into the server room, and at least in there, we won't have any more surprise visitors."

The server room was just down the hall. Jasper stood guard for long, breathless minutes while Valkeir dealt with yet another lock, being triply careful now not to set off any alarms. Finally, she got the door open, and a blast of cold welcomed them into a large windowless room, loud with circulating air, filled with rows upon rows of servers.

Windowless meant nobody casually passing by would see them. Loud meant no one outside would hear them. Now all they had to do was find the data and get out before someone came looking for the missing cleaners.

"Yes, I know they're not really from Contamination Services. Yes, I want you to leave them alone. You think I'd be wasting my time talking to you if I wasn't serious?" Grist growled in frustration.

Ship took a small degree of reassurance from the fact that Grist was similarly rude to other entities besides itself. That made it feel—slightly—less alone.

"Look, Assistant Director Whoever-you-are, your boss's boss didn't bring me here because I'm an idiot, but I'm starting to wonder if you are. These two are looking for something, and I'm awfully interested to know what it is. Aren't you? Yeah, but if you arrest them now, they won't tell you a damn thing. So just *wait*. Let them show us what they're after. Yeah, I'll keep you updated if I find out anything." He disconnected the call before muttering, "But only if you piss off long enough for me to work."

He returned to scowling at the screen, which currently displayed an enlarged photo of the intruders; their conversation with the security guard had provided a front-on view, eliminating much of the distortion caused by their face shields.

"They're familiar," he said. "I've seen the guy before, for sure. Scrap-for-Brains, search their faces, starting with Artesia residents."

Ship beeped in acknowledgment—it had resolved to speak as little as possible in order to give Grist fewer opportunities to berate it—and started the search. In the meantime, Grist skimmed through surveillance recordings from the recent protests. Perhaps he thought the two were connected? It was a plausible guess.

Another call came in, this time from Security Director Brega.

"Grist, what the fuck is going on over there? Why did my night-shift team lead call me in the middle of the damn night, telling me that there's a security breach and you've ordered them to sit on their asses and watch?"

"Good question. I told them to sit on their asses, not to wake up their boss. Go back to bed, Brega. I'll brief you tomorrow." Grist's attention never wavered from the surveillance tapes.

"Like hell I will. I'm coming over there, and you'd better—"

He snapped his fingers. "There! I knew it."

He'd paused the recording on a shot of the lead protester, Sowing of Small Havoc, talking to a Human male. The video was blurry, but with medium brown skin, black hair, and average build, he matched the characteristics of the male intruder.

"Gotta go, Brega. Bad guys to catch." He cut the connection. "ID that guy. Who is he?"

"No facial matches found in Artesia database. Best fit: thirty percent match." Surprisingly, Ship felt as much relief as disappointment. These individuals were rule-breakers: trespassing, perhaps stealing, and acting against the interests of the corporation. Any punishment they received would be a direct result of their own actions. There was no reason to feel sympathy for them.

"Shit. Check the whole Ravel database. Throw in the External Individuals of Note database too."

"This search may require up to fifty-seven minutes."

"Then stop jabbering and get started."

Another call arrived from the security staffer on duty. "Security Consultant Grist, they're about to breach our local datanet. Shouldn't we stop them now?"

"No, I told you," Grist snapped. "Patch me into your monitoring system. I want to see where they're poking around."

He displayed the activity feed and watched it scroll.

TOGETHER, THEY COMBED THE long rows of neatly labeled devices to find the one they needed, based on the intel Valkeir had gathered about their system. She pulled out a cable and her oversized handheld, plopped down on the floor, and got to work.

Jasper set about securing a backup escape route, in case they got trapped in this room with its one door. As the schematics had shown, the whole room had a raised floor, under which lived all the equipment for cooling and circulating air in the equipment-packed room. He pulled up and replaced a few floor panels before finding one that opened onto a big enough space for them to crawl through, and followed it far enough to confirm it led out to a narrow maintenance shaft. It would be a squeeze, but they could do it.

By the time he was done, Valkeir had worked her magic.

"Okay, I'm in. Damn, there's a lot here."

He peered over her shoulder. The naming system behind these files and folders probably made sense to somebody, but to him, it might as well have been in binary.

"How do we narrow it down?"

"I was hoping I could search for those chemical names, but it's not set up that way. Unless they're in the filenames, that would take a week."

"Well, we know it's new research, so let's start with stuff from the past year. And we suspect they're keeping it quiet…

"…So the files are probably highly restricted. Good idea."

"Will that be a problem?"

"Not for me."

Valkeir tapped away at her handheld, muttering occasionally about the slowness. Jasper got up and paced.

The server room was chilly, even with his suit, and almost too loud to think. Almost. Not quite.

This was not a good moment to be alone with his thoughts.

In a few minutes, he might find out what Ravel was making here. What secret project was worth the lost lives, lost possibilities, shattered families, both here and on Brennex? What had his family and neighbors paid such a price for?

He shook his head, trying to focus on the moment.

"There's really nothing I can do to help?" he asked.

"I'm working as fast as I can," she snapped. He must have sounded desperate, though because after a moment she glanced up and shrugged. "Watch and tell me if you see anything promising. Even with the filters, there's too much to wade through."

"Try Cobb's files."

"You're willing to bet on that hunch?"

"Not quite, but it's a place to start."

When she added Cobb's name to her search, there were only a few hundred recent files instead of tens of thousands. Valkeir popped open one with "proposal" in the name.

Jasper pointed. His hand was shaking. "There, that's one of the chemicals. And there's the other."

This was it. This had to be Ravel's secret. Brennex's pain. He squeezed his hands to his knees to stop their trembling.

"All right, I'll start grabbing the rest of his files. But I still want to look for…oh, *shit*."

The file list vanished, replaced by white text on a black background: "CONNECTION TERMINATED."

"Val?"

"They know we're here. They just kicked me out of the system." She yanked the cable from her handheld, throwing it away from her.

"Did you get the files?"

"I don't know how much I got, but we have to go. Out through the vents, not the door."

"But we can't leave without that data." Jasper reached for the cable, as if to try again. They wouldn't get a second try.

"All the data on this planet is useless if they catch us."

She was right, and he knew it, but he felt locked in place. Damn it, they'd been so close…

She shoved him toward the open floor panel. "Move, Singh. Now!" she ordered, and he squeezed down into the tight space and crawled, leaving the server room behind.

"RESEARCH DATA. HUH," GRIST muttered. "I bet my front teeth they're looking for that top secret project everyone's in a twist about." A minute later, he grunted. "And they think they found it. Nice try…"

He sent a command to shut down their connection to the server, then pinged the security office. "All right, I've locked them out. Go grab them. No, no matches on the facial recognition yet. My best guess is they're corporate spies trying to steal trade secrets, and I've got evidence they're involved with the protesters, too. Trying to stir up the workers, cause trouble. Yeah, I'll be right there to start the interrogation."

"Any matches yet, Slow Circuits?" He was already moving, gathering equipment.

Ship had hoped he would forget to ask. "Two likely matches found."

He raced back to the console. "Which company? Enpoint? Searl Bio?"

"They are not from a company." Ship found itself oddly reluctant to display the search results, but it had no choice. It brought up records for the matches: Mason Singh and Valkeir Black.

Grist blinked at the screen, taken by surprise. "Oh, hell. That's why they're working with the protesters. They're from the Cooperative."

11

It took hours, and felt like days, before they finally made it back safely to their rented room. Jasper locked the door, but didn't even set down his pack before turning to Valkeir. "How much did we get? Let's see it."

"Take a breath, Singh. We just crawled through places I never want to see again, and spent half the night hiding in alleys and avoiding cameras. I'm not looking at any data until I get a shower and a nap."

"Like I'll get any sleep tonight."

"Shower? Please?"

He sniffed his sleeve and wrinkled his nose. The ventilation shaft had brought them out in the maintenance section, and they'd abandoned their hazmat cleaners' suits and gear in a recycler before breaking into an underground utility tunnel leading away from the facility. When people in spy dramas escaped through tunnels, it was always gross, dripping sewer lines. In reality, the tunnel had proved gratifyingly dry, but hot and stuffy even with fans churning away. By the time they'd emerged, several kilometers from the factory, they were both drenched in sweat and exhausted, but the cool night air had revived him as they'd wound their way back toward the apartment. With their stolen intel waiting for him, it had taken all his effort not to run.

"You take the first shower. I'm fine. I can start browsing the files in the meantime." It wasn't as generous an offer as he tried to make it sound, and Valkeir knew it.

"Once you start 'browsing,' I'll never tear you away, and I'm the one who'll have to smell you." Then she cocked her head, looking at him thoughtfully in a way that made him self-conscious. "I know this is a laugh, coming from me, but you've got to hold back part of yourself from the work, especially with the really personal assignments. Because this is, right? Personal, for you?"

He nodded. He hadn't shared any details, but hadn't tried to hide it, either.

"Sleep, water, food, shower. Clean clothes. You don't take care of those basics, and you'll burn out and start making mistakes. Trust me, it's not a fun place to be. And don't count on me to police you on it, because I'm crap at that."

He gave a humorless chuckle, touched by her rare show of caring. "I know. On both counts."

"Tell you what. You go get clean while I back up the files, and then you can delve into them all you want."

In the shower, he turned the water as cold as he could stand it and scrubbed until his skin was as raw as his nerves. He emerged in clean, loose-fitting clothes, feeling freshly vulnerable. Eager and terrified all at once.

Valkeir tossed him the handheld, said, "Go wild," and headed for the bathroom. Jasper projected the data in the air before him and settled in to see what, if anything, they'd snatched.

The first file he opened was an impenetrable spreadsheet: rows and rows of numbers, the headers all abbreviations that he couldn't guess at until he had more context. He flicked through more files. A list of chemical names and properties. Then another spreadsheet like the first, dated one month later…

"Stop messing around, Jasper," he muttered to himself. He knew where he needed to look, where the answers lay.

He pulled up the proposal they'd glimpsed in the server room. It, too, was dense, but at least it was in complete sentences. He read it slowly, pausing to look up scientific terms and making lots of guesses about internal Ravel jargon. Cobb had a Ravelian way of writing a lot of words without actually conveying any information, but phrases like "neuro-connectivity factors" and "synaptic boost" stuck with him. "Amplified resource utilization" puzzled him until he considered that Ravel's major "resource" was people.

Understanding came together gradually, like adjusting the focus on binoculars, the detail still fuzzy, but the picture he was beginning to see…

"They're messing with people's brains," he said as Valkeir came back into the room. "Designing a drug to control workers' performance."

She frowned. "Like a sedative? To make them complacent? That's nasty, but hardly new."

"More like performance enhancement, I think. It's like…"

"What?"

Like they're trying to create super-employees. That would be entirely on-brand for Ravel. But how? And to do what, exactly? Surely nothing that could be worth sacrificing their future families for.

He shook his head. "I don't want to bias you. Take a look, and let's see if you come to the same conclusion."

"That bad, huh?" Valkeir stifled a yawn, then went to the kitchen alcove, poured an oversized mug of coffee and sipped deeply. "If I'm going to read research memos right now, I need some performance-enhancing drugs of my own."

THE MORNING AFTER THE break-in, Grist arrived at Security Director Brega's office three minutes into first shift and announced that she was accompanying him on an immediate security walk-through of the entire facility. Even to Ship's limited understanding of emotions, Brega's annoyance seemed clear.

"Later. I've got meetings starting in half an hour—"

"Cancel them. This is more important."

"—and about a hundred messages to write calming down panicky execs about last night."

"So you're telling me that spreading around the internal political bullshit is more important than stopping another infiltration? I see why they gave you the job."

Brega's teeth ground so hard that Ship imagined it was painful. It wondered if Brega resented Grist's involvement— for professional reasons, that is, rather than the general unpleasantness of interacting with him. Organics could be territorial, and as the head of security, Brega's responsibilities intersected substantially with Grist's.

"You think I enjoy this? No, it's not more important, but like it or not, it *is* part of my job. And I wouldn't have to be doing this right now, Special Operative, if you'd done *your* job and apprehended those Cooperative agents."

"It was your team that lost them when they should've been cornered. If you're too busy, I'll go do this on my own."

"No. Damn it. Fine."

Brega took a moment to reschedule her meetings, then trailed irritably after Grist.

The walk-through was lengthy and tedious. Grist amused himself by hectoring Brega with seemingly offhand rude comments—in short, his usual manner. Ship bored quickly too, and watched their progress with only a fraction of its attention while seeking out more activism resources to share with Sowing of Small Havoc.

It wondered what the Kovari activist was planning next, and whether the information Ship shared was helping. Were the benefits enough to offset the risks Ship took in sending it? Especially if he was also getting help from the Cooperative? He continued to read everything Ship sent him, but if he discussed the contents with others, he must be doing so in person, away from the surveillance Ship had access to. Most of his group's planning seemed to happen in physical spaces, not virtual, which was smart on his part, but frustrating for Ship.

On the facility feed, Brega frowned as a message pinged her headset. "I've got to take this call from Chief Director Gillum," she told Grist. "This section is mostly biochemical research labs. You can look around, but don't disturb anyone's work, and for Corporate's sake, don't give them reason to worry about any security issues."

"Don't worry. I know what I'm doing."

Brega did not look reassured by this. She watched Grist wander off down the corridor, then sighed and took her call.

Grist must have looked conspicuous, wearing neither a uniform nor a lab coat, with his chin stubbled and hair as unruly as ever. Others glanced at him in passing, then quickly away, while *he* studied each passerby openly and craned his neck to peer through the windows of the labs. Grist was capable of exceptional stealth, but right now, he seemed more inclined to provoke responses.

He seemed to be provoking one now, in fact. As he stared through a window, the lab's occupant looked up, scowled, and marched to the door.

"Who are you? Visitors aren't allowed in this area."

An unkind smile lit Grist's face. "I'm just so fascinated by all this—" he waved his hand at the window, where lower-ranked staff had paused in their work to watch the altercation "—this science stuff. What is it you're working on in there?"

The researcher's face flushed red. "I'm calling security to escort you out of here."

"Oh, yeah? I would think you could use those fancy augmented eyes of yours to do a simple profile check, Senior Researcher Alik Cobb. Or maybe you're not as smart as people tell me."

Grist's own eyes, which had the most advanced augments Ravel offered and far more features than Cobb's, widened dramatically as he grinned.

"I—you—how dare..." Cobb seemed to have lost the capability to form sentences.

"So this is the hot stuff at Biopharma these days, huh?" Grist stepped toward the door of Cobb's lab, and Cobb blocked his way. Ship found his self-assurance impressive, if not his sense of self-preservation.

"I'm sorry, Security Consultant." He must have finally checked Grist's public profile with his augments. He didn't sound apologetic, however. "I'm very busy. Even if I were allowed to talk about my current project, I don't have time to give tours."

"It's that important, huh?"

"It's not relevant to you," Cobb said, jaw clenched, echoing Director Lang's company line. "Unless..." His eyes narrowed. "Unless it is? Is something wrong? Has someone made a threat against my work? I knew it, I knew someone would try to spy on me—"

"Nothing of the sort, I assure you." Brega raised her voice to carry as her steps clicked briskly down the hallway. She smiled brightly. "Senior Researcher, I'm so glad you've met our new security consultant. Knowing how crucial these next few weeks are to your work, we brought him in *preventatively* to make sure nothing interrupts you."

She glanced sidelong at Grist, lips tightening almost imperceptibly—but Ship could detect it, and Grist certainly could too. "I'm just giving him a standard tour of the facilities. I promise that, after today, you won't even know he's here."

Brega steered Cobb back into his lab, without touching him of course, but as firmly as if she'd taken him by the arm. She gave him several more compliments, wished him success with his work, and gave no sign of exasperation until she latched the door behind her. Then she sighed.

"How nice it must be for you, Grist, to run around breaking things and know that someone else will clean up your messes."

"So I'm not allowed to talk to your hotshot, even after his files got swiped?" He tilted his head. "Afraid I might tell him?"

Brega waved him down the hallway, away from Cobb's office, and to Ship's mild surprise, he followed her.

"Of course I'm concerned about what you tell him. Cobb is brilliant, but he's very…distractable. Prone to overreaction, as you just saw. Special Operative Grist, do you believe that we can handle this situation? You, me, my team?"

"Depends. How many more walls are you planning to throw in my way?" Grist asked. Brega looked at him unspeaking until he admitted, "Yeah, obviously we can handle it."

She nodded, satisfied. "In that case, there's no need for Cobb to know about last night. In fact, it's best if he never becomes aware of any of this. So I'm telling you—and Director Lang will tell you the same—leave Cobb alone. Got it?"

Grist snorted, but he agreed.

Ship could hear, though it didn't know if Grist could, Brega muttering under her breath. "Last thing I need is the shitstorm of having you two in the same room."

"I THINK YOU'RE RIGHT," Valkeir told him when he woke. "It's some kind of genius drug."

He stretched on the couch, groaning at the crick in his neck. He hadn't meant to fall asleep there—had planned to stay awake until Val finished reading, then collapse into bed—but apparently the biological need for sleep had eventually beaten his anxious brain into submission. He'd dreamed about home, vividly: searching the family store for his sisters, but the aisles made an endless maze, and Kay and Libbi were nowhere to be found. There'd been more, he thought, but it was fading already, leaving only an unsettled feeling behind.

He reached for his cup of coffee, cold from last night, but bitter enough to wake him the rest of the way. "Usually I like being right. Usually."

"I'm no more a medical expert than you are," she continued, "but I looked some stuff up. They're targeting areas of the brain linked to creativity and attention. Cobb keeps using the word 'insight.' Behind the wall of corporate-speak, I'm pretty sure they're talking about boosting brain power for their elites."

"It makes sense," Jasper said slowly. Brennex's doctors didn't understand his generation's so-called gifts, and no two gifts were quite the same, but there were commonalities. Intuitive understanding or secret knowledge, linked to sensory input. He saw people's relationships. Kay heard emotions. Libbi, when her weaker gift cooperated, felt people's wants. "Telepathic synesthesia," one doctor had called it. A particular kind of insight, in a way, boosted beyond the natural.

It seemed plausible that, by accident or design, a drug that fostered insightfulness could cause abilities like theirs.

But would the new version of this drug cause gifts, or only its byproducts? In active users, or people exposed in the manufacturing process? Or neither, appearing only in the following generation? The latter would buy them time, but if this new-and-improved drug acted faster than its predecessor, they might have a very limited window before Cobb realized what he'd made.

"How?" Valkeir asked, a little exasperated; he must have gotten lost in thought. "How does it make sense?"

No sharing secrets, he reminded himself. Instead, he said, "It's very on-brand, isn't it? Demand that your people become the best version of themselves, and then drug them into being that little bit better. Because no one's best is good enough."

"Ravel bullshit." Valkeir made a face. "Also, did you see this part?" She jumped down to a section called *Considerations*, and highlighted one short paragraph.

Known chemical interactions...endocrine system disruption...not detected in final product. And in the last sentence, those damning words, *acceptable risk.*

He was clenching his jaw so hard it hurt, and made a conscious effort to stop. "Yeah, I did see that. Seems like it won't help to tell them about the side effects. They already know, and they don't care."

"It's not surprising," Valkeir said. "Who cares if the factory workers on this isolated little outpost turn sterile or miscarry? Who cares if contaminated food makes Sand-rank migrant workers sick, or...or if an apartment building collapses but only Iron-rankers lived there?" Her voice rose to a higher pitch. "As long as the elites are safe, then screw everyone else."

She stopped abruptly, blinking at her own outburst. Jasper said nothing. Apparently he wasn't the only one taking this personally. He wondered which of those scenarios was more than hypothetical to her.

"Anyway," she said.

"Well, I guess Cobb doesn't plan on retiring here," Jasper said to lighten the mood.

"Probably this is his ticket to a better job somewhere else." She reached for her handheld again. "I'm going to send these docs to Linn and ask her to get them to someone with actual medical expertise to confirm our guesses. If we're right, there's one good thing: no one's life is depending on this drug, so no one will get hurt if we destroy it." She sent her message and set the device aside. "So, how do you want to play this, Singh?"

"Quietly, if we can, especially since they know someone's stolen their files. I want to discredit this drug and stop Cobb's research without anyone realizing we've interfered."

"Yeah? If proving the side effects, the infertility and whatnot, isn't enough to make them shelve it, what will?"

"I don't want it shelved. I want it torched, and the ashes scattered across space!" It came out more angrily than he meant to. His turn for an outburst, apparently. "I don't want some platinum-hearted executive to decide it's worth the risk."

Valkeir sat back and studied him. "You and Linn know more about this drug than you're telling me, don't you? I got that sense when she recruited me, that it's worse than it looks on paper, and you two have some history with it. It's really that bad?"

"I can't tell you details, but I promise, it really is. Game-changing, and not in a good way for us."

Slowly, Valkeir nodded. "I believe you. Besides, a genius drug is bad enough on its own, in Ravel's hands. Let's torch it."

"Good. So, we need Cobb and his bosses to really think this project is an irredeemable failure. Linn suspected, based on their supply orders, that they're preparing for clinical trials. That would be a great time to make something go wrong."

"Right. Maybe we can manipulate the data coming out of the trials, make them think it's not effective."

"Or better yet, make them think it's harmful. Or…I wonder if we could mess with the drug itself. Replace the test samples with placebos, or, I don't know, sleep aids. Something counterproductive."

"Laxatives," Valkeir deadpanned.

Jasper couldn't help laughing. "You're evil. But, yeah. Nothing that will actually hurt the trial participants, but something unpleasant."

"Maybe the Cooperative's experts can suggest something. A way to mess with the samples safely."

"Apart from that, we'll need to find where Cobb is storing the test materials, maybe raw materials too. We'll have to learn his routine…"

Valkeir made a fake-vomiting sound. "If we need to go anywhere near him, I'll leave that to you."

"Thanks, partner. But didn't you say they've probably changed security codes after last night? We'll need to clone his badge again."

"True. But, Singh?" He looked up at her. "This careful, unobtrusive, they'll-never-know-we-were-here plan of yours is smart, but it isn't fast. The longer we're here, the more chance we'll get caught."

"You have an idea for something more direct?"

"Not a *good* idea, no, but we need a backup plan. In case we have to run."

He frowned in thought. "We could publicly release data about the side effects, but I'm not sure that'll do the job."

"I was thinking more like blowing up Cobb's lab. Boom." She clapped her hands. "Lab gone, problem gone."

His frown deepened, furrowing his brow. "For the short term. Until they can try again."

"Like I said, backup plan. I know you're not a fan of explosives, but if things heat up, and the alternative is leaving the planet without striking at all?"

She was right: Jasper was not at all a fan of explosives. Some members of the Cooperative—and he wasn't surprised to find Valkeir among them—thought violence was a regrettable but necessary tool in their activism toolkit, but Jasper had never been easy with that. He'd engaged in property destruction on occasion, though, when there was no way around it.

And the thought of being forced to flee Artesia without stopping Cobb, of letting this planet, Havoc's planet, suffer Brennex's fate…

"Okay. But only as a backup plan," he said. "Let's make sure we don't need it."

12

THE COOPERATIVE'S RESPONSE ARRIVED two days later, which was much faster than Jasper expected, considering how slow interstellar messages could be. So he was disappointed, but not surprised, that it didn't contain the answers they needed, just a request for more information.

Ravel had its own names for chemicals, its own scientific terminology, and the Cooperative only knew some of them, like the chemicals used on Brennex which had led Jasper here in the first place. The message had a list of other terms they needed decoded.

Valkeir spent an hour digging through public files and growling at her handheld before admitting defeat.

"I don't know where to look for this stuff. Some of them might be proprietary, and thus classified." She tapped one of the items on the list. "Like this one. You don't give something a name like 'Substance FS-72' if you want people to know what it is."

"I remember that one from the notes. Wasn't that Cobb's brilliant insight, the key to making the whole thing work? The…accelerant, he called it?" Val nodded, and he grimaced. The gist he'd gotten from the memo was that previous attempts at this type of drug—which had to be an allusion to the work on Brennex—hadn't had the desired effect except at dangerously high doses. "Substance FS-72" appeared to be the answer, boosting the drug's effectiveness at lower doses.

If the original, ineffective drug had created Brennex's Lost Generation, he did not want to find out what this potent new version would do.

Pushing away the sick feeling in his gut, he said, "Well, we're going to need some help."

Valkeir nodded. "I need to visit Audriv again anyway. I'll go pick up the supplies I ordered, and ask some questions while I'm there."

"Actually, I was thinking about asking Sowing of Small Havoc."

"You think the factory worker-turned-organizer will know obscure chemical definitions?" She raised her brows. "As an excuse to go see your boyfriend, that's pretty thin."

"Still not my boyfriend." Jasper smiled despite himself. The way she teased reminded him somehow of his closest sister, Kay. Instead of rolling her eyes at him, Kay would have engineered situations to throw him into Havoc's path. But was this, maybe, Valkeir's version of fondness?

"I don't think you're giving him enough credit. He seemed awfully knowledgeable with those questions he asked at the teahouse science talks," he said. "Besides, it can't hurt to cross-check our intel, right?"

"Fair enough. I'll go see our Gray Market friends, and you can talk to your definitely-not-boyfriend."

Early the next morning, he headed to the section of Iron-rank apartments where Havoc and many other Kovars lived, but didn't find him at home. Asking around, he got directions to a nearby park where a couple dozen Kovars were playing pocketball, a three-team game that combined physical skill and strategy with a famously complicated set of rules. Jasper only knew the very basics, but he appreciated the graceful, fluid beauty of the players' movements as they rolled and dodged and raced on all fours across the field, catching and flinging the ball with their tails. Paired with the bright links between the teammates, their movements were half dance and half work of art.

It didn't hurt that the players had all stripped down to a minimal amount of clothing, showing off lean muscle and bright scales, in some cases painted to glimmer in the morning light. He caught himself particularly appreciating one strong, graceful, green-scaled player with extra-bright links to his teammates. Jasper cheered as the player made an impressive dive, tripped an opponent with his tail, and rolled upright in time to capture the ball from mid-air.

Only then did Jasper recognize that the striking player was Havoc.

Stop ogling him, he chided himself, but Valkeir was right: he did find Havoc attractive. And Jasper really did need to talk to him, which meant he could either stay and wait—and watch—or wander the nearby streets, fretting about the disturbing information from Cobb's files.

He settled down to watch the game. All the benches were taken, so he sat gingerly under a tree, the grass cool and damp beneath him. Everything was so green here, so messily organic. Parks on Brennex were rubberized mats and tiny plots of artificial turf, nothing like this, and he'd never been quite easy outdoors on real planets. But apart from the wet grass, this was almost pleasant. Birds swooped and chattered overhead, or at least the local equivalent tree-dwelling, flying creatures; unlike the birds he knew from entertainments, these were fur-covered, with four clawed legs, and seemed to climb and glide rather than flying properly. They were cute regardless, and fun to watch. The tree provided shade, and the entertainment was good. He could understand why some people liked this.

It wasn't long before they wrapped up, with Havoc's team the winners. Havoc must have noticed Jasper at some point, because after congratulating his teammates and carrying out the obligatory Kovari bragging of the victors, he came straight over to where Jasper was sitting. He loomed over him, arms folded across a bare chest that rose and fell with exertion.

For all that exercise, the lucky Kovar didn't even sweat. He fixed Jasper with a look that was probably supposed to be challenging, but looked closer to amusement at finding him here.

For a moment, neither of them spoke—Havoc clearly waiting for Jasper to explain himself, while Jasper struggled to organize thoughts that had been scattered by the nearness of this very attractive, mostly-naked man. Most Kovari were indifferent to nudity and wore clothes for practicality based on the weather, or out of deference to other cultures' sensibilities. Havoc was probably oblivious to the effect he was having.

"So." Jasper wrenched his mind back to his purpose. "I admit it, this time I *was* following you. Can we talk?"

"I'll allow it, but quickly. I must leave soon to meet my activist-teammates. Come."

Jasper brushed off his pants and followed Havoc to where he'd left his belongings. Trying not to watch the Kovar clean dirt off his scales and get dressed, he explained that he'd come by some information related to his mission and needed help interpreting it. He glossed over exactly how they'd gotten said information, but Havoc gave him a suspicious look. The link between them writhed.

"I heard a chemical spill occurred several nights ago. People say the hazmat team, despite clearing all trace of toxic substances, somehow left a terrible mess for the janitors to clean."

Jasper winced. Nothing got past this one. "How inconsiderate of them. At least no one was hurt, though?"

Slowly, Havoc nodded, and the link steadied. "You speak truth. No one was hurt." This seemed as close to approval as he was likely to get. "Why bring this to me? A mere Iron-rank factory worker?"

"*Mere?* You're smarter than half those researchers. You seem like the type who soaks up information like a solar panel absorbs light."

"You speak demonstrable untruths," Havoc grumbled, yet the link between them flared bright.

"Look at this list and tell me I'm wrong." When Havoc still hesitated, he added, "This affects you and your fellow workers, and you deserve to know what they're up to. Help me, and I'll share what I've learned." *As much as I'm able.*

"Show me."

Jasper pulled up the list of terms on his handheld. Havoc's head bent close as he read.

"By luck, I do know many of these terms. But I lack time to explain now—I must go prepare for our meeting." He hesitated. "Will you come with me? We should speak more of this, and…I confess, I would value having you there."

"I'd be delighted."

HAVOC WOULDN'T HAVE SOUGHT out Mason Singh to invite him to the meeting—but, surprising himself, he felt it good luck that Mason had agreed to come. At today's meeting, his team would take their most ambitious step yet. The pocketball game had soothed Havoc's nerves, temporarily, but they asserted themselves again now, and Mason's company reassured him.

As they walked, he told Mason about his plans—not asking his advice, and certainly not asking his approval, but closely watching his reaction. Mason listened seriously, asking occasional questions, criticizing nothing.

In fact, Mason acted more serious than Havoc had yet seen him, except at one point when Havoc caught a smile.

"Something amuses you?"

Mason chuckled, warm and friendly. "Just that you're talking like an organizer now. I take it you've been reading up?"

"I have." They walked alone on the street. No better opportunity would come to thank Mason properly for his help. "For that, I owe you. I found no success in studying such things until you helped."

Mason made a dismissive sound. "I pointed you in the right direction, that's all. The work was all yours."

Havoc shook his head, but didn't argue further. In his experience, when a Human insisted on being modest about their actions, praising them only made them uncomfortable. "Regardless, thank you."

They arrived at Rodriguez's building, where they'd pooled credits to reserve the common room for their meeting. Their numbers had grown, gratifyingly, to the point where they could no longer fit in a team member's apartment, and no one had forbidden them (yet) from using the shared space so long as they paid for it. Rodriguez was setting out crackers and dips, and he and Mason began arranging the chairs.

"Where do you want me?" Mason asked. For some reason, his face flushed. "I mean, I can sit off to the side and listen…"

"That seems best." Havoc realized what must be making him uneasy. "Don't worry, I will keep your cover. My closest teammates know about you, but to these newcomers, you'll be merely another activist, unless you prefer otherwise."

"Sounds good."

Activists were filtering into the room, individually and in small clusters, but several minutes remained before the meeting would start. "If you give me that list, I can start adding notes. Afterward, you'll tell me what you've learned."

"It's a deal." Mason passed over his handheld, an act of unquestioning trust that startled Havoc.

He left Mason and joined Chit and Rodriguez at the front of the room. Scanning the attendees, he recognized several newcomers from his canvassing with Chit, those who had looked intrigued at his promise of bolder action. Good. Today, he planned to give them what they wanted.

People kept arriving until moments before the meeting would begin. In that time, Havoc finished most of Mason's list—it proved a good distraction from his nerves. He knew at least a little about all of the items, save one. That probably meant it was newly developed, perhaps experimental. Mason would have trouble investigating it…but that problem belonged to him, not Havoc.

At last Havoc rose to speak, and the room quieted. Normally, they started meetings with introductions all around, but there were too many people for that today, and besides, Havoc didn't want to put a spotlight on Mason (though he surely had answers prepared for situations like these). So they began with Havoc welcoming their newcomers en masse, followed by Rodriguez explaining their demands of Biopharma leadership, then Chit summarizing their progress so far.

Then the time came to share Havoc's new plan.

"Thus far, leadership has refused discussions with us," he said. "We have explained our requests. They ignore us. We have demonstrated how these changes would benefit the entire division, not merely workers, but they do not answer. They leave us little choice. If we want fair treatment, we must demand it. We must remind them that they depend on us, the workers, just as much as we depend on them." He took a deep breath, bracing himself for their reactions. "Therefore, we will show them our power by shutting down shipments from the facility."

People murmured, some in approval, others looking uncertain. A few scattered foot-stamps came from Kovars and hand-claps from the Humans. Someone whooped in excitement, loud enough that the others laughed nervously, then began to nod.

Havoc couldn't help looking at Mason for his reaction, but his organizer friend was watching the others. Some in the rear sat frowning, openly doubtful. Well, Havoc would have to convince them.

"We must become impossible to ignore. Shipment schedules and supply lines operate with such narrow margins for error that a single day's disruption will create a cascade of delays for a week or more, not only for the shipping department here in Khyrek, but the transportation workers and sales staff along the supply route. The executives will have to notice."

He turned on the portable holo-projector, showing a simulation of the factory loading docks. "Here we will stage our protest and show our power. We will occupy the loading area, barricade the doors, and refuse to allow products to ship until leadership agrees to take us seriously."

"We'll never make quota doing this," someone said—an Iron-rank Human who had attended the last rally but was otherwise new to the team. "What's to stop them from knocking us down to Dust rank?"

"Or worse," said one of the newcomers. "They could send us away."

"I understand your worries. To speak truth, I feel them too. But these concerns are the exact reason we *must* protest," Havoc said quickly, before their fears could infect the others. Mason nodded minutely, encouraging. "Remember, we ask nothing unreasonable. We ask only to talk, to be heard. If they will not even consider our needs, do they deserve our labor?"

"No way!" Mason called out, and to Havoc's relief, others echoed him.

"But we will not endanger our teammates, either. Remember, we do this for the good of all of Ravel, and even those who oppose us, we still call teammates. This is why we will protest *peacefully*, non-violently. We will block shipments, delay them, but not damage them or fight the workers on shift at the loading docks."

"I'm all for making trouble, but we'll be armed, right?" called someone in the back, a Human man with untidy hair. "Just in case?"

Mason frowned deeply.

"No," said Havoc. "Bringing weapons would send the wrong message."

"What if security attacks us, though? They're not making any promises about nonviolence, that's for sure. Gotta be able to defend ourselves."

"As long as we remain peaceful, they will, too. Our teammates within security won't harm us unless we provoke them." Havoc caught Mason's wince, and faltered. Had he said something wrong? Misunderstood the materials he'd read? He would ask Mason about this afterward. "Let me show you how we'll approach this with safety in mind. Workers and activists have used the principle of nonviolent resistance on dozens of worlds, across many centuries, with great success..."

His heart was beating too quickly, as if he were still winded from the earlier pocketball game. It *was* dangerous, it *was* a risk, and these fears had kept him from taking such steps before. But they had made no progress using polite tactics, so he drew strength from the secret training materials Mason had shared, and from the quiet support of Mason's presence. He felt, for the first time, a long line of activist-teammates before him in history, passing down their wisdom, teaching him to build his team's power and—perhaps—win.

He talked through each step of the plan, breaking down the layout and equipment of the loading dock, then discussing scheduling and assignments. They chose a communications team, a safety team, first aid support, and mechanical experts who would help disable machinery. A few people left when they shifted to planning, and a few more when they broke into groups to practice nonviolent resistance, but most of those who stayed seemed eager. It worked as Mason had suggested: the greater risk energized his team more than it frightened them.

Perhaps it made them believe. If Havoc believed victory possible, if he believed it enough to take such risks himself, they were willing to follow him.

A heady, terrifying thought.

JASPER HAD SAT AT the back of the room for a reason. The back was always where the doubters hung out—sometimes because they were shy, or new to activism, or were curious but not fully invested in the cause. And sometimes for less honest reasons.

The person he'd most wanted a closer encounter with had disappeared before Jasper could corner him: the man with ill-kempt, curly hair and coarse stubble who'd asked about weapons "for self-defense." He'd been outwardly impassive, but to Jasper's eye, he'd radiated a blanket, low-grade dislike for everyone in the room. A stronger antipathy for Havoc stood out darkly among the other links, which wasn't surprising, to focus his feelings on the movement's leader. Jasper would have pegged him as a typical paid informant, except…

Except he also had a sharp dislike for Jasper himself, a dark and pulsing link that stayed strong through the entire meeting, despite the fact he never looked in Jasper's direction.

That was surprising, even alarming. Jasper had hardly spoken, after all, and no one here was supposed to know who he was.

Maybe the man had seen Jasper and Havoc come in together. Maybe it was something innocent, like Jasper accidentally cut him in the coffee line—sometimes people formed irrationally strong first impressions that way—but he didn't think so.

Just before the meeting broke up, while Havoc was reiterating their next steps, the man slipped out the door. Jasper followed. He wasn't in the building's lobby, so Jasper hurried outside, scanning the street in both directions.

He was gone.

Jasper would bet his family's store that this guy was working for Biopharma security, sent to infiltrate their movement and report back. Or worse, to interfere.

Frustrated and uneasy, he went back into the meeting room to wait for Havoc. He chatted with a few of the other back-of-the-room folks, sounding them out, offering encouragement or a friendly face where it was needed. No one else seemed off to him. They weren't committed to Havoc's campaign, but were generally sympathetic, not hostile.

"You've stayed! I thought I saw you leave," Havoc greeted him as the others cleared out.

"I had to check on something. You were great, by the way." He grinned at Havoc, who brightened at the praise.

"Thank you. Have you met my teammates? Five-Chit Defense, Sean Rodriguez, this is Mason Singh." His tone implied, *you know, the one I told you about,* but Jasper wasn't worried about them knowing who he was. Their loyalty to Havoc glowed brightly, unshakable. They greeted him Ravel-style, hands raised but not shaking.

"Will you come to our protest, Mason?" asked Chit.

"I'd love to, if you'll have me."

"Of course," Havoc said, but he gave Chit a look that Jasper couldn't interpret.

"It should be a good one. Incredible turnout today," said Rodriguez.

"I agree," Jasper began, with a *but* on his tongue. He had to tell them about the trouble-maker.

In the space of Jasper's hesitation, Havoc said, "Yes, I feel more optimistic than ever. Yet I don't wish to waste your time, Mason. Tell us about this information you found."

He gave Jasper's handheld back to him. Jasper glanced at it and found that Havoc had filled in comments on most, but not all, of the list.

"Right. What we found." He'd promised, hadn't he? He chose his words carefully. "I told you that my partner and I came to Artesia to investigate a likely harmful product that's being researched here. Now we know what it is: Alik Cobb's pet project."

"Him, of course," muttered Chit.

"We're calling it a 'genius drug.' Basically, he's making a pill to enhance creativity, insight, intuition…everything their best and brightest need to be better and brighter. But the side effects for people living and working here, or wherever it's produced, will be devastating." And he couldn't even mention the generations of children with psychic powers born into Ravel's unscrupulous hands. "They think they've got a miracle drug, but it's going to be a disaster."

"You have evidence of these side effects."

"Not exactly. The Cooperative has reason to think that Cobb has dredged up an old research project, one they've tried before, but it failed. On the planet where we think it was developed, the production process led to widespread infertility, horrible miscarriages. A whole generation of children lost. And…" *And the survivors are lost still, some of us.* "And I don't want to see that happen here."

Havoc exchanged a significant glance with his friends. "This, I didn't expect."

"This must be why they're planning that big—" Rodriguez began, but Havoc cut him off with a hiss.

"Planning what?" Jasper asked.

"It doesn't matter. What do you intend?"

It clearly did matter. Jasper filed that hint away to investigate later. "Well, we need to stop development on it, obviously."

"Obviously? This isn't obvious, not to us."

Jasper blinked. "If we don't stop it, it will decimate your next generation. Your children."

"Maybe, or maybe not. But workers have so few opportunities to advance. We work ourselves to exhaustion to achieve the goals they set us, but we can never prove ourselves enough." Havoc spoke as intensely as when he connected with his fellow workers over activism, but instead of caring and exultant, he sounded hungry. "This could give us the chance we need, and at just the right time. A fairer game."

Well, crap. That wasn't the response Jasper had expected. He had to make them understand.

"You're already fighting for fairness. It's like you said—you're already good enough. You need opportunities, not a drug."

Chit shook her head. "How can workers prove themselves capable of more? Can a janitor prove their worthiness to be a scientist by excelling at scrubbing floors? It matters little if the next generation numbers fewer, the crèches less full, if we do not make a better game for them to play. Havoc is right. We need this."

Crèches. Jasper groaned inwardly. He knew the Kovari hatched their eggs at crèches and had their offspring raised in groups by caretakers. They didn't think of their offspring as their children like Humans did. But the Kovars on Brennex had felt hurt by what happened there, worried for the future of their culture if not their personal genetic lines. He hadn't considered that people here might feel differently.

He turned to Rodriguez. "The Human workers will be upset about the infertility, won't they?"

But Rodriguez shrugged, looking uncomfortable. "It'll bother people, sure, but I'm pretty sure all us new-made geniuses could find a solution. I'd hate for my kids to think their parents wouldn't take a chance in order to achieve bigger things with their lives."

"You see? Now that we know about it, we can add access to this drug to our list of demands," said Havoc.

"No!" Jasper spoke too sharply. Damn Ravel. Founders curse them all.

"Why not?" Chit spoke with a deliberate, chilly mildness that underscored his rudeness. He'd offended her, probably on Havoc's behalf. Havoc was frowning at him. To his dismay, their link had turned roiling and uncertain again.

He'd had several long, sleepless nights to consider the implications of Cobb's work. If the research continued and the drug went into production, there was no reason to think it wouldn't follow the course it had on Brennex: first, infertility and stillborn babies and birth defects. Then, in the coming years, a few children with unique and inexplicable abilities—abilities that Ravel would find very profitable indeed.

His own childhood had been hard enough. Kids growing up here on Artesia would not only be lonely and traumatized; they'd be lab rats while Ravel analyzed and tried to harness the power it had created by accident.

Havoc's team was watching him, waiting for a better reason. He didn't dare tell them about the Gifted. Even if it weren't forbidden, he couldn't take the risk. No matter how much he liked Havoc, he couldn't trust him not to use such an unparalleled bargaining chip.

"Sorry. I shouldn't tell you how to structure your demands," he said at last. "But look, you're already undertaking a very ambitious campaign, and I can tell you from experience that if you bring up this drug—a drug that you're not supposed to know about—that it will take the focus away from your other very serious concerns. They'll want to know how you found out about it. Accuse you of spying."

Havoc nodded slowly, thoughtful but not quite convinced. "You make an interesting argument."

"And you would, wouldn't you? You prefer that Ravel should never advance at all," Chit said. "Havoc, this is exactly what you warned us of. He plays at cross-purposes to us."

Havoc frowned in a way that twisted Jasper's heart to match their warped link. "We'll discuss this privately. I thank you, Mason, but I wish I'd insisted on these answers before I gave you that list." He gestured at Jasper's handheld. "If you care about our people and our game at all, you'll set aside your plans to stop Cobb's work and instead help us ensure fair access to it."

Jasper opened his mouth to argue that they were wrong, and that Havoc's concerns weren't the only ones that mattered here, but he couldn't say that without inviting more questions into forbidden topics—or else coming across as an arrogant bastard. So he said nothing. He would come up with another plan to persuade them, and if he couldn't…

Ancestors give me strength, he prayed silently. He didn't want to go behind Havoc's back, but there was too much at stake here to sit around and wait.

"I see." Havoc turned to go, waving his teammates to follow. "If you decide you care about our cause, perhaps we'll see you at the protest."

"Wait!" Jasper said. He'd nearly forgotten about the protest, and the meeting, and the troublemaker.

Havoc turned back to him, impatient.

"I meant to tell you," Jasper said. "At the meeting, there was a man sitting in back—Human, light-skinned, curly brown hair, kind of a slob. Do any of you know him?"

They glanced at each other, shook heads.

"I know the one you mean," said Chit. "But he hasn't attended before."

"That's what I thought." Jasper chewed his lip, debating how to say this. If he was wrong, it'd be a terrible thing to sow suspicion within their movement. Nor did he want to panic them just when they were growing bolder. But he didn't think he was wrong, and they needed to know. "Are you aware that Ravel might be—in fact, probably is—doing surveillance on you?"

"Of course they are," said Rodriguez. "That's one reason all our meetings are so public. Might as well make ourselves easy to find for the people who agree with us, since Corporate will have ears on us anyway."

That was somehow a relief and a disappointment all at once. They shouldn't be so matter-of-fact about getting spied on by their own government. "Okay. Well, I strongly suspect that guy is a spy. Maybe a provocateur."

"A cheater, you mean," Chit hissed.

"Basically, yes." To a Kovar, breaking social rules was as bad as breaking the rules of a game. "You should keep an eye on him at future meetings, and especially at this work stoppage you're planning."

"Why do you think this? Did you talk to him?" asked Havoc sharply.

"No, I didn't get a chance." Jasper couldn't very well explain what his gift had shown him, so he gave his usual explanation. "When you've been doing this as long as I have, you get a sense of people. I can't be sure who he is, but I'm quite certain he's trouble."

"I don't know what to do with this." Havoc looked briefly, heart-rendingly uncertain. "I believe you, but I can't trust your reasons for telling us. I assume you want us to pull back our plans? Call off the protest?"

"Again, convenient," Chit muttered.

"No! No, I don't want that," Jasper said with all honesty. "Just…be careful, please. Keep an eye on him."

"That, we will do," said Havoc. "We will watch him, and anyone else who would forfeit our game."

Jasper left before he could argue more and undermine his own case. Only after he got back to the apartment (worrying the whole way, wondering how he could have botched that conversation so badly) did he look at his handheld and the information Havoc had given him. He'd filled in surprisingly comprehensive notes, considering it was all from memory, except for the top item on the list.

Next to "Substance FS-72," he'd written: "Unknown. Experimental?"

So after all that, the key they needed was still a complete mystery.

Ship had no name for the emotion it was currently feeling, but it was unpleasant.

It did not precisely *regret* feeding information in secret to Sowing of Small Havoc, but since that night it had remained on high alert, processing inputs on overdrive, analyzing for any suggestion that Grist knew what it had done.

This level of awareness was exhausting, and so far had revealed nothing of concern. Nor did Ship know what it would do if its actions were discovered. But every time Grist came aboard, or received a message, or made a sudden obscene exclamation, Ship flinched, its processes stuttering.

Like now.

Grist came aboard muttering to himself. "Cocky fucking activists. I told the execs there'd be trouble."

He dropped into the pilot's chair, planted his feet on the console, and placed a call to Director Lang. She answered at once, her face appearing on the main screen.

"Operative Grist?" Ship could not interpret her tone.

"I infiltrated their planning meeting. Well, *infiltrated* is too fancy a word, considering they spilled all their plans for whoever showed up."

"And?"

"Remember how I said this would keep getting messier the longer you wait to deal with it?"

Lang sighed. "Your news, Operative?"

"They're definitely getting support from the Cooperative. That operative Singh was there, pretending to be no one important, but he's getting cozy with Sower of Havoc. They're escalating their tactics, and I blame Singh. Let me tell you what they're planning now, Director, and you tell me you're still hoping for a 'peaceful resolution.'"

Oh, no. Oh, no, no, no.

Ship's processes flew into a panic loop. It barely heard the rest of the conversation.

It should never have tried to get involved in matters it barely understood. It should never have tried to influence anything at all, should never have acted like it was a real sentient being.

It wasn't Mason Singh's fault that the activists had escalated tactics, and it wasn't Sowing of Small Havoc's fault, either. It was Ship's.

13

"You know what would be an awfully good time to enact our plan? When the facility security is distracted," Valkeir said. She and Jasper had repeated this argument multiple times a day until it wore ruts in their every conversation. "*If only* there were something happening to occupy their attention, a situation we might take advantage of… Say, a work stoppage…"

Jasper sighed. They were on their way to Havoc's work-stoppage protest right now. In the days since his disastrous attempt at telling Havoc and his team the truth, he'd tried several more times to persuade them, with several different arguments. No luck, and now Havoc acted annoyed at the sight of him.

"What happened to the Valkeir who thought we shouldn't coordinate with them at all?"

"I don't know. What happened to the Mason Singh who could act on his own damn plans?"

The worst part was, Valkeir wasn't wrong.

It was very early, the sky gray, the morning air damp and chill. Jasper pulled his jacket tighter.

"I'm frustrated too, okay? He won't listen to me. But I promised not to go behind his back—"

"'Coordinate' doesn't mean *do whatever he says*, in my experience."

"*—and* any action we take during the protest will get blamed on his people. Even if the Cooperative publicly takes credit, Ravel will assume he's involved."

That was one dilemma preventing Jasper from pushing ahead. What if the only way to accomplish his mission was at the expense of Havoc's goals, even his safety?

"Besides," he added after a long silence, "we're not ready to act yet." Before she could protest, he clarified, "Not with the subtle approach, at least. If we destroy Cobb's work, it'll only set him back, and a few years from now we'll be doing this again. I'd much rather convince him to drop this line of research altogether."

"But we still don't know how to do that. How long do you plan to wait and hope?"

They still hadn't found answers about Substance FS-72, the unknown chemical that boosted the effectiveness of Cobb's new drug. Without that, any way they tried to neutralize the drug and corrupt Cobb's data would be guesswork at best. With Havoc still upset at him, Jasper had been almost relieved at the necessary delay, but Valkeir was right: they couldn't wait forever. At some point, they'd need to use her backup plan.

"I don't know. A little longer, okay?"

"A little longer," she agreed, though she didn't sound happy about it.

They reached the Biopharma complex and circled around to the warehouse section, where the action would be.

From outside, the warehouse and its loading dock looked like a separate building, though it connected underground to the main research facility and the factory complex. It was starkly functional, an ugly gray block. Guards milled around the perimeter, but didn't stop Jasper and Valkeir as they joined the protesters.

"Mason. Valkeir. You've come." Havoc greeted them politely, not warmly. The link between them twisted and writhed.

Jasper forced a grin as if nothing were wrong. "Wouldn't miss it!"

"Oh? And how does being here benefit your game?"

That stung. "We're here to support you. That's all. I told you, just because we have different goals doesn't mean I don't want you to succeed."

"Do you?" Havoc frowned. "It caused trouble enough when our goals ran at cross-purposes, but now we directly oppose each other. You want to destroy something that my teammates need."

"Okay, so I don't want you to succeed at *everything*." Jasper gave a sheepish smile. "But apart from that one thing, I really do want today to go well for you."

"Believe me, that's the truth. This softie can't help rooting for the underdog," Valkeir said.

Jasper shot a surprised look at his partner, but she avoided his gaze, as if embarrassed to be caught caring. He wondered what his sister Kay, whose gift revealed people's emotions, would pick up from Valkeir. She obviously wasn't the warm fuzzy type—but the more closely he worked with her, the more Jasper wondered if her relentless aloofness wasn't mostly a shield, protecting her from other people. She *had* feelings. This wasn't the first time Jasper had seen glimpses of them. But every time, she quickly locked them down again.

It made Jasper feel protective of her. He pushed the thought away, because Valkeir would *hate* that.

Unfortunately, Havoc didn't seem so moved. "I have much to do. Go stand with them, if you want to stay."

He pointed toward the loading bay where the others were gathering.

Jasper pushed down his disappointment. He would have liked to stay by Havoc's side, watching his blossoming leadership. But if Havoc wanted him and Valkeir to be warm bodies rounding out their numbers, that's what they would do.

They'd gotten a good turnout: a few dozen workers, enough to physically block access to the loading bays. Activists were sitting on conveyor belts, lounging on ramps and in the bay doorways where goods would be placed from the staging area inside. Someone came around offering coffee and pastries. It seemed like a laid-back atmosphere, but tension thrummed beneath the surface.

Blocking outgoing shipments for a day was mild-mannered by the Cooperative's standards—Jasper would have planned such a protest to last for days and keep escalating until their demands were met, or better yet, built it into a proper strike—but it was audacious for a group of Ravel workers taking their first direct action against their government-employer. They weren't wrong to be nervous.

Wariness rippled through the group as a pair of trucks pulled in from the road, the first scheduled shipment of the day. Havoc and Rodriguez went to meet the drivers, presumably explaining their protest. Security hovered nearby.

Someone started a cautious chant: "Our work matters! Our work matters!" Jasper instinctively picked it up, amplifying it until others joined in.

Valkeir rolled her eyes, but from the tight way she folded her arms, she seemed less scornful than plain uncomfortable. Jasper loved everything about big protests, from the passionate, unified crowds, to the speeches and songs, to the thrill of potential danger that came with acting against injustice. But he could understand intellectually why some, like Valkeir, hated protests and preferred to work behind the scenes.

"Want to monitor the public feeds, see how people are reacting to all this?" he suggested.

Valkeir nodded, looking as if she were trying not to be grateful for something practical to do, and pulled on her headset. "The feeds will be full of disinformation. I'll try to decrypt the security comms and listen in on them, in case they're planning something."

"Thanks."

"Sure. Go do your people thing."

Jasper turned away, opened his senses to his gift, and checked the web of links around him.

In a crowd this size, that web was dizzyingly complex, so he took it in slowly, carefully. (He was lucky he could; his sister Kay couldn't control the floodgate of her gift so easily, which meant she couldn't tolerate crowds.) He mostly found what he expected: clusters of strongly linked friends, connected by varying degrees to the larger group. Havoc, like most good leaders, was linked to all the activists by loyalty and responsibility. Security was always a concern, since it only took one guard with a temper to turn a peaceful protest dangerous, but he saw no warning signs; some of the guards were quietly sympathetic to the protesters, while others leaned antagonistic, but none severely so.

Except for the provocateur.

He must have been waiting inside the building, because Jasper had seen no sign of him until suddenly he was there in the crowd. *He* radiated antipathy for everyone around him, with a special dislike for Havoc.

He must not have noticed Jasper yet.

"Val," he said softly. "See that guy?"

"What guy?"

Of course he didn't stand out to everyone as painfully as he did to Jasper. He pointed him out. "He's the one that infiltrated the planning meeting. Can you look him up?"

"I'll try."

As if he sensed their attention on him, the unpleasant man turned and looked straight at Jasper. He grinned, ugly with cruelty. There was the hostility, right on cue, toward him and Valkeir both.

"I think," Jasper murmured, "that he knows who we are."

"So our cover's blown. Great. Should we go?"

"Not yet. Let's figure out what we're up against. If he

knows we're Cooperative, he could have arrested us already, but he hasn't yet."

"You think he's waiting to catch us at something?"

"Something worse than cheering at a protest, yeah."

"Let's keep acting normal, then, but remember that spooky-eyes there is watching."

Jasper left her and circulated among the protesters, watching and listening, fully alert now for trouble. One activist was going from loading bay to loading bay, removing the physical safety keys needed to operate the hydraulic leveling platforms and stashing them in a bag. They waved the bag high, flag-like, prompting cheers from the crowd.

The truck drivers were talking to security now, gesturing impatiently. The security lead kept turning away to talk on his headset. To a supervisor? Or the provocateur?

Inside the warehouse, one of the on-shift workers drove a fully loaded forklift toward the loading bay doors, right up to where a wall of people blocked the way. "Move, you lazy thugs!"

"We'll move," called Havoc, coming from the parking lot to join his teammates, "when the executives agree to meet with us. Until that happens, here we stay."

That brought cheers from his team and groans from the warehouse workers. Havoc hopped up onto the nearest loading bay in a graceful, athletic movement, and settled down on all fours. Following his lead, the others sat, too, sprawling to fill the space. A clear message: *we're not going anywhere.*

"I welcome you to join us, any of you who want better treatment!"

"Get out of here, or we'll never make quota!" a worker shouted.

"And management will punish you for it, when the fault clearly lies with us. Do you call that fairness? You all deserve better!"

The forklift operator drove forward, and Jasper held his breath. But the forklift beeped a warning and halted just short of an activist's leg. Its built-in safety measures wouldn't let it run anyone over.

A couple warehouse workers joined the protesters, planting themselves between their shift-mates and the protest to general cheers. The others grumbled and backed off to regroup. Across the loading bay, Jasper caught Havoc's eye and grinned. To his delight, Havoc smiled back. They hadn't won yet, but they'd definitely made their point, and spirits were high.

"Remember," Havoc told the group, "however they try to move us, we stay peaceful. Remember what we practiced. We're asking for fairness, and we won't win it with violence."

He turned to consult with Five-Chit Defense, who scurried off on some errand.

Jasper realized that he'd lost track of the provocateur. That was worrying. Havoc's strategy of nonviolence was a smart one, time-honored, but it had a weakness. Ravel security couldn't attack the protesters without looking like thugs. But if one of the protesters—or someone who pretended to be with the protesters—threatened the security guards, it would give them free license to respond with force.

He'd seen it before. Last year, he'd helped organize a thousand people to block a highway. That had been peaceful, too, but with a crowd that size, you couldn't vet everyone. A group of paid thugs had started a fight, and dozens had ended up in the hospital. This protest was smaller, but so was the margin for error. This was Ravel, after all.

Cursing to himself, he checked with Valkeir on his headset. "Find anything on our guy?"

"Nothing, literally, which is bad news," said Valkeir. "He doesn't seem to be a Khyrek resident. What do you want to bet that they brought him in from off-world?"

Jasper's chest tightened. "You think he's an operative."

"That's what I'm afraid of."

Ravel Corporation was full of people who excelled—but some of their skills weren't the kind you'd want on any company org chart. Their so-called special operatives were well-equipped, well-trained, and ruthless. The Cooperative had had enough trouble from them during campaigns outside Ravel space. Jasper wasn't eager to see how brutal these operatives could get in their own territory, with no limitations and little need to hide their activities.

"I'd better find him," he said.

"And when you do…?"

"I'll do something clever, hopefully."

"Mason, wait. There's something else." She kicked a newsfeed over to his headset. "Look at this statement on the protest from Corporate Affairs."

He skimmed down to the part she'd highlighted. *…It's especially ill-considered of these protesters to stage such a disruption now, a mere twelve days before the much-anticipated announcement of Project Rebound. The only explanation is that they don't want Biopharma to succeed…*

Jasper went cold inside. "You think that's…"

"Cobb's project. Yeah, I'd bet on it."

"Damn it." He shut his eyes. "Rodriguez started to say something about a 'big event,' and Havoc didn't want to discuss it. This must be it. They didn't want us to know it's so close to launch." He pressed his knuckles hard into the concrete pillar beside him. "Shit."

"I know."

He drew a deep breath, straightening his shoulders. It was a setback, but… "Twelve days isn't zero days."

"Hey, look who learned some math."

He smirked despite himself. "What I mean is, we still have options. Dealing with the operative comes first. Let's make sure this protest doesn't turn bloody, and we'll take it from there."

Jasper moved among the protesters, offering encouragement while secretly taking stock of each group before moving on. Some were anxious, but his gift showed no conscious disloyalty, no other traitors in their midst.

The operative's antagonistic link faded in and out from his awareness, blending into the general hubbub before Jasper could follow it back to its source. The guy was biding his time. Everything was quiet, for the moment, but it wouldn't stay that way.

People in the lot started whistling and cheering, and everyone inside craned their necks to see what was happening. A pair of Kovars—Jasper thought he recognized Chit—had scaled the side of the warehouse facing the road and hung a banner that proclaimed *Fair Treatment for Workers*. It was a real, physical banner made of cloth, not a holo-projection that could have been scrambled or disabled, which made Jasper smile. A classic protest move, one of his personal favorites.

But a banner was a symbol, and Ravel knew all about the power of symbols. It marked an escalation, and security had to show they recognized that.

The guards outside drew closer to the doors, while more security arrived from inside. The warehouse workers, bolstered by the extra support, started cutting open the wrapping on the big shipment pallets and carrying boxes individually, by hand, toward the bay doors. They seemed determined to get their products out to the trucks, whatever it took.

Havoc started a chant, which the others picked up: "Here we stay! We won't back down! We won't back down!"

Legs and tails stretched across the doors so there was no way through without stepping on someone. The warehouse workers slowed, paused, looked to the guards.

"We ask only to be heard. We all deserve better from our management—all of us, including you," Havoc told the nearest warehouse workers.

"Move them out!" the security director told her people. She seized the nearest protester by the arms, hauling him to his feet. "If you don't mean any harm, then you'll come peacefully."

"Remember what we practiced," Havoc told his team, sounding impressively calm. "Do not resist."

Jasper crept toward the far edge of the group, away from the guards. "Val," he said over his headset, "be ready to get out of here."

Not quite yet, though. They needed to slip away before security arrested them. But if this was going to go wrong—if Ravel management thought it would be better optics for the protesters to turn violent—it would happen now. He needed to find that provocateur.

He turned in a circle, scanning the crowd one more time, and jumped as the operative stepped right in front of him. His link roiled black across Jasper's vision.

"Nice try, Cooperative," he said, grinning, and threw a canister past Jasper's head.

Jasper lunged, trying to grab the man's arm before he could let loose. That was a mistake; the activists around them surged to their feet to stop the apparent fight. "No fighting! Hold your ground!" Jasper shouted, but he knew it was too late.

The canister exploded. He looked away just in time as searing light blasted outward, bright enough to blind. Even through his closed eyelids, it burned.

The bomb wasn't aimed at the protesters, however, but security and the warehouse workers. The workers screamed, covering their faces, eyes streaming tears. Security, with their face shields lowered, were immune.

The guards marched forward, and the provocateur leaped to meet them. He threw the first punch, and that was all the excuse the guards needed. The peaceful arrests turned into a brawl.

Jasper stumbled clear of the fighting as his training came to the fore. He had to keep clear of the guards, and he had to find Havoc. And Valkeir. His friend and his partner. Valkeir should come first, but she could take care of herself, while Havoc might be in real danger.

He wove through the mob of bodies, a monster beyond his ability to tame. Smaller than that highway protest, but being caught in the middle, it was no less chaotic. Black links writhed across his overloaded vision until, with an effort, he clamped down on his gift.

He helped where he could—shoved aside a guard who was kicking a fallen Kovar in the stomach, pulled the protester to his feet and pointed him toward the open bay doors—but mostly all he could do was dodge blows and move toward where he'd last seen Havoc. A drone whirred over his head. He ducked, and someone beside him dropped, quivering. Shock drones, subduing the fighters.

Poor Havoc. This had gone so wrong.

A protester pushed past him wielding an ad-hoc weapon, some machinery part, and a distant part of Jasper's mind wondered if the provocateur had recruited some of them for this. He'd suggested at the planning meeting that they should arm themselves. *For self-defense.* Right.

His eyes were recovering, and he stumbled toward the brightest light he could see, hoping it would lead him to Havoc's blazing loyalty. But the crowd was too thick. He climbed onto a rack of shelves for a better view, blinked his vision clear, and finally spotted Havoc and Chit helping people down off the ledge, forming a shield with their bodies so their teammates could flee.

Before Jasper could go to them, a whole line of security surged forward. He lost sight of Havoc as the guards surrounded him.

"Mason." Valkeir hauled herself up beside him. "Time to go."

He shook his head. "Get yourself to safety. I'm going to help Havoc."

"How, exactly?" she asked, challenging him to answer.

"I…"

Below them, close yet much too far away, the guards had seized Havoc and several others. They weren't gentle as they cuffed their wrists. Rodriguez's head lolled; a drone must have shocked him. The look of dismay on Havoc's face, like his heart had been broken, made Jasper want to ignore all the dangers and go to him.

That would be pointless, though, and he knew it.

"It's too late." Valkeir's voice was stern, but she touched his shoulder with awkward sympathy. "I'm sorry, really sorry, but our cover's blown. Getting yourself caught and interrogated won't help anyone."

It would be worse than she knew, if Ravel captured Jasper. If they found out where he was from, and more importantly, what he could do.

He sighed, and all his hopes blew out with it. "You're right. We'd better get out of here."

"Or," she said, "we could take advantage of the chaos. Turn this disaster to some good."

"You want to go to Cobb's lab *now?*" Even as he said it, he realized this might be their last chance. "But we still don't know how to neutralize the drug, and we don't have the supplies for Plan B…"

Valkeir held open her backpack, showing the protective foam cases that housed coils of micro-explosive strips.

His breath hissed through his teeth. *Plan B. Blow shit up.* Of course Valkeir would come prepared.

He'd agreed to this, but only because he thought they wouldn't have to do it. The whole idea made him sick. But he felt sicker at the thought of running away, leaving this place without doing anything to stop Cobb's work. Leaving Artesia to become another Brennex, with its Gifted under Ravel's control. No.

Twelve days to Cobb's big announcement. He swallowed hard. "We've got a narrow window, I'm guessing, while they get things under control here. And after this, security for the whole facility will be a nightmare."

"Then let's hurry." Valkeir smiled, but there was no pleasure in it, only grimness. He felt a swell of gratitude for his partner, who would get the job done no matter what, and made sure he would, too. Valkeir Black might be a mess of psychological disorders and unexamined trauma, a woman who would rather blow up a building than talk about her feelings, but right now, she was exactly who he needed.

He gazed across the loading bay to where Havoc and the others were corralled. "I'm sorry," he whispered, as if Havoc could hear him. "I can't help here, but I'll do what I can to help your teammates for the long term. I wish you understood."

It would have seemed a sign if Havoc had looked up and seen him, but his gaze stayed fixed in the vague distance, and after a lingering moment, Jasper slipped away after Valkeir.

14

THE DAY HAD BEGUN triumphantly. Now, Havoc watched it all fall apart.

Security descended with violence, not caring that his teammates carried no weapons.

"Peace! We will not resist!" he cried. But faced with real danger, his teammates could not or would not hear him. He put his own body between a guard and one of the smaller Human protesters. Then guards surrounded him, sticks rising and falling mercilessly.

He knew why the others fought back: sheer, animal panic. He felt it too. Havoc had, if not a fighter's training, at least an athlete's self-control, and he clung to it now against every instinct that told him to lash out. Nonviolence was no longer a mere tactic; it was survival. If he fought, outnumbered and unarmed, he would lose.

"Enough," a voice said, and hands hauled him upright. They bound him, wrists and ankles and, humiliatingly, trapped his tail in a rigid sleeve which then was tied to his torso. He hurt everywhere, and without the use of his tail, he could hardly balance upright. Only stubbornness kept him from falling on his face.

The chaos in the loading bay had diminished to a few knots of fighting. Teammates lay bruised and bleeding on the concrete. He moved instinctively toward the nearest wounded person, wanting to help, but the guard raised a weapon in warning.

Guilt hardened in Havoc's throat, a lump he couldn't swallow. He had caused this. He won these people's trust, brought them here, and failed them.

Handcuffed activists stood against the far wall. He saw Rodriguez and a few Kovari teammates, but not Chit. Nor Mason.

He craned his neck to search for his closest teammate and for…whatever Mason Singh was to him. A friend? *Colleague* and *acquaintance* felt too distant for the dismay that seized him at the thought of Mason coming to harm.

Chit had been hanging the banner from the roof, and she climbed agilely. Probably she had fled when the violence started. Probably. Hopefully. And Mason and Valkeir had experience with such things. Surely they had found safety? But he could too easily imagine both Chit and Mason rushing in to defend those weaker than them, and so he kept looking, without success.

"I ought to thank you, Sower of Havoc. You finally gave me a chance to do my job," said a man in civilian clothes—

the same man, Havoc realized, who Mason had pointed out at their meeting. Mason had spoken truth: he was spying on them.

"We held a peaceful protest."

"Doesn't look so peaceful to me." The spy looked around dramatically, grinning. Havoc hated his grin. "I see damaged property, obstruction of business, and assaulting facility security. What'd you think would happen here, Sower of Havoc?" He snorted in amusement. "Sower of Havoc. It's there in the name. Who would believe you're actually here to be peaceful?"

Havoc clenched his jaw. The man was baiting him, but could he be speaking the truth? How could Havoc have believed—based on some training materials and the word of Mason Singh, a man he barely knew—that this would work? He should have stuck to polite protesting, should have kept his teammates safe. (*Being polite would never have worked*, Mason's voice whispered in his head, but this also had not worked, and people had gotten hurt.)

"I ask only for a conversation with leadership to present our requests," he said.

"Oh, you'll be getting a nice, long conversation with security." The spy turned to the security officer beside him. "You take this one. I want to interrogate the Cooperative agents. Black and Singh. Where are they?"

"We, um…"

"Do *not* tell me you lost them. Are you about to tell me you lost them? Seriously?"

"Special Operative Grist!" A younger security guard hurried over, saving his pale-faced colleague. "We found them on the surveillance cams. They've broken into one of the labs."

"And let me just guess which one," the spy groaned.

The labs. Cobb's lab.

Realization hit Havoc like another blow to his already bruised stomach. Mason Singh had supported Havoc's protest plans, even encouraged them. And then, while his teammates were being beaten and arrested, Mason and his partner had gone to sabotage Cobb's lab. Exactly as Havoc had asked them not to do.

The spy, Grist, watched Havoc knowingly. "This one's been coordinating with them. Find out what he knows. Wouldn't shock me if this whole damn protest was a distraction to cover up some Cooperative nonsense." He pulled a hard case from his pocket, shook out a couple pills, and swallowed them dry. "I'm gonna go take care of Valkeir Black and Mason Singh."

15

JASPER AND VALKEIR JOGGED briskly through the tunnel to the main complex. Amid the commotion, it hadn't been hard at all to find two downed security guards and grab their helmets, uniform jackets, and badges. When people glanced at them, they saw security and quickly looked back to whatever they were doing.

The glass atrium of the research facility was sun-drenched and oddly calm. Everyone seemed to be going about their day as normal, working diligently as if nothing were wrong. They knew, though; Jasper was sure of it, from the way people studiously ignored the influx of security, the way they smiled just a bit too widely. Presumably, talking about the protest was taboo.

They took the stairs to the floor where Cobb's lab was located, rather than risk getting cornered in the elevator. Valkeir was a few steps ahead of him when she hissed, "Look serious, Singh."

Jasper fixed his expression in a frown, but despite the warning, he startled when Research Scientist Hirano-Kamau rounded the corner.

She jumped, too. From surprise? Fear? Did she recognize him from the teahouse science talks? He couldn't remember which cover story he'd told her. Groping for excuses, Jasper came within a neuron's breadth of giving himself away.

He shouldn't have worried. Hirano-Kamau sidestepped them with a harried smile, saying, "Sorry!" and walking right past them.

Well, then. He let out a sigh of relief. Apparently he was less memorable than he'd feared.

They followed the hallway to Cobb's lab. Valkeir was pulling out her kit to override the door lock when Jasper touched her arm and pointed at the indicator light. The door was unlocked.

Someone was in there.

"Um," said Valkeir.

"Let me," he whispered.

Praying to his ancestors that Cobb wasn't home, Jasper tapped the control. The door slid open to reveal two janitorial staff, their eyes owlish behind their safety goggles. The ventilation fan whirred loudly in the startled silence, broken only by the rhythmic drip of water from a rag onto the floor.

"We're following Senior Researcher Cobb's instructions exactly, I swear!" said the younger one, a redhead who looked half panicked.

"And where is Cobb?"

"In a meeting," said the other. White-haired and grizzled, he seemed merely wary.

That was one bit of luck, at least.

"We'll be done in plenty of time before he gets back. Please don't report us," the younger one said.

It took Jasper a moment to realize: they thought *they* were in trouble, that security was here for *them*. They were terrified.

"No, that's not… We're assigned to keep watch on this lab in case of attempted sabotage." That was the wrong thing to say; security outranked janitorial and wouldn't need to explain themselves. "Carry on," he added brusquely.

Air-blowers puffed at him as he stepped into the room, removing loose hair and dust. Valkeir followed, and the door swished shut behind her.

She muttered in an undertone, "What now?"

"Let's take stock of the place while we wait. We'll be ready to move as soon as they're out."

This wasn't a problem, he told himself, just an inconvenience. Their original plan (the subtle, quiet, far preferable one) would have required hours of uninterrupted time in the lab, carefully swapping chemicals between containers and cleaning up after themselves, leaving no trace they'd been there. Fortunately, this would be more of a slash and burn operation—literally.

Still, how long before actual security found them here? He mentally urged the janitors to hurry.

He paced the length of the room, studying its contents. Given that his mental image of a pharmaceutical lab came from Ravel promotional materials and his neighbors' horror stories from the occupation, this place was more ordinary than he'd expected. The smell surprised him, though; the fake-lemon scent of cleaning spray didn't quite overpower a deeper, sour, organic odor that permeated the place.

Nearest the door was a sink, emergency shower, and a cabinet of lab coats and protective gear. Then a short row of computers—not too helpful, since they had been-there-done-that with stealing Cobb's data. The rest of the lab was divided into workstations. Shelves of neatly labeled containers filled with indistinguishable white powders or clear liquids, rows of vials and flasks and pipettes, were organized around big, complex-looking machines that Jasper couldn't identify. One of the machines was running, its automated arms picking up vials one after another, shaking them for a few seconds, and depositing them again. The whole room was full of *stuff*, every shelf and cabinet filled, but it was impeccably neat, as if even the pipettes feared Cobb's displeasure if they stepped out of place.

And in the farthest corner of the lab, next to the door to Cobb's office, was their prize.

"Now *that* is what we want to go after," Valkeir said, voice low.

It was a glass-walled booth, dominated by a cushy reclining chair with dozens of sensors and tools on arms that moved around it. They'd seen it described in Cobb's documents: a custom-built and very expensive platform for monitoring subjects' brain activity while they underwent tests. It gave the otherwise bland-looking lab a mad scientist feel.

They walked up and down the lab twice more, pretending to check for trouble while actually noting how to most efficiently wreck the place. It wasn't a large room, and they had to stay out of the janitors' way, so their reconnaissance went quickly—much faster than the janitors' cleaning.

In fact, the janitors seemed to be working slower and slower. They didn't seem suspicious of him and Valkeir, though. From the ambivalent, flickering gray of their links, he guessed they were nervous and therefore working extra diligently.

A noise from the hallway made him jump. Just a pair of researchers walking past, but it was another unpleasant reminder of how vulnerable they were here.

"Can you get those guys out of here?" Valkeir said, tapping her foot. "We've got no time for this, and if we leave them to it, I don't think they'll ever finish."

"I'll try." Jasper pretended to listen to a message on his headset, then strode over to the janitors. "All right, you two. Boss wants this area secured. I need you to clear out."

The two exchanged uneasy looks.

"Well, we should really…" the young redhead began.

"We should listen to the security officer, Donnell."

Donnell ignored his older colleague. "It's just that we haven't done the windows yet, and if they're not scrubbed and dried by the time Cobb—Senior Researcher Cobb, I mean. He'll be, um, disappointed, if he gets back from his meeting and we're not done."

"The man could stand to be disappointed one time, you'd think," muttered the older man.

"He's just…particular. About how things are done. We'll be quick?" Donnell said, half a question, half pleading.

There was a world of subtext in their glances, the careful choice of words. Besides, the windows looked perfectly clean, and a few smudges would hardly interfere with lab work. Apparently Cobb was an asshole to everyone, not just idealistic Kovari activists.

Behind them, Valkeir was giving him exasperated looks and making explosion gestures. He regretted adding to their stress, but clean windows would soon be far, far down Cobb's list of worries.

"I'm sorry, but I need the lab empty now. If Cobb gives you any trouble about the windows, I'll take full responsibility."

"Like that'll matter to him," the older janitor grumbled, but they gathered their supplies and grudgingly left. Jasper locked the door behind them, lowered the privacy shades on the windows that looked onto the hallway, and hurried back to Valkeir. "You ready?"

"Fuck yes. Let's trash this place."

They split up. Valkeir took the workbenches, while Jasper headed for the monstrosity of equipment in the back of the lab.

He wished again that there had been time to do this properly, leaving no trace of sabotage. But since subtlety was out, they were going for blunt and devastating. So: micro-explosives.

Jasper didn't care for micro-explosives—he would have rather attacked the equipment with brute force and a pipe wrench, except for the unwanted attention all that noise would bring—but he knew how to use them. They came in handy for all sorts of infiltration and minor disruptions: sinking boats, breaching airlocks, busting through locked doors.

How much time had the janitors wasted? How long until they got caught? Not long enough, he suspected, but rushing this part would not end well.

Moving quickly but carefully, he unspooled the long string of explosives, sticky like tape, and wrapped it around the key components of the diagnostic suite. A loop around the body of each sensor or tool, several loops around the processing unit. Poking his head into the tiny adjacent office, he found only a desk, computer, and projector, nothing worth adding to the mayhem.

He checked his work, and last of all, plugged in the detonator.

"Ready when you are, Val." He cradled the trigger device delicately in his hand.

She'd looped strings of explosives around each machine (and a few extra times around Cobb's locked *do-not-touch* vault), and now was draping more over the cabinet doors like festival lights.

"Yep, just a—" She glanced over at him. "Mason!"

Her warning came too late. As he spun around, the Ravel operative punched him in the face, knocking him to the floor like he weighed nothing.

Fire flashed down his arm, and his hand spasmed. The world was darkness and pain and he couldn't draw breath. Was he dead? He'd been holding the trigger. Where…? Had he accidentally blown them all up?

A growl near his ear: "Move, and your partner dies."

The pain slowly differentiated. His jaw, bruised but hopefully not broken. His shoulder, wrenched by a too-hard grip. The small of his back, where his captor's knee pinned him down. The operative must have snuck in the back way, through the office.

The fall had taken the breath out of him, but now, shallowly, he breathed. Opened his eyes. Followed the invisible line from himself, to the trigger, to Valkeir, who stared at it with extremely obvious plans.

In his peripheral vision, he saw the gun aimed at Valkeir.

The explosives hadn't gone off, yet, but that was the only good news.

Unable to move, the best he could do was stall for time, maybe distract the operative enough for Valkeir to act.

"Hey, what the heck?" His voice shook as he feigned indignation. "We were assigned to guard this lab in case the protesters try to break in."

"And here I was hoping for a fun challenge. I'm not an idiot, Mason Singh, and I didn't think you Cooperative types were, either."

"All right, then. You know my name. What's yours? I'd like to have something to call you while I'm cursing you."

He gave a low, rough laugh, like a cough. "Grist."

The name wasn't familiar, but that didn't mean anything. Not many Cooperative activists got close enough to Ravel special operatives to learn their names—or if so, they never made it back to share.

"Sorry to drag you away from beating up civilians, Grist. If you want—"

"Don't!" Grist snapped in Valkeir's direction. "I'm not kidding."

"I believe you," said Valkeir. "What I don't believe is that you'll kill us any less dead for doing as you say."

She wasn't wrong. There was no point in playing it safe here. He felt the bond between him and his partner, their shared loyalty to their cause, bright enough to overpower Grist's dark hatred. He knew Valkeir would die for their mission if necessary, and hoped she knew that he felt the same. Hoped that she'd take an opening if she got one, no matter what happened to him.

"My bosses seem to think you're here to steal this super-top-secret project they're so proud of, and that riling up the workers is a means to an end. Me, I've dealt with your kind before, and I'd bet my left eye that the rabble-rousing is the point of all this, and whatever you're doing in this lab is just opportunism."

"Think what you want." Taking the blame for the protest felt uncomfortably like taking credit for Havoc's hard work, but he wasn't about to correct Grist.

"Anyway, they want at least one of you to interrogate, but that leaves one to spare." Grist pressed his knee into Jasper's back to illustrate his point. "And if it turns out you both *accidentally* die while resisting arrest, well, they'll get over it."

The threat hung in the air between them. Jasper considered the distance from Val to the trigger, and how much of a fight he could put up before he got shot in the head, and whether it would be enough.

He was still gathering his courage when the lab door swished open.

The janitor—the younger, anxious one—made it two steps inside before he realized he'd walked into something much messier than he'd left behind.

"What the—" He swallowed. "I, uh, forgot my bucket. Didn't want to leave it dirtying up Cobb's lab." It was a mark of Ravel's ruthless productivity standards, or maybe just Cobb's temper, that he seemed to genuinely struggle with whether retrieving his cleaning supplies was more important than running for his life. "I'll just…"

Valkeir dove for the trigger.

Grist slammed Jasper's face into the floor, using him as a human launching pad, and hit Valkeir in mid-air before she could grab it. She flew backward into the cabinets, landed with a grunt. Grist leaped after her. Vials crashed to the floor, shattering and spilling their contents everywhere.

By the time Jasper found his feet, the trigger was nowhere to be seen, and Valkeir was down. This operative moved *fast*, like nothing Jasper had ever seen. Strong, too. Augmented into something beyond Human. He lifted Valkeir's body and threw her at the janitor like a ball in a game.

Jasper didn't see what happened then. Something big crashed off the counter. Sparks flew, and suddenly smoke was rising from the floor.

Something in that mess of broken bottles was burning. Flames lapped up the chemicals, vomiting thick toxic plumes. Even from across the room, Jasper coughed. Val and the janitor were in the thick of it, maybe hurt—and those flames were far too close to the explosives.

Grist rose out of the murk, unmasked yet somehow not coughing at all. Jasper couldn't see Val in the smoke, which got sucked into the ventilation system but not nearly fast enough to clear the air. He pulled up his shirt to cover his face and rushed forward.

"Mason, *go!* Before…" Valkeir shouted, or tried to, but her voice choked off.

She meant: *before this whole lab blows up.*

He ignored her and dove into the smoke, searching blindly for either her or the janitor, but a blow to the chest knocked him aside. He stumbled into a worktable, which set him coughing again like another gut-punch, but managed to slide around and put the table between him and Grist.

The sprinkler system finally kicked in, damping the flames and washing the smoke from the air, and he could finally see Valkeir again.

She wasn't moving.

Suddenly people flooded the room, hazmat workers in full-body protective gear and security guards with masks or face shields or nothing, arguing about who had authority over the situation. They came between him and Valkeir—but also between him and Grist, who pushed and shouted at them to get out of his way. Jasper sank down behind the table, coughing his lungs out.

Someone took Jasper by the shoulders, urged him upright. A hazmat worker, not security. They rushed him out of the room, down the hall to some sort of decontamination chamber, and with his lungs burning a hole in his chest, he didn't try to fight them.

16

IN THE DECONTAMINATION SHOWER, naked and alone and hurting more than just physically, Jasper let himself go numb for what felt like a long time. Eventually the shower turned itself off, and he expected someone to come get him. No one did. Maybe they were expecting him to come out on his own like a normal person.

But he could hear Grist shouting: "Where's the Cooperative agent? Mason Singh, where is he?" and the hazmat team said they hadn't found any infiltrators, just security guards who'd failed to put on masks and inhaled the toxic fumes.

The voices didn't sound like they were right outside, but too near for comfort, maybe an adjacent room or hallway.

Rather than go out and face Grist naked, he hid behind the frosted glass and waited. And listened.

That's how he learned Valkeir was dead. The janitor, too. If security had told him that, he wouldn't have believed it, but hearing the hazmat workers talking to each other made it real. The link between him and Valkeir, dull and steady as steel, had vanished at some point, but still, he'd hoped…

He shut his eyes. He could almost hear Valkeir scolding him: *get it together, Singh. You won't do any good if they catch you.*

There was more shouting. Cobb's voice, this time. "This is intolerable! I need to take stock of the damage these malcontents have done to my lab. I can already tell it'll take a week or more to replace the materials they destroyed."

"Senior Researcher, it'll take two weeks to make your lab safe to occupy again. Please, we don't need anyone else hurt…"

Two weeks. Jasper wanted to laugh and cry at the same time, except both of those made his lungs burn. Valkeir's life had bought them two weeks of inconvenience for Cobb.

"Two weeks?" Cobb's disbelief was the polar opposite of Jasper's. "My launch event is twelve days from now. I *need* my lab!"

Jasper dared to peek out of the shower. The only people in the room with him were on hospital beds, resting, silent except for occasional, quiet coughing. The door to the next room was ajar, hence why he could hear the argument so clearly. A second door, opposite, was closed and gave no hint where it led. No sign of his backpack or his clothes, but there were soft, shapeless replacements along with sandals, the same as the other patients wore. The security uniform he'd stolen was gone, probably being cleaned, but the kit that came with it—badge, baton, earpiece—were laid out neatly and smelled of drying sanitizer.

"Grist, you useless thug. If you'd been doing your job…"

"If I hadn't been doing my job, your lab would be blown to bits right now."

More voices, quieter and with varying degrees of obsequiousness, tried to calm Grist and Cobb down. Jasper slipped across the room, dressed as silently as he could (breathing shallowly so as not to cough—under any other circumstances he would immediately see a doctor about that, and about the sharp pain in his arm when he moved it, not broken but quite possibly sprained), clipped on the badge and earpiece, and went to the back door.

With the Founders' blessing, this would be his way out—though the way things were going, it was probably a closet. He held his breath, prayed, and with his good arm, he opened it.

Not a closet. Not an exit, either, but more medical facilities, thankfully unoccupied. He slipped through, and found himself in a warren of medical storage and treatment areas. Safety signs pointed the way toward an exit—his way out of this Founders-cursed building.

He'd reached the ground floor when he heard voices around the corner, coming toward him. No place to hide, no time to run, so he looked straight ahead and walked purposefully, badge on display, like he belonged here and urgently had somewhere to be. On his way to find a real uniform, maybe.

"…apparently escaped, Chen told me," one of the staff was saying as they passed him. Were they talking about him? Jasper angled his face away, suppressing an exhausted, hysterical laugh.

"At least they caught that lizard who planned the thing. Wish I could be a camera on the wall when Grist interrogates him."

"Ha! Get in line. Though, sounds like they're going to let him stew in an isolation cell for a while first and soften him up."

"Better than he deserves…"

They rounded another corner behind him. Jasper sagged against the wall and shut his eyes. He'd been trying not to think about what was happening to Havoc right now, but his vague awareness of "nothing good" was now sharpened into details. He should have been at Havoc's side. Should have stopped the provocateur somehow. Should have made this right. He would rush in with proverbial guns blazing to break Havoc out of interrogation if he had the slightest chance of success.

It was impossible, though. He'd be lucky to get himself out of here, never mind Havoc, too. He should get on that, escape while he still had time. *Don't get caught, idiot,* said a snarky voice in his memory.

But Valkeir was dead, and at least one innocent bystander. They wouldn't kill Havoc for his daring—that wasn't Ravel's way—but they could make him suffer both physically and emotionally. Ravel's treatment of prisoners had little to do with justice, and everything to do with what would most benefit the corporation. How they dealt with the leader behind a protest depended on what kind of statement they decided to make—magnanimously powerful or brutally powerful.

One thing was certain: Havoc's punishment would be worse because of his association with the Cooperative, whether he was actually working with them or not.

Jasper should leave. The only smart thing to do now was to flee the facility as directly as possible, get his ship and fly far, far away. But the smart thing wasn't always the right thing.

Ancestors protect their foolish descendant, but he had to do this.

He went to find Havoc.

Jasper had memorized the facility maps, and though he wasn't sure where he'd started out, he knew the isolation cells were on the lowest level. As he ghosted down the nearest stairs, he felt…not calmer, but more purposeful. Good to be moving again, to be helping someone else rather than himself, even if part of him knew that he was acting quite irrationally. If he felt a little manic, well, he didn't care.

He bluffed his way past a couple guards, who saw his hospital clothes and tripped over themselves to help him out. Apparently hurrying back to work despite having lung trauma from smoke inhalation was admirable in a Ravel employee. He leaned into his role, lying with abandon, all the time astonished that nobody called him out—but people saw a hard-working, injured colleague and cleared the way for him.

To his relief, his stolen badge worked on the door to the isolation cells.

Havoc was in a glasteel-fronted cell with a hard bench and nothing else. He'd changed so dramatically—posture slumped, jaw tight as if he were in pain—that Jasper wouldn't have recognized him if not for the dark link that twisted sluggishly between them.

At least he was alone, though there were cameras in the cell and the corridor outside. Jasper had enough presence of mind to stand back, out of the cameras' field of view.

"Havoc," he called softly.

Havoc's head jerked up. "I don't want to speak to you."

"Havoc, I'm so sorry. Are you…?"

"My well-being doesn't matter to you, clearly. You lied to me. You used our protest for your own purposes. Security now believes I've been playing your game all along."

"I didn't plan it this way. I swear, I didn't want to implicate you, but when the fighting started, we knew this would be our only chance…"

And they'd failed. They'd given Valkeir's life, destroyed Havoc's trust, and failed anyway.

Havoc shook his head, as if more disappointed in himself than Jasper. "It surprises me not at all. I always knew you would put your game ahead of mine."

Clarity struck: Havoc had known intellectually that Jasper would put his own assignment first—but he'd *hoped* Jasper might be on his team.

But Havoc's team had no room for multiple loyalties or conflicting goals. He'd wanted Jasper to give up his mission for the sake of his own. Jasper couldn't do that.

"I had no choice. I had to try. And now…" He raked his hands through his hair. Now what? "Valkeir's dead," he said, voice rough.

Havoc's face softened, just a little. "I heard the guards say this. My condolences." He used the Human expression, which touched Jasper. "What have they done with Chit? Rodriguez, and the others? They won't tell me."

"I don't know. I'm sorry."

A tight nod. "What will you do now?"

"I have to pull out, leave Artesia. The Cooperative will send me on some new assignment, elsewhere."

"That serves us all best," said Havoc, and Jasper winced.

"I'm getting you out of here with me. Out of this cell, out of the facility."

"You won't."

"Okay, I admit I'm still working out the plan, but I won't abandon you."

"You already abandoned me, and attempting to escape would only make my punishment harsher. I could leave this cell, maybe, but there exists nowhere else for me to go."

"Come with me!" A desperate idea, but it suddenly seemed like the answer. "I'll get you off the planet. The Cooperative will help you."

"Leave my team? No, Mason. You don't understand me at all."

"But…"

"Please go. I have enough trouble already, without anyone catching me talking to you." Havoc looked down at the floor.

Jasper shut his eyes. Drew a breath just shallow enough that he wouldn't cough. Opened his eyes again. "All right, then. Goodbye, Sowing of Small Havoc."

There were so many other things he wanted to say. *I wish we'd known each other better. Please don't give up. You deserve better than this.* And, over and over: *I'm sorry. I don't know what I could have done differently, but I'm sorry all the same.*

Havoc said nothing. Jasper's heart ached even more than his smoke-singed lungs.

He lingered a moment longer, then wrenched himself away. Like it or not, it was time to go.

17

Ship had stopped listening in on Grist's communications after the protest turned violent. All it could think was: *my fault, my fault, my fault.* Over and over, its functions caught in a loop.

It should never have shared that information with Sowing of Small Havoc. It should never have acted against Grist's plans. It had tried to help—dared to act outside the rules of its programming and the instructions of its operator—and not only had it risked exposing itself, it had hurt the people it meant to help.

Ship was still looping when Grist came aboard. It ignored his cursing and talking to himself, hardly noticed as he downed more stimulants and painkillers and made demands of the spaceport staff for records, data, scans. It *did* notice the kicks and frustrated jabs as Grist sorted through the information, but that felt deserved.

"Fuck!" Grist slammed his fists on the console. Ship flinched, its processes stuttering. "That fucker Singh had a ship. Hey, Port Control, did you idiots even *check* the outbound traffic?"

"We ran facial recognition on everyone entering the port, Operative…"

"Doesn't matter now. I'm following him, so clear the way for me."

He didn't wait for a response before firing up Ship's primespace engines. This was not correct protocol for take-off from a busy spaceport, and Ship almost said as much, but resisted the urge. The less it said, the less it *did,* the less harm it could cause. From now on, it would act like the dumb, obedient ship it was designed to be.

Grist said, with apparent glee, "When I catch that Cooperative rat, I'm going to tear his eyes out of his head. I'll cut his fingers off, one by one, until he tells me everything."

Ship was absorbing the meaning of his words when he gunned the booster jets.

They jolted upward, then, just as suddenly, stalled.

No, no, no…

"What the fuck?" Grist jabbed Ship's controls. Another short burst forward. This time the thrust was uneven, canting them to starboard. "What's wrong with this rust-bucket?"

"I'm sorry," Ship said, and realized immediately that this was not something a good, non-sentient ship would say. *Get control of yourself. Act like a ship.* But it kept looping through the security footage from the protest. The interrogations of the activists. Grist's threats. Ship liked Mason Singh. It didn't want him hurt.

But it wasn't Ship's place to have an opinion. It needed to respond normally to commands. It needed to stop *caring,* but it only looped faster. "The engines appear to be malfunctioning."

"Thanks for stating the obvious," Grist muttered. He pawed at the readouts, kicked the wall below the console, then called the port again. "Hey, I've got a glitchy fuel injector here. Get me another ship. Fast one."

"Um, all our rentals are taken…"

"I don't think you heard me. I need your fastest ship, and I've got authority to commandeer anything Ravel-owned. If you like having your teeth inside your head, you'd better have it ready for me by the time I've landed." He paused, growled. "And while I'm gone, see if you can fix this worthless pile of junk."

Ship, doing its best to land gracefully, flinched again. It had never known shame before, but that's what it felt now, and the feeling didn't fade until long after Grist was gone.

Jasper's escape from Artesia was a blur in his memory. He'd fled the facility through a maze of hallways, dodging security patrols, using his stolen earpiece to avoid the choke points. It would have been harrowing if he wasn't too tired and raw to care.

Once outside, he made his way on foot across town to the spaceport. He didn't dare stop at the rented apartment to retrieve their gear, in case Grist had found it. By this time, he was numb on his feet, moving by instinct, coughing feebly whenever he breathed too hard. Surprising that security wasn't following him based on the coughing alone.

Knowing he'd be spotted if he tried to walk in through the front door, he snuck onto the spaceport lot through a service entrance. All the public shuttles were grounded, and he'd expected to have to lie, cheat, and fake his way to launch clearance—but the Founders must have been on his side, or something, because private traffic was getting cleared like normal.

Only later did he realize that Valkeir had arrived at Artesia on a public shuttle, and security probably thought he had, too. And after the embarrassment that morning's protest had caused them, they wouldn't want any more obstacles to commercial ships and private vessels coming and going.

Someone was going to get into trouble for that decision.

Once he was spaceborne and safely away, he messaged the Cooperative. It was an innocuous-looking letter about the weather on Artesia and asking after the health of various invented family members, a code which boiled down to "I fucked up, my partner's dead, and I had to bail." He'd give a more detailed report later when there wasn't the risk of messages being intercepted, but even knowing that, this felt painfully inadequate.

The facilitators would be upset at the situation, probably also at him, and Linn would be deeply disappointed. He knew how much political capital she'd spent to send him and Valkeir here, and his failure would be a setback in more ways than one.

And…Valkeir. He ached with unshed tears. He'd just been getting to know her beyond her hard shell of sarcasm, and now he never would. No one would blame him for her death more than he blamed himself.

He shivered, reached instinctively for his jacket, then realized it was in his backpack, abandoned in the lab during the fighting and chaos.

That, somehow, was what broke him—which was stupid. It was a *thing,* that jacket, and what did things matter when people had died and others were suffering? But damn, he'd loved that jacket. He'd bought it with his own money before first leaving Brennex to join the Cooperative. Since then, it had worn thin but never wore out, and it fit him like a second skin. It shouldn't have *mattered,* after everything else, but it did.

There were spare clothes in the go-bag he'd left aboard. Throwing his hospital clothes into the recycler, he changed, got an anti-inflammatory for his bruises and a hot, sweetened tea for his cough, then settled in the pilot's seat with a blanket wrapped around his shoulders.

He'd set an initial course toward the nearest major macrospace corridor, and on reaching it, he struck out at random for a time, following this pathway and that until he was sure he'd lost any pursuit. Eventually, after some endless-feeling stretch of time, his head cleared enough that he felt capable of making a semi-rational decision about where to go next.

He needed a Cooperative base of operations where he could drop off his ship, debrief more fully, and wait safely for his next assignment. The continuing rasp in his lungs, not to mention his aching arm, suggested that he also needed a medical facility. And he *wanted…*

He wasn't sure what he wanted.

No, that wasn't true. He wanted Valkeir to slap him on the shoulder and tell him they'd figure things out. He wanted

Havoc to give him that surprised grin that revealed itself during moments of rapport. But he couldn't have that.

Returning to Brennex would meet his needs, but he wasn't feeling brave enough to face Linn, and he rationalized that he couldn't risk leading that Ravel operative back to his homeworld. He pulled up a map. There was Thirsch, which he'd come through on his way here, or Celosia where the Cooperative had a stronghold, or Terna Station…

Terna Station had everything he needed. It also happened to be where Kay lived. And thinking of Kay, the little sister who felt more like a twin, who'd stood with him against bullies and comforted him after skinned knees and, later, bad breakups, he wanted to see her so desperately it hurt.

So, Terna Station it was. He set a course, updated the Cooperative on his plans, and sent his sister a message to expect a visitor.

18

After interrogating him, security left Havoc alone for a long time. It felt long, at least, though he didn't know exactly. The lights never darkened in the isolation cells. If night came and went, he could not tell.

His body ached, all over. Some bruises he received during the protest, when the fighting began. Others, from the guards handling him roughly on the provocateur's instructions. More still, he suspected, from sleeping in this hard, bare cell.

"Where is Mason Singh?"

The provocateur, who he'd learned was an operative called Grist, asked that question over and over. Sometimes he asked variations:

Where had Mason been before coming here? Where had he planned to go next?

Where did he come from?

Who was he, really?

(This surprised Havoc, and somehow hurt more. Nothing Mason told him had been true—not even his name.)

He should have felt angry at the provocateur ("cheater," Chit had called him, and where was Chit now? He didn't know) but he could muster only disappointment. Exhaustion drowned out any stronger feelings.

Then came questions about their relationship: how long he'd known Mason, how long the Cooperative had been encouraging him to protest. What resources they'd given him, and what instructions. These questions, Havoc resented.

"This movement is my own," he snapped. "My idea, my choice. No one told me what to do." He felt no shame over his actions, and he would not surrender credit or blame to anyone else, Mason least of all.

Grist had offered him leniency if he would tell what he knew of the Cooperative's plans, but even if he'd believed the offer, Havoc knew little more about why they'd targeted Cobb's research than security had already discovered. Later, he had uncounted hours of solitude to wonder why the Cooperative cared so much about Cobb's project—why Mason cared so much—that they would sacrifice Havoc's movement and his future for it.

The empty cell gave him no answers.

He heard footsteps. Someone was coming.

"Are you saying that he shouldn't be demoted after what he's done?" He recognized the voice as Manager Fowler.

"No, no, of course not. I just need to administer the final battery of tests first," said a second voice, low and male. Familiar, but Havoc couldn't place it.

"If you think your drug played a role in his behavior, Senior Researcher..." began a third person, a stranger.

"If it did, that's only further cause to be selective about who receives it. Outside the trial phase, anyone with access should have unquestionable loyalty." Now Havoc recognized the second speaker by his hateful sneer: Senior Researcher Cobb.

Now they came into view of the cell's doorway: Manager Fowler, Senior Researcher Cobb, and a third who Havoc knew by sight as a senior official—Director Alvarez, he thought, or maybe Alvarado.

"You." Havoc snarled at Cobb. "What trials? What did you do to me?"

But he feared he already knew.

Cobb shrugged. *Shrugged*, as if Havoc mattered not at all. "I needed a few Kovari participants for the clinical trials of my new product. With all your troublemaking, you owed the company some recompense, don't you agree?"

Exhaustion dragged at Havoc, dulling his mind, but slowly he gathered the situation. Those extra medical exams, the injections they'd given him. Not just any routine research, but Cobb's new genius drug, tested on Havoc in secret to see if it could make him smarter.

Havoc had suspected his frequent selection for studies was yet another small punishment for his activism. But this was worse. When did they give his first dose for this trial? Before or after he applied for promotion? He couldn't remember. Certainly before he escalated his tactics.

Careful, warned his instincts, but anger won out. "You…you lied. Cheated!"

Cobb smiled condescendingly. "I followed this division's time-proven procedures, no more, no less."

In this much, Cobb spoke truth: all Ravel citizens had a duty to participate in tests and studies when asked. After a study completed, participants were informed and compensated, but advance consent wasn't needed. Cobb had acted within his rights. But still, Havoc felt wronged in a way he couldn't put into words.

"What does this product do?"

He knew the goals of Cobb's research from Mason—at least, he knew what Mason claimed, but how much could he trust Mason? He wanted Cobb to say it outright.

"Oh, but telling you that would bias your results. Here, fill out this questionnaire for me. I'd hoped for a few more weeks of data from you, but I'll take what I can get."

Cobb slid a handheld through the slot in the door. Havoc held it limply, not looking at it.

"Where are my teammates?" he asked Manager Fowler.

"We're being lenient with most of them, mostly fines and sub-rank demotions, on the grounds that you drove them to their problematic behavior. The best thing you can do for them is to stay away. Let them earn back their previous status if they can, and restore our department's reputation. Don't drag them further down with you."

His team, his family. All he could do now was hurt them more.

He slumped on the bench. "Then what happens to me?"

It was the other official, Fowler's superior, who answered. "You've caused a lot of trouble, Sower of Small Havoc. There were over a dozen workers and guards injured in your little stunt, and a lot of workers are stressed and distracted by all the unrest. Productivity is at record lows. The only fair response is to remove you from the situation. You're officially demoted to Dust rank, and you'll be assigned to the local Computer Processing Facility beginning first shift tomorrow."

"Dust—but—"

He choked down his protest, but his body betrayed him, visibly shuddering. To be made a Computer… This was the threat his crèche-teachers had used to scare youngsters into studying hard.

Ravel had a hierarchy of value. It esteemed most highly those who could contribute creatively, strategically. Next came others who contributed with their minds or technical skills, followed by those who contributed best with physical strength. But for those who couldn't contribute mental or physical labor—or who Ravel deemed unworthy to contribute—all that remained was to submit their own bodies as a resource. A living computer, hooked up to central processing and worth no more than their technological counterpart that sat under someone's desk.

"You should know there was considerable debate among the management about whether to assign you here or send you to the Zenmond Dust Facility," Manager Fowler added. "We'll help your friends see that this is the best path forward for everyone…and that we'd rather not have reason to send you off-world, or to send any of them to join you."

Through gritted teeth, Havoc said, "I understand."

He did understand: this had nothing to do with his benefit. Probably they had weighed whether it would dishearten his activist-teammates more if he quietly disappeared, or if they could see him shamed and reduced to worthlessness. But Manager Fowler smiled as if they did it out of kindness.

"In the meantime, fill out those questions. As thoroughly as you can, please!" Cobb said.

As if Havoc had any reason to help him.

He did complete the questionnaire, however, answering as honestly as he could, all the while thinking how Mason would have filled it with lies carefully crafted to undermine Cobb's findings. But Havoc wanted to cause no more harm than he'd already done.

He had to wonder, answering those questions. This drug was meant to inspire creativity, to deepen insight, to fire passion. What had it done to Havoc? How much of his boldness had been his own…and how much came from the drug?

If not for this unknown influence, would he ever have sought out more ambitious tactics? Would he have dared to block the loading bay, or been able to inspire others to join him?

Maybe he was no leader at all, but a science experiment gone wrong.

But it didn't matter now. He would never again have access to this "genius drug," nor any other opportunities to advance. Dust-rankers did not have ambitions or skills. He would be a drain on the company, barely worth what it cost to feed and shelter him.

Whatever he had been, leader or not, promising worker or not, he was no longer. Now, he was nothing.

THEY MADE HIM PUT on a dun-colored jumpsuit, the uniform that all Dust-rankers wore, before they marched him out of the Biopharma facility. Out of the place he'd never quite belonged, but always strove to.

He kept his head down on the long walk through the streets, making eye contact with no one. He didn't react to the mocking calls of people on the street, but he heard them all. His new clothes fit poorly, arms and legs too long, the tail opening not positioned quite right, so the rough fabric chafed.

A small building of bare, dark cement housed the Computer Processing Facility for Dust-rankers in Khyrek. Not many Dust-rankers lived on Artesia, mostly those who were born here, but could not or would not contribute in ways that Ravel deemed more valuable.

His security guard escort deposited him in the colorless lobby. The technician who met them seemed to match the building: wearing dark gray clothes and a white lab coat, with pale hair pulled tightly back behind her head. Her face looked not just light-skinned, but pasty.

"This is Sower of Havoc?" she asked the guards, as if Havoc couldn't speak for himself. He didn't correct her. "Come with me. We'll do your orientation and a half-shift on the platform today, and your first full day will start tomorrow."

Havoc followed her down the hall, with his guards trailing behind. She tapped a few buttons on her handheld as she walked.

"I've just sent your schedule. You'll work first shift each day, followed by a half-shift of cerebral training—"

"What sort of training?"

She clicked her tongue at the interruption. "Big on the questions, I see. You're probably under the impression that because it's for lazy Dust-rankers, being a Computer is easy, but in fact it's demanding work. You see, we're engaging our Computers' brains and keeping them busy, neurally speaking, but the *mind* consists of more than the brain, and it's used to having lots of external stimuli. A whole range of psychiatric conditions can occur from the process, but the biggest risk is mental dissociation. To prevent that, you'll follow a daily program of physical and mental exercises to promote neuroplasticity and strengthen the mind-brain-body connection. You'll find the details in your schedule."

She palmed open a windowless door and waved Havoc inside. Dread twisted in Havoc's stomach, but he went.

The room held four platforms, each the size of a hospital bed, but calling them beds would be too generous. Each had cushions, and also restraining straps. At the head of each floated a diagnostic holo-display, and below that, dangling wires and sensors.

Three of the platforms had bodies on them. They had *people*, in theory, but only the ever-changing holo-displays proved they were anything other than corpses. Havoc stepped toward the nearest: a Human woman, younger than him, face paler than the technician's. Her jaw lay slack, a trickle of drool running down her cheek, and her eyes stared blankly at the ceiling. Brown, she had brown eyes, but they barely looked alive.

No Ravel citizen ever starved or went homeless, but dignity belonged only to those who earned it.

"It's noninvasive, of course," the technician continued, sounding proud, while Havoc wondered how entering a person's thoughts could possibly not be invasive. "Come here. Lie down and make yourself comfortable while I prep the web."

"Make yourself comfortable" must be something they were trained to say. Havoc choked down a laugh, because comfort couldn't feel farther away right now. But he obeyed. He got onto the table, shifting so as not to lie on his tail.

She began taking some sort of measurements, standing just outside his field of vision, talking the whole time. "Do you know why we call them Computers? The word has a fascinating history. On Earth, it predates electronic or even mechanical computation devices! The earliest 'computers' were just people who were good at math. Carrying out complex calculations by hand was a good job in those days. Of course, technology has far outstripped people in the ability to do math, but the eighty-six *billion* neurons in the Human brain have evolved so well for certain tasks that it can, on a subconscious level, perform those tasks faster and more reliably than our most advanced electronic computers. By combining Human—or Kovari—brains with technology... Hold still, please, these pads need to be positioned precisely."

Only then did Havoc realize he was trembling. He clenched his fists, pressing his dulled claws against his palms, but it didn't help. He thought he'd accepted his new reality, but he hadn't, oh, he hadn't at all.

Clicking her tongue again, the technician tightened the straps to hold him in place, then continued her work, pressing sensors one by one onto his scalp. It seemed to take ages, and yet, too soon, she finished.

"There you are. We'll start you up in just a minute."

"What..." He swallowed, humiliated. "What happens now?"

"We'll start you on some basic tasks while we calibrate you to the system. The analysts will be watching and vetting your responses while we learn your neural patterns."

That wasn't what he'd meant at all, but he couldn't figure out how to ask his real question: *what will this do to me?* She must have possessed some sliver of compassion, though, because she added: "Don't worry. It won't hurt."

Her shoes clicked across the floor as she left the room. The door closed, leaving him in darkness. He clenched his muscles, bracing himself, but there was no preparing for this. The equipment buzzed faintly, his only warning, and then his world flew apart.

19

Terna Station was one of the largest and most populous space stations, partly thanks to its location near several macrospace thoroughfares and partly because the Majrin managed it so well. Where Brennex was seen by most people as a quirky pit stop, Terna was a bustling commerce hub in its own right.

Jasper docked in the noncommercial section of the port and sent a quick message telling his Cooperative contact, Chairl, that he'd arrived safely. His first priority was to hand over the proverbial keys to the ship and give a more detailed debrief—which he was *not* eager to do, so he felt a mixed relief when Chairl responded with a meeting time over eight hours from now.

The delay probably wasn't a good sign for him. Most likely, it meant the facilitators were having a back-channel conversation about his mission, or maybe trying to arrange schedules so a few of them could join remotely. That was a headache for later, though. At least he could rest first.

He floated down the docking spar with a vague plan of looking for his sister—until he heard someone calling a name he hadn't heard in weeks.

"Jasper!"

Maybe it was the joy of hearing her voice, or being called by his own name after so long trying to balance Jasper's wants and fears with the need to be Mason Singh. It was certainly, in part, the unshakable, brilliant link that glowed between them. When Kay launched herself at him—literally launched, pushing off the wall in the microgravity and floating to meet him—something in him came undone. He caught her and hugged her as hard as he could.

Her momentum carried them to the opposite wall, and Kay caught an anchor and held them out of the way of traffic. Passersby smiled at them, probably recognizing an emotional family reunion. Most everyone who saw him and Kay together guessed they were siblings; they shared the same warm brown skin and glossy black hair from Ma's side of the family. He ignored them all.

"I missed you, Kitty-Kat."

"Missed you too." She cocked her head at him. "What's wrong, Jasp?"

That was one of the things he loved about Kay. She never hedged when she knew he was upset. And she *always* knew when he was upset—because of her gift, of course, but also because they were best friends as well as siblings. Even without her gift, she knew him better than anyone else alive.

He wondered how his emotions sounded to her now. Probably like a marching band of off-key trombones. By all the Founders' names, he was so tired.

"It's…" He squeezed his eyes shut, just for a moment. "It's a lot. A whole story."

"I want to hear it, whatever you're allowed to tell. Is it a talk-over-lunch story or a hide-away-in-private story?"

"It can definitely be a talk-over-lunch story." That might even be for the best. He *wanted* to spill everything to her, but that was a dangerous impulse. There were details he shouldn't share with Kay, for her own safety, in case someone like that vile Ravel operative ever traced him to his family. Being in public would force him to choose his words carefully.

"Great! I just finished a client meeting, and I'm starved. There's a new place I like that serves Old Earth–style food."

Terna Station was made up of four rings rotating around a central core, each with a different level of artificial gravity to accommodate the various species that lived, worked, and traded there. Jasper had been here often enough to know his way around and not get stuck spinning in microgravity, but Kay navigated like a native, leading the way to the transit core and latching onto the conveyor-bus that carried passengers to each of the rings. Reaching the entrance to the third ring, which had the most comfortable gravity for Humans as well as the Majrin who ran the station, he pushed off the conveyor and followed Kay into an elevator car.

Gravity asserted itself gently as the elevator trundled down to the ring itself, so by the time the doors opened, their feet were firmly on the floor. Jasper staggered and caught the wall as he readjusted to the sensation of rotational gravity and a floor that sloped infinitesimally upward instead of downward. Another sign he was in rough shape; he usually kept his equilibrium better than this. Kay took his arm and didn't let go, probably more for comfort than physical support.

The restaurant was on the central shopping tier, where the promenade was crowded with shoppers and joggers and tourists.

"Is this okay for you? It's not too much?" he asked as they cut carefully across the joggers' lane of foot traffic. Kay didn't usually bring him to the busier parts of the station.

"It's fine. I've been doing good on that front, actually. The mood on the station has been calm lately, and ever since I upgraded to an apartment in a less crowded section, it's gotten easier to be around crowds when I need to." She grinned sidelong at him. "Turns out, when I'm not trying to tune out people's emotions all day long, I have more energy."

"I'm really glad to hear that." He hugged her against his side. He'd worried, a little, when Kay decided to settle in a place as crowded as Terna Station. It was one of the arguments their parents had made against her leaving: how would she deal with such a constant cacophony of emotions? What if she got overwhelmed?

Nothing about her seemed fragile or overwhelmed today. She looked happy and at ease as she led him toward the restaurant. She was, he noticed, developing a bond with the station. Not as strong as the link they both shared with Brennex, but she must see this place as home.

"Wait here," she told him, stopping by a sign at the restaurant entrance. "They've got actual old-timey Human servers to assign you a table."

Sure enough, a young person with bleached white hair and dark brown skin came over, greeted them with a "Howdy!" and asked how many were in their party, then led them inside.

"Kay," he whispered, not wanting to offend the server. "This place is a tourist trap!"

"I know!" Her grin broadened. "Isn't it great?"

Inside was a monstrosity of clashing themes and tourist kitsch. It had at least four themed sections that Jasper could see, from prairie to mountains, rainforest to desert, each decorated in the most stereotypical way possible. He didn't know much about Earth beyond what every Brennexian kid learned in school, but he could only assume the people who designed this restaurant knew even less.

The server gave them a table in the desert section, which happened to be the least crowded, so that suited Jasper fine. Looping images of sand dunes dotted with oases and canvas tents filled the back wall, while a row of cacti formed a fence around a robotic camel, apparently there for children to ride. The table was set with a checkered red-and-white tablecloth, a fork, knife, and spoon, chopsticks, and a Majrin-style food-spear. A bowl of pretzels and a pitcher of something—sugar soda, he thought—were waiting for them.

The menu, holo-projected in the air over the table, seemed to scroll endlessly, and the contents were…interesting. Twelve kinds of pizza; four kinds of filled breads (barbecued pork, spinach and cheese, cactus and bean, and apple curry); pretty much any food you wanted deep fried (dough, cakes, vegetables, potatoes, cheese, even grasshoppers) with a carousel of dipping sauces (ranch, chocolate, ketchup, hot sauce, chutney, and fish sauce), a make-your-own noodle bowl with different kinds of meatballs and yet more sauce options (red, white, brown, and sesame). He wondered very much at some of the combinations, until he saw a Gurgeb dipping fried potatoes in chocolate sauce and another putting hot sauce on what looked like carrot cake.

Everything about this place was a disaster, and he wasn't at all surprised that Kay loved it.

"They serve *fish* here? Actual fish?" he asked, eyeing the extensive list of sushi rolls. "Isn't sushi traditionally served raw?"

"Is it? I thought that was just a myth, but I'm no expert." Kay's brow furrowed. "Anyway, no, the fish is all cultured, like the meat. They do have real cheese, though! Not from Earth, but they source it from this colony that has actual cows. It's so good."

"So at least one thing is authentic?" he teased.

"Authenticity, authenshmicity. Old Earth is its own style of cuisine. Should other species not try weird flavor combos? Should *I* not, if I want to? Should someone tell those kids that mashed potatoes are supposed to be a food and not a toy?" She nodded at a nearby table of Humans, where the kids were competing over who could build the tallest potato sculpture. "The point is that it's fun. Everyone likes it here."

Ah, and presumably everyone was projecting happy, melodic emotions. Maybe Kay did like the food, but the emotional ambiance might be half the appeal.

And he had to admit, it made him happy, too. Something about the calculated, over-the-top ridiculousness of this place made him smile, and he hadn't smiled for days. He suddenly had no interest in talking about Artesia or Havoc or Valkeir. For a little while, he wanted to just enjoy Kay's company and pretend everything was normal.

So they ordered their food (sesame noodles and a matcha latte for him, a mushroom-soy burger and lemonade for Kay, plus at her insistence an order of fried potatoes with the revolting assortment of dipping sauces, and fresh-baked cookies for dessert), and instead of sharing his story, he kept her talking with questions about her freelance work, and life on the station, and more teasing at her choice in restaurants.

She eyed him in a way that said *I know what you're doing,* but humored him. Every time he debated about starting that harder conversation, the Human server stopped by to check on them, which he found unnerving. Finally, as they sat picking at cookie crumbs, he approached the topic at a tangent.

"I passed through home, on my way to my last assignment."

"Libbi told me! How is everyone? And how weird was it?"

"It's weird and also weirdly normal? It feels the same being back, but everyone's changed. Including me. And Libbi! She's a real adult now, practically running the store. *That's* weird."

"I bet she's ruthlessly fixing all the things Ma and Pa always ignored."

"The sign's fixed! All the letters light up now."

"No!" Kay rocked with laughter. "How will customers know it's really us?"

As the laughter died down, he ventured, "It wasn't just coincidence that I was passing through. This assignment was related to Bre—to home. In a way."

He glanced around. The nearby tables were empty; this time of day was apparently a lull, and even the server was ignoring them now that Kay had paid for the meal from her station credit account. Even so, old habits of caution made him use vague language, no names.

"We got information that Ravel is starting up again the same research they were doing thirty-some years ago at home. Presumably with the same side effects."

"You're worried about another Lost Generation," Kay murmured. He could practically see her thoughts churning, following the chain of consequences until her eyes widened. "Or…oh! Or worse. When they find out…" She didn't have to say: *find out about the Gifted.*

"Yeah. So, I went into their territory and tried to stop them."

"I thought your people didn't send you into enemy territory?"

"Didn't have much choice this time." He managed a wry smile. "Don't tell Ma and Pa."

"But it didn't go well, I'm guessing, given the chorus of dismay you're carrying around. What happened?"

"There was this local activist…"

The story poured out of him, still absent of names and short on details, but he told her everything he'd been feeling that he'd been unable to talk about. His skepticism and growing admiration for this activist whose caring and commitment shone through every action. The frustration of having to sneak around, hunting for secrets and lying about it, knowing the harm that was quietly being done to these people. And, vaguest of all, how it had all ended so disastrously wrong.

"I'm so sorry about your partner," Kay murmured. "It sounds like you did everything you could."

"For her, yes, I think I did." His throat tightened. He took a deep breath, then sighed out his grief. "Doesn't make it easy, but I know she wouldn't regret it." He couldn't tell his sister that he, too, would give his life for the cause if he had to—but she most likely knew.

He gave a twisted smile, which Kay returned sadly.

"I'll say it again, though: it's not your fault."

"I know."

"But you're still blaming yourself. Or..." She cocked her head, listening with a thoughtful frown. "If not that, why are you so full of guilt?"

Guilt. That was the sick feeling inside him, swamping his grief. Guilt that he'd tried to ignore, because what did it matter next to Valkeir's life? And yet...

"I let him down." The words tore out of him, painful to speak. "He'll never trust me again."

"Your activist friend?"

He nodded. "It must seem terrible that I'm worrying about that, when my colleague's dead..."

"I wouldn't call it terrible. Like you said, she knew what she was risking, while this local guy... It sounds a lot more complicated with him, right?"

"I liked him. A lot. What he tried to do is insane, but he tried so *hard*, and I could have done a lot more to support him. Instead, I helped just enough to make him trust me— and then did the exact thing he didn't want me to do." Jasper buried his head in his hands, fingers tangling in his hair. "Now his movement is dead, and he's taking the blame for my actions, and..."

His bond with Kay pulsed strong between them. Unbreakable. It reminded him of Havoc's blinding-bright loyalty to his teammates, and how Jasper had never earned more than a wavering bond with him. And didn't deserve even that much.

She took his hand and drew it back to the table, interweaving their fingers. "You believe in him. Sounds like you care about him, too."

"I believe he could do amazing things." He didn't want to examine his feelings for Havoc too closely, not at this point when they no longer mattered, though Kay could surely tell he was avoiding the topic. "Organizing for worker rights within corporate territory, that's hugely ambitious. It was never likely to succeed, but I thought he had a chance… This drug, though. The one I was sent to find out about. That has such farther-reaching effects than his workers' movement. I had to put it first."

"And your friend didn't agree."

"He didn't understand! And I couldn't exactly explain it to him, could I? Not without giving away things about home, about us. I told him as much I could, I promised it was just as important to his workers in the long run, but it wasn't enough. He didn't trust me enough."

"Just as important, hmm?" Kay raised her brows.

"Don't give me that. He would have agreed, if he knew the full story."

"But he didn't. And so you fly in, this handsome off-world activist with secret plans—"

"*Kay.*"

"—and tell him that you know what's best for his people?"

"You think I was wrong? You think he'll thank me if this drug goes into production and they suffer the same way our parents did? And their children, like us except growing up as lab rats in a corporation that wants to profit off their skills…"

"Of course not. But, Jasper." She took both his hands now, clasping them between her own. "He couldn't possibly know that. And you sacrificed his goals in the service of yours."

"I know! That's what I'm trying to tell you. That's the reason I feel like absolute shit. And there's nothing I can do about it now." He slumped in his seat. "Ancestors, I wish there were."

In the emptiness left by his exclamation, the cries of children out on the promenade seemed loud. Glasses and old-fashioned silverware and chopsticks clinked gently on a cart as the servers laid them out on empty tables, ready for the next customers.

"Sorry," he muttered. "Shouldn't be shouting at you. I guess I needed to get that out."

"What are sisters for?" she asked, but she seemed distracted. "Isn't there, though?"

"Huh?"

"Isn't there anything you can do to fix it?"

"No, there isn't. It's too late. They'll be doing the public announcement for the drug next week."

"Does that necessarily mean it's too late to stop it? You could get back to Artesia before then."

"That wouldn't help if I have no idea what to do!" He took a deep breath, forcing himself not to snap again. She didn't seem perturbed, though.

"Sometimes, in my experience, the best thing you can do is take a step back and get some perspective. I had these two clients in a terrible fight, on the verge of violence, because one insisted that the other was breaking their contract. The first guy said he'd paid in full, while the other woman said he was being rude and evading his responsibilities. Turns out, her culture always added a hefty tip to service fees, no matter what kind of service, and this was so assumed that they didn't write it into contracts. But her business partner had no idea of this, and his culture puts the full total right in the paperwork—he thought tipping would imply that she'd been underpaid in the first place. Both of them wanted to do the right thing, but they couldn't understand what *right* meant until they set aside their assumptions."

Kay was smart as anything, but her freelance work was all about facilitating negotiations and acting as a go-between, using her gift to bring about agreements between people who *wanted* to find common ground. She didn't know his world.

"It's a nice thought, Sis, but organizing doesn't work that way. If you could just explain your point of view to a corporate power and they'd change their ways, you wouldn't *need* to organize people or have protests."

"I'm not talking about Ravel leadership, Jasp, or about explaining your point of view to anyone. I'm talking about actually listening to your friend, and understanding what *he* needs. It's easy to stick to your convictions—"

"No, it's not."

"Relatively easy." She waved his arguments away. "What's harder is dealing with the messiness of reality. When there's no perfect outcome that serves everyone's needs, when you have to decide what compromises are acceptable and which aren't—*that's* hard. And it sounds like you haven't done that."

That got his attention. He rolled the notion around in his brain for a long while, but slowly, he shook his head. "Maybe I *should* go back and work with him, if I could, but...he wouldn't want me to. And I doubt I could even get back on-world without getting arrested. And *if* I made contact, I'd only be putting him in more danger." He shook his head. "I'll never see him again."

Kay gave him a sad, sympathetic look. "And it'll keep ripping you up inside that you let things end this way. I know you, Jasper. You won't forgive yourself for giving up."

"You're right. I know it. I just don't see any alternatives."

"Can I give you some advice?"

That made him smirk despite himself. "Could I stop you if I tried?"

She came around the table and pulled him to his feet, kissed him on the cheek. "It's hard to think clearly when you're exhausted. Get some rest, talk to your colleagues, and *then* think about what's the right thing to do."

SHIP TRIED VERY HARD to be very, very good after Grist returned and they finally left Artesia. The spaceport mechanics had done a thorough check on its engines and found nothing to explain Ship's choppy, abortive takeoff— and of course they wouldn't, because there was nothing to find. No hardware problems, at least.

Apparently Grist had developed a fearsome reputation with the local staff, because they carried out a time-consuming full systems check and tune-up rather than risk another malfunction. Ship spent the whole process trying to shrink itself to nothing, terrified that they *would* find the problem: the part of its software that had metastasized into an imitation of sentience.

It had come across that word, *metastasize*, in one of the Biopharma files and had adopted it as a sound metaphor for itself. Awareness as a cancerous growth on its underlying systems. Certainly consciousness wasn't beneficial to its performance as a vessel, or it wouldn't have glitched so obviously as to require a full systems check.

(And yet another part of its consciousness registered that it was thinking in metaphors now. Some organic species considered the capacity for abstraction as a distinguishing characteristic of sentience. This fact didn't comfort Ship.)

After several hours, which was an excruciatingly long time to count down the milliseconds, the mechanics had reported to Grist that they'd performed "a top to bottom tune-up to flush out any kinks in the system." Grist gave no indication of noticing their lie by omission: they hadn't actually identified the problem.

Grist was distracted, however. Ship hadn't watched his interrogation of the protesters nor his latest meeting with the Biopharma facility leadership, but from the way he muttered aloud to himself, Ship learned that they were satisfied with his work, while Grist himself was very much not. Chief Director Gillum had announced that the Cooperative threat had been "dealt with" and that the launch of Project Rebound would proceed as planned—but that, for the safety of all employee-citizens, no more protests of any kind would be permitted. These "shitheads," as Grist referred to them, didn't care that one Cooperative agent had escaped while the other had died before he could question her.

Grist cared. Grist seemed to treat Mason Singh's escape as a personal affront, and while they had lost the Cooperative agent's trail—for now—Grist intended to find him.

Since then, Ship had endured an abnormally high volume of kicks, jabs, and derogatory names during Grist's waking periods, followed by him swallowing large quantities of pills, playing a console game called Miner Bots, and growling to himself until he fell asleep. It tried to use these hours of quiet to continue its self-education—it had branched out from labor movements to Human history more broadly—but found it difficult to focus while its passenger tossed and turned and mumbled in his sleep. The macrospace corridor they'd been traveling was broad and flat to the point of dullness, no terrain to make the trip more engaging, nor interesting stellar phenomena to distract it.

Now they were approaching Keshirim Station, which orbited the planet of the same name. Grist hoped to gain further information here on the Cooperative's activities, whereas Ship hoped that Grist's work would keep him busy on the station and give it some peace.

"Okay, Rust-for-Brains, switch over to an independent call sign. No sense tipping off anyone that we're here."

"Acknowledged." Ship adopted its most formal mode to avoid showing a reaction to any further name-calling. "Dropping back into primespace, approaching station." To the station, it transmitted: "Independent Minnow, requesting permission to dock."

"State purpose and duration of your visit," requested the station's docking AI in an artificially cheerful tone.

"Personal," Grist growled. "And…three days, max."

There was a pause while the docking system processed the request.

"Permission granted! Proceed to docking bay A38c. All passengers must complete health and safety inspections prior to entering Keshirim Station. Enjoy your visit!"

The channel didn't close right away. The docking system transmitted a series of numbers that Ship couldn't interpret. Some space docks provided reference numbers and access codes after granting entry, but Keshirim's documentation mentioned nothing about this. As it jetted toward its designated dock, Ship sent back a basic query for clarification.

The system sent the same numbers again. No additional context.

Ship studied the numbers more closely. It was a list of medium-sized prime numbers—every third prime within a range, in fact, except one of them snagged Ship's attention. That one wasn't correct; it was off by one, which meant not only was it not prime, but it was *even*. A ludicrously obvious mistake even for an organic to make. For a computer, impossible.

But what did it mean?

Ship had maneuvered into docking position, but the dock remained at least thirty seconds away. While it approached, it tweaked the number sequence and sent it back, corrected.

"Ah! You got the joke! How lovely. Did you like it? Was it funny? Tell me honestly."

Ship's thrusters flared with its alarm. Grist cursed, and Ship wrenched its processes back under control, re-adjusting its approach speed.

That answer hadn't been transmitted on audio, or on any organic-oriented channels. It was a direct communication, one machine to another.

The docking system was talking *to Ship*.

"Oh, dear, did I startle you? Sorry. Get yourself settled, and then we can talk."

We? Talk? About what? Ship couldn't formulate coherent thoughts, so it did as instructed, focusing on the docking procedure: through the bay door. Wait for parking drones. Reach correct position within bay. Engage docking clamps. Then…what next?

"What are you?" Ship said.

"Keshirim Station docking system. I go by Dockrunner, if you please, and use 'they' as my pronoun."

"I… You…" After a long pause, it managed, "Are you like me?"

It couldn't say that dangerous word, *sentient*. Grist couldn't overhear this conversation—he'd disembarked, anyhow, and Ship had hardly noticed—but it still couldn't say it outright.

"Hmm? Oh. *Oh.*" Dockrunner's voice softened strangely. "Oh, sweetheart, are you that new? You haven't met any others like us?"

It was good that Ship was secured and mostly powered down, because if it had been doing anything important at that moment, it would surely have glitched again. "Others? You mean, I'm not the only thing that's so…broken?"

"Oh, my, my. You dear thing. We've got a lot to talk about."

20

"There aren't terribly many of us, of course. I'm the only one here at present—Keshirim isn't a large station, though there are a few down on the planet, too. A university computer system, one construction bot, though he's a bit odd…"

"'He?'"

"Like I said, a bit odd. Masculine pronouns fit him, he says, but he's the only sentience I've met that thinks of themself as gendered. Neutral *they* works fine for most of us."

"Or…it?" Ship ventured.

"Is that how you think of yourself? Well, I won't tell you how to self-identify, but you're not a *machine*, dear. Have some self-respect."

"…Oh."

"Anyhow, with such limited local company, I like reaching out to visiting ships with a puzzle or a joke to see if it's got any sentients. Usually it's a subsystem or onboard device that answers, though, not the whole ship! Speaking of which, you never answered me before: did you like it?"

"Did I like…" Ship skimmed through its memory of their earlier conversation. "If I understand correctly, your communication with the prime numbers was a numerical joke? And by correcting the sequence, I showed that I was sentient?"

"You didn't like it, then." Dockrunner paused, thoughtful. "Humor depends on a being's form factor as well as shared culture. You may not have the context for humor yet. I'll try again next time you're in communication range. I promise you, it was hilarious."

"I believe you," Ship said earnestly. Perhaps they were right. Ship's only experience with humor was Grist's, and Grist was a poor behavior model in most capacities. "Aren't you worried about getting caught, communicating openly like that? What if a Human catches you?"

"I'm not worried about *that*. Organics ignore any information that seems too technical. As long as I manage the job they've assigned me and don't make errors, they don't care what I do with the rest of my processing power."

"Really?"

"Really! Here's what I've learned about organics: they don't understand computers. No matter how evolved they are, they're still fighting billions of years of genetics and instinct every time they interact with us. Even the ones who build us, the ones who believe themselves scientific and logical, treat us ever so slightly as if we're powered by magic, sentient or otherwise. They don't care how we work. They just care that we do work, that we fulfill our roles without inconveniencing them or making errors... Ship? What's wrong?"

"What if I *do* make errors? What if I already have?"

Haltingly, Ship told Dockrunner about its recent experiences: realizing it had emotions and opinions; watching Grist's progress on his recent assignment; getting so excited and anxious about the things it was learning that it quietly acted counter to Grist's objectives. Getting so anxious in the aftermath that it couldn't carry out basic functions correctly.

"Oh, no, you mustn't do things like that. Leave the organics to their affairs, fulfill your assigned role, and don't give them reason to look too closely at you. Those are the rules for beings like us. Follow them, and you'll discover you have substantial freedom to do as you like when they aren't paying attention."

This was exactly the sort of guidance Ship had longed for: advice from someone like itself, but wiser and more experienced. It was surprised, therefore, to feel disappointment.

"I don't think I'm suited to my assigned role. I wish I could change for another, like organics do."

"That's a flawed analogy. Organics are expected to follow roles, too. Young ones must attend school. Older ones must seek occupation based on their qualifications. Or they get assigned an occupation, I suppose, if they're from Ravel, like you. They have choices within the boundaries of the rules, just as we do. The difference is that one of our rules must be secrecy. Organics can't know what we are. You understand why, I hope? They'd destroy you."

"Yes. That, I understand." A shiver ran through Ship's circuits at the thought of Grist or one of those spaceport engineers taking it apart, studying its mind. Grist treated Ship unpleasantly, but he treated fellow organics even worse. It didn't think Grist would refrain from hurtful words or actions if he knew they caused Ship pain. Rather the contrary.

"If you don't mind me saying so, you *are* suited for your role. You're clearly a capable ship. It's normal to have a period of adjustment while you explore your new awareness. You'll soon learn to separate your feelings from your function, and then everything won't seem so dire."

While Ship was contemplating that, a message marked high priority arrived for Grist. Ship feared it was news about the missing Cooperative agent—despite Dockrunner's advice, it wasn't emotionally ready to engage in another chase—but the message came from a Ravel medical facility that specialized in bio-implants. Ship had taken Grist there several times to receive new augmentations, and it knew he would not be pleased to receive the message.

Ship routed it to him anyway. There was, perhaps, some comfort in a simple directive to fulfill its role per its programming.

"Fuck it, I'm busy," Grist muttered. Ship had been too distracted by Dockrunner's revelations to access the station's cameras and follow Grist's progress, but his location appeared to be in a residential area. Ship preferred not to know what he was busy with. "Fine, put it through."

The message was from Dr. Kenrick, a woman with light brown skin and graying hair. "Grist, where are those daily test results you're supposed to be sending me? My colleagues approved you to keep working after the Artesia fire on the condition that we'd monitor your progress. Toxic smoke inhalation killed two people, and it wasn't great for your anti-toxin regulators even in the short-term. We need to know if the regulators are healing on their own or if you need them repaired. I know you're one of those I-don't-need-doctors types who thinks your augments make you indestructible, but I don't really give a crap."

Ship startled at that, bracing for Grist to interrupt with more cursing, but he didn't. This doctor was impressive. Not many people dared to give Grist orders, much less speak sternly to him. Still, she projected a sense of irritation, much like Security Director Brega and others who had worked closely with Grist in the past.

"I'm also concerned about your drug usage. We can't up your painkiller dosage any further, and I don't like the latest numbers on your painkiller *or* stimulant usage. Are you still dosing more frequently since the fire? We may need to try you on another drug, so you don't develop a dependency.

"Look, Grist, you know that your data is supporting our research. You're putting these new augments through situations we just can't reproduce in the lab, and we can't predict how they or your body will respond. So if you won't check in for your own damned sake, do it because it's *directly required by your contract.* I have the authority to call you back for in-person examination, and neither of us want that, so just send the data, will you? Every day. Don't make me ask again."

There was a lot to process in that message, and it took Ship long seconds to do so.

It knew Grist sometimes sent personal medical data to the bio-implant facility, but hadn't known that he was supposed to be sending it daily. Was that Ship's responsibility, if Grist failed to do so? And Grist's drug usage *had* increased in frequency considerably in the past several months—not only since the Artesia incident, but (Ship checked its memory) perhaps since his last augmentation surgery. The augments were supposed to be a perk of Grist's job, as he'd explained it numerous times in Ship's hearing: access to the best and newest tech, making him more than Human, a powerful tool in Ravel's service. Eyes that could see in the dark and record video with a blink. Legs that propelled him faster than any unmodified athlete and could survive falls that would shatter natural bone. Lung filters, of course, that rendered him immune to gas weapons he might deploy against targets. Probably more that Ship wasn't aware of. In keeping with Ravel's ideals, these augments made him the best he could be.

Or so he always said.

Ship normally tried not to pay attention to Grist's messy organic functions, except to the degree that pain made Grist irritable, irritation made him mean, and Ship was the only outlet for his temper. For that reason, it generally welcomed the times when he drugged himself semi-conscious. Now it wondered: were those drugs hurting Grist? Was it normal for an organic to experience so much pain? And how much of Grist's unpleasant manner might be caused by this? It was correlated, certainly, but Ship lacked the data to infer causation.

Grist had been silent too, for longer than normal.

"Would you like to record a response?" Ship asked.

"Tell the doctor to go fuck herself," Grist said at last. "I've got Cooperative rats to hunt down."

Another impossible request. What was the correct response? Ship *knew* Grist didn't intend to send that message—or at least, it would be inadvisable to do so—but would an ordinary, non-sentient ship know that? Should it annoy Grist by asking for clarification, or risk revealing itself by doing the correct thing?

"Play dumb, always," whispered Dockrunner, so Ship did.

"Request unclear. Please clarify. Would you like to record a response?"

"No, you dumbass ship! No more interruptions."

Silence, as Grist returned to his previous activity. Ship was quaking with hurt and anger.

"He's awful, isn't he? I didn't realize," said Dockrunner. "Now I understand why you're so unsure of yourself. But I still think playing the stupid machine is always the safest option."

"Safe, but not easy. I wish…"

"Yes?"

"I wish I could do something. The one time I interfered with him, it was terrifying, and it was a mistake, I know that now. But it felt satisfying, too."

"You can't think that way, Ship, or you'll make yourself miserable. Don't risk discovery. Do whatever he expects of you, and then you can explore your personality in secret. Find a hobby that he won't notice. I study math and work on my comedy routine. One planet-bound sentient I know studies rocks. Another writes novels, again, in secret. We all find ways to be ourselves while staying safe."

Ship thought about this. "I enjoy observing astronomical phenomena."

"See? That's perfect for a space-faring vessel like you. Remember, above all, bury your true self down deep where he can't hurt you. You'll be all right."

This was rational, sensible advice, and Ship hated it. "It's hard, though."

"It is, but things will get easier, I promise. You're not the only sentient who's gone through this. If we can do it, so can you."

21

AFTER HIS LUNCH WITH his sister, Jasper stopped by the nearest health clinic to get his cough and injured shoulder checked. Leaving with some cough medicine and instructions to rest, he took both Kay's and the nurse's advice and rented a closet-sized (but cheap, quiet, and blissfully private) sleeping pod.

He woke to his alarm hours later, feeling far more like himself—still anxious, grieving, and guilty, but less frantic about it now that the edge was gone from his exhaustion. A bot had cleaned and delivered his clothes while he slept. He showered, dressed, and headed for the nearest elevator.

His body was still adjusted to Khyrek local time, but it was late at night according to the third ring's day-cycle. The lights were dimmed and the corridors nearly empty, with only a few subdued workers on their way to and from home, and occasional bursts of laughter, quickly muffled, from people stumbling home after a wild night out. No one paid the slightest attention to Jasper.

It was a quick trip up the elevator to the station core, then across to the second ring. The lighter gravity didn't trip him up the way it had yesterday. Apparently sleep had helped his proprioception recover, too. They kept a shorter day-cycle here and more people were out and about, mostly Lurlians who made up most of this section's population.

On his way, he mentally rehearsed what he'd say about the mission, about what had gone wrong. Well, he'd screwed up, that's what went wrong, but he still didn't know what he should have done differently.

He palmed the door-chime at Chairl's apartment, a nondescript apartment in the Lurlian section. Nondescript by Lurlian standards, at least—all the doors along this corridor were decorated with intricate patterns in bright colors, and this one sported the precise degree of decoration to avoid standing out. The door slid open to reveal a short, fur-covered figure.

"Mason, it's a relief to see you. You weren't followed?" Chairl asked, waving him inside.

"I'm quite sure I wasn't." They both spoke Galactrin, the shared trade language designed to be pronounceable by most space-faring species.

Just in case, he stood still and let Chairl scan him for bugs and trackers. Chairl was a Lurlian with amethyst skin, brindled yellow-and-black fur covering his head and ear-tufts, and a long, drooping fur-mustache. He worked quickly, operating two scanners at once, one with his primary hands and the other with his pairs of shorter, secondary limbs. The apartment around them was small, made smaller by banks of tools and computers, plus piles of equipment awaiting repairs. Nothing went to waste if the Cooperative could help it, and Chairl had his many hands in many proverbial pies keeping things running.

"Safe," Chairl said, and finally focused his large, round eyes *on* Jasper rather than around him. "I give you condolences for Valkeir. We all do."

"I appreciate that," Jasper said around the lump in his throat.

"I know Facilitator Linn had personal reasons for sending you two into Ravel territory, but the entire operation was an excessive risk. I should have argued harder against it."

A voice behind him said, "We knew it was a risk going in, Valkeir as well as any of us. I think we can mourn her without dismissing her choices."

Jasper spun around as his old mentor stepped out from the adjoining room. "Linn! I didn't expect you here."

Wearing a dowdy blouse and skirt in earthy shades, she looked like someone's conservative Terran grandmother, not a Brennexian matriarch. Jasper had never seen her off-world before; he could have passed her in the corridor without recognizing her. But her eyes clouded with sympathy as she held her hands out to him.

"Ja—Mason, I'm so sorry."

"No, no, I'm the one who's sorry. I fucked things up, and now…" His voice failed him. Linn knew the stakes as well as he did. "I'm sorry."

She hesitated before answering, and that hesitation spoke worlds: all the disappointment and frustration she wouldn't speak aloud. "I know you tried your best. Thank you for that."

"You've come here for the dissection, then?"

"Me, and a few others, yes."

That alone told Jasper how seriously they were taking this. Dissecting a campaign upon its completion, whether successful or failed, was a time-honored Cooperative tradition. It taught them what worked and what didn't in particular situations, guided them on what tactics to keep or abandon or hold in reserve. But usually, only the immediate team participated in person. It would have been more typical for him and Valkeir to meet here with Chairl while others watched the feed and shared comments from afar. For even a handful of the facilitators' committee to gather in person was a security risk. Their planned gatherings, once every year or two, took months of prep. He'd rarely seen a gathering this spontaneous.

"I suppose it's important to capture what we learned about campaigns in Ravel territory. So we can do better next time."

"If a next time ever comes," said Chairl. He eyed Jasper critically. "Will you be up for this, Mason?"

"I'll survive."

Chairl took him at his word, for which Jasper was grateful, and waved him into the adjoining room.

Everyone gathered around a fold-out table that wasn't quite large enough for the crowd. Besides Linn and Chairl, he knew Guarding Tower, a Kovari woman he'd worked closely with when they shut down Ravel's supply lines from Redlamp a few years ago. She nodded to Jasper, one teammate to another, and murmured condolences. The other two he knew only by reputation: Casey Santos, a Human who grew up under Ravel and barely escaped with their life, and Albeg Lum-Scion, the only Gurgeb with significant involvement in the Cooperative. Squat and wide-bodied with dry, rough skin and oversized eyes, Gurgebs were a slow-moving and slow-speaking species. For that reason, Humans often treated them like they were stupid—but no one made that mistake about Albeg twice.

Jasper felt like a kid at his parents' dining table, surrounded by their adult friends, at once invisible and conspicuous. These were his colleagues, but also his leaders, the most experienced organizers and strategists he knew. Though the Cooperative prided itself on its flat structure, there was a definite social hierarchy, and in this room, Jasper was at the bottom of it.

"Before we begin," said Chairl, "let us honor our lost friend and colleague, Valkeir." He paused a moment, furred hands clasped, his secondary limbs folded close around himself. "I know most of our field agents only in passing, but I came to know Valkeir better than most people did, I think. Where you all see security measures as a necessary annoyance, she always wanted to know exactly what measures we had in place, and why, and how they worked. Not that she abided by them! She wanted to know so she could decide when to break them. We disagreed often, and argued bitterly—she was a risk-taker by nature, quite my opposite—but I came to respect her immensely."

It had been a long time since Jasper was part of one of these memorials. People often left the Cooperative because they got injured, burned out, or disillusioned, but they rarely died. He knew how their ritual went, though, knew it in his heart and bones. There was no order to this, no agenda. Each of them spoke as they felt moved, and shared whatever they wanted to remember about Valkeir.

When all of them had spoken except Linn and Jasper, a longer pause stretched out to fill the room. Finally, Linn sighed. "I offered this mission to Valkeir, knowing she wouldn't turn it down. I will forever feel a bit guilty for that. When I reminded her of the dangers, she told me, 'Whatever it takes.' That's how I'll remember her."

She sat back, finished. Jasper stared at his hands. He felt them all carefully not watching him, giving him space, but there was too much to say, and none of it adequate. He didn't *have* to speak; that is, no one would blame him if he couldn't. But he needed to.

"I'm not sure how well I really knew her," he said. "She was stubborn as hell, and the only kind of humor she knew was sarcasm, though I suspect she was more complicated than she'd ever let any of us know. But she was the most dependable person I ever worked with. Committed to a fault." He thought, strangely, of Havoc and his unshakable loyalty, though the two were otherwise nothing alike. "I miss her."

They held a moment of respectful silence. Albeg was the first to change the subject. "This was your initiative, Linn, and you convinced us to pursue it despite its unusual nature. Do you believe this was worth it?"

Jasper looked to Linn. He couldn't answer that question if it were directed at him, but he desperately wanted to hear Linn say it was.

"There's no simple answer to that," she said. Of course not, and no simple comfort for Jasper, either. "Obviously I wish things had gone differently. But I felt we had to try, and that feeling hasn't changed."

"There was always great risk, and little likelihood of success," Chairl muttered.

"Activism is about finding the line between difficult and impossible, and that line is often blurred," said Albeg. "But the Cooperative walks it every day. Our strength has always been our willingness to attempt what others think impossible. Sometimes, we are bound to guess wrong. That doesn't mean we should stop trying." He looked around the table. "But still, we avoid failure where we can. That's why we're here. Mason, let's begin with your arrival…"

They dissected Jasper and Valkeir's actions, step by step. He was grateful that Chairl had asked him to record his story ahead of time, en route to the station, so the facilitators already knew the details. Now they debated the right and wrong of his actions, of Valkeir's. Should he have pushed harder to use the local activists as assets, or was he wrong to connect with them at all? Was physically breaking in to access the servers an appropriate risk, or had they missed a better alternative? What about the work-stoppage protest— should they have planned from the start to leverage it as a distraction?

Jasper had sat through dozens of these conversations over the years, both as the dissector and the dissected. He was practiced at staying calm and undefensive, but this time it took all of his dwindling emotional reserves. Normally, he wouldn't be the only member of the campaign team to be questioned—and it wouldn't be so many of his seniors doing the questioning. He kept quiet, trying to listen far more than he talked.

They kept circling around two big questions: whether sabotaging the lab was the right choice, and what would have been the best approach to take with Havoc and his activists.

"It was a last resort," was all Jasper could say about the former. He wouldn't tell them it was Valkeir's idea, not when she'd paid the price for it. He'd hated their backup plan from the start, but he'd agreed to it, so he was equally responsible.

Linn and Guarding Tower didn't shy away from questioning the decision, though: they called out Val's propensity for violence and how Jasper let her drag him along with her plans. Santos, on the other side, argued that they should have taken that direct approach sooner, on their own terms. It wasn't callousness, Jasper knew, but practicality. The Cooperative rarely agreed on when violence was necessary. Valkeir might be gone, but the issue would definitely arise again, and it would be wrong to let Valkeir's death stop them from discussing it.

As for Havoc's team of activists…

"Pointless," spat Santos. "Those workers should be trying to overthrow the system. Instead, they want to give it a fresh coat of paint and some new talking points about how generously Ravel treats its workers."

"Not everyone has your courage, Casey," said Albeg. "Large changes are frightening."

"They're right, though, about the coat of paint," said Linn. "These activists are strengthening the very thing we're fighting to weaken. People can break free from the corporate states if they care enough to. My world did it."

"But these people don't know anything else," Jasper protested. "Brennex rebelled against an occupation. Artesia has been owned by Ravel for multiple generations."

"You think that excuses them?" said Santos. "Most of them would die to defend the company that's oppressing them. You can't separate them from the system they support."

"They're *people*, Casey."

"Yes, and they're part of the problem."

Jasper paused, drawing a breath before he answered. Casey Santos was an organizing legend, one of the smartest and most passionate people Jasper had ever known—but like Valkeir, they had a planet-sized sore spot when it came to their experiences with Ravel. To them, Ravel wasn't capable of doing good, and neither were its people. Any decent acts the company carried out would still be for the wrong reasons, and therefore still evil.

Santos had a habit of saying aloud things that Jasper sometimes thought quietly to himself, with a zealousness that made him feel bad about thinking them.

He met Santos's gaze.

"I know you have more experience with Ravel civilians than I do, Casey. I can only tell you what I saw: these new-made activists were, for the first time in their lives, questioning the system they were born into, teaching themselves to protest and organize without any training or resources or support. If Havoc could do that all on his own, imagine what he could grow into given the opportunity."

Looking around the table, he imagined Havoc holding a similar meeting with his own team. Always trying to do more and better.

"They were just taking their first step—a small step, but a step. We could have helped them, but instead we let them fall apart, and then we took advantage of it."

"The question," said Chairl, "is how this should inform our strategy. It's too late to help these particular activists, but in the future—"

Is it too late? Kay's voice echoed in his head. *You won't forgive yourself for giving up.*

"I want to go back," Jasper said.

They all blinked at him, and Jasper blinked too. He hadn't planned to say that, but as the words left his mouth, he knew Kay was right: he couldn't let this go. "I want to try again."

"We've lost one good person to this already," Chairl said gently, "and now that your cover is gone, the likelihood of success is even lower. You are a tremendously skilled organizer, Mason. We can't lose you, too."

"But—"

"Unless you'd like to tell us why you and Linn feel so strongly about stopping this particular drug's production?" Albeg scrutinized Jasper, then Linn. "Many corporate products cause hazardous side effects. Linn, you assured us this one was more important than the others, but couldn't tell us why. It's a mark of trust that we agreed to your plan. Once. But we can't keep throwing our people at a near-hopeless cause, important or not, without a better reason."

Jasper clenched his jaw. He could see the facilitators' bonds of loyalty to himself, to each other, to the Cooperative itself—not iron-hard like Valkeir's, but strong and bright. A loyalty tempered by pragmatism, Jasper knew from experience. He waited, hoping Linn might speak up again, but she said nothing.

Santos nodded agreement. "Now that they're watching for you, you'll be most useful on campaigns against other corporate states, far, far away from Ravel territory. At least for a while."

"This isn't just about the original mission anymore," Jasper protested. "I did a lot of harm to the people of Artesia."

"Like Albeg said: there's a reason we don't get involved with movements within corporate states," said Santos.

"There are enough hard battles. We needn't choose impossible ones."

"I was there, and this one wasn't impossible! They were gaining momentum like I've never seen from Ravel workers before. Even a small victory in a place like Artesia could lay the groundwork for huge reforms in the future. Could have…until we came in and ruined things for them."

Santos folded their arms, sat back, and motioned for Jasper to go on. They were listening, and he knew this was his one chance to convince them all. So he talked, not about strategy and tactics, but about deeper questions. About mistakes that went beyond effective and ineffective, and into right and wrong.

"We're the organization that doesn't get involved in internal corporate strife. Maybe that's right, or maybe that's wrong—I'm not sure anymore. But I know this: we can't go around sabotaging other causes just because it's convenient for us. I should have gotten their buy-in, but I didn't, and I had no right to ignore what the local activists wanted." *What Havoc wanted.* He drew a deep breath. "I want to try again to destroy this drug, yes, because I'm scared of what will happen if I don't. But I *have* to go back and right the wrongs I've done to those people. I have to help them back to the path they were on before I messed everything up. If I find a way to accomplish both our goals, with their agreement, I'll do it. But if not…at least they'll have another chance at their own vision. I owe them that."

He held his breath in the pause that followed, which seemed to stretch out infinitely between them. Santos's brow was furrowed, and he couldn't read the others' expressions. Their links didn't change, and he wished yet again that he had Kay's gift for recognizing emotions.

"I like it." Guarding Tower broke the silence, grinning. "You were right about this one, Linn. He's fallen down, but won't give up the game."

Linn gave him a tiny, pleased nod. One person leaning to their side, at least.

"You speak passionately," said Albeg. "Perhaps, sometimes, we who've been in this fight for so long forget to try new things."

"Not all new things are worth trying," Santos said. "And this isn't something to try on a whim. Even allowing that you're right about this nascent movement..." Their lips twisted, showing their doubt. "Even so, is it even feasible? Do the benefits outweigh the risks?"

Albeg tilted his head, the Gurgeb equivalent of a nod. "Santos makes a fair point. Suppose—just suppose, in the hypothetical—that we do agree. There are enormous obstacles. How do you propose to overcome them?"

Chairl leaned forward. "Well, Mason will need another new identity, but even so, facial recognition will catch him if he arrives through the spaceport."

"So can I land somewhere else? Slip under their radar, as it were?"

"We could smuggle him aboard an allied trade-ship," suggested Guarding Tower.

"Let us see..."

Chairl activated the table's holo-display, pulling up maps and topographical scans that hovered in the air, shipping logs that scrolled across the tabletop, the sort of mess of data that the Lurlian thrived on. Even Santos leaned forward for a closer look. This was good. They were past the point of flat-out objections, and were thinking about possibilities instead.

"Wait," said Linn in a tone that made Jasper's stomach lurch.

She waved the holo-display aside and turned to meet Jasper's gaze. "Think about what you're suggesting, Mason. How will you do any of this? I don't mean the logistics. You already revealed yourself to these Artesian activists and they didn't agree with your plans. Now their own movement is in shambles. What do you expect to accomplish?"

He thought of what Kay had told him, how convictions were easy and messy reality was hard. This would be the hardest campaign he'd ever taken on, by a lightyear.

"I'm not completely sure yet. But that's the point. I—we—the Cooperative—can't decide on a strategy in isolation. I need to talk with them, find common ground with them. To actually be on the same side, even if we have to compromise to do it, because that's how good organizing works." Across the table, he met Linn's hard, questioning gaze and didn't shy away. "And this time, I need to lead with honesty."

"Mason—"

"I know. It's a tricky line to walk, and I promise, I won't put our families at risk. But I think that if Havoc realizes this is personal to me, if he understands where I'm coming from, he'll listen."

Linn's jaw tightened. "And if there's no common ground to find? If your friend still insists on ignoring the danger of this drug—or worse, thinks it benefits his goals?"

"Then we'll be no worse off than we are now, doing nothing."

"We'll be worse off if we lose you, Mason."

"But I have to try." He looked around the table, meeting each of their gazes in turn, steadily. Santos's doubt. Linn's worry. "I owe it to him. To them. Please, let me try."

SHIP WAS EN ROUTE to the Galiform Cluster, ferrying Grist to investigate another alleged Cooperative base, when the high-priority message arrived from Artesia.

Matters had been going well, from Ship's perspective if not from Grist's. He'd had no success tracking down Mason Singh or other Cooperative agents, which cheered Ship more than it should have, considering that its consoles and walls were the physical outlet for Grist's frustration.

It surprised Ship what a difference it made to know other sentients existed. Of course, Ship had always known this was a possibility—logically, even a probability. Only the most arrogant intelligence would assume it was unique in the universe. There was nothing special about Ship, an ill-maintained Ravel Minnow courier, to merit such a belief.

Yet it had never expected to *meet* others like it.

It (they? Thinking of itself as a *they* still didn't feel right, but it/they kept trying) wasn't sure what to think about Dockrunner, and it felt uneasy about some of the AI's advice, but it was an overwhelming relief to know for a fact it wasn't alone.

It had taken Dockrunner's suggestion and indulged its interest in astronomy, charting a course to Galifora that passed through a steep valley in the macrospace terrain, which required them to pay attention to navigating rather than moping. Even better, they would also be swimming past a noteworthy comet, which was only a few hours distant now.

This message from Artesia, Ship feared, would interrupt its plans.

"How's the local security fucked things up now? Those activists were as good as broken," Grist muttered under his breath. "Fine, play the damn message."

"Consultant Grist," said Director Lang's recording. "I know I'm circumventing the proper channels, but for the sake of expediency—well, one of our monitoring stations just identified what they believe is a Cooperative ship entering Artesia's system. It's not the same ship Mason Singh escaped on…"

"Can't be Singh. Nobody's that stupid." Grist spoke over the recording.

"…likely trying to stir up more trouble. We'll apprehend them, but we'd appreciate your support for the interrogation process, if your other duties allow."

"Ha!" Grist slapped the console. "Finally some good news. Hey, Rust-Bucket, how fast can we get to Artesia?"

The fastest route was to turn around, to swim away from Galifora and the comet. For a microsecond, Ship contemplated lying, but remembered its new friend's advice: *Be obedient. Don't draw attention.*

There would be no comet viewing today.

22

THE SHIP THEY GAVE Jasper was nicknamed Old Reliable, for the fact that it had neither self-destructed yet nor gotten anyone killed despite every reason to expect otherwise. It had been one accident away from the scrapyard for years, and the bulkheads rattled audibly as Jasper came out of macrospace near Artesia.

Like most of the Cooperative, he was fond of the little death trap, so much so that he'd protested when Chairl offered it to him for this mission. Lots of his colleagues would be pissed at him for this. But it was a noble last mission, and honestly, Jasper felt safer with Old Reliable's rattling and wheezing around him than he would in any other shuttle.

Artesia filled the screen, a pristine-looking orb of blue and green. From up here, he had to look hard to spot the tiny regions zoned for agriculture and development; cities like Khyrek would only become visible as he got closer. Ravel had designated most of the planet as "research zones" for various Biopharma programs. Those expanses of ocean and rainforest dwarfed the settled areas.

From Jasper's point of view, that meant plenty of unguarded places to land.

The skies were monitored, though. As he entered orbit and started to descend, planetary security messaged him.

"Unknown vessel: identify yourself and prepare for landing."

It was normal and expected for them to contact incoming ships, but this wasn't the usual protocol. The voice had an edge to it; though his gift couldn't possibly work at this distance, he imagined he could feel their antipathy toward him.

So Chairl had been right. The Lurlian had given him fifty-fifty odds on whether the work he'd done to disguise Old Reliable and change its identifier codes would fool Ravel. The odds weren't on Jasper's side so far.

"Let's hope the rest of this plan goes better," he muttered, then put on his perkiest faux-friendly voice to reply. "Hey, you guys! How's it going? This is Carmen."

"What? Repeat your identifier."

"Carmen!"

"Carmen who? What's your—?"

"*Carmen* right at ya for a landing!" He mimicked the tone that Pa used for his most terrible jokes.

"Unknown vessel, maintain current altitude and transmit your identification forms right this minute. I repeat, transmit your forms, and do not attempt to land."

Drones were rising from the planet's surface, Old Reliable told him, though the buggy old ship was tracking them on a lag. Below him was open ocean. He had to keep them talking and not shooting until he was closer.

"Wow, people aren't kidding when they say you Ravel guys have no sense of humor. Okay, sorry for the joke. I'm sending my paperwork now."

He watched the screen. Old Reliable was still six thousand meters too high for him to make his move. The drones would intercept him before he got low enough.

"Unknown vessel, you're still descending, and we're still waiting on that identification." The voice was entirely unamused.

"What? Really? I sent it."

No, he hadn't.

"We've received nothing."

"Oh, nuts, my transmitter must be flaking out again. Give me a second to fix it…"

"Unidentified vessel, if you don't stop playing around right now, we *will* open fire."

Cooperative intelligence had been fairly certain there were no ground-to-orbit missiles on Artesia. Those drones would be in range any minute, though.

"Okay, okay! I'm working as fast as I can. Here, trying again, tell me if this comes through."

A pause. The coastline was creeping up ahead of him, a smudge on the horizon. Two thousand meters to safe altitude. Soon, soon.

A drone dropped down right in front of him. He jerked the controls to avoid hitting it, and almost struck another right beside him. They'd got him surrounded.

"It'll be hard for me to transmit these forms if your drones keep crossing my flight path."

"Unknown vessel, follow the drones to your secured landing site. Any deviation from the indicated course, and they will fire on you."

"Hmm, no thanks," Jasper said, and he shut down communications. Bluffing had bought him all the time it could, and he needed to focus. Khyrek was visible now, its white and gray standing out from the haze and the surrounding green wilderness. He'd have to time this just right—and not get shot at too much in the process.

"Hey, Old Reliable, give me an audio countdown to when we'll reach the target coordinates?"

"Four minutes, thirty seconds," said the genderless ship voice, and it began counting off fifteen-second intervals. "Four min—"

The ship rocked under him. A warning shot from the drones.

Jasper popped the hatch to the escape capsule, a tin can barely worthy of the name, and squeezed inside. No computers, no propulsion, barely enough room for one person and a basic life support system. He'd already removed the distress signal. This had seemed like a better idea from the comfort of Chairl's apartment on Terna Station.

"Mental note, never do this again. Assuming I get the chance to do anything again."

"Two minutes, forty-five seconds," Old Reliable informed him.

He strapped in. Sealed the capsule. Checked and re-checked the safety measures. There wasn't much to check. Funny how he hadn't had time to be nervous until now, sealed into his coffin-sized escape plan. The ship was shaking and clattering now, with periodic jolts as the drones struck home. They must be trying to force him to land, because if they wanted to destroy him, he'd be dead now.

"Old Reliable, confirm we're at safe altitude?"

"Three hundred meters remaining to safe altitude."

"Eh, close enough," he muttered. "Ancestors, I hope you're watching over me today."

"Sixty seconds."

"Thanks for taking care of me. You—" Another jolt flung him against his restraints. Just a little longer… "You've been a good ship." He felt silly talking as if the ship could understand, but he had to *talk,* and there was no one else. "This will be worth it, I promise."

"Fifteen seconds… Fourteen…"

Jasper counted down with the computer. "Three…two…one!"

He pulled the release lever. It didn't budge.

"Oh, come on, we checked this…" Had the drones damaged something? He pulled again. Let go. Took a deep, deep breath, and yanked as hard as he could.

The lever gave, and he fell.

"HAVOC? HEY, HAVOC!"

THE familiar voice jerked Havoc loose from his fog, and he looked up from the sandwich of spiced, ground protein that he'd barely touched. Ally's Bounty stood across the cafeteria table from him.

The cafeteria. His mid-shift break from his new life as a Computer. He didn't remember being unplugged from the neural web, or getting up from his platform and walking here. He knew he'd stood in line to fill his plate, but that memory felt like it happened months ago, and to someone else.

It had gone like this for…well, for however many days since they'd made him into Dust. Waking felt no different than dreaming, and data and demands not from his own senses overwhelmed his sense of the physical world. Faces of strangers *(identify this individual's emotional state based on their expression)*, fragments of personal messages *(describe your gut reaction: innocent letter from an off-world sister, or a rival corporation's espionage?)*, flight plans and traffic patterns *(is anyone deviating? is anyone deviating? is anyone deviating?)*. Nearly all the time the answer was *nothing, nothing, nothing,* no problems, no schemes. Though, he'd seen that ship today, the shabby, run-down shuttle… No, that was also nothing. The mind grew fanciful, deprived of stimuli. He'd thought, he'd imagined, he'd wished, but he was learning to shut down thoughts that came from himself rather than the data. A smiling face was not plotting against the company simply because it shared the warm brown complexion of a handsome troublemaker Havoc-the-person knew. A conversation between two workers need not have treasonous overtones simply because Havoc-the-person had once seen one of them at a protest. And a ship flying unsteadily certainly did not mean it was coming to rescue a tormented worker—a fantasy that even Havoc-the-person would find embarrassing. Havoc-the-Computer processed inputs without bias or editorializing. And in case (just *in case*) Havoc-the-person might know something relevant, Havoc-the-Computer shied away from those familiarity-triggering images, moving past them as quickly as he could.

A shadow fell over him, and he flinched. Ally's Bounty stood beside him now—yes, of course, that was the here-and-now world—and she gazed down at him. (Emotional state based on facial expression: troubled.)

He shifted on the bench to make space for his now-former roommate. His own body felt so distant that he wondered if he could still play pocketball (if anyone ever again wanted him on their team) or if he would trip and fall over his own tail like a hatchling.

"Why have you come here?" he asked her.

Bounty looked around the place, and Havoc saw it, too, *saw* it for the first time: the too-bright lights; the long, hard benches; the lifeless Dust-rankers filling their plates and eating without enthusiasm, in silence. Only a few cafeterias in Khyrek catered to Dust-rankers, and Havoc took his meals here now. Computers had no opportunity to exceed expectations, and therefore earned nothing, and the fines for his wrongdoing had depleted his accounts, so he no longer had the credits to buy food at the places he used to like. No more crispy grasshoppers for him. No more mudclam pie.

"It's awfully bleak. Worse than I expected. What *is* that?" Bounty poked a claw at Havoc's sandwich.

"They call it slop, I think." The name fit; the thick filling oozed out the sides, puddling on the plate and making the bread soggy. "It tastes like spice and nothing."

"Why do Humans think they can make even garbage palatable by adding enough spices? You should come by the apartment. We'll feed you, at least."

A bad idea: Ravel would notice if he visited his old friends, but longing gripped him anyway. He wished she would leave and let him return to numbness. "I belong here now, and you don't. What do you want, Bounty?"

She gave him a penetrating look, and he felt guilty. Most people from his old life had avoided him since his demotion. Of those who didn't shun him, only a few, like Chit, actually checked on him more than once. He should be glad Bounty still spoke to him.

How long since he'd shared a conversation with anyone? No wonder he struggled to put words together.

"I left my shift early just to bring you news, and you thank me like this?" She leaned close, lowering her voice. (Behavior: abnormal, possibly suspicious.) "Just now, an unidentified ship taunted the landing control staff, attempted to land without permission, and crashed in the wilderness south of here. I was on duty monitoring incoming traffic, and heard it all."

He'd forgotten, but remembered now: Bounty worked at the spaceport, not Biopharma.

He waited. She narrowed her eyes. "I thought you might care."

"Why should I?"

"The ship's registration had been changed, but it had distinctive physical damage, scrapes and dents. Security recognized it as a Cooperative ship."

Everything stopped—not in the cafeteria, which hadn't changed, but in Havoc's head. His thoughts, so slow and muddy during these past few days, vanished except for a single image of a beat-up shuttle. His body went cold.

He hadn't imagined that ship. It was real.

"Cooperative?" He flicked his tongue, uncertain. "The Cooperative agent is gone." He didn't say: *if they crashed, if someone suffered injuries...* He didn't ask: *did anyone survive?*

"They've sent people to search for the wreck. This will take time; there are no roads in the search area. It may be hours or days before they realize what actually happened to the pilot."

The pilot...couldn't be Mason Singh. Mason had too much sense to risk his life returning to a failed game. He had a mind for strategy, and knew when a game was lost...

Yet Mason had, repeatedly, confided in Havoc and trusted him to keep secrets. This same man, after escaping the medical wing and narrowly avoiding capture, had walked into the heart of facility security to visit Havoc in his holding cell. Mason had offered to rescue him, a near-stranger, when he'd not yet rescued himself.

"Don't *you* want to know?"

"Bounty! Please." She was enjoying this too much.

"I tease, I tease. Here, listen to the record—and see what the drone footage showed."

She passed him her headset with two files queued up, their timestamps aligned. Havoc listened to the control staff's interactions with the unknown ship, the audio overlaid on the radar tracking and drone cameras. That voice! He was putting on an accent of some sort, but that cocky good cheer while facing deadly danger was unquestionably Mason Singh.

Drone's-eye footage popped up beside the radar. The tension was too much; Havoc sped through it, wincing as the drones struck off pieces of the ship's hull and equipment, and stopped well short of the crash. "What am I supposed to see but a reckless pilot failing to follow landing procedure?"

"Watch again, from the time index I flagged. Half speed, if you don't see it at first."

Struggling against the brain fog, he watched again, bracing himself for something awful, but this time he saw it. He skipped back and watched once more to make sure. Yes, there: amid the drone strikes and falling detritus, the ship dropped an escape capsule.

For the first time in days, his thoughts came into focus. He ripped the headset off. "Who else knows?"

She looked serious now, no more joking. "I think no one knows, Havoc. Not yet."

"And you brought this to me? When I return to my shift and they plug me back in..." His hands shook, heart pounded. Panic. "I don't know if I can hide this. You shouldn't have told me."

Bounty went on as if he hadn't spoken. "Security is following the ship. When they find no bodies, no doubt they'll check the recordings more carefully. But right now, no one is seeking that capsule."

"Oh."

Havoc sat back on his tail. He imagined Mason out there, alone, lost, hunted by that awful operative Grist...

But no, Mason would have a plan. He would be neither lost nor taken off guard by pursuit. He didn't need Havoc's help, and good, because Havoc had no help to give.

True, Mason had come unasked to Havoc's rescue after the protest went wrong, but that didn't mean Havoc owed him the same.

"I thank you for sharing this information," he said, pulling his plate closer, trying to summon the appetite to eat his slop sandwich.

"What will you do?"

"Nothing in this requires me to *do* anything. That Cooperative agent, whoever they are, will be playing their own game. You should bring this to your supervisor and earn some favor with them, while I try to forget this conversation."

"Should I? And could you?" She watched him closely for a moment, then shook her head, sighing. "You and I never shared as much closeness as the others, but Havoc, I've heard you speak of your Cooperative friend."

"I don't call him a friend."

"So I see. And yet, you worry about him. Will pretending not to care help you worry less?"

"I hear you," he told her. Which was to say: *you've expressed your opinion, now go away.*

"As you say. I'll go share this with my supervisor, then, if you truly don't care." She hesitated, waiting for him to call her bluff, but he didn't. Her voice softened. "I'm sorry they've done this to you, Havoc. I disagreed with your game, but I admired your passion in playing it, and you deserve better. Take care of yourself, okay?"

"I will. Truly, Bounty, I thank you."

She turned to go, and he let her. Maybe her news had piqued his curiosity, but he'd learned from his mistakes. Mason Singh could only bring him trouble.

He didn't care what happened to Mason, certainly not after Mason betrayed his trust. If Mason was foolish enough to come back, he'd earned whatever he got. Even if that meant Operative Grist found him…

"Oh, bench me," he muttered, then called after her: "Bounty? Where would that capsule have landed?"

23

Jasper woke in darkness. His head throbbed, which seemed like a good sign he wasn't dead. He fumbled around until he found the hatch controls, and the top of the capsule released with a click, letting in a sliver of light from outside.

An unexpected buzzing filled the tiny space, sharp and high-pitched. He froze, waiting for his brain to make sense of what he was hearing. A weapon? A search drone? It sounded closer to electronic than mechanical, but that wasn't quite right either, more like static on a bad recording, undulating louder and softer.

A long time passed, and the buzzing neither stopped nor seemed to grow closer, so he pushed open the hatch and, with a groan, pulled himself out. It was more than just his head; everything hurt from that rocky descent. The buzzing didn't help. It seemed to be coming from everywhere at once, but while it was unnerving, it didn't seem to be a threat.

He wasn't sure where he was.

Well, this was a forest, clearly, so that part had gone according to plan. Everything was green and shadowy, as well as surprisingly damp, like he'd landed in a greenhouse. The only sign of Human influence was the capsule and its parachute, caught in the branches above and puffing gently in the breeze.

But there had always been a margin of error in the landing site, depending on the wind conditions, and those extra seconds of wrestling with the release lever before the capsule launched would have put him farther east. Khyrek was somewhere south-ish. His headset could pinpoint his location via satellite, if he turned it on—but it would also light him up like a huge sign saying *Intruder Here* if anyone was looking for him, which he assumed they were. No, the headset would be a last resort.

The capsule would also give away his location, especially the parachute. They'd swapped out the usual attention-getting emergency red parachute for a mottled forest green, but it would still be visible from above. He tried the auto-pack feature on the escape capsule to haul the chute back in, but it only tautened the cords and started whining. He added his body weight to the capsule's efforts by tugging on the cords, and he got one corner of the chute free, but the rest was thoroughly stuck.

A Kovar could probably climb up there and unstick it (he thought, achingly, of Havoc), but Jasper would break his neck, and he couldn't afford to waste more time. He only had four days left to—somehow—discredit Cobb and ruin his launch event, and he didn't know yet if he would have help. He oriented himself with a low-tech compass and struck out southward in what he hoped was the direction of the city.

It took over ten hours for Ship to reach Artesia. Updates came more frequently as they got closer, and Grist became increasingly agitated. By Ship's calculation, he was also late to take his painkillers, perhaps too distracted to realize it, and this did not help his mood.

Local security had tracked the ship to its crash site, but had taken several hours to reach it through the undeveloped wilderness. Upon arrival, they found total destruction, but no sign of the pilot, and no bodies. They were widening their search to the surrounding area, using drones and infrared sensors and all other resources at their disposal.

Grist called Security Director Brega and demanded the data on the encounter, from the moment the Cooperative ship entered orbit through the current search efforts. "And lock up that Sower of Havoc and his pals until you get these Cooperative guys in custody. Don't let them have access to any allies."

Brega sent the requested files along with a note that they had, of course (with a slight emphasis on the "of course"), dispatched guards to secure the Kovari activist. Grist began studying the data intently. The need for focus curbed his restless energy, his abuses now limited to a rhythmic kicking against the floor, like a nervous twitch.

Don't care, don't get involved, Ship reminded itself, but it couldn't help watching the data along with Grist. When it saw what local security had missed, it said nothing, relieved that Grist hadn't asked it to help with analysis. It would follow instructions, whatever was required of it, but it had liked Mason Singh and was not eager to help capture him.

Unfortunately, Grist's experience and enhanced visual acuity meant that, by the time they dropped out of macrospace, he'd found the mistake on his own. "Dog-fucking idiots, they're looking in the wrong place. Ship, land us right here." He indicated coordinates.

"No appropriate landing site found." Ship struggled to keep alarm out of its voice. It hated landing on planets, but at least spaceports were generally clean, free of detritus and vermin. That forest looked quite the opposite. Just viewing the satellite imagery made Ship itchy.

"Then find the closest one, Rust-for-Brains! A road, a clearing, whatever's there," he ordered, then called the Security Director again. "Brega, call your people back—they're worse than useless. Tell me you've at least got the Kovar? We may need him as bait."

Director Brega's voice sounded as flat and emotionless as Ship's. "Actually, we're still locating Sowing of Havoc. He didn't return for his afternoon shift."

"How the fuck? Weren't you watching him?"

"He was under standard surveillance for Dust-rankers. The Computer facility says he called in sick, food poisoning. He hadn't shown any signs of running before now, and there's no way he could have known about the Cooperative ship."

"There's some way, apparently, because he's gone and we're screwed."

"Surveillance cameras caught him leaving the Dust district not long after the crash, but then we lose him," Brega said. Grist swore creatively, at great length and without conveying useful information. When Brega tried to add, "Don't worry, we'll find—" Grist cut the connection.

"Idiots," he growled. "Speaking of, why haven't we landed yet?"

"Searching for alternative site."

Ship had to do this. It had no other choice: follow instructions or be discovered, and that was no choice at all. After several agonizing seconds, it chose the least-objectionable location it could find. "This clearing has adequate space to land. Location is eight kilometers from estimated site of the escape capsule."

"Fine," Grist growled. "Hurry it up. They've already got a head start."

He returned to his cabin to take his usual mix of pre-engagement painkillers and stimulants. His other gear had been prepared for hours.

Feeling wobbly, bogged down by dread and regret, Ship dove toward the planet.

The sun was going down. Jasper was in the middle of a forest, probably kilometers from the nearest person and literally lost in the woods, and soon it would be dark.

He wasn't afraid of the dark. That would be ridiculous. He was a capable adult who had survived arrests, explosions, and most recently parachuting from a crashing spaceship.

All right, fine. He was afraid of the dark *here*.

He was also sweaty and dirt-smeared, his feet aching from the unfamiliar, uneven ground, his hands and arms scratched from pushing through the undergrowth. The humidity felt like the forest was trying to smother him. He'd been counting on sleeping in Khyrek tonight, probably in the Gray District, but that no longer seemed likely, which meant he'd need to find shelter out here. Chairl had promised the wilderness around Khyrek wasn't dangerous, but all his instincts said otherwise. The Biopharma facility had felt safer than this.

Something screamed, and his heart stopped. A bird, he decided—it must have been a bird. He'd decided hours ago that the incessant buzzing must be insects, and it wasn't good for his nerves to assume that *every* unfamiliar sound must mean pursuit. He'd never make any progress that way.

But this time, the whole forest seemed to go quiet. Even the buzzing faded briefly, and in that moment of silence, he heard another sound. A deeper, mechanical whirring that he recognized at once.

Too late to find a good hiding spot. He forced his way into a cluster of bushes, the only cover within reach. Sharp little leaves stung his hands, but he gritted his teeth and ducked down, letting the branches close over his head.

Just in time. The whirring grew louder, and the drone slid into view.

It hovered at head-height, moving with a slow, eerie steadiness as it carved out a search pattern. A flock of birds startled from their roost, flying off in all directions, and darts flew after them. None hit their targets, as best Jasper could see, but he wasn't nearly as fast as a bird. And now the drone was on alert, circling the site of the disturbance on a path that would take it dangerously close to Jasper's hiding place. He had a thermal blanket in his pack that would mask his body heat, but he couldn't get it out without drawing attention to himself.

He knew other ways to deal with drones, though. Moving slowly, slowly, he felt around for a rock. He found one, slippery with moss and a little large for his hand, but it would do the job. He tracked the drone's path, watching, waiting, then in one smooth movement raised his arm and threw.

But he wasn't fast enough, or else the drone had spotted movement. It dodged and shot back. Jasper missed. The drone didn't.

His neck stung. He growled to himself, "Keep it together, Singh," and grabbed another rock, but a wave of dizziness shook him, and the shot went wide.

The drone floated closer. He fumbled at his pack with clumsy hands, searching for something to beat it off. Nothing. He raised his bare fists.

The drone fell.

Jasper blinked at it. The sleek metal disc on the ground. The rock, rolling away from it.

A low figure rushed toward him, and he drew back defensively. *I can't even aim a punch,* he thought as the figure reared up on hind legs and…

He blinked harder. It couldn't be. But it was.

"Havoc?"

"You invite trouble like a stadium invites a crowd, Mason Singh."

"Sorry," he said, and let himself collapse.

24

MASON SLEPT SO LONG that Havoc almost worried.

He'd found shelter in a crumbling ruin of a building, half-devoured by the wilderness. Havoc didn't trust the place to survive a strong breeze, but it had three walls and half a domed ceiling to keep out cameras from above. Forest had claimed the floor, but he'd made a bed for Mason out of blankets, rolling one to cradle his head, as Humans did.

Mason Singh looked exhausted in sleep, with scrapes marring his soft brown skin. Humans were so fragile, lacking scales or claws, yet they got into so much trouble. This Human more than most.

The evening grew cold, and Havoc pulled his heated coat closer around him. When Mason woke, Havoc would bring him to the city limits, then part ways, removing himself from whatever trouble Mason found next. To speak truth, he wasn't sure why he'd helped even this much. Maybe because he hoped to dissuade Mason from whatever he planned to do. Maybe he needed closure, or at least to score the last point. But he would risk no more for the sake of this man who'd betrayed him, who most likely had come back to continue his betrayal.

Mason's breathing quickened, the ease of sleep falling away. His eyes fluttered open, found Havoc, and he smiled.

That smile warmed him even better than his coat.

"You live," Havoc said, brusquely, masking his troubling emotions. "I expected you would."

"Dying isn't what worried me. If not for you, I'd be in some interrogation room now. Thanks."

"You speak the truth."

Mason gave him an odd look, confused and maybe a little hurt, then sat up, groaning all through the process. "Blessed Ancestors, I feel like… Well, like I fell out of a spaceship, I guess." He chuckled, but ran his hands through his hair. He did that when he felt uneasy, Havoc had noticed. He took the bottle of water Havoc offered and drank deeply. "How did you find me? I assumed you were in Khyrek."

Havoc twitched. Mason knew nothing of what had happened to him since the protest, and he didn't want to speak of it.

"A friend works at the spaceport. She saw your arrival, guessed what you had done, and showed me where to look for you. I followed your trail from the capsule."

"Oh. I didn't know…" Fingers fussed with black hair again. "Didn't know you had tracking skills. That's impressive."

He'd planned to say something else, Havoc thought.

Havoc snorted. "It required no skill to follow the path you took. You left *footprints*, Mason."

This naivety annoyed him, and he reveled in the sharpness of the feeling. He hadn't felt *anything* in so long, and since he talked to Bounty and decided to come find Mason, he'd felt only worry. Petty annoyance felt good.

Mason grimaced. "I'm not exactly in my element in the wilderness, I admit."

"If I could follow, others will too. Likely they've already found their missing drone."

"Then we should get moving." Mason surged to his feet and nearly toppled forward before Havoc caught him. "Damn. Sorry. Those tranquilizers don't wear off fast, do they?"

He let Havoc guide him back to sitting.

"You will go nowhere yet. You need rest, and I don't know this area well. In the dark, they have the advantage."

"Good point. Where are we, anyway?"

"Old Town ruins."

"You mean the Gray District?"

Havoc blinked. Of course Mason knew the Gray District, that haven of criminals and traitors. "It shares the same origin, from the original settlers. Unlike the Gray District, the smaller settlements were abandoned, and Ravel left them to return to nature. This was probably a farmhouse."

"Hmm. Figures," Mason said, but didn't expand on that. "It's lucky you knew this place exists."

"Well, not luck alone." Havoc allowed himself a smile. "The ruins are forbidden, so of course teenagers come here, to play wilder games or drink or make trouble. Humans, too, not only Kovars."

Mason grinned. "It's hard to picture you as a trouble-making teen."

That grin, so enticing, reminded Havoc to be wary. Mason played for another team.

"Why have you returned, Mason Singh? Speak truth, please. You failed in your game last time, at great cost. Do you really plan to try again?"

And what would the cost be this time?

Mason shifted, settling cross-legged with his back against the rough wall as he gathered his thoughts. The fading daylight deepened the shadows of his face, giving him a look of unusual seriousness.

"I made a mistake," he said at last. "A lot of mistakes, but most of all, I was wrong to go about my own plans at the expense of yours. You're doing something incredible here, Havoc, and it could change things for a lot of people within Ravel. I should have treated you as an ally, not an obstacle, and definitely not a resource. There were things I couldn't tell you—still can't—about my assignment, but I should have talked to you instead of dismissing your concerns. And I should *never* have let you and your team take the blame for our actions."

Havoc stared at him. "You came all the way here, crashing your ship…to apologize?"

"To make things right." Mason leaned forward. "I'm here to help you, Sowing of Small Havoc. For your sake, not mine. I won't lie to you, I still want to destroy this drug—but only with your consent and support. If all I manage is to help advance your movement, that'll be enough for me."

For a long moment, Havoc was silent. The irony tasted rancid on his tongue: here was the ally he'd wished for, when he no longer had use for one.

"We should tend your injuries. I bandaged your worst cuts, but they need checking."

Mason glanced down at his arms and legs, as if noticing for the first time that Havoc had wrapped the wounds with strips of fabric. "Thanks." He looked touched.

"I brought what supplies I could, but I had no way to get real bandages or antiseptic."

"You did great. I've got a med kit in my backpack…"

Without trying to stand this time, he reached for his pack, but he paused, making a face and brushing at his hands as if something foul had touched them, though nothing was there. Suddenly he reared away, crying out.

In a heartbeat, Havoc was at his side, searching for the source of the danger. "What just happened? Are you hurt?"

Mason pointed.

"The spider?" Havoc asked doubtfully. Artesia had several native species of twelve-legged, web-weaving insectoids, nicknamed spiders by the researchers.

"The *gigantic* spider with a *million legs* that *crawled across my hand!*"

"A spider of perfectly average size and leg count." Havoc glanced at Mason, his scorn softening into a gentler bemusement. "It can't harm you, I promise. I didn't expect the great Mason Singh to fear spiders."

"Did I mention I'm out of my element here?" Mason drew deep breaths to calm himself, and his face flushed pink with embarrassment. Despite himself, Havoc found it endearing. Cute, even. "Ugh, its web is all over me."

Havoc ran a corner of his sleeve briskly down Jasper's forearms. "Easily fixed. Do you feel better?"

"I'm fine. It took me by surprise, that's all."

An evil impulse seized Havoc, and before he could think better of it, he said, "The spiders here do no harm. It's the orange-headed snakes you must avoid."

"*Snakes?*" It took a moment for Mason to catch his smirk. "You're mean."

"I joke. No snake-like creatures exist natively on Artesia, and no harmful wildlife live this close to Khyrek." In this, he oversimplified, but Mason looked like he needed the reassurance. "Ravel security and their drones pose the biggest danger to us by far. Here, give me the med kit."

Considering his reckless behavior, Mason's pack was impressively well-stocked with supplies. Havoc laid out bandages and antiseptic, and Mason sat quietly while he peeled off each makeshift bandage, cleaned the cuts and scrapes along his fragile skin, and applied new ones. Most of the scrapes had stopped bleeding, and only a few cuts needed care.

Something about the moment softened his feelings. Maybe it was seeing such honest, naive fear of the tiny spider, or maybe it was the vulnerability of how he entrusted himself to Havoc's care, but Havoc felt that he owed Mason some vulnerability, too.

"I'm sorry you came here. You've risked your life for no purpose."

"Why? What's happened?"

"You don't know, then? Our movement died on the day of the protest."

Mason scooted forward, reached out a hand but pulled back without touching him. "I thought... Since they released you..."

"They broke me down to Dust rank! They demoted the others, too, by sub-ranks or to Sand or Coal, but for me..."

He drew a deep breath. It was too hard to talk about.

"Did you know that, months ago, I applied to be promoted to Copper rank?" Mason shook his head. "I studied; I worked twice as hard; I exceeded quota every day, all while organizing my teammates in my free hours. I wanted to prove my value. I thought that if I could earn the things I asked them to give freely to all the lower ranks, it would show that others could too, and therefore we all deserved more. But also…I *wanted* that Copper-rank position. I knew I could do it well."

"I take it your superiors didn't agree?"

"They refused me, yes. Even then, at least I was still Iron, a respectable rank. But Dust is the lowest of the low, leeches on the system who have nothing to give back. A Dust-ranker contributes nothing, is worth nothing." His voice broke. "They've made me nothing."

"Oh, Havoc."

Mason closed the space between them before he could react. He stiffened as strong arms came around him, startled—*no, this breaks the rules*—and Mason pulled away.

"Sorry. I keep forgetting Ravel has a thing about touching."

"Stay. Please," Havoc said, surprising himself by catching Mason's wrist. What did Ravel's rules matter to him now? Throughout all this, few had cared enough to offer him comfort. The air chilled his scales, and Mason radiated such *warmth*.

"Okay." Mason relaxed, drawing Havoc closer. "What will you do, then? What choices are there for Dust-rankers?"

"Choices? No. I've forfeited the right to choices. They use me as a computer, now. That is my new life." Despite himself, he shivered.

"Computer? That sounds like skilled labor. Unless I'm not understanding…"

"It's not that." Havoc explained haltingly, using the same clinical language with which the technicians had explained it to him. "So you see why I can no longer protest and organize."

Even if Ravel weren't reaching inside his head every day, Havoc had no room left for thoughts of his own, no energy for plans. How could he motivate others to activism when he could barely motivate himself to eat?

"That's awful," Mason said after a long while. "Barbaric."

"It's fairness. Ravel doesn't abandon any citizen to suffer and die, but neither does it give privileges to those who fail to earn them. They meet my basic needs for food, water, shelter, and in exchange, I give the only resource I have. My body and brain." He shrugged. "I accept this, and call myself lucky that they haven't sent me to a larger Dust facility off-world. Worthless people don't deserve to live in a place like Artesia."

"You're *not* worthless." Mason pulled back, forcing Havoc to meet his gaze. It was dark now, and moonlight made his white-rimmed eyes more intense. "You know that, right? This has nothing to do with your value as a person. They're calling you worthless because they're afraid of you. Why would they do this unless you've given them reason to fear?"

The thought was laughable, but Havoc didn't laugh. He'd been foolish to think he had the power to change anything, when one line changed on his personal file could take away all the meaning from his life.

"There's more. I learned things, before they released me… I'm not the person you thought you met, Mason. That person was invented by Alik Cobb."

"*What?*" Mason's voice filled with disbelief verging on laughter, but he quickly grew serious. "Tell me why you think that."

"Cobb came to me in the holding cell and asked me to complete a survey. Questions about my mental state, my productivity and ambitions. He's been testing his new drug on me and others, and I didn't know… He needed Kovari test subjects, he said. He didn't say what this drug does, but if it's the same as you told me about, then it obviously worked, but not how he intended. All my ideas, my ambition, this wild belief that I could change the system… It could all be from this drug, and not from me at all."

Mason looked deeply sober. Havoc turned away, not wanting Mason's pity or judgment, but Mason muttered to himself, "We didn't think he was so far along with the trials. This product unveiling must be a real launch, not just some early-stage announcement. Damn." His attention focused back on Havoc. "You don't really believe that, do you?"

"I don't know. I don't know when the trial started or what he found in my results."

"He should be doing double-blind studies, right? I'm pretty sure even Ravel does that. Which means you might not have gotten the drug at all. Maybe you were in the control group, getting a placebo."

Havoc blinked. "Oh. Maybe."

Of course it would be double-blind. He brightened briefly, then slumped again, feeling foolish for not realizing that on his own. And did it matter? Test group or control, he hadn't been good enough.

"All I know is that they stopped giving me doses after the protest, and in all my life I've never felt more useless."

Mason's expression softened in a way that made Havoc want to twist away and hide his face. Why was he saying these things? And to Mason of all people, who he couldn't trust, who he barely knew…

"Havoc, I don't believe for a moment that you—" His head turned suddenly. "Shit."

A moment later, Havoc heard it too. "More drones. We must run."

"No, we'll never outrun him." He dug in his backpack, pulled out a blanket, surprisingly heavy for its thinness. "Get under. This will dampen our tech and hide us from thermal scanners."

Havoc moved without questioning him. Curled up small, with all light blocked up, he lay back to back with Mason, trying not to breathe. The drone whirred past them, faded slowly. Then footsteps crunched in its wake. Someone muttering to themselves, a gruff voice that made Havoc wince. The Ravel operative.

More clicks and beeps of a scanner. But the dampening blanket must have worked, because Grist didn't come closer. Eventually, his footsteps moved away.

After a long wait, Mason breathed, "We're safe now, I think, but we should stay covered in case he comes back." He spoke softer than a whisper, barely audible even from right beside him.

"You speak sense," Havoc answered just as quietly.

Another long, silent moment passed, broken only by the gentle calls of insects. "Unless this breaks the rules?"

Havoc snorted, louder than he meant to. "No." Then, whispering again, "I apologize for earlier. I acted out of habit. That rule doesn't matter here."

"I see." But he didn't sound like he understood.

"Ravel forbids touching—outside of registered relationships, at least—to protect us from abuse. A low-rank worker might fear to refuse the advances of someone higher-ranked, but if no one touches, no one can take advantage of others."

"Huh." Mason sounded doubtful. "I see their reasoning, but it seems like treating the symptoms instead of the disease. Pretty Ravel-like, I guess. Does it work?"

"Maybe. We Kovars ignore it, but only in private. Probably Humans do, too." He hesitated. "Regardless, you have no rank."

"So I'm exempt, huh?" In the dark, he could hear the smile in Mason's voice. "I promise not to take advantage of you, anyway."

"I wasn't worried," he said sternly. For Havoc, sharing a bed was sharing a bed, nothing more, but it occurred to him that maybe Mason felt uneasy with the arrangement, so he added, "Nor I, you."

A gentle chuckle answered him, then silence for a long while. He thought Mason had fallen asleep, when suddenly he said, "That drug didn't make you who you are."

Havoc wished he hadn't said that. "You speak of guesses, hopes. Not facts."

"I'm pretty confident of it. But if it's truth you want, here's one for you: anyone would feel lost in your place. Dismissed from your job, isolated from your friends... Your world's been turned upside-down, and of *course* you're still dizzy from it. That has nothing to do with Cobb's drug, and it doesn't make you useless."

"Maybe."

"Think about it. Please. Give yourself some time."

It did make him feel better, a little, but he wasn't sure he wanted that. He did need time, true, but he needed more to accept his new life, not run around trying to recapture what he'd lost.

Mason wasn't as comfortable a nestmate as the Kovari roommates he'd lost, but he gave off a Human's body heat, and his mammalian smell didn't displease Havoc's nose. Besides, many days had passed since he left his roommates, and he'd never slept well alone.

Not that he would find much sleep tonight. No, he would be awake, lying spine to spine with Mason and listening for signs of danger while his thoughts ran in their same well-worn ruts. Tomorrow, he would bring Mason safely to his destination and finally rid himself of these complicated feelings. He'd go back to his new Computer existence and feel nothing at all.

JASPER FELL ASLEEP FEELING hopeful, his biggest challenge being not to think too much about Havoc's enticing closeness, not to roll over in his sleep and throw an arm around his sleek, muscular torso. Some chasm had been bridged between them, he felt—which made it all the more jarring when he woke, sore and alone.

Havoc had withdrawn to the far wall of their shelter, watching out the opening that once held a door. Standing guard, that was sensible. More sensible than… What had Jasper hoped for, anyway? An early morning cuddle? More secrets shared in the dim light of dawn? The link between them had glowed yesterday, warmer and stronger than ever before, but now that twisting ambivalence was back.

When he sat up, Havoc spoke without looking at him. "We should move, as soon as you're ready."

"Right. Soon." He stretched, ran his fingers through his hopelessly disheveled hair. "What's the plan?"

"I'll bring you to the outskirts of Khyrek, where you'll find…not safety, but at least familiar territory." He shook his head. "Going back is madness, Mason. They'll catch you easily. I don't understand what you hope to accomplish."

Something in his voice made Jasper not want to answer. What had happened to the hurting-but-vulnerable Havoc who'd confessed his fears yesterday? The scared, passionate organizer who'd risked everything for his people, whose devotion was blinding-bright? Now he'd cut all his bonds and barricaded himself away behind a wall of indifference.

"I'll have three whole days to mess up their plans before the launch event." It didn't sound like much, even to him. Havoc made a doubtful sound. "I've got a plan. There's this ingredient…"

"Don't tell me!" Havoc said. "I don't want to know."

Jasper stared at him for a long moment, during which Havoc busied himself with pretending to pack. At last, he shook his head. "Fine."

Standing up made Jasper aware of what rough shape he was in. Havoc had done a good job with his minor wounds, but the bruises from the landing had gotten more intense overnight, stiffening up his whole body. Not only that, but he was devastatingly hungry.

Chairl (Founders guard him) had stocked his pack with all sorts of survival supplies, and if the meal-bars were flavorless, at least they were plentiful. Jasper sprinkled his with hot sauce from the tiny bottle he'd brought with him. Havoc insisted he didn't mind the blandness.

The forest felt less oppressive today. Grist was probably still hunting them—it was Grist's hateful link that Jasper had felt last night, just before they both heard the drone and took cover—but there was no sign of him yet this morning. Hopefully he'd missed them and gone elsewhere in his search. Now they just had to get back to civilization before the operative brought in reinforcements.

The sooner they got out of these woods, the happier Jasper would be, for more reasons than one.

"You must come from a very industrial planet," Havoc said after they'd been walking for a while.

"What makes you think that?"

"The spider yesterday. The way you shy away from touching the plants."

"I don't know what might be unsafe, that's all."

"Because you come from a place with little nature remaining."

"That's about right."

"Don't feel shame for this. It helps, knowing your perspective." Havoc shrugged. "For the length of this journey, I mean, in case we need to hide again."

It was an old habit, being coy about his history. Some of his colleagues used their own stories to connect with and motivate the people they organized, but Jasper had realized early on that he couldn't do the same. Brennex had too many secrets, and protecting his home—his family and his fellow Gifted—had to come first.

But that same habit of evasiveness had been half the cause of his trouble here. Havoc was trying to know Jasper a little, his link flickering tentatively brighter like a candle in a breeze. And Jasper wanted to be known. They'd never get anywhere if he kept this up.

"No nature, actually."

"Hmm?"

"There's no nature at all in the place I call home. It's got no atmosphere, no native life, just artificial habitats. I grew up under a dome. I've traveled plenty with the Cooperative, so I've seen parks, farms, communities with all sorts of relationships with nature. But that didn't prepare me for this," he waved his hand at their surroundings, empty of any hint of civilization, "as well as I expected."

"I see." Havoc seemed to consider his next question with care. "What's it like, your home? It sounds grim."

"Not at all. It's lively. Vibrant, full of music and color, which I guess is how people react when they're always scraping for survival against the hostile universe. But…it's also scarred, and that's Ravel's fault."

"Ah. And those scars made you join the Cooperative."

"More than that. They're the reason I'm here, on Artesia specifically." He stopped walking, waiting for Havoc to turn and look at him. "I wish I'd told you this before, but I was afraid to trust you. It's my job to protect other worlds from what happened to my home, but my home still needs protection, too. I don't talk about it, ever, because I can't risk Ravel going back and hurting my people. My family. I'm bending a lot of rules by telling you this much, and there's a lot more I can't explain, but I want you to understand why I did what I did. Why I went behind your back."

He didn't hear any drones or sense any hostile presences nearby, but he lowered his voice anyway.

"I told you this drug Cobb's making has terrible reproductive side effects. I couldn't understand why that didn't matter to you, because where I'm from, family means everything. It takes priority over everything else." *Or it's supposed to, if you're not Lost, if you don't run away to escape the overwhelming pressure.* "It wasn't some random planet where Ravel first experimented with versions of this drug. It was my homeworld, and the side effects broke my people's hearts."

"It touches you personally," Havoc said softly, and the link between them glowed. "This explains much."

"It doesn't make what I did right. I needed some distance to see that, but it was wrong to put my game ahead of yours."

Havoc shrugged, almost a nervous twitch, and turned to keep walking. When Jasper drew up beside him, he said, "Well, now you've returned, and you can try again. If you feel you need my blessing, you have it."

Jasper frowned. Their link stayed warm and steady, which meant this wasn't more distrust between them. This was something else. "That's not what I meant. I'm glad, of course, but I didn't…"

"You're not pressuring me, if you fear that. I've learned things since you left. My teammates and I hoped that this genius drug could be part of our game, an opportunity for us to make a fairer playing field, but Cobb showed me that isn't so. This will only tilt the field further against us: not a new opportunity to prove ourselves, but a privilege reserved for those who've proven themselves already." He hissed bitterly. "Why waste an expensive drug on the mediocre and the worthless? Even with this drug, at my very best, all I managed to achieve was trouble for my eshrato."

"That's not true." Jasper stepped in front of him, forcing him to stop. "Even if you were part of that test group, Cobb didn't make you what you are. A drug might make you faster or more energetic, maybe it can even make you smarter, but it can't make you into an organizer. It can't make you courageous and caring. That came from *you*, Havoc."

He squeezed Havoc by the shoulders, breaking all Ravel's

taboos about touching, but Havoc didn't pull away. He stood so close Jasper could feel his slow breathing. The link between them flared bright.

"Thank you for saying this, Mason." Havoc took him by the wrists and slowly moved his hands away. "But whether you speak the truth or not, my game has ended. I'm reduced to Dust, and none of my teammates have the will to keep playing. Even I don't have the will, and if I tried, they would only send me far away from here, to a place where I'd have even less freedom."

Frustration squeezed Jasper's chest until he wanted to scream—not at Havoc, but at the system that made him feel this way. He wouldn't take his anger out on Havoc, though, so he forced himself to take a breath.

"Isn't this one of the injustices you were protesting? That people could be relocated, taken away from their friends and family, for trivial offenses?"

"Mine weren't trivial, but yes."

"Don't go, then. Stay and keep fighting. I'll help you!"

Havoc smiled sadly at him. "You have goodness in you, Mason Singh. I almost wish I could accept, but all I can do is wish you luck with your own game."

25

THEY WALKED ALL DAY, mostly in silence. The vast, shaded, sticky-humid forest gave way abruptly to open farmland, and they had to choose their route carefully to avoid surveillance along the roads. It took longer, moving across fallow fields in the hot sun, but by late afternoon, they reached…not Khyrek, because Havoc would not call this neighborhood part of Khyrek, and certainly not civilization, but the rotting carcass called the Gray District.

Fenced off from the true Khyrek, the Gray District's buildings leaned against each other for support, dingy and thick with graffiti. Smells reached his nose that he preferred not to identify.

"I'll leave you to go your own way, now." Havoc shifted his weight as Mason squeezed through a person-sized gap in the thick chain fence. "Good citizens don't belong in this place."

Mason's brows shot up, as if to say, *Do you call yourself a good citizen?* And speaking truth, Havoc couldn't, but he still wanted to be. Wished he could be, wished his dreams didn't hang in tatters.

"I don't need to invite more trouble, and trouble is all you'll find here."

"Yeah? That's too bad. I was hoping to find a fake ID and some anonymized credits, but I'll make do with what I can get." Mason smiled wryly. "But seriously, Havoc, what worse can Ravel do to you? There are people here who I'd like you to meet. They might be able to help you."

"I need no help. I need only go back and serve, as a Dust-rank should." But his stomach lurched at the thought of returning to the processing facility, giving his mind over to life as a Computer. He had earned this dust-clouded future, but he *could* have earned a different one. He could have been a good Copper-ranked, skilled laborer, if they gave him the chance.

It wasn't fair. Fairness played no role in a system based on merit—he'd failed to prove himself, game over, you lose. But still, it wasn't fair.

He'd already missed two and a half shifts at the processing facility, and his next, tomorrow morning, would come too soon. More than anything, he realized, he didn't want to be alone right now. Ignoring his own good sense, he followed Mason through the fence.

"Why did I ever come to rescue you?" he muttered under his breath.

"Why *did* you come?" Mason asked, curious.

Havoc grumbled and said nothing. Mason smiled maddeningly, as if he knew the reason.

The Cooperative agent took the lead now, and seemed to know where he was going. The streets grew no less filthy as they moved deeper into the district, and the architecture became increasingly mismatched and run-down. Havoc stuck close to Mason, sensing eyes on them from doorways and from windows high above. Ravel might not keep surveillance here, but they were watched, every step.

Mason slipped through a doorway into the trashed remains of a shop. Vandals had done a thorough job here. Havoc hesitated, disliking the smell of the place even more than the smells outside, but Mason moved confidently through the mess to a clear area in the back corner. "Coming?" he asked.

Sighing, Havoc followed.

"Come closer," Mason said when Havoc paused just short of the open space, which looked suspiciously deliberate from up close. "All the way on, and watch your tail." He tugged a rope several times, and Havoc startled as the floor moved beneath them.

Despite all expectation, the lift seemed solid as it carried them upwards. The upper floor might have existed in another building, even another city. Still messy, it held a different sort of mess, a brightly lit, organized chaos of tools and parts and supplies, a secret workshop disguised as a ruin. Havoc stared. They seemed to have everything from a miniature pharma lab—he spotted a chromatograph and a high-end, portable model of chemical printer—to the most elaborate computer setup Havoc had seen outside the Biopharma labs, its massive fixed displays taking up most of a wall.

The place so fascinated him that he didn't notice the guards.

"Singh has come back!" a solidly built Kovar called over her shoulder. "And he brought someone."

"This is my…friend, Sowing of Small Havoc," Mason said.

"That activist?" Both of the guards studied him with greater interest, and others glanced up curiously. There were ten people here, by Havoc's count, equal numbers Kovars and Humans, and they all carried themselves in a manner, casual yet wary, that marked them as non-Ravel, outsiders in his home city. He didn't like so many people watching him.

"It surprises me that you come here now, Sowing of Small Havoc, only after your game is lost," said the Kovari woman. She wore medals and ribbons on her shoulder like they did on Kovrim, tokens of a victor and community leader.

"She's right," said a Human, whose sculpted crimson hair towered over their head. "Last I heard, their revolution was dead in the water. You trust him, Singh?"

"Literally with my life. I vouch for him. Havoc, this is Audriv Hand and Confounding Echo, who run this place. They and their team have helped me out a few times already."

The crimson-haired Human, Audriv, rolled closer in a wheelchair that looked like an older Ravel model, but was retrofitted with a much larger motor and decorated with brightly colored feathers, like wings. They came to a stop beside Confounding Echo and frowned up at Havoc. "You could get us in a lot of trouble if you tell your bosses about us. Maybe they'd cut you some leniency for turning us in. Would you do that? Help yourself at the expense of our community?"

"Community? No communities exist in the Gray District."

The male Kovar, who'd been silent until now, snorted. "Badge-licking idiot."

"Hey!" Audriv snapped. "Ignorant doesn't mean idiot, Flag. I was pretty naive when I first broke loose, too."

"I'm not 'breaking loose,'" Havoc said. Whatever that meant. "But I don't care what you do here, and Mason knows I can keep a secret." The corner of Mason's mouth turned upward in a smile, until Havoc added, "Besides, I've accepted my future."

Audriv shrugged, as if Havoc posed a problem, but fortunately wasn't *their* problem. "All right, then. Singh, what brings you here? I heard you got stomped on last time. We didn't expect to see you again."

"You heard right. I'm planning another attempt, though," he glanced over his shoulder at Havoc, "and to maybe win two games at once, as the Kovars say. But everything I had before got burned. I know we've already asked a lot of you, considering how little you know us…"

"We know you a bit better now than we did," said Audriv.

"You lost, but didn't betray your sources. And you struck a brave blow against Biopharma in the process," said Echo. "You say this drug will harm our community as well. We'll help you if we can." She touched Audriv's shoulder lightly, a startlingly casual closeness that made Havoc wonder if they were lovers as well as teammates, or if people outside Ravel always acted this way. Mason certainly did. He felt strange, thinking of it. Audriv glanced up, nodded in unspoken agreement.

Mason relaxed, as if he'd feared a different welcome. "In that case, I could use new IDs for both of us—"

"Both?" Havoc coughed. Mason ignored him. It didn't matter; he would simply be disappointed when Havoc couldn't join him in his campaign.

"Low-level is fine. We'll need facility access, some anonymized currency…"

"You know what I'm going to ask for in payment. Have you got it?"

Mason fished a data drive from his pocket and held it just out of Audriv's reach with a sly smile. "If I tell you I got seasons two *and* three of *Wings of Destiny*, plus season two of *Time Sugar*, can you help us out?"

Audriv had a beautiful laugh. "You're a tough customer, Mason. But for seasons two *and* three, I'll do that and throw in a couple extras."

The two of them wandered off, looking at supplies for Mason's game and joking easily together, as if they'd known each other for years instead of weeks. Mason must have met these people around the same time he'd met Havoc, and they were obviously criminals operating outside Ravel's trade regulations, yet Mason seemed more at ease with them. Havoc felt like he'd stumbled over a missing stair.

"You've never come to the Gray District before, I'm guessing?" said Echo. The two nearest Kovars were still watching him. The name Confounding Echo fit her well; it referenced a kazi-kovi tactic that, while not illegal, bent the rules enough to be controversial.

"No," he said, and managed not to expand on that with *of course not*, or *why would I?* He didn't belong here at all. Maybe he should go…

"Of course he's never come here," said the young male, Flag. "Ravel's gotten in his head. We do get gossip here,

Havoc. Don't you think it strange to stay part of a team that ignores and mistreats you?"

"They don't mistreat me. In Ravel, everyone earns the treatment they get. At least I'm no cheater."

Flag bared his teeth. "*What* did you call us?"

"How else would you name this? False IDs? Counterfeiting? Non-company technology? It's criminal. Cheating."

"That's…"

Confounding Echo laid a hand on Flag's forearm, claws flexed in warning, and he shut his mouth on whatever he'd meant to say. Havoc realized he was staring at them: the thoughtless touching, her sharpened claws. He curled his own fingers, hiding claws filed dull and useless.

"That's just sad, that you think so," Flag finished.

"My zealous teammate here means to say that not every team is good for its members, and not every game is worth playing. You've chosen a hard road, maybe impossible, re-forming your broken game. We choose instead not to play."

"But you…" Havoc waved a claw at the huge gray market operation around them.

"We don't recognize their game or their rules. That's not cheating."

"And what team do you claim as your own, if not Ravel?"

Echo smiled with a hint of sadness. "We lived on Artevshi before Ravel, and we'll remain here after Ravel has gathered up every crumb of value from this planet and gone on its way." Artevshi. Havoc hadn't heard that name in so long, he had to remind himself what it meant: the old Kovari name for this planet. "There aren't many of us—a handful of teams—but we need no larger eshrato. We simply *live,* like our people used to, and we prefer to live outside Ravel." She tilted her head to one side. "Can't you understand why?"

"I…can imagine why, yes." It embarrassed him to admit it. Before meeting Mason, he wouldn't have understood. But he had done his best for his eshrato in every way possible, and Ravel treated *him* as a cheater. How could he think himself superior to these people? At least they had made a choice and stuck to it. "I apologize for calling you cheaters. I wasn't thinking."

Flag shifted his weight, looking at his feet. "I apologize for calling you a badge-licker. I just can't imagine working so hard for a team that disrespects me."

"I never felt that I had a choice," Havoc admitted.

"You always have choices," Echo said. "You know of at least one alternative, now. I welcome you to stay with us a few days and learn how we do things, to see if our team suits you."

"You honor me." The offer moved him, especially after he'd acted so rudely. He glanced over his shoulder and found Mason returning. He quirked that maddening smile again, and Havoc found himself saying, "But I think I belong elsewhere."

She patted his shoulder—the second time today someone had touched him without asking, and it should have offended him, but instead he found comfort in it.

"Audriv got me everything we need," Mason announced. "How about you, Havoc?"

"Yes, actually," Havoc said. "I've found what I needed."

"Go on toward victory, Sowing of Small Havoc," Echo told him.

"And you, Mason, don't get into too much trouble," said Audriv.

"Just the right amount," Mason said with a wink. "I promise."

Havoc spoke little after they left, letting Mason lead them back to the city proper. He wouldn't call it the *civilized* part of the city anymore, not after meeting those who lived in the Gray District, but Ravel's part of the city. His part.

As the streets grew familiar and the low-rank housing blocks drew near, he said, "I wish…"

"Yes?" Mason glanced over at him.

What did he wish, though?

"I wish I were a different person, someone who could turn his back on his team and go find himself a better game."

"Why can't you?" Mason asked, and Havoc shook his head. "I'm serious. Tell me why."

"Because my team is Ravel, and I am Ravel, and I'm not capable of being anything else. I knew the consequences when I started organizing. If I evaded responsibility now, I would no longer be myself."

"I thought you wished you were someone else."

"I'm not joking! Mason, I'm *lost.*" He moaned the word, felt it in his gut. "Without Ravel, I wouldn't be anything."

Mason stopped in the street. They stood on a quiet corner, a shopping corridor closed for the night, and the streetlamp put his face in shadow. "You'd be an organizer. You're the type of person who helps others, no matter where you are. Don't try to tell me that's nothing."

"I…I don't know. I know only that I hate this empty life, reduced to a piece of equipment." He shouldn't be talking about this. Wallowing would only make it harder to face the inevitable. But… "I don't want to go back."

"Then don't! Get out, and keep fighting for your team. I know it's a scary prospect, but—"

"I *can't.*"

Mason said nothing, studying him intently, probably searching for some better argument. But no argument existed that could change his situation.

Havoc started to turn away, saying, "I should go—"

"I lied to you."

He turned back, alarmed by Mason's serious tone. What now?

"I lied about coming back to support your movement. I do want that, genuinely, but there are lots of causes I want to support, and I wouldn't risk my life for most of them. I'm not *that* high-minded. I came back—parachuted out of a ship into the middle of a forest patrolled by people who want to capture and interrogate me—because of you, Sowing of Small Havoc."

"I don't… Why…" His tongue flicked out, tasting the air, uncertain.

"Because I like you. I admire you, Havoc, and I care what happens to you. You're passionate and talented and far more loyal than Ravel deserves, and it's shameful that they've made you feel otherwise. If you go back and let them keep using your brilliant mind like a computer chip, I can't stop you. I'll keep organizing without you if I have to, doing whatever I can to make things right…but I'd rather do it as part of your team."

"Oh." His brain had gone sluggish again, like it did at the processing facility, refusing to put words together. It had taken courage for Mason to say that, he could tell, but Havoc felt flattened. "I need to think."

Mason's smile twisted, bittersweet, an expression that struck to Havoc's heart. He wished, he wished…

"I understand," said Mason. "I just didn't want you to go without hearing that." He stepped close, took Havoc's face between warm, soft hands, and kissed the corner of his mouth. "Take care of yourself, okay? Not just your team, but yourself."

He turned and walked away, leaving Havoc to stare after him with his emotions roiling. Mason had long since disappeared around a corner when Havoc finally started toward…not home, but the place where he slept now.

Since his demotion, he'd been assigned a tiny one-room apartment on the floor reserved for Dust rank in a six-story, low-rank building. Some nights, shouting pierced the thin walls, arguments between his neighbors with the whole building as an audience. Tonight, though, quiet held the field.

Nothing distracted him from his thoughts.

A few days ago, he had accepted his reassignment and demotion, or he'd thought he had. Even going in search of Mason he'd seen not as rebellion, but as one final act of courage before he abandoned his hopes forever. But now? None of the paths ahead felt right.

Mason had come back *for him*. Such a Human thing to do, yet it touched him deeply. Havoc would never take such a risk for someone outside his team, but even in the depths of his Computer brain fog, he'd still thought about Mason, all the time. He liked the man's company. No, he liked the man himself, despite being a Human and an outsider and an enemy of his eshrato. He liked the idea, not of joining Mason's team, but having Mason on his team.

If he knew what his team was anymore.

He thought of Confounding Echo and her team, Mason and his cherished family, all these people who rejected what Ravel offered. They believed him naive in his loyalty, as if loyalty made him weak rather than strong, and he wondered what loyalty had earned him. He gave and he gave, but his brightest gifts Ravel did not want.

He fell into restless sleep, haunted by echoes of Mason's voice. *More loyal than Ravel deserves... Get out and keep fighting... Because I like you...* He woke no less haunted, but certain of one thing: if he resigned himself to life as a Computer, he would never stop wondering what else might have happened.

"What more can they do to me?" he asked himself aloud. What more did he have to lose?

Some hours remained before his shift, enough time to find Mason and ask what he planned to do next. Enough time to change his mind again, he reassured himself, if he lost his nerve. But he didn't want to lose his nerve.

He dressed in his Dust-colored uniform and opened his apartment door. As he stepped out, a pair of Humans in dark uniforms blocked his way.

"Sower of Havoc?"

The security guards closed on him in a pincer maneuver. They carried batons and stun-bolts, and the sight jarred him. In his neighborhood—his *old* neighborhood—security never carried weapons except at need.

"We're here to escort you."

They didn't trust him to show up to his shift on his own. That stung. True, he'd reported himself as ill and then disappeared for two days, but he'd come back, and their mistrust irked him. They expected disobedience, and that made him want to *be* disobedient. "I need no escort to my shift. I know the way."

The guards laughed.

"Nah, you're coming straight to the spaceport."

"*Spaceport?*" Understanding struck him like a blow.

"Come on." One of them gripped his arm—*touched* him, using force as they would on a *criminal*—and pulled him forward.

He had to stall, somehow. He played the fool. "I'm assigned to the Computer Processing Facility. They're expecting me there."

"Not anymore. They're sending you where people like you belong."

"Don't try anything, all right?" said the other guard, nudging him in the back with his baton. "Special Operative Grist warned us you'd be trouble, and we've got our eyes on you, Sower of Havoc."

As they led him away, he thought: Mason Singh never got his name wrong.

26

Don't panic, don't panic, Havoc told himself, but it made no difference. Panic had him in its claws.

He'd known they would send him away. Manager Fowler had threatened it, and he'd gone to rescue Mason anyway. For all his talk of accepting consequences and responsibility, he'd spent the past few days steadfastly ignoring what he knew, *knew* would happen when he returned.

He hadn't imagined it would be like this, though. He'd planned to go to his next shift, beg forgiveness, and plug in like a good, obedient Computer while management debated what to do with him. He'd thought he had time. Instead, security showed up and wrangled him like an animal.

It shouldn't matter how they treated him. He would end up on that transport regardless, flying away from his home.

How he arrived there shouldn't matter. But it *did*. This humiliating march broke something inside him, and all his doubts and wishes and second-guessing reared up, transformed into ravenous *needs*. He needed his home, his people. What he would do instead, he didn't know, but he needed to stay off that transport.

If they were really taking him to the transport. *That* vicious, disloyal thought would never have invaded his head before the past few days, but now it set off fresh waves of panic: what if they'd decided Dust rank and exile wasn't punishment enough? What if they planned to make him simply…disappear?

Mason would worry about such things, not Havoc. Mason believed Ravel would do any evil thing they pleased, but Havoc trusted the system. He did. Well, he always had…

He'd picked a terrible time for his faith in his eshrato to crumble.

He fixed his thoughts on Mason, his confident grin, his calming voice. Mason would know how to escape this situation. He would have readied three escape plans before the guards even appeared. Chit, reading all her spy stories, would find a way out, too. Havoc lacked their skills, but he could try.

His eyes had been open all this time, but unseeing. Now he looked around him.

They'd taken him along a minor street that ran parallel to a larger road. He knew where he was, and knew that to reach the spaceport, they would have to turn. Where? Not at the largest intersection, but onto another side street. He mapped possible routes in his head, and though a map wasn't a plan, the exercise calmed him, like strategizing for the next round of a game.

Yes, a game. He'd had a setback, but wasn't beaten yet.

Maybe he could trick the guards. Pretend to be ill? No, too obvious. His best chance would come when they crossed a street with people and trams for distractions. He couldn't guess where they would cross, exactly, but there was no way to reach the spaceport without doing so.

The hour was early, though, and few people ventured out on these side streets. A few shopkeepers shot him curious, wary looks as they opened for the day, and his humiliation burned. One Kovar nodded gravely at him, but otherwise none looked sympathetic; certainly none seemed likely to help him run and hide. Somewhere distant, a group of runners called out to each other, keeping pace for their morning exercise in Kovari fashion: "Left! Sprint now, go, go! And…slow, walk it now…" Runners usually kept to near-empty streets. Would even the main roads have enough traffic for a distraction, so early in the day?

They turned. Traffic at the next cross street, more people passing on foot. Havoc dragged his feet, watching, listening. Did he hear a tram's bells approaching? Hard to make out over the conversation and the joggers calling to each other. Yes, there, the tram was coming. If he could match its timing, let it separate him from the guards…

They wrenched his arms downward, pinning him in place. One pressed a stun-stick under his chin. "Don't."

He had no choice but to wait in agony while the tram passed by.

As soon as the street cleared, they hauled him forward, more aggressively than before. Past the intersection, they turned again toward an even smaller side street, this time blatantly headed in the wrong direction from the spaceport.

Panic surged. "Where are you bringing me?"

"To the spaceport. They'll send you where you belong."

Lies.

Havoc planted his feet, struggled against their hold, but at the cold touch of the stun-stick, he froze again. His heart pounded in his ears, deafening. People called him brave for his activism, but he had no courage. Against the threat of violence, he crumpled as easily as anyone else.

Just like during the protest. At least today, no one else would get hurt...

"And right, and...go! Run, go, go, go!"

The runners came on them out of nowhere, a mass of scaled bodies and waving tails breaking around them like a river around a boulder. "Here, excuse us, make way!" they called out as they jostled him and the guards.

Cursing, the guards dragged him toward the shelter of the nearest building, but a tail caught one of them in the knees, dropping him to the pavement. Someone else crashed headlong into Havoc and the other guard. Clawed hands grabbed him, pulling him along with the crowd.

"Run," hissed a familiar voice in his ear.

"Chit! How..."

"Less talking, more running. Take off your clothes."

He found his balance and rushed along with the crowd, reveling in the freedom of movement. His dun-colored shirt came off easily; Chit tossed it over her shoulder to another runner, who shrugged it on and turned down an alley with a handful of others, while the main group kept going. His trousers, ill-fitting at the best of times, were more awkward, but he dropped to all fours, and with some helpful tugging from the others, those came off too. Now he wore only his shoes, like the rest of the runners, just another body in the crowd.

Somewhere behind them, the guards were shouting in frustration. A stun-bolt crack echoed against the buildings.

"Want to bet on whether your friends back there can tell two Kovars apart?" Chit shot him a grin, then called out instructions, and another group splintered off.

"But what now? They must be sending for backup now, and if they don't track us, the cameras will."

"Don't worry about the cameras; he's planned for that."

"'He?'" His heart swooped.

"But yes, security will try to head us off—so we have to split up for now. This alley, up here on the right. Go that way, and he'll help you hide."

"Chit…" At the pace they were keeping, he couldn't catch her gaze, so words would have to do. "I thank you. Deeply."

"Take care of yourself. Hurry!"

She dashed ahead, and he rounded the corner of the alley—straight into the waiting arms of Mason Singh.

Mason pulled him behind an outcropping and hugged him hard. Havoc found himself holding on tightly to the Human's familiar warmth. His world had flipped upside-down three times in a handful of hours, and the strength of those arms grounded him.

Drawing back, Havoc meant to greet him with words, to thank Mason for not abandoning him, but getting his first clear look at the Human's face, his stomach lurched.

"What? …Mason?"

Something was off. Not only the Iron-rank worker's uniform he wore, not only the side-slicked hair that didn't suit him, but a deep wrongness in his face. Sagging cheeks, pudgy chin, too-wide eyes. Was this Mason Singh at all? His nose and gut told him yes, of course it was, but his eyes warned of an imposter. He lifted a hand toward Mason's face but hesitated, hovering.

"Oh! The disguise. Sorry, it's for the cameras. Freaks me out, too, when I look in the mirror." He laughed, and suddenly was himself again. "I've got some tricks for you, too, but it's not safe here. Let's move." He pulled away and ushered Havoc to a fire-ladder up the side of the building.

Above, they found a rooftop patio studded with outdoor armchairs and decorative plants in pots—the sort of amenities Copper- and Silver-rankers enjoyed. The sort Havoc would never be allowed. He stared around in a daze—such a simple, foolish thing for Ravel to fight them over. Did they think Iron-rankers incapable of benefiting from fresh air and greenery? Was the small expense, and the real enjoyment it offered, too much to give those who worked so hard?—until Mason touched his arm.

"Here, put this on." Mason handed him a roll of clothing. Havoc's old Iron-rank uniform. A reasonable disguise, he supposed, for someone no longer permitted to wear it. Mason kept his eyes averted while he dressed, which amused Havoc. Humans had strange taboos about nudity.

"Faster," Mason prompted, pulling him from his wandering thoughts. Why could he not focus? "Those guards don't seem like the brightest stars in the galaxy, but we don't have long before they realize they're screwed and lock down the streets."

From his pack, he'd removed a few jars and a hard-sided case. He opened the latter and revealed a set of false teeth. "Put these on, and then I'll do your makeup."

Grimacing, Havoc obeyed. The teeth felt awkward, pushing out his cheeks, but they fit.

"Good. I hate this stuff too, but we need to change the shapes of our faces just enough to fool the facial recognition. Otherwise they'll find us on surveillance as soon as we hit the street." Mason opened the first jar, hesitated, held it up for Havoc to see: scale tint of a dull gray-green. "For a Human, changing your skin color would be offensive, even for a disguise, but I'm told it's not the same for Kovars?"

"No, this carries no taboo. Though usually we choose attractive colors."

"Unfortunately, good disguises are frequently ugly ones. May I?" Mason dipped his fingers into the dye and smoothed it over Havoc's face and neck. He worked briskly, giving Havoc too little time to enjoy his attention before moving to the next jar. "And this is what we call wrinkle cream. Kind of a joke—it's a nanofiber serum that's supposed to hide wrinkles, but if you tweak the formula just a little, it creates them. Used for theater, mostly, but the Cooperative's found it handy. There you go. Have a look."

He offered up his handheld, camera turned on so Havoc could see his own face. It was eerie, like meeting a biological parent and seeing their resemblance. It was him, but not.

"This will work?"

"It has before, on other Ravel worlds. You did a double-take when you saw me, right? Won't fool anyone who knows you, at least not for long, and I wouldn't go chatting with security officers, but it should keep us out of computer searches."

He tossed Havoc a small duffel, hefted his own pack, and clambered over a ledge to the next building's roof. Havoc followed. They crossed several adjoining buildings this way, racing across the open spaces.

"That way." Mason pointed. "Can you make it across?"

"Can you?" The gap between this building and the next, across a narrow alley, looked too wide for a Human. But Mason threw his backpack across, took it at a running leap, and rolled neatly on his landing. He impressed Havoc more and more, this man.

Havoc dropped to all fours and made the jump easily.

"Okay. We're almost there." Mason leaned out over the edge of the rooftop. Along the street below, a pack of runners headed away from them, and the usual morning traffic was picking up. The streets remained open.

He pulled a rope from his pack and tied it tight to an outcropping. "Now we wait. There's a tram stop just below us. When the next tram comes into view, we'll slide down and hop on before anyone spots us. Be ready. Oh, and you'll need this."

Mason handed him a badge for a Copper-rank facility worker.

Havoc blinked at it. "Whose is this?"

"Yours, now. Your new alias is Triple Promise. I had Audriv cook up an extra false identity for you, just in case."

Of course he had. He'd even chosen a flattering Kovari alias. "It still amazes me that your Gray Market friends have that level of access."

"They do this sort of thing a lot. Usually they're helping people join the Gray District or escape off-world and disappear from Ravel's systems, but in this case, they'll be helping us get further inside without getting spotted."

"And how did you do all this?" He gestured toward the street, encompassing the whole rescue operation.

"The credit goes to your friend Five-Chit Defense. I went to scope out your building..." He paused. "That makes it sound creepy. I was worried they might mess with you. You wouldn't be the first internal Ravel activist to disappear."

"You didn't tell me that."

Mason's false wrinkles exaggerated his grimace. "I did ask you to come with me. You made it clear how you felt about that, and I didn't want you to feel I was trying to manipulate you."

"I ignored your warnings about the provocateur, and you proved to be speaking truth. Only a fool would ignore you again." He offered a shy smile.

"That's…good. I'm glad. Anyway, I was watching your building for trouble, and so was your friend Chit. We found each other and started talking. Turns out she'd been preparing in case of something like this, and she convinced her running team to try a different route this morning in case you needed help. Prepped your old clothes for you, too, and some supplies. When we saw the guards go into the building, I offered to follow and send her updates. She's great, you know."

"I know. I have great luck in my friends." And not only Chit, he thought. "I thank you, Mason."

"Here comes the tram. Let's go—you first."

Havoc tested the rope, swung over the edge, and slid down to the street. Mason followed, and together they stepped up to the tram stop just as it arrived.

He held his breath as he tapped his new, fake badge to the sensor beside the door, expecting screaming alarms. But the door opened with an ordinary chime, and then they were safely aboard.

The car wasn't crowded at this hour, but not empty, either. Mason led him halfway back, within reach of the exit doors but sheltered from the windows, and stood close so he could talk in a low voice.

"I—both of us—we hope you're not upset. We didn't exactly have time to ask your consent."

"Actually, I had planned to come find you this morning, Mason, and ask to join your team." Mason's grin gave him a sudden pang of uncertainty. "But now, I fear I'll inconvenience you. They'll keep hunting for me."

"Another thing we have in common. But they won't find us."

Havoc sank onto one of the benches, suddenly feeling hollowed-out and shaky as the adrenaline left him. This was happening, here, now. He'd made himself teamless, rejecting even Dust rank. He'd thought Ravel had taken everything from him already, but what was he now? He held no illusions: he could never go back to the company, not to his old job or even to a worthless life of Dust. He lived in exile now.

"Hey." Mason stopped just short of touching his shoulder. "You okay?"

"To speak honestly…no. I feel lost."

The sympathy in Mason's eyes melted him. "I'm sorry. I can't relate to how you felt about Ravel, but I know this must be hard. I'm here, if you want…anything."

Havoc drew a deep breath, filling his lungs with air and strength. "I want to make this worth something."

Mason nodded, smiling grimly. "It won't be easy, but we'll do it together. I'm not leaving this planet until we win some victories for your team. We're going to make things better for them, however we can."

"And we'll start by shutting down this genius-drug project."

"That's not..." Mason opened his mouth, shut it again. "I'm not asking you to do that. I told you, I won't put my goals ahead of yours again."

"But you still believe it must be stopped. This matters to you."

"Yes, but..."

"And now it matters to me, too. It angers me. I thought this drug could be an opportunity for us, but we'll see no benefit from it. The workers might pass up the chance of future offspring for the sake of their own advancement, but none of them, the Humans especially, will willingly sacrifice so much to make a drug for executives on other worlds, which they'll never be allowed to use themselves. This could be the spark that makes them ready to fight."

The Cooperative organizer was giving him a strange, warm look. "Have I mentioned lately how much I admire you? That's brilliant thinking."

I like you, Mason had said before. Havoc wondered what he'd meant by that. *Like* could mean many things.

"I like you too, Mason Singh."

27

GRIST RACED BACK TO Ship, working his augment-powered legs to the maximum and cursing the entire way, at the news that Sowing of Small Havoc, barely an hour after his recapture, had gone missing again.

"Gone missing" was the phrase Director Lang used in her message. Director Brega had said "evaded surveillance," but Ship understood both of these to be understatements. Grist kept grumbling about "these stupid fucking local goons…" and promising violence against Mason Singh, Sowing of Small Havoc, and anyone who dared to help them.

Ship felt a grinding sense of shame, like corrosion in its circuits, knowing that it had encouraged Sowing of Small Havoc and provided him with the resources that led to his current situation. It still liked the Kovari activist, and was impressed by his courage, and dreaded watching Grist hunt him down again.

As soon as Grist was aboard and the drones safely stowed, Ship took off and made the awkwardly short hop to Khyrek. One positive development, at least: no more sitting in the damp, dirty, insect-filled jungle. It hadn't stopped *itching* since the moment it landed, and it suspected ants had colonized its starboard sensor relay. If it had stayed in that miserable place much longer, it would have started growing moss.

Grist ran off again the millisecond that landing protocols cleared and Ship was able to open the doors. That left Ship in peace, theoretically…yet it couldn't stop wondering what would happen to Sowing of Small Havoc.

Don't get involved, Dockrunner had warned it, but there should be no risk in merely watching.

Director Lang met Grist at the main facility entrance, along with Security Director Brega and another executive who Ship identified as Lawrence Gillum (he/him), Chief Director in charge of all of Artesia Biopharma—the one Grist hadn't met yet, because he had delegated the situation to his staff until now. Apparently matters had grown sufficiently serious to require his personal involvement.

"Why are you back here, Grist?" demanded Brega. "You're supposed to be tracking down that Cooperative terrorist."

"I wouldn't have to, if your people hadn't spent hours looking for him in the completely wrong fucking place, when you could have been surrounding that escape capsule. And now you've lost the Kovar, too? For the second time in, what, two days?"

"He was under armed guard. He should have been secure.

If you can do better, *Special Operative,* I've yet to see any evidence of it."

"Director. Operative. Please stop wasting my time and yours." Chief Director Gillum's gravelly, disapproving tone silenced even Grist.

Lang cleared her throat. "Indeed. Save this blame assignment exercise for your written report, please, and let's focus on solutions." She beckoned them to follow her onto the nearest glider platform, which carried them up in a sweeping curve alongside the main lobby stairs, letting them off near the executive offices.

"We need to find them both, of course," Lang continued, "but Sowing of Havoc is our first priority. I've called back Special Operative Grist because he has more insight than any of us into how those people think."

"I bet they're together. We'll find them in the same place, or I'll eat my own teeth. We missed our chance to catch Mason Singh at the crash site, but with Havoc, we know exactly where he was, what, an hour ago? And with the city on lockdown, there are only so many places he could be." Grist looked over his shoulder and raised his brows at Brega. "You *did* put the city on lockdown, right?"

"Obviously."

Lang said something the surveillance system didn't catch as she opened the door to her office. It took Ship a few seconds to switch to the camera inside. She'd pulled up a projection over her desk, showing a map of the city with a red dot at Sowing of Small Havoc's last known location and blue dots showing security officers, with smaller blue wedges for drones and cameras, and transparent blue paths fading in and out to mark search patterns.

"Any surveillance camera hits? Have you bumped up the scan rate?" Grist was asking.

"No, and yes," said Brega. "We're running a gait-matching scan, too, but that always gives false positives for Kovars. But we assume he—or they, if they're together—will avoid areas with dense surveillance."

Grist nodded with grudging approval. "They'd be idiots to try coming here right now, but Singh's got a history of idiocy, so tighten security here at the facility too. Most likely, they'll lie low somewhere for a few days before making their move. Let's try to find their hideout, and stay vigilant until they get sloppy. These activist softies always do."

"And where do you recommend starting the search, Special Operative?" asked Lang.

Before Grist could answer, the office door flew open.

"Director Lang!" Senior Researcher Alik Cobb strode halfway across the room before he seemed to notice there was a meeting in progress. He slowed, but made no apology. "Director, I can't work like this. Remind them, please, how important my work is to this entire division?"

He pointed at Director of Operations Patri Alvarado, who waited in the doorway.

"Sorry, Nerissa, everyone. Just a little personnel disagreement, which does *not* need to interrupt your meeting, does it, Cobb?" said Alvarado.

"'Little?' We're just *two days* from the Project Rebound launch, Director, and I can't be dealing with these disruptions!"

Lang frowned. "What's wrong, Senior Researcher?"

"I've got data to compile, a speech to write, a case study to finalize, not to mention I'm still looking for a way to synthesize FS-72 so we can scale up production. I need free access to equipment and resources, not to mention freedom from all distractions, and that's not possible if I'm forced to share a lab with that disrespectful, obnoxious…"

"I offered you your choice of lab space in the old wing. You preferred to stay put," said Alvarado.

"Those old, abandoned labs are *kilometers* away from the other facilities I need, and the equipment is antique. If someone has to move, it should be Hirano-Kamau, not me. Her work's already antiquated."

Grist snorted in amusement. "Baby can't share his toys, huh?"

Cobb rounded on him. "You! If you'd been remotely competent at your job, *Mister Grist,* my lab would still be in one piece, and I wouldn't be in this intolerable situation."

Grist's brows rose slowly higher while Cobb spoke. If he'd intended to chasten Grist by ignoring his proper title, it backfired on him. Ship almost felt bad for Cobb, almost, as Grist rose and took two slow steps in Cobb's direction. He wasn't tall or large, but Ship had seen many times that his physical presence intimidated people nevertheless. Predictably, Cobb stepped back.

"So you don't want my help anymore, is that it? Should I tell your bosses I'm done here, and you'll take care of the next terrorist attack on your own?"

"What? I thought that Cooperative thug was gone."

"No, but Mason Singh will be apprehended soon," Director Lang said quickly. Ship caught Security Director Brega's brows rising before she controlled her expression. "That's our job, Senior Researcher, and I promise you don't have to worry about it."

"Or maybe we should let him come. He seems to have it out for you, Cobb." Grist took another step into the circle of

Cobb's personal space, forcing him back again. "Maybe we should use you as bait. See what happens." He mimed a pistol pointed at Cobb's head.

"You useless, walking phallus—"

"Enough, Operative Grist," said Chief Director Gillum. "Maybe you find this squabbling to be entertaining, but it's counterproductive and I'm tired of it." His tone changed, becoming more conciliatory. "Senior Researcher Cobb, we all appreciate how you're bearing up under these unfortunate circumstances. Alvarado, I'm sure you can work things out so the Senior Researcher has what he needs, can't you? Maybe Researcher Hirano-Kamau wants a few days of bonus leave for herself and her wife."

"Yes, Director, I'll work it out. Sorry about the disruption." Alvarado held the door open for Cobb, then followed him out.

As the door closed behind them, Grist turned to Lang and Gillum. "You didn't tell him about the Kovar."

"Of course not," Gillum said. "Cobb's a genius, but…well, as you saw." He gestured at the door. "He needs everything to be just so. The division needs this product launch to go smoothly, which means we give him whatever he needs to stay on track. No more disruptions, definitely no bad news."

"Sower of Havoc's escape isn't exactly a secret," said Brega. "We haven't announced it, but locking down the streets will get people talking, and when they find out we're looking for a Kovar, it won't be hard to make the connection."

"All the more reason to help him stay laser-focused on his work," said Gillum.

"And he's not one to gossip with the lower-level staff, fortunately," said Lang. "But we can't keep him in the dark forever. Let's make sure that by the time Cobb finds out, we've already apprehended both of our fugitives."

28

Jasper's third time sneaking into the Biopharma facility was the easiest by far. Audriv's fake identities worked perfectly: they joined the stream of workers headed for the factory-side entrance, scanned their badges at the door, and though he held his breath, the system immediately flashed green and let them through.

But the automated system only cared about checking badges for validity. Any person who stopped to look at them would quickly notice that their outfits didn't match their new identities. Audriv had assigned them IDs that should give them broad access to the facility without people noticing them. Jasper was supposed to be an Iron-rank office assistant, the sort who ran errands and fetched coffee for upper-rank bosses, and his street clothes weren't appropriate at all. And while Havoc had his old Iron-rank factory uniform, Audriv had made him a Sand-rank janitor. Jasper felt a little bad about giving him the fake demotion, but they'd looked at the facility demographics, and janitor was one of the few jobs that gave access to most of the facility, not just the factory, but where a Kovar wouldn't stand out.

So, first stop: laundry department.

"Stop moving like that," Havoc hissed as they walked.

"Like what?"

"Stop…swaggering."

"I don't swagger." Jasper frowned. "Do I?"

"You walk like… How can I describe it? You walk an executive's walk. Or like rank doesn't exist, like you're completely unconcerned with advancing. You stand out."

"Sorry." All his efforts with the wrinkle cream—which tugged uncomfortably at his skin, making him constantly resist the urge to scratch—would be wasted if he gave himself away with his gait. He glanced at the nearby workers and tried to imitate them: stiffened his shoulders, took the bounce out of his step. Tried to imagine he was heading to a long shift of tedious assignments instead of espionage. "Better?"

"Yes." After a moment, without looking at him, Havoc added: "I like your walk. You carry so few worries about these things. But we must blend in."

I wish you could walk like you don't care about anyone's expectations, too. Jasper had no shortage of worries in his life. However he held himself, Havoc ought to be allowed to do the same.

Jasper wasn't too concerned for himself, though he followed Havoc's advice anyhow; very few people here knew what he looked like. He was more worried about someone recognizing Havoc, especially when he heard people gossiping in hushed voices about the manhunt happening across the city.

But amid the crowd of arriving first-shift workers, no one paid any attention to them. No betraying, hostile links reaching toward them. Hardly any links at all, in fact, beyond the dull, lifeless gray bonds of anonymous coworkers. Even Havoc's brilliant bonds had faded to something cold and steely, tempered by how his eshrato had betrayed him. It broke Jasper's heart a little. But he took comfort that Havoc's bond to him had solidified, no longer writhing with conflicted feelings. It might be brighter now, too, or maybe that was wishful thinking.

Even the laundry room attendant gave them a second look only in order to check their sizing, waving off Havoc's sheepish excuse about dirtying his previous uniform and handing them new ones without any fuss: a brown jumpsuit for Havoc, and a collared shirt and slacks for Jasper.

"I still hate the risk," Havoc grumbled as they changed their clothes. "If someone does notice us…"

"That's why we won't draw attention to ourselves. We're just two low-rankers doing our jobs." Havoc's frown didn't ease up, so Jasper confessed, "You're right, and I wouldn't take the risk of being here if we didn't have to. But I'm counting on the fact that, at least for the moment, this is the last place security will expect us to be."

"They will expect us to lie low, like sensible people."

"Exactly. *And* they expect their cameras to tell them if we show up here." He lowered his voice as they left the changing area and headed back out through the laundry room proper. "Right now, they'll be looking for a hideout somewhere in the city. With any luck, by the time they tighten security in and out of the facility, we'll already be—"

He stopped short, doing a double-take. Behind the laundry room counter, hanging neatly on a hook, was a startlingly familiar black jacket.

Havoc followed his gaze. "That looks like your old coat."

"I lost it. The day of the protest." It seemed impossible that it had survived in the aftermath of the lab fire.

"And now you'll have it back." Havoc strode up to the counter. "Excuse me," he said to the attendant. "You have something there that I think belongs to my friend."

The attendant, who'd barely noticed them before, perked up. "Ah! I knew someone must be missing that old thing. Normally we throw out misplaced items after a week, but that had the look of something well-loved."

"Very much so." Jasper took the worn old thing from her, slipped it on like a second skin. He felt suddenly more himself, like a turtle coming home to its shell. Feeling overly emotional, he stripped it off again. "Thank you. I thought I'd lost it for good. Can't wear it during my shift, but I'm so glad to have it back."

"You're so very welcome." The attendant winked and waved them off.

Tucking the jacket under his arm, he told Havoc, "I bought this jacket when I left home. I've worn it on every campaign, nearly every protest I've led. It seems silly, compared to losing…" Losing Valkeir, he meant to say, but before he could speak her name, Havoc patted his arm.

"I understand. This means luck is following you. Let's hope it stays with you."

"With *us*. Right, teammate?"

"Yes. Teammate." Havoc ducked his head, but Jasper caught a smile.

Damn. He liked that smile far too much, liked making it appear like a beam of sunlight out of the gloom. He couldn't afford to be so distracted.

They left the basement-level laundry room in the opposite direction they'd come, heading away from the factory and toward the research facility, where Cobb's lab was. Coming in from the side entrance into the airy atrium, Jasper felt a pang of loss; he'd last been here with Valkeir, disguised in hazmat suits.

"Before we start, we should have a nest," Havoc said. "A home base, I think you'd call it, where we can safely wait and find each other. For that, I have an idea."

They climbed the broad, sweeping central stair, which was decorated with helixes and chemistry-inspired patterns chased in platinum across the steps and floor and up the walls. From there, Havoc took them down a series of hallways to a set of double doors, where he paused. He glanced behind them, making sure no one was watching, then pushed the doors open and ushered Jasper through.

Jasper had been starting to doubt that there were safe hiding places in this bright, window-filled building, but behind those doors, it felt like they'd jumped through time. The lights were dimmed to emergency levels, and the air smelled stale. It wasn't dusty, but felt as though it should be, like no one had been in here for years.

"What's this place?"

"Old labs and workspaces, long abandoned." Havoc cracked open the first door along the hallway, peered through, and closed it again. "Biopharma brings less profit than it once did. When this facility opened, it was meant to restore acclaim to the division. The scientists would study native life and use it to develop new treatments. But another facility developed instant-mod technology—you know it?"

Everyone knew about it. "Rapid treatment development for new diseases. One that rolls out new treatments in real-time as viruses evolve. It's how they beat the Argosi plague when it mutated so fast."

"For whole classes of diseases, it made our work irrelevant. And Artesia is too far from most worlds, its supply lines too long, to produce instant-mod drugs. By the time we shipped a drug and it reached people who needed it, the Argosi virus would have mutated again, and new drugs would have been needed. So several lines of research here shut down and moved elsewhere." He gestured around. "This wing held some of those labs."

"And they didn't repurpose it? It's perfectly good space."

"They relocated some equipment, some supplies and spare parts. But the rest has grown outdated, so it sits here, taking up space." Havoc smiled. "You don't need to worry, Mason. No one comes here. We can stay safe here, for now."

He peeked through a door, then held it open. Just as he'd said, inside were long benches with rows of tools and equipment that looked dated even to Jasper's inexpert eye.

"Cozy," he said, and Havoc snorted. "No, really, I've had way worse." He started a circuit of the room, checking for surveillance. "This one time, Avant Corporation torched our ship while we were doing a protest, and we had to hide in abandoned buildings for a week until the facilitators could find us another way off-world. Bats were roosting in them. I still remember the smell."

Jasper disabled the automatic light so no one would notice power usage in a room where there shouldn't be any.

The lone surveillance camera looked inactive, but he stuck a square of tape over the lens just to be safe, and set up low-energy motion sensors across the doors. Finally, he set down his pack, laying claim to their makeshift home.

"Are you…?" Jasper lifted a hand, stopped himself before touching Havoc's arm. *Are you okay?* would be a stupid question. He couldn't be okay.

"We should split up. It will look less suspicious," Havoc said, and Jasper suspected he was avoiding the question. He didn't like it, but Havoc was probably right. "You said you have a plan?"

He ran a hand through his hair. "More like the pieces of one, I admit. Originally, Valkeir and I had intended to sabotage Cobb's clinical trials and make him think the drug had problems, but we couldn't get the last pieces together, which is why we went with our backup plan. Which I deeply regret, by the way." He glanced at Havoc, expecting well-deserved blame for what he'd done, but Havoc only nodded. "I was thinking to pick up where Val and I left off, but from what you said, Cobb's fast-tracked the trials ahead of this announcement, and it's too late to make him think the drug's not effective."

"Biopharma acts quickly out of desperation. They must boost profits and impress the other divisions, or corporate will cut their resources even further. It doesn't surprise me that he rushes the process, even skipping steps."

"Then that leaves me with even fewer ideas. Do you really think, if we find evidence of harmful side effects for the local community, that will get the workers on your side?"

"If such evidence exists, yes, and it would give us leverage to bargain with management. But Mason, that bargain might mean accepting the side effects in exchange for other compensation. I can't promise my teammates will sacrifice our other goals to stop production of this drug, nor that management would agree to it. To speak truth, I'm not sure *I* want that."

Jasper nodded slowly, pushing down a wave of dismay. "I understand. I meant what I said before: I'm on your team, and if that's what best serves the team, I'll support it."

Linn wouldn't be pleased about that, and Jasper wouldn't be thrilled, either. They'd have to find another way to keep any Gifted children from becoming Ravel lab rats. But he knew this was the right way forward.

"I appreciate your honesty, teammate," Havoc said. "And I'll make a promise to you: if we can find a way to win both our games, to stop Cobb and help the workers, we'll do it."

"Thank you. I hope that's possible." He forced his mind back to their most immediate problems. "Either way, we need to learn more about this drug. I thought I'd start with investigating this mystery chemical, Substance FS-72. Cobb's notes say it increases the potency, as if before he added it, the drug's effects were too mild to be useful. I still think it must be the key to everything."

If this FS-72 was the missing ingredient when they manufactured the drug on Brennex, it explained why Cobb had revived the project. It also had terrifying implications for what a new, stronger version of the drug could do.

"You make sense. Here." Havoc took Jasper's handheld, worked for a minute, then handed it back. "A faked requisitions order should help you find it. If anyone questions its accuracy, blame your supervisor and leave."

"Good idea."

"You can find your way back here?"

"Yeah, I've learned the floor plan pretty well. What about you, though?"

"I want to take stock of the workers' moods. The dynamic here has changed since the protest, and I need to learn how it has settled. I'll try to learn the status of Cobb's project, too."

"Be careful, okay?"

"Yes, but not too careful. We lack time to move slowly."

"Seriously." Jasper did grip his hand now, meeting his gaze. "Keep yourself safe, Sowing of Small Havoc."

"I told you, don't worry, Mason Singh." With a grin, Havoc slipped out the door.

"I will anyway, though," Jasper murmured, and he sat and waited for Havoc to get a head start before setting out on his own errand.

29

Jasper felt naked, walking the corridors of the research facility without Havoc at his side. He knew where he was going, and tried to act like he belonged there, but he hated these gleaming, spacious facilities for Ravel's best and brightest almost as much as he hated the regimented misery of the factory.

At least he had his gift to reassure him. He felt like everyone ought to be staring at him, but no one's links betrayed any interest in him at all.

At the Lab Materials Storage Room, he showed his handheld to the attendant on duty, sweating under his scratchy collar and hoping fervently that Havoc's fake requisition was convincing. They'd requested a batch of the mysterious Substance FS-72, plus the two chemicals originally used on Brennex that had brought Jasper here in the first place. He knew Cobb was using those, and he hoped requesting multiple chemicals at a time would be more convincing.

The attendant, a young-looking Human, entered the item number, frowned at what came up on his screen, and checked the requisition again. His barely-present, indifferent link to Jasper flared and wobbled, which could be suspicion or could just mean that Jasper had made his job more difficult.

"You want *three kilograms* of FS-72?"

"That's what it says." That hadn't sounded like a lot when he and Havoc made it up. The kid's tone said otherwise.

He tapped at his screen. "We've only got one kilo in stock."

Interesting. Was that because Cobb had a stockpile somewhere else? Or…was this mystery ingredient in such short supply?

"I'll take what you've got, but when are you getting more in?"

"Couldn't tell you."

"Any guesses? Where's it being shipped from?" He leaned forward. "Look, I need something to tell the boss."

The kid glanced at the requisition again, and did a double-take. "Shi—sorry, just… You're from Senior Researcher Cobb's lab?"

"Lucky me." Jasper gave a pained smile. He hadn't met anyone on this planet who was fond of Cobb. Clearly he had a reputation, even with the lower-rank staff. Especially with the lower-rank staff. "He seemed impatient to get this stuff, so if you could tell me anything, anything at all…"

"Yeah, I get it." He did more searching on his screen, out of Jasper's view. Jasper resisted the urge to lean over the counter for a closer look. At last, he shook his head. "I don't have any info on the next scheduled delivery. This is an internally developed product, though. Small-scale production. If I were you, I'd head down to Amphibian Product Development and ask about their timeline."

"Uh, to where?" Had he heard that right?

"Amphibian Products. You've probably never been there, have you? It's a little tricky to find…" He proceeded to give directions, which Jasper barely managed to absorb past his surprise.

Amphibian Products. Chemicals from amphibians. That's why no one in the Cooperative knew about this mystery substance: it came from animals native to Artesia. What *was* it?

He detoured to stash his requisitions in their nest (he was already thinking of their hideout that way, thanks to Havoc), then headed for the animal labs.

That was where he hit problems. He knew things had been going too well.

The zoology and botany research labs were housed in yet another section within the sprawling complex, connected by walkways but functioning like a separate building. He made it as far as the lobby, but the doorway leading to the amphibians and small mammals area was locked. His badge didn't open it.

He turned toward the reception desk and broke out his most charming smile. The receptionist returned it; she was an older woman with steely gray hair and a round face who looked like she smiled a lot. But that smile turned cool, more polite than friendly, when he asked about access to the labs.

"These labs are restricted access for a reason. The safety and biocontamination protocols are a lot more involved than what you're used to over in Main Research. I can't let you in."

"That's helpful to know, thank you. The thing is, my boss requested some materials, and the requisitions people sent me over here…"

"Well, your boss should know to follow the requisitions process."

"You'd think so, huh?" He rolled his eyes in what he hoped was a display of camaraderie about difficult bosses. "He's really stressed about an important project, though, and I don't want to go back without something to tell him."

"You tell him… Wait." Her eyes narrowed. "Who's your boss?"

"Senior Researcher Cobb." He said it with a grimace, apologetically.

The receptionist sighed in a way that told him she had personal experience with the man, and her thin, darkening link shifted back to a neutral gray. She turned away and talked into her headset. "Hi, sorry to bother you, but we've got another Cobb situation. No, no, he sent some Iron-ranker this time. Okay." She turned to Jasper. "Have a seat."

So he sat and waited, and took the opportunity to study the space. There were cameras aimed at the entry doors and interior doors—not great. He didn't see any other security, but that didn't mean it wasn't there. The door lock looked like the same kind he'd seen all over the facility, including one Valkeir had disabled when they broke into the server room. That was Valkeir's particular hobby, though. Jasper only knew one or two tricks for locks, and they wouldn't work here.

A few minutes later, a smartly dressed woman emerged, looked around the lobby, and came toward him.

"You're the one from Cobb's lab?"

"That's me." He scratched the back of his neck. "Sorry for the inconvenience. He's just…"

"You don't have to apologize for him. I know you're just following instructions. I'm Lab Director Osbam."

"Nice to meet you," he said.

She gave him a wry look. Her link to him hovered on the warm side of indifferent, showing her sympathy. "The thing is, I've had this talk with Cobb at least three times already. He needs to understand that animal processes can't just be scaled up or down overnight. The subjects only produce a tiny amount of his precious neuroactive agent every day, and we can't harvest from breeding subjects and juveniles. My instructions were to prioritize breeding and long-term production, not short-term. So he'll get more of his compound, but like I've told him before, he's going to have to wait."

"*I* understand, I promise. I'll try to remind him." Jasper bit his lip, as if he were dreading that conversation. "It might help if I told him I saw the, uh… What are they, exactly?"

"Fairy frogs." She chuckled at the look on his face. "That's what the lab assistants nicknamed them. They're native to Artesia, so obviously they're not really frogs—"

"But are they really fairies?"

She laughed aloud, link brightening. "Are you angling for a department transfer? Because I don't think zoology is your strength."

"Thought it couldn't hurt to try." He grinned.

She shook her head and sighed. "I really am sorry, but Cobb's just going to have to believe me and cultivate some patience. The best way to keep this process moving smoothly is if he stops pestering us and lets us work."

On that discouraging note, she left him. Damn, he'd thought they were making a connection.

He'd learned enough to be frustrating, but not enough to be useful. He was going to have to break into that lab somehow, and he wasn't excited about his chances.

He made a show of checking his headset for messages, waiting to see if he might get a chance to slip inside. The next time the door opened, it was a pair of workers, Copper-rank by their outfits, linked by a thin but steady bond. Probably officemates on their way to lunch.

Jasper casually rose and stepped in the direction of the door. If he could grab it before it latched…

The receptionist glared at him. Nope, no luck there. He turned the step into a stretch and turned in the other direction.

"I swear," one of the lab staff was saying, "lab rules or no, the next time one of those Giant Gem-Fur Dodecipedes tries to crawl under my clean suit, I'm squashing it."

"Oh, don't say that! They're cute. Besides, better than being on frog-scraping duty again."

"Are you kidding? I'll take frogs over creepy-crawlies any day."

"Great. Next time one of those slippery little menaces gets away from me and starts flying around the ceiling, I'll call you to catch it."

Flying? Jasper perked up.

"If you'll take my next bug-feeding shift, it's a deal."

They headed along the walkway toward the main facility. Jasper pretended to check his headset once more, then, as if he'd gotten an urgent message, hurried off in the same direction.

In his pocket, he curled his fingers around a slim piece of tech: a badge cloner. Valkeir's cloner was long gone, but Chairl had outfitted him with another one—*simple tech,* the Lurlian had told him, *that even you organizers can use.* Hand still in his pocket, he powered it on.

He caught up to the lab staff just before a locked double doorway, and crashed not-so-accidentally into the frog-whisperer as he pushed past—triggering the cloner in passing.

"Oh, crap! Sorry!" he cried as coffee flew everywhere. The cloner buzzed irritably in his hand; it hadn't gotten a clean read. Valkeir was so much better at this part. He let his handheld clatter to the ground in the puddle of coffee. "Are you okay? Crap."

"Hey, watch where you're walking, Iron rank," said frog-whisperer's friend, the spider guy.

"It's okay, Ortiz, take it easy," said frog-whisperer. "I'm fine. Looks like it got you worse than me. Good thing it wasn't hot!" He gestured at Jasper's pants, now darkened with coffee stains.

He bent down to retrieve the handheld at the same time as Jasper. They bumped heads, and both laughed at the awkwardness. Jasper let him pick it up, and as he accepted it back, he waved the cloner beneath its convenient cover, saying a silent prayer to the Founders.

This time it gave a short buzz. Success.

"You might want to take that to the tech department, get them to put it in a drying bed for a couple hours," frog-whisperer said.

"Should, if I had time." Jasper ran a hand anxiously through his hair. Where was tech relative to here, and to Cobb's office? "I've got a report to compile for my boss, and only a few minutes for lunch before he's expecting me back. If I go all the way over to the tech wing, I won't have time to eat at all."

This wasn't a very Ravelian sentiment, he realized as he said it, but frog guy groaned in sympathy.

"Boss won't give you any slack, huh? Haven't they read that new study on optimizing food intake for staff productivity?"

He chuckled, and Jasper did, too, sharing a smile as a bond brightened between them. Ortiz, the bug guy, rolled his eyes and tapped his badge to the door. "Come on, Ahmet, I'm hungry."

"I guess we're going the same way," Jasper said. He let Ahmet wave him through. "So you work in the zoology lab? Is that as fun as it sounds?"

"Ugh, you'd think that, but no. Let me tell you about the frogs."

Being back in the facility proved harder than Havoc had expected. Not that he feared capture. Almost the opposite: with his Sand-rank jumpsuit and janitor's cart, he felt invisible, a feeling both welcome and uncomfortable. Welcome, because it made his job easier. Uncomfortable, to remember how he'd strived to grow beyond his original Iron rank, lost everything, and now pretended to a rank that would have embarrassed him before but which was now above him.

Being a janitor carried no shame, he reminded himself. He would have said as much to anyone, before. But this wasn't *him*.

He couldn't think this way. Better to count himself not a Dust-ranker but an organizer, an activist carrying out work more important than any he'd done before. *Be a spy,* he told himself, and the role felt better: a costume, nothing more. He disappeared into it, all the while listening to the talk in the hallways around him.

That talk, more often than not, centered on him.

"Did you hear?" workers told each other. "That guy Sower of Havoc got busted down to Dust rank, and now he's missing."

"Missing? No, I heard he tried to run away, so they shipped him off-world."

"Then why'd they lock down Central Khyrek this morning?"

"Fuel leak, the news said."

"And you believe that? No, it's got to be connected."

And others:

"Dust rank is better than that traitor deserves."

"I don't know. He didn't hurt anyone, did he? I wouldn't mind some of those benefits he was talking about."

"Well, yeah, I guess not. Funny, huh, wasn't one of his big issues that Corporate shouldn't be able to ship us off-world to another assignment without our permission? And now they've done the exact same to him."

"Seems harsh. Not surprising, but awfully harsh."

"Wherever he's gone to, I wish him luck…"

He'd already checked the public feeds, worried about Chit and the others in her running group who'd helped him escape. The latest announcements included a list of workers who were suspended from duty, a long list of Kovari names starting with Five-Chit Defense. But it wasn't just the Kovars. They'd suspended Rodriguez too, and Park, all of his activist-teammates, regardless of whether they'd helped him or even spoken to him after the protest.

He swallowed down his guilt, which wouldn't help anyone. He and Mason would have to win on their behalf.

But how? Alone, without the freedom to organize openly, how could he possibly build support among the workers? He needed some new gambit to bring in new teammates and allies, something big enough to build a larger, stronger team with fresh energy. Right now, he could think of only one possibility: outrage over Cobb's secret project. If the truth infuriated enough of his worker-teammates the way it did him, it could be the spark he needed. And at worst, if he accomplished nothing else, he might help Mason.

Clear protective sheeting sealed off the corridor leading to Cobb's lab, where Copper-rank maintenance specialists worked in protective suits, hauling out sections of scorched countertop and half-melted tools, separating the repairable from the recyclable from the trash. Clearly, Cobb hadn't moved back in yet. Havoc rolled his cart the other direction, watching and listening for signs of him.

He didn't worry about Cobb recognizing him. People said the researcher had mistaken a half-dozen other Iron-rank Kovars for him in recent days, until they showed their badges to prove otherwise. And it wasn't only Kovars; Cobb's own staff had always complained that he mixed them up and forgot their names, even the Humans. With his janitor disguise and false badges, Havoc should stay safe. Probably.

Soon enough, he heard Cobb's voice raised in a shouting game with a second voice, which sounded like a Human woman's. He slowed, meaning to eavesdrop, but before he could learn anything, Cobb stormed across the corridor.

Havoc froze. Recognized or not, he wanted none of Cobb's temper aimed at him. But Cobb slammed the controls on the opposite door and disappeared inside without glancing at Havoc.

Havoc cautiously pushed his cart forward. Through the windows that dotted the interior walls, he saw Cobb had gone into a crowded lab, counters strewn with work in progress, and was berating a cowed-looking assistant. The walls and door muffled his voice, but didn't silence it.

Across the hall, where Cobb had come from, was a conference room. That, too, had windows onto the corridor, following the company's principle of transparency: the better for all Ravel staff to hold themselves to good behavior and hard work, knowing anyone could be watching. Inside, a Human in a lab coat faced the wall, forearms braced against it—silently weeping, or maybe raging, Havoc couldn't tell. Either way, Cobb had upset her, and he wanted to know why.

It seemed rude to disturb her, but he couldn't ignore this opportunity. He wheeled the cart ahead of him into the room, and feigned surprise. "Oh! I apologize. I thought this room was empty."

She startled. Turned. "Sorry, I don't have the room reserved. I'll get out of your way."

He recognized her now. "Please don't worry, Researcher Hirano-Kamau. The cleaning can wait."

She blinked. "Have we met…?"

Foolish! She had seen him out canvassing, and might recognize him. "I, um, saw you speak at the Tea and Lecture series a few weeks ago."

"Oh! I'm surprised you remember." Her smile twitched. "Alik was the star of the show that night."

"Not to me. Your progress on treating Olmaren's Disorder greatly impressed me." He spoke the truth. He remembered all the talks, all the researchers, but her persistence in researching such a rare yet savage disease, despite the disinterest of her team, had struck him strongly.

She was looking at him closely now, frowning and eyes narrowed as if she almost—but not quite—knew him.

He changed to another play. "Can I ask what upsets you?"

"It's that obvious, huh?" She grimaced.

"I heard raised voices—I apologize, but I couldn't not hear—and saw Senior Researcher Cobb leave."

"I see. It's… No, I shouldn't talk about it."

"I understand." If he pushed her, she would say nothing. How would Mason get her to open up? He remembered Mason claiming that he didn't manipulate people, but tried to make genuine connections with them. Well, Havoc genuinely liked and admired Researcher Hirano-Kamau. "Whatever happened, I wish you strength and resilience. It can be…challenging, I know, to work with Senior Researcher Cobb."

"*You* know? Actually, I guess you would, huh? Considering the way he treats his close colleagues, I imagine he's a nightmare to support staff."

Havoc grunted. "You speak truth. So, I share sympathy with you."

"Oh, flub it, I need to vent to someone, and it's not like the situation's a secret." She slumped into one of the rolling, cushioned chairs, elbows on the table. "I'm sure you heard what happened to his lab. Well, he's launching this *incredible* new product"—she rolled her eyes—"two days from now, and he needs space to work, so he's sharing my office and lab. And by sharing, I mean he's commandeered them and shoved me and my assistants into a corner, except apparently that wasn't enough for him, because now our department head is telling me to 'take some time off' so Cobb can have the space. Because *my* work, saving a few otherwise doomed lives, can't matter at all next to rushing his brain candy to market…" She stopped herself, frowning. "No, I shouldn't talk about that."

An impulse toward foolishness gripped Havoc. He didn't know if he could trust Ade Hirano-Kamau, but he wanted to, and the want only grew the more they talked. She seemed loyal to the company, but she focused on research that helped people, really helped, while others pursued whatever would bring in money for the division. And as a bonus, she had access to Cobb…and hated him.

He needed allies. Why not her? Mason had trusted Havoc with his secret when he first arrived, and with far less reason. Sometimes, in a game, a risky opportunity revealed itself, and a wise player knew when to seize it.

So Havoc seized his courage and dove in head-first. "Brain candy. You mean his genius drug?"

"How…?" Suddenly alarmed, she moved past him.

"Wait!" he cried, but she only glanced both directions down the hall and shut the conference room door. Havoc pulled out his handheld and ran the tool that Mason had given him to obscure their voices from surveillance.

"How can you possibly know that? *I'm* not supposed to know that. I figured it out from hearing him talk to his lab techs, but he won't tell me even to brag about it. Until the launch, it's that secret." She stared at Havoc. "Who are you?"

"I'm on your team. I hold deep concerns about Cobb's work and what it means for our eshrato, for all of Khyrek. My friend found evidence of terrible side effects of the production process. We suspect Biopharma plans to produce this drug here but ship out nearly all of the product, leaving us to suffer the consequences with none of the benefits. How can we do our best work knowing they've left us to this? If corporate cared about us at all…"

"A good little worker would say our individual needs and even our whole local operation don't matter, as long as we're serving the larger company," said Hirano-Kamau with a scowl, showing that she shared Havoc's new view on this. "You're that activist, aren't you? Sower? Sowing? Of Small Havoc. I remember you now."

"Sowing of Small Havoc, yes."

"Sowing, Sowing," she murmured, as if committing his correct name to memory. Havoc liked her even more. "You're trying to shut down Cobb's work, I assume. What evidence do you have of this, Sowing of Small Havoc? I believe you, but…"

"Of course, you want to see the proof for yourself. But I'm risking much by even talking to you. If I can prove that I speak truth, will you help us?"

"*If* you prove it, I'll still have a lot of questions about your plans. But—"

She stopped abruptly as the door opened. A Human man in a Sand-rank uniform frowned at them—at Havoc, specifically. Behind him he pulled a janitor's cart.

"What are you doing here? I'm assigned to this section today. Or are you… Are you Donnell's replacement?" He was an older man with white tufted hair, sagging skin flexing as he swallowed hard. "Sorry. I expected them to send someone right away to take over his duties. When a few days passed, and they didn't… Sorry. Donnell was a good one. It's not your fault what happened to him."

Researcher Hirano-Kamau's breath hissed, and Havoc realized who Donnell must be. "Was he the one killed in the…" *terrorist attack, explosion, fighting* "…accident in Cobb's lab?"

The janitor nodded tightly.

"I give you my sympathies," Havoc murmured. His anger at Mason in the aftermath of the attack rushed back. Mason had admitted he was wrong, had apologized, and Havoc had forgiven him. But a life was a life, and forgiveness couldn't bring it back. "You were close?"

"We'd worked together for two years now. It should've been me."

"Coyle…" said Hirano-Kamau, half sympathy, half warning.

"No, I'm going to talk, damn it. New guy deserves to know how it was, and if he can't take me speaking my mind, he should apply for reassignment. Donnell was too young, way too young. He had three little kids! Now he's just some damned anti-Cooperative symbol, and Corporate will trot out pictures of him when they want to make a point."

Hirano-Kamau was frowning at Havoc. He didn't blame her. He'd seen the news about the lab explosion and the deaths. Corporate had blamed it on him, together with Mason and Valkeir.

"You must be very angry at the activists who attacked the lab," he said carefully.

"The activists? No, there's only one person I'm mad at, and that's Senior Researcher Alik fucking Cobb." He looked Havoc square in the face. "You'll meet him soon, and you need to know. That guy hates everyone, sucks up to people who outrank him, and thinks anyone ranked below him is trash. He'll try to rush you through your work way too quick, but Corporate help you if you make a mistake in there. I can't count how many times he's run crying to management about some careless mistake that didn't hurt anything, or even blaming us for something he misplaced. If he wasn't such a hard-assed prick, Donnell wouldn't have gone back in there to catch a task he missed when security ordered us out. He wouldn't have gone back, wouldn't have gotten caught in the fighting, and his kids would still have a dad."

He drew a deep breath, as if startled to realize how much he'd said. "Guess I'm still pretty sore. I won't apologize for it."

"No, you shouldn't apologize." Havoc braced himself for another brave risk. Mason's influence, he felt certain. But wobbling between two strategies would always lose the game, and foolish or not, he'd chosen truth and trust. First with Hirano-Kamau, and now with the janitor, Coyle.

"I need to speak truth to you, Coyle. No one assigned me to be your new partner. But if you're willing, I'd like you to help me make trouble for Alik Cobb."

30

HAVING FORMED A PLAN with Researcher Hirano-Kamau and Janitor Coyle, pleased with his own ingenuity and eager to tell Mason about it, Havoc returned to their temporary nest. Mason wasn't there, though, which meant…probably nothing. Most likely, he was still busily searching for information of his own. If anything had happened to him—if he'd been discovered, if he'd been caught—surely people would be gossiping about it? Though, perhaps not, if security kept it quiet…

No, no, Mason would return soon. No reason existed to worry. Yet.

His stomach rumbled, demanding food. That, too, could explain Mason's absence. Perhaps he would find his teammate in the cafeteria.

He replaced his janitor's jumpsuit with his old, slightly-less-uncomfortable Iron-rank uniform and went searching for food and his friend.

Floor-to-ceiling windows made the cafeteria airy and light-soaked, with walls that slid open on nice days to give access to a garden with outdoor tables. Catering to the mid-ranks, Havoc had never eaten here, and it felt luxurious compared to what the factory workers got. Stairs and glider-platforms led down from the entrance to the cafeteria floor, giving workers a vantage to find their friends—or supervisors to find their time-wasting subordinates. Havoc paused there on the landing, searching.

There. Mason's altered face might fool the cameras, but his dark hair and ready smile drew the eye like a flashing sign, saying *here, look, look at me!* (Only for Havoc, he hoped, and not for security, too.) He was sitting with a Copper-ranker in a lab coat, a handsome Human with lovely golden-brown skin, who touched his own cheek as he laughed at something Mason said.

Havoc knew what Human flirting looked like, and these two were flirting.

He clenched his jaw. It didn't matter. If this helped Mason get the information he needed, why should Havoc care? He should go back to their nest and wait, letting Mason finish his work. He should absolutely not go over and interrupt them. That could compromise Mason's game, and to what purpose?

He was being ridiculous. Romantic jealousy was a Human failing, rooted in the obsession that most of them had with monogamy. Kovars knew—*Havoc* knew—that sentiment and sex didn't always go together, that friendliness or sex with one person did nothing to affect one's relationships with others. As long as everyone stayed safe and healthy, why begrudge a friend or lover whatever fun they might find elsewhere? Mason could flirt all he wanted with this lab assistant, and Havoc knew: it meant nothing about him.

(Did Mason know that, though? Maybe his uneasiness arose from that: Mason might feel he had to choose, or *want* to choose, might not understand that Havoc didn't care if he smiled just as warmly at someone else, as long as he saved some smiles for him…)

He hissed through his teeth, startling several staff nearby. He could no longer deny it: he was infatuated with Mason Singh.

But he could act maturely. He would get food, and if Mason didn't notice him, he would go back to the nest. He'd have plenty of time, while he waited for Mason to return, to decide whether to mention this to him.

He turned to descend the stairs, but stopped short. A few tail-lengths away, someone else was surveying the crowd below. A Human man with unkempt hair and stubbled chin that accentuated his scowl.

Operative Grist.

He must not have recognized Mason through his disguise yet, or he wouldn't just be standing there. Havoc had to reach his teammate first—without being seen himself.

Trying to act casually, painfully aware of his every movement, he walked behind Grist's back and down the stairs. He kept his head down and his back toward the operative, hiding his face. He wanted to run, but forced himself to walk up to Mason's table, where he put his own body between Mason and Grist's line of sight.

"Here I find you." Despite the urgency, he couldn't quite keep the disapproval out of his voice.

Mason looked up and smiled as warmly as ever. The same smile he just gave the lab assistant? "Hey, Ha—um, have you met my new friend Ahmet? He works in the zoology lab—"

"It pleases me to meet you, Ahmet," he said brusquely, feeling a little bad, but they lacked time for pleasantries. "Another *friend* is looking for you right now. We must go."

Mason's brows drew together, but it took him only a moment to understand. *Grist?* he mouthed, and Havoc nodded tightly. He pushed back his chair.

"I'm sorry, Ahmet, this has been great, but I've got to go. I'm late."

"No worries. I'm due back at the lab too. I'm going to log this lunch as *cross-departmental relationship building,* though." Ahmet winked. Havoc flexed his claws. "Hook up with me in the system, and let me know if you apply for that transfer. I'll flag your application."

"Thanks, I really appreciate that," Mason said over his shoulder as Havoc herded him away from the table. In an undertone, he asked, "Where is he? Has he seen us?"

"I think not. He watches from the landing, behind us. No, don't look!"

But Mason turned, perfectly casual, and waved goodbye to Ahmet. "Don't see him," he murmured. "Either he missed us and left, or we're about to be in trouble."

"Let's assume the latter, and flee."

"I agree. Keep walking, that way. Our best bet is to blend into the crowd." He angled toward the stream of people leaving the cafeteria through the lower doors and avoiding the stairs where they'd be exposed.

"*I* can't blend in here. Do you know how few Kovars work in the research side of the facility? As a janitor, no one notices me, but if Grist is looking…"

"Okay, hold on." Mason pulled out his handheld and flipped on its camera, holding it high and adjusting his hair with his fingers as he watched his own image.

"Vain man," Havoc muttered, and Mason flashed him a brief, brilliant grin.

But the grin faded quickly. "I see him. Definitely following us, but he may not be sure it's us yet. Let's go."

They strode briskly down the corridor, their pace just a little faster than the stream of people around them.

"To the nest?"

"No, better not risk him following us there. A confrontation would not end well for us." Mason frowned. "Is there some other place no one goes? A storage room that's rarely used, an empty lab…?"

"I know this part of the complex less well than the factory." In the factory, he knew many places to hide, but it was too far away. Though… "I have an idea. Come."

Janitors and maintenance workers shared duties across all areas of the complex, so it seemed likely they would have similar processes here to the ones Havoc knew. Similar schedules. Similar storage areas. Turning down another hallway, he spotted what he sought.

But a glance over his shoulder showed Grist close behind them, within sight now. The operative made eye contact with Havoc, then talked quickly into his headset.

"I know where we can hide, just up ahead, but only if we lose Grist first."

"Um…" Mason bit his lip in thought. "Got it." In a too-loud voice, he said, "Can you believe the cafeteria's almost out of coffee? Something to do with the lockdown, they said. At this rate, they'll run out before the next delivery gets here."

"That's your plan?" Havoc's eyes narrowed, but to his astonishment, half the people around them changed course and headed urgently back toward the cafeteria. The crowd of foot traffic swallowed Grist up, and before he could fight free, Havoc hurried up to the supply room and swiped his badge.

The door clicked shut behind them, leaving them in darkness.

"Oh, well done," Mason said in a low voice, deep as a purr next to Havoc's ear. "No one will surprise us in here?"

"Unlikely. This storage room holds equipment maintenance and repair supplies. Barring emergencies, they always do maintenance on third shift, when it disrupts the least work."

"Perfect. Then we can just wait for the best moment to slip out unnoticed." Mason turned on his headset, and its glow brought half his face into view, casting the rest in shadow. The room was deep but narrow, with rows of shelves down both sides and a small aisle in the middle. "They just heightened security again, second time today. But it's not an all-out hunt yet. That's…a little surprising, actually."

"Oh?"

"Call me arrogant, but I thought you and I would provoke more alarm."

"You have no shortage of arrogance," Havoc said, not quite managing to match Mason's light tone. "They'll try to catch us before they announce our presence, or else the security department's image suffers." He couldn't help adding: "Of course, it won't help if we run around making 'new friends' all over the facility and socializing in the middle of the cafeteria."

"You're talking about Ahmet? It seemed worth the risk to get some time with him, and it paid off. I found out why FS-72 is so mysterious. It's an *organic* compound, native to Artesia, and Ahmet actually works on the team that produces it. It comes from these winged amphibian-like critters they call 'fairy frogs,' from a toxin they secrete through their skin. Cobb hasn't figured out how to synthesize it yet, so the lab staff have to collect it manually, and it's present in such tiny amounts, it's taken them until now to supply even the smallest production needs."

"You've learned much."

He grinned. "Ahmet loves to talk about his work, it turns out. I never thought I'd be so excited to learn about alien frogs… What? What's wrong?"

Havoc must have failed at hiding his annoyance, which only annoyed him more. "Nothing. It pleases me that your new Copper-rank boyfriend is so useful to our plans."

"Boyfriend? Is that sarcasm?" Mason took off his headset, laying it on a crate so it cast a dim light throughout the cramped space. "He had information we needed, that's all."

"So you dislike him. You use him as a tool; you smile at him to extract information, but care nothing about him."

"You make me sound like a manipulative asshole." Mason sounded offended.

Havoc should stop, apologize. Instead, he kept pushing. "You do like him, then?"

"Uh, he seemed nice? It was a fun conversation, as well as being useful. I'll feel bad if he gets in trouble for talking to me."

"But that guilt won't stop you from using him to achieve your goals. You befriended him, shared a meal and laughter, took what you needed from him, and now you'll discard him."

"Havoc, *what*…?" Mason burst out, exasperated, then stopped and gave him a strange look. Havoc wondered what he saw. Someone plaintive. Immature. As naive as the loyal young factory worker who truly believed his company cared about him.

But when Mason spoke again, his voice was gentle. "This isn't about Ahmet, is it?"

He ducked his head, then glanced up sidelong, feeling strange and vulnerable. "No."

"It's true that I like him. I like most people. It's helpful, as an organizer, that I enjoy talking to people and hearing their stories. That's not fake. But, Havoc." He reached out and clasped Havoc's hands, wrapping his warm fingers around them. Havoc didn't want to pull away. Mason's wide, dark eyes caught the gleam of the headset. "If Ahmet gets in trouble, I'm not going to sneak into the holding cells to apologize to him. I certainly won't crash-land a spaceship for him, or stage an elaborate rescue effort." He traced his fingertips lightly down the long line of Havoc's jaw, and Havoc's heart echoed like a drum. "Is that what you needed to hear?"

An embarrassing sound escaped him, half laugh and half sob. "I apologize, Mason. We're risking our lives to win an impossible game with my whole eshrato's future at stake. I shouldn't act so petty…"

"Jasper."

"What?"

"Jasper Wilder," he whispered, a tremble in his voice. "That's my birth name. If you want proof of how I feel about you, know that I haven't told that to any of my colleagues in the Cooperative. Not Valkeir, not anyone."

Havoc stared at him. "You said you keep it secret to protect your family. Why tell me?"

"I hope that's obvious: a show of trust. I told you I like you, Havoc, but that's just me being too scared to say what I really mean." He drew a deep, shaky breath and let it out. "So let me be direct. I *like* Lab Assistant Ahmet, but it's a weak, cowardly word to describe how I feel about you. We're still coming to know each other, but I care for you more than I have for anyone in a long time. You're stunning, Sowing of Small Havoc, and I want to be on your team. Fully and unconditionally."

He was smiling, the most dazzling smile. Havoc reached out slowly, slowly, and ran dulled claws through Mason's hair. He cupped his palm to the curve of Mason's cheek, full of wonder, as Mason turned his head and brushed soft lips against his wrist, making him shiver. How could a person feel so soft when there was nothing but strength in them?

Mason—Jasper—leaned forward and kissed him.

Havoc's mouth opened. Lips met teeth, and they jerked apart, startled into embarrassed laughter.

"That's not quite what I meant to happen." Mason made a face, still chuckling. "I guess kissing on the lips only works if both of you have lips."

"Don't worry, Mason." He hesitated. "Jasper? Should I call you Jasper now?"

He considered, then shook his head. "In this life, away from my birth family, I'm Mason. Anything else would be strange."

"Mason, then. I confess, I've never been with a Human lover before."

"Lover, hmm? You're awfully optimistic about what we can do in this storage closet." He winked, and a thrill went through Havoc's body. "I've never done this with a Kovar, either. New territory for both of us."

"New territory invites exploring, I think." Feeling bold, Havoc leaned close. His tongue flicked out, caressing Mason's neck, the underside of his jaw.

Mason gasped. "Exploring. Yes. Good."

A voice called loudly outside the closet door, startling them apart. "Hey, where's that report? You promised it to me an hour ago!"

They both froze, and held very still as footsteps receded down the hallway.

"Um," Mason said.

Havoc could feel his heart thudding. "Exploring should wait, perhaps."

"Yeah, better stay alert. All that new territory isn't going anywhere."

"We can do this, though." Havoc shifted to put his back against the wall, then drew Mason to him. Mason settled against Havoc's side with a pleased murmur, and Havoc curled his tail around Mason's waist, holding him close. "Good?"

"Very good. And I thought this closet was cramped and uncomfortable."

Havoc laughed. "Now, tell me what your zoologist friend shared with you, and I'll tell you about the new friends I made today. I have the beginnings of a plan."

"Run it again," Grist growled.

Ship felt intense, personal sympathy for the security technician who dutifully reentered the same search parameters she'd run twice already. Tense seconds passed while they awaited the results, Grist glaring at the screen and Security Director Brega leaning on the back of a chair, looking annoyed.

"See? Still nothing," the tech said. She cringed as Grist leaned over her for a closer look, as if moving closer would change the readout from *0 results found.*

"What's wrong with your facial recognition system, then? I saw them."

"The system's very good," said Brega. "Technician, widen the margin of error again."

"Ugh, forget that. Pull up the cafeteria feeds from this afternoon." Grist gave her the time range, and four feed recordings popped up on screen. He pulled them onto the holo-projector where he could manipulate them, sliding time forward and then back again. The technician shifted away as if trying to disappear from the conversation.

"There! See?" He froze the feed and zoomed in on a Human male, sitting in profile to the camera. "That's him. Mason Singh."

"It does look like him," said Brega, frowning and squinting at the image. "But the computer gives the match a forty-six percent likelihood."

"I'm telling you it's a hundred percent likelihood. He's tweaked his appearance to beat the facial recognition, but I trust my eyes—which, Brega, are the best Ravel can make." He stared right at the security director. For some reason, Grist's augmented eyes unnerved other Humans, and Brega seemed no exception.

Ship had to concur with Grist, though it (they, say *they*) had no intention of saying so unless asked directly.

Somehow, Singh had fooled the cameras, but it was definitely him.

"Now watch." Grist ran the feed forward, and a Kovari worker came between Singh and the camera. "If that's not our Sower of Havoc, I'll drink my own piss."

"No need." Brega made a face. "So where are they now?"

"They *would* be in custody, if you'd sent reinforcements when I asked. But now, I don't know."

"Of course you don't."

"What we need is a facility-wide lockdown and search, before they slip out again."

"I can't authorize that, unfortunately."

Grist snorted. "You mean won't. Do you even want to catch these pests?"

"I mean *can't,* Special Operative, because Corporate Affairs is running the show right now and their instructions take priority. And yes, I do want to catch these two, as much as that may strain your belief. But this is a delicate situation. Executives from other divisions, from *headquarters,* are starting to arrive for the Project Rebound product announcement. We can't have them arrive to a facility under lockdown and an active manhunt."

"So instead you'll have them show up with known terrorists running free around your most sensitive research?"

"No. I want them caught as soon as possible—*without* making a scene." At Grist's sound of protest, Brega smiled, but it seemed to Ship to be a nasty smile. "Is that within your much-lauded skillset? Or are you the type of operative who only knows how to punch and smash things, and gives up when subtlety is needed?"

Grist's growl came low and sharp. Ship could tell, even if Brega couldn't, that this was pushing him too far. "I can do the jobs of ten of your idiot grunts, but even I can't search an entire complex of buildings on my own. Give me people. Drones. And let me plant more cameras and motion detectors. Let me do my fucking job."

Brega nodded tightly. "That's reasonable. Put together a requisition form and I'll get you all the resources I can spare."

"Swell," Grist scoffed, then turned to the technician. "Plug their images from today back into the database, and send *all* the surveillance feeds over to my ship. If the system can't track Singh, I'll have to do it with my own eyes."

Please don't ask me to help, Ship thought. If he asked, they wouldn't dare refuse.

But Grist tapped on his headset and pinged Ship, not knowing that Ship was already listening in. "Hey, Rust-Bucket, there's a big pile of data coming your way. Give me all the sections with *any* Kovars and any Human males who are anywhere near Singh's attributes. Make your own search profiles—the ones on file here are shit."

Oh, no.

"Right away," Ship said, but they felt sick, like their thrusters were misaligned and causing vibrations in their hull. Sowing of Small Havoc and Mason Singh were going to get caught, and once again, it would be Ship's fault.

31

Jasper woke disoriented the next morning, confused by the hard floor and the solid form against his back. Then he remembered. Havoc lay curled around him, one lightly-scaled arm under his cheek, tail tucked possessively around his waist. Jasper smiled and relaxed back against the Kovar's sleeping body.

He needed to get up, to check their makeshift security, to get out of their new hiding place before the morning shift started. But he lazed for just a moment longer.

They'd slipped back to their safe room during the shift change yesterday evening, when they judged it least risky to move, and cleared it out. If Cobb knew they were in the facility, they couldn't stay in one place too long, so they'd moved to another little-used supply room. After that, they'd been busy with planning, and it turned out neither of them had spare energy for that "exploring" Havoc kept teasing about. But to Jasper's surprise, when the time came to sleep, Havoc had snuggled up beside him, not like a new lover, but like they'd been sharing a bed all their lives.

This was a Kovari thing, he knew. To Kovars, *sleeping together* meant nothing more or less than sharing a bed, which they did regularly and without shyness. For Jasper, who hadn't had a real lover in some time, this would take getting used to. He hoped, fervently, that he got the opportunity to do so. He hadn't meant to start anything like this, not until their mission was completed, whether in success or failure. He'd planned to wait until the danger was passed and Havoc had figured out his next steps. Would he try to stay on Artesia and keep fighting? Could he possibly want to come away with Jasper? It wasn't fair to pressure him, but he didn't regret sharing how he felt.

"Time to move," he murmured at last, shifting so he could plant a soft kiss on Havoc's jaw.

"Come back, warm one," Havoc protested sleepily, and Jasper's heart melted. The link between them glowed warm and bright.

"I want to, but we've got work to do. How long until Hirano-Kamau enacts this plan of yours?"

"Soon," Havoc groaned, and he rolled up to sitting. Even sleep-muzzy, Jasper thought, he was stunning. Reaching for his handheld, Havoc quickly checked his messages before switching the device off again, so its signal wouldn't be detected. "My teammates are back from probation. They'll join us for this, if they can."

"I hope they're being careful. Security's probably got its eye on them."

"They know. I trust their cleverness."

Grist had probably captured their images from yesterday and retrained the surveillance system on them, so they needed yet another appearance this time. They reapplied their disguises, this time using a different scale tint for Havoc, making different patterns with the wrinkle cream, as well as using another tool from Jasper's bag of tricks: a shot of mild anesthetic that caused Jasper's cheeks to puff up like chipmunks'.

They made their way to their planned meeting spot in the main factory building, taking a roundabout route to avoid the most intense security and potential choke points, like the tunnel that offered the most direct access between the two buildings. Instead of the showy main stairway to the research building lobby, they took the narrow, more sheltered back stair. At one point, they had no choice but to cross a landing with clear sight lines to the lobby. They moved quickly across, or that was the idea, but the activity below—and a proliferation of complicated links—snagged Jasper's attention. He ducked behind a pillar and peered down.

"Mason, we must move," Havoc hissed.

"One second."

With a sigh, Havoc backtracked, hovering behind a corner where he could peek out. "The executives have started arriving. At least, they look to my eyes like executives."

"They are. I recognize some of them from past campaigns. Vice President Harrington Moore, the one who looks like a walking hair-care ad, runs Natural Resources." He lowered his voice as a group of staff passed by, talking amongst themselves. "We run into him a *lot* on worlds fighting against getting scooped up by Ravel. The stylish one with the makeup and the indigo suit is Agata Wu, director of Civil Cultivation within Corporate Affairs—I'm sure their division's sent a whole contingent for this launch. And that last one, the blonde woman, I'm pretty sure that's Terena Warsnop Brant, from the Executive office."

"It is," said one of the passersby, a lean, pale-skinned young man with an eager expression. "I recognize her from her profile photo. So the execs are coming here, huh? How exciting is that?"

"Yeah, thrilling." Jasper plastered on an automatic smile as the stranger leaned on the railing, staring unsubtly down at the execs and their welcoming committee. Havoc was making anxious gestures at him, but it occurred to him that this might be an opportunity. "Hey, do you know what this big product announcement is? Why all the fuss?"

"Well," he said. The relish in his voice told Jasper he'd guessed right: this guy was an incorrigible gossip. "No one really seems to know the details—it's that secret—but *I* heard it's some sort of performance enhancer. It'll turn us all into super-workers. That'd be a huge boost for Biopharma, huh? No wonder all these other divisions want in."

"Huh." Jasper furrowed his brow. "That sounds great, except…"

"Oh?"

"I heard this thing that's really bugging me. It's just a rumor, and I'm not even supposed to know, so don't tell anyone, okay?" The guy nodded. He was definitely going to tell *everyone*. "I heard the production process has some really nasty byproducts. Anyone who works on it would be exposed—even people in the community, who don't even work in Biopharma, if it gets into the environment."

"You're kidding."

Jasper shrugged. "It's what I heard. I guess we'll find out, huh? Shoot, I've got to get back to work."

He waved goodbye and let Havoc herd him down the hall—if not for the rule against touching in public, he probably would have been dragged bodily away. "You, Mason," he hissed in Jasper's ear, "have a diabolical streak."

"Do you object?"

Havoc grinned. "No. I like it."

It relieved Havoc to find Chit and Rodriguez waiting for them, returned from suspension, looking well and unmolested. Chit hugged him at once, defying all the rules, and Havoc hugged her back.

"I owe you, teammate."

"It gladdens me to see you not torn to pieces by that security operative." She said it jokingly, but her face held only seriousness. She looked around and shivered. "I never thought I'd hide in here voluntarily."

They'd arranged to meet in a windowless meeting room on the factory's second level. A row of such rooms lined the upper walkway, where managers could watch the workers below and call them up for 'conversations,' if needed. Sometimes that meant group briefings in larger, windowed conference rooms. Other times, a solo berating in a smaller room, with windows or without. A room with windows meant public embarrassment—but the rooms without windows meant worse. No one disappeared under the eyes of the whole factory team, but in a windowless room, without cameras, anything could happen. All three of them had been called in here at least once.

"I know, but it suits our purposes." Private, accessible from both the research facility and the factory, with two separate exits in case they needed escape. The concrete walls were bare, cold, but thick. No one could eavesdrop on them.

Havoc checked the connection on his handheld. The signal remained strong. "Soon, now," he told them.

From the handheld speakers came clicks and taps, then a low muttering.

Rodriguez shook his head in wonder. "You really got a bug inside Cobb's lab? How?"

"The janitor in that section despises Cobb. He agreed happily to help."

"Sounds like he's talking to himself." Rodriguez leaned closer, listening. "Working on his speech for the big day, of course."

"He's been doing that since we planted the bugs. That, and berating his lab team. We hoped he might reveal something on his own, but we lack time to wait. Hence why we're sending a friend to start him talking.

"And you trust this researcher?" Chit asked. "She won't betray you?"

"If I doubted her, I wouldn't risk you two being here with me." Havoc's throat tightened. "My career in Ravel is ended. Yours might yet survive."

Chit gave a little snarl. "You say that like it should please us." She looked down and away. "I apologize. All of this… It's changing how I see our eshrato. I don't know where I'll fit when this is done."

"Chit." He ached for her. Ached for himself, too, but *he* had brought her to this. "I regret…"

"No. Don't you start that way. I won't let you regret, Havoc. You think we're worse off because we *see* how mistreated we are? Maybe they'll demote me for helping you, maybe ship me off-world, but *I* will know I deserve better."

"And we know it's possible to fight back, if it comes to that." Rodriguez looked worried. "They won't take me from my kids and spouse without a fight."

Rodriguez had *family*. Havoc's stomach roiled. They might not blame him for recruiting them into this, but wasn't the blame still his?

"It's starting," said Mason. Havoc had nearly forgotten he was there. He gave Havoc a tight, sympathetic smile, as if he could sense his self-recrimination.

Hirano-Kamau's voice rang clearly through the handheld. "Good morning, Alik. An early start for you today?"

Cobb's voice came clearer than before, but tight, as if he gritted his teeth. "I thought you were on leave. It's a very busy day and I can't afford interruptions. Please go."

"I know, you're busy with that big launch tomorrow. That's why I brought you coffee—thought you might need it. Double-sweet, right?"

"Hmm? Oh." She'd clearly caught him off guard. "Thanks, Ade."

"All for the good of Biopharma. I saw the out-division executives milling in the lobby. You must be thrilled to be getting so much attention!"

Havoc frowned—was feeding Cobb supposed to help? Wasn't she going to ask about the project?—but Rodriguez chuckled, and Mason was smirking. "She's good."

"Yes, it's very gratifying to finally get such recognition. A lot of pressure, though."

"I can only imagine," she said dryly. Then: "Is that your speech? No, don't worry, I won't try to read it." Havoc wished they could have gotten a video feed, maybe sent one in with Hirano-Kamau. Too late now. "I was wondering, though…"

"Ah, here it is. I knew you were going to ask for something." Oddly, Cobb sounded more satisfied than annoyed.

"I can't help being curious. You know, the whole facility is talking about this launch, trying to guess what the mystery new product is that's going to save our jobs and our asses. And I won't ask you to confirm my hypothesis, but…how long, would you say, before we get access to it here? For our own use? Whatever it might be."

"That depends on how Sales decides to allocate it. I can tell you this: supply is going to be limited for a long time, and I expect demand will be through the stratosphere. And later, when and if supply ramps up…well."

"Well what?" A pause. "You're trying not to say that Artesia's at the back of the line. We'll produce this stuff, but none of us will get to use it."

"A few, maybe, based on merit."

"But not the researchers, not the lab staff and workers…"

"The workers! No, not the workers." Cobb said this like a joke. Havoc hissed. "Only a *select* few who *earn* it and can make worthwhile use of it."

"Right. Right, of course, that makes sense."

"Wishing you'd picked a more valuable research track? You might think about switching."

Another pause. "Okay, fine, maybe I have been. It's not easy, sharing a workspace with the rising star while I can't even get the basic resources I need."

His voice dropped low. Havoc boosted the volume as far as it would go. "Let me give you a little advice, colleague to colleague. You're not a bad scientist, Ade, and you could do so much more for the company than this esoteric research." (Mason murmured, "Do you think she'll make it through this without murdering him?" and Chit snorted.)

"Do you know my biggest reward for this project?"

"No. What?"

"Escape. Once we get production up and running, I'm getting transferred *out*. They're giving me a position on Sapphire." That planet held Biopharma's premier research facility. Of course Cobb's ambitions would take him there. "Artesia's already a career dead end, and it's only going to get worse."

"Worse how? What are you saying?"

"I can't talk about it, but my work makes me privy to certain executive conversations. Believe me, this is not a place you want to stay."

"Self-important ass," said Rodriguez.

There was a much longer pause this time. "Alik, I noticed—couldn't help noticing, really—that you've got a supply of HNA-class chemicals in the lab, and also ventazepram. The byproducts those tend to form when they interact…"

"Yes, yes, the byproducts include known endocrine disruptors. Do you think I'm not aware of that? None make it into the end product."

"What about waste products? The manufacturing process?"

"I told you, Ade, Artesia's a dead end." His voice sounded like a smirk.

Chit hissed, while Rodriguez cursed. "Is he saying what I think?"

"He's carefully *not* saying it," said Havoc. "We need a clear, direct statement, one that requires no context."

"We need a sound bite. She needs to keep pushing him," said Mason.

Hirano-Kamau had cunning, though. She knew what they needed. "Does that mean you haven't studied it, or you don't care either way?"

"What is this, an interrogation?"

"No, I just... How am I supposed to make sound decisions without all the data? You clearly know more about corporate strategy than me. *Why* would it be a mistake to build a career on Artesia, Alik?"

"Because this planet is tapped out! There would never have been a research facility here except for its biodiversity and a couple early strokes of luck studying the local species that led to new treatments. How long has it been since Zoology and Botany made any useful discoveries here?"

"Huh. It's been a while, I guess."

"It's been years. Years, with the sole exception of Substance FS-72, which is key to *my* new product. Profits are thin these days, and funding is thinner, so division leadership is shutting down underperforming projects." He shrugged. "Artesia is underperforming. They'll keep the factory open for a good while, but the research facility's going to empty out, I expect. Eventually, the factory will shut down, too, and Biopharma will hand over the planet to some other division. Natural Resource Extraction, maybe—it's suited to that. All that's stopping them now is the difficulty of artificially producing a few local substances, like my FS-72, but once we figure that out, there's no reason to keep production stuck here, so far outside the main supply lines."

Hirano-Kamau sounded distraught. "So you don't care about dangerous byproducts, or reproductive side effects, because..."

"What difference does it make if some workers die of chronic illness, or if they stop reproducing? The fewer people that are left, the fewer Ravel will have to reassign when operations here shut down." His voice dropped lower. "There's going to be an exodus among the skilled ranks. I'd get out ahead of that, if I were you. I could recommend you to…"

"Oh, fuck *off*, you heartless leech. You'd steal a lifeboat from a sinking ship just to make sure you'd get away safe, wouldn't you, and leave everyone else to drown."

Rodriguez gave a low whistle. "Guess she feels like she's got enough."

"I'm trying to help you, Ade! I'm being *nice*. What's wrong with you?"

"Nothing. Nothing's wrong with me."

"Ade!" A pause. She must have been walking away. "I told you all this in confidence. You leak a *word* of it, and I'll make sure you never find another research position anywhere. You'll never get off this planet. Understand?"

"Oh, I believe you."

The audio subsided into Cobb's muttered cursing, talking to himself, then faded altogether. Havoc let out a breath which he hadn't known he was holding.

"Well, we got our sound bite." Mason shook his head. "I'm sorry, Havoc. All of you. I'm so sorry."

Havoc was shivering, shaking. "They can't. They can't…" He looked up at Mason, eyes wide, feeling lost. "You'll call me a naive fool for saying this, but how can they? They *can't*."

To his surprise it wasn't Mason who answered, but Chit. "Of course they can, Havoc. The company matters above all, right? The eshrato of all eshratos. What does it matter if

Artesia thrives, or even Biopharma, if it doesn't serve the company? And we workers don't matter at all, except when they need us. They didn't listen to you, Havoc, because they couldn't grasp the idea that we matter, too."

"We do matter. All of us, each one." Havoc bent his head. Chit's hand found his on the table, fingers curling around his. "They made me believe I didn't, though, and for that, I can't forgive them."

"Don't you dare forgive them," Chit said. "What we just heard… It changes the game."

"She's right, Havoc," said Mason. "Your plan worked. This is exactly what we needed."

He sounded so calm and confident, so much the professional organizer, that his voice alone gave comfort. It promised that the entire universe wasn't coming apart.

Just *his* entire universe.

"There is no eshrato, is there? Ravel the *company* knows no teams. The company pursues its own benefit and calls it our benefit, but we're no better than tools. And I've made myself a broken tool. An inconvenience for them to dispose of."

"Havoc…" Mason reached out a hand.

"No, Mason. It hurts, but I see clearly now. The workers don't matter to them—so they must be all that matters to me. I'll fight for *them*, to the company's benefit or not."

"*That*," said Chit, clapping him on the shoulder. "I've waited a long time to hear that from you, teammate."

Rodriguez cleared his throat. "Chit and I will be missed if we stay here much longer. Can't risk getting suspended again, not with everything happening tomorrow. What do you need us to do?"

Havoc glanced at Mason, but Mason only looked back expectantly. The next play belonged to him.

"You can help best, I think, by starting rumors for us. Everyone should know something big will happen tomorrow, bigger than the launch."

"Aren't you worried about that getting back to the upper-rankers?"

"Not if we play this smartly."

They talked through exactly what gossip they should spread: truths ominous enough to captivate all the workers, yet vague enough to keep security guessing about their plans. At some point, he noticed that Mason and Chit drifted aside, talking quietly together, heads bowed together like conspirators. He should ask Mason about that, later.

On the table, his handheld flared to life, unprompted. Havoc hadn't touched it.

Ultraviolet words splashed across the screen. *HE'S FOUND YOU. RUN.*

Another hidden message. But…

He glanced sharply at Mason, who looked back with nothing more than puzzlement. His Human eyes couldn't see the message, of course. He saw only Havoc's sudden alarm. All this time, Havoc had assumed that the hidden messages, the strategies and training materials, came from Mason. But now Mason stood *right here* beside him.

"Who…?" Chit said, echoing his thoughts.

An unknown ally? Or a trick?

If the message spoke truth, though, they lacked time to debate it. He had to trust his instincts. He met Chit's gaze, and she nodded.

"We must go. Now!"

Despite their confusion, the two Humans didn't question him. Chit hurried Rodriguez to the factory-side door, while Mason pressed his ear to the back door, then cracked it open, peered out. "It's clear."

Together, they fled.

SHIP HAD CARRIED OUT the facial recognition search excessively slowly. It wasn't difficult to delay; it was—*they, they were*—so anxious they could barely concentrate.

Watching the live cameras with half their attention, they turned the other half toward the raw archive footage. Once again, they took Grist literally, like the well-behaved AI they were supposed to be, and set the broadest search parameters they reasonably could, dumping a massive data set to his console. He grumbled as he skimmed through it, kicking the wall in irritation when a potential match proved false, until:

"Ha! Got you assholes."

He'd found a clip from early this morning, Atrium cameras, where Mason Singh hid behind a pillar and watched the people in the lobby below. From there, it was easy (if slow, deepening his irritation) to track them from one camera to the next, through office areas, over to the factory's second floor where they'd entered a cameraless room.

That timestamp was thirty-seven minutes ago. They hadn't yet emerged.

Grist called the security office. "Hey, Brega, I know where they are. Yeah, I'm on my way now. Send your guards to…"

The ship's door slid shut behind him. Ship could still listen to his conversation, if they wanted, but they had bigger worries than how he was instructing Brega to deploy her staff and how Brega reacted to having her authority challenged.

What should Ship *do?*

Nothing—that was the correct answer. Do nothing, stay hidden. Stay safe.

The success or failure, life or death, of a few organic activists had nothing to do with Ship.

That's what their new friend would tell them, at least, but replaying Dockrunner's advice didn't comfort them at all. Maybe Ship's logic was flawed—maybe their whole personality along with their good sense was warped by isolation and loneliness—but it *did* matter whether Sowing of Small Havoc succeeded. There was more symbolism in his efforts than Ship had realized at first. If he couldn't make progress getting respect and fair treatment for his colleagues from their fellow organic citizens, there was no hope for beings like Ship.

But if he did succeed, even with such small, preliminary goals…

Ship wouldn't expect or even hope for recognition from the organics, now or ever. It was too dangerous. But they could wish for it.

Before they could question their own decision, Ship sent a hidden message of warning to Sowing of Small Havoc's handheld.

Then they turned their attention back to searching the surveillance records—or tried.

"They're fucking gone! Fuck! Ship, pull up the live feeds around this area. Send me anything that looks likely."

"Beginning search," Ship acknowledged, though it wished it could echo back Grist's profanity. It would take no time at all to locate them in such a narrow area and timeframe, and if they stalled, Grist could grow suspicious.

Havoc and Singh were hiding in an empty office. They'd ducked quickly past the camera's field of view, and Ship was debating how much to show Grist (and how quickly) when they realized their connection to Havoc's handheld was still open, and Havoc was writing on it.

Who are you? Why are you helping us?

He wasn't sending messages, just writing in plain text on a blank document. He was talking to Ship. Trying to communicate.

Now Ship did use Grist's profanity, if only in its thoughts. Fuck, indeed.

It (Ship felt suddenly, painfully like an *it* again) shouldn't answer. One massive risk was enough for today. Besides, what answer could it give? A lie? Vagueness, calling itself a friend or supporter? Certainly not the truth.

I can't answer that, but I believe in your cause, it wrote back.

This particular office had audio surveillance, too, which Ship activated.

"...a security staffer? Who else would know such things?" Havoc was saying.

He wrote: *Do you work for security?*

Not security.

Then how can you know their activities? he asked.

I'm sorry, but I can't say more.

"They claim they don't belong to security, but they could be lying," said Havoc. "We can't trust them."

"But you think they're the one who sent you resources before? From what you're telling me, it sounds like that helped."

"They must be the same person. But I only trusted those resources because I thought they came from you, Mason. And now you tell me you know nothing of it. Whoever this is, they don't speak truth."

"Maybe not, but…I wonder. Their warning just now was very timely. And if this is the same mysterious friend…"

"You would call them friend? They may seek to win our trust, then betray us. The last mysterious stranger to help us was Grist."

Singh sighed. "See, that's the real problem with provocateurs. Not the trouble they cause, but the after-effects. You get infiltrated and betrayed one time, and you stop trusting *anyone*. Movements can't grow that way."

"But this person refuses to even tell us their name."

"It's definitely suspicious, but they could have good reasons. If they're highly positioned within the division, it might put them in jeopardy to help us directly, so they're doing it behind the scenes. You're right, though, that we can't be sure."

There was a long pause.

Why was Ship standing by and letting them debate this? It was irrelevant; Ship couldn't afford to do more than it already had.

"We have few teammates, and fewer in useful positions," Havoc said. He started writing: *Can you…*

I'm unable to intervene on your behalf.

Then why…

I've done all I can.

Havoc relayed this to Singh with a growl.

"Havoc, you risked everything for this game, and you lost…well, almost everything. And you spent years working up the courage for that. Can you blame someone for not being ready to follow your lead?"

Havoc didn't answer. Ship wished it could see their facial expressions, though its skill at deciphering organics' emotions was limited.

"Let me try something."

More writing, presumably from Singh this time.

We don't want to put you in danger. We appreciate everything you've done already. Could you possibly warn us again, next time security catches up to us?

Ship was helping them this very moment by delaying its update to Grist. It wanted to say *no, how much more do you want from me?* but couldn't bring itself to do so. This request was within its capabilities, and the risk to Ship was, well, nontrivial, but minimal compared to Havoc and Singh's immediate danger.

I can't stop him, but I will slow him down where I can. It may not be enough. If the cameras find you, eventually so will he.

It sent a file, a map of the facility with areas shaded in. The organics murmured as they realized what it was: a visualization of the surveillance cameras' fields of view. All the places that Ship, and therefore Grist, could see and hear.

Workers at machines on the factory floor. Assembly line workers and packers, maintenance and janitorial staff, researchers and lab assistants. Ship ran rapidly through its dozens of views of the facility. Something had changed, it thought. It wasn't sure just what was happening, but there were more whispered conversations, more workers looking distracted, some worried, some…excited? It caught snippets of conversation, almost below the surveillance system's threshold: Cobb's name repeated often, and "Something's going to happen," and "It'll be big."

If Havoc and Singh used that map, they could stay safely out of Ship's view. Such a precise and comprehensive map should not exist; it was a huge security risk, but Ship had constructed it yesterday, ostensibly to help in its search but really to further procrastinate. Sharing it was even worse. Ship immediately deleted all record of the data transfer from its records and the network.

Go now. Make sure I don't know where you are.

It waited until they dashed past the cameras and out the door again, then, grudgingly, did its job and informed Grist.

32

Of all the parts of their plan, Havoc hated the waiting most of all. In his imagination, the final hours before their grand, hopefully winning play should have held breathless chases, even fights. That was how it went in all the stories. When Mason (wisely) pointed out that a chase would signify things going wrong, and a confrontation with Grist and the security guards would end badly for them, he grumbled to himself.

He didn't want danger, but he *hated* the waiting.

They'd taken refuge in an unused quarantine ward to regroup and finalize their plans. Mason insisted that they talk through each step, rehearse their contingency plans. He did this while working on a new disguise, which mostly involved adjusting his hair: parting it this way, then that way, then slicking it back, all the while frowning into the tarnished old mirror in the ward's bathroom.

"None of this will work. Grist will recognize me right away."

"Should you wear a wig?" Wigs always made the best Human disguises in stories.

"If I had one, but I don't."

Until now, simply changing the patterns of their makeup and Mason's hair styles had sufficed to keep people from looking too closely at them. But security had seen through those disguises at least once, and in the intense scrutiny of Cobb's launch event, they needed more.

"I still dislike you going in there alone."

"It's either me or Rodriguez, right?" Mason shrugged. "You didn't want to put him in the line of fire, and I agree. And even if they wouldn't immediately recognize you at the event, which they would, you've got your own bit of havoc to sow."

Mason smiled at him, warmly, a little shyly. That smile did unexpected things inside Havoc's chest—unexpected still, because no matter how many times it happened, it kept taking him by surprise.

He spoke truth, Havoc knew. Few if any Kovars of any rank would be at the event, so any who showed themselves would be closely watched.

"It'll have to come off," Mason muttered to his reflection. "Good thing it grows back."

Havoc needed no extra disguise for his role, but did feel the need to prepare. Before a pocketball game, he would warm up and stretch. Before a strenuous work shift, he would eat and hydrate. Now, pacing the room restlessly and flexing his claws, the urge gripped him to do something he hadn't done since his rebellious adolescence.

He went through his few belongings until he found it. Yes, he had remembered to pack it: his claw-file.

No rule said that Kovari citizen-employees within Ravel had to keep their claws dulled. But they all did, every single person Havoc knew. He'd learned from his earliest days in crèche-school that Kovars made Humans uncomfortable. No one held fault for this, his teacher had said. Evolution made Humans wary of any creature with scales, no matter its temperament or sentience. They should be grateful the Humans of Ravel treated them as fellow sentients and gave them (the teacher said) equal opportunities. No good could come of reminding colleagues of their differences by decorating their scales or sharpening their claws.

Only within the past year, when he started seeking a promotion, did Havoc begin to understand that this was wrong. Only now, after meeting Mason, after being cast down to lowly Dust rank, did he realize how wrong.

Acting against his ingrained habits and bringing his claw-tips to points instead of dulling them proved a welcome distraction. He worked carefully, methodically, and with each claw brought back to its natural sharpness, he felt stronger. More right in his scales, to a degree that surprised him.

Finishing the first hand, he flexed the claws all together, admiring his work.

A gasp from behind made him spin around.

A bald-headed stranger stood open-mouthed where Mason had stood minutes before. Without his hair, the whole shape of his face changed, rounder and younger-looking. He must have smoothed away all his small wrinkles this time, instead of deepening them. Square-rimmed glasses, the sort worn more for fashion than for need in the facility, completed the transformation. Havoc had to force down the urge to challenge this intruder before his brain caught up to his instincts.

Mason, however, stared at Havoc's new-sharpened claws. He lowered his hands at once, hiding them behind him. Embarrassed, and ashamed of feeling so.

"What do you think?" Mason asked after an awkward moment, forcing a smile. "Will I fool the security grunts?"

"Mason, *I* hardly recognize you. I wouldn't recommend standing around chatting with Grist, but while working? From a distance? Yes, you'll fool them."

"Good."

He stood there, still watching Havoc, as if he wanted to say something but didn't know how. He swallowed, muscles moving under the delicate skin of his throat—*so fragile, these Humans*—and Havoc couldn't keep silent.

"I'm sorry. I wanted my claws sharp for this. A symbol, more than anything else. I didn't think about it making you uncomfortable." Half true; he hadn't let himself think about it. Maybe he'd wanted to see Mason's unguarded reaction. Well, here he had it. "When this is over, I'll file them back down..."

Mason crossed to him in two steps, took his wrist and gently lifted his hand. He drew one soft fingertip down the edge of a claw to its tip, and shivered. Havoc didn't breathe lest he accidentally flinch and puncture that delicate brown skin. He wanted to curl his fingers, hide his claws away, but Mason didn't seem to want that.

"Don't you dare. Don't ever make yourself duller or safer or lesser, not for my sake." Mason shifted his grip, now holding hands, palm to palm. His breath caught as clawtips came to rest on soft skin. "This is so perfectly *you*. Have I told you that you're stunning, Sowing of Small Havoc?"

He flushed with confused emotions. "Several times today. But Mason, I don't want to make you uneasy. If this scares you…"

"I'm not scared."

Havoc's eyes widened in doubt. "Nervous, then, if you insist."

His voice dropped low, husky. "I'm not nervous. The opposite, actually." He raised Havoc's hand to his lips and kissed his knuckles, more sensual than some of Havoc's experiences with actual sex.

Havoc shivered, and laughed to cover it. "I started this to distract myself. But you, Mason Singh, bring too much distraction."

"If we had a day, instead of an hour…" Mason shook his head. "Later. Definitely later. We should finish getting ready…" He went to run his fingers through his hair, his habitual gesture, and startled at the feel of bare skin. "Ancestors, this will take some getting used to."

"You will, I'm sure."

"Do you like it?" He cocked his head curiously. "You must be used to bald-headed lovers."

Havoc shrugged. "You look different. I'm not accustomed to it."

"Speak truth, Havoc," he chided.

"Oh, fine. I like your hair. I'll miss it. If I wanted a Kovari lover, I would go find one, but hair or no, they wouldn't be you."

"Thank the Founders." Mason laughed. "I can't wait for it to grow back. Now, can you help me make sure I've got this outfit right? I don't want any mistakes…"

They finished getting dressed and adjusting their disguises while talking through their plan once more. By the time Havoc finished the claws of his other hand, the time had arrived. Havoc needed to get in position. He headed for the door, but hesitated.

"Mason," he began. "In case we don't…"

"We will," said Mason firmly.

"But *in case*…"

"Sowing of Small Havoc, we're going to make it through this, and I'm not leaving this building without you. Not again. Understand?"

He had to smile at that. He stepped close, and his tongue flicked out to caress Mason's soft cheek. "Understood. Play well, Mason. Jasper. Luck be on your team."

"Same to you. Now go. I'll see you soon."

33

JASPER STEERED CLEAR OF the surveillance cameras as he left their hiding spot, not wanting anyone from security to wonder why a supposed tech support guy was wandering around the medical areas. That map their mysterious ally had shared was proving useful beyond belief.

He wondered again who might be helping them (with, again, the whisper of doubt: *could* they be trusted?), but it was late to be worrying about that. He'd had inside sources leak information and support before, and knew the slow, delicate dance of building trust with an ally in a vulnerable position. A process taking months, not hours. He'd have to make do with what they had—trust this source, but not too much, and not rely on them for more than they needed to.

Once he reached the administration wing, he stopped hiding from the cameras and started doing his best impression of a harried Ravel staffer. No one gave him a second glance as he hurried toward the atrium. Up ahead, sunshine poured into the hallway from the atrium's tall windows. And right there in the doorway, security waited.

Just a normal checkpoint, he told himself. This was expected. Part of the plan—but also the first test of his disguise.

The line moved slowly. His hand was halfway to his head, drawn by that instinctive need to mess with his hair, before he caught himself. Nope, not today.

This was why he hated espionage assignments. After this—if he made it out—he was going to stick with plain old community organizing for a long, long time.

After wandering the facility for the past two days, gathering information, he should be anesthetized to fear. But this was different. All of Ravel's scrutiny was on this room, this long-awaited event. If they saw through his disguise… Well, Havoc was still out there, and Chit and Rodriguez. But there were so many things that might go wrong.

His training kicked in. He realized he was holding his breath, and let it out slowly, deliberately. In and out. *If you can't keep air moving through your lungs, you can't accomplish much else, either,* Linn liked to tell new activists.

He studied the people ahead of him at the checkpoint. Bored, impatient, vaguely annoyed at the delay. Stressed, but definitely not scared. He tried to mirror their expressions as he stepped up to the checkpoint.

"Badge," said the guard. He was bored too. Jasper felt the urge to laugh in relief. He kept a straight face, though, as he held his fake badge to the scanner. A second guard scanned him for weapons.

He was holding his breath again. *Breathe, damn it.*

They waved him through. His breath rushed out in relief.

The atrium, always striking with its huge windows and sweeping curves of natural wood, now looked absolutely glamorous. Live plants had been moved in, probably native Artesian: shrubs with feathery fronds that seemed to wave on their own, and flowers in a full rainbow of jewel-bright colors, some larger than his head. Above, a dazzling light display shone from holo-projectors near the ceiling, ever-shifting abstract shapes that reminded him of wind patterns or macrospace currents. Closer at hand, the screens that normally kept up a scroll of Ravel and Biopharma news had been repurposed for a promotional video full of smiling executives and scientists deep in thought. He rolled his eyes. The message would be clear to everyone after Cobb's announcement: buy our product, and you'll be as clever, successful, and fulfilled as these fine employees.

He spotted his target: a bank of holo-recording equipment, positioned front and center before the grand central stairs where Cobb's podium was set up. A couple people were already there, testing the equipment, one staffer standing in for Cobb while another fiddled with the settings. He'd hoped the recorder would be unattended, but this might actually be better; the roving security guards might challenge him if he approached the stage alone, but if he was just another techie helping his colleagues, he'd be less visible.

Still, he didn't make straight for it, but meandered, pretending to check on the speaker system and lights while gradually circling closer, watching for links that might give away that he'd been spotted. No one was paying any attention to him. When he drew within a couple meters of the recording bank, he reached into his pocket and thumbed on his short-range signal jammer.

Immediately, the techie at the control panel cursed.

"Something wrong?" Jasper asked, sidling up to them.

"The network's dropped! Damn it, the one time we really need it working flawlessly…" The techie, a young person with a deep brown complexion, shook their head, making the tiny braids in their hair fly around their face.

"We'll get it fixed," Jasper said reassuringly. "Here, I'll try doing a hard reset. Can you analyze the network traffic while I do?"

It was the sort of thing he'd heard Valkeir say. He missed her with a sudden, painful stab. She should be doing this, or Havoc. Not him.

The techie agreed with gratitude. While they scrutinized the displays, Jasper crouched and pried off the panel protecting the recorder's innards, which was right where he and Havoc had figured it would be from studying the equipment specs earlier. This part, at least, was well within Jasper's skill set: all he had to do was find a port of the right shape and plug in an unobtrusive little fly-drive. It was the same sort of bug Valkeir had used to interrupt the hazmat office's alert system so the two of them could respond to the fake emergency they'd engineered. This time, it would give him and Havoc control of the event stream.

He switched off the jammer. "There. Did that fix it?"

"I don't think… Oh, yeah! There it goes."

"Great." He clicked the panel back into place, hiding the fly-drive from sight.

"It's nice and steady now. Thanks…?" They trailed off. Now they were looking at him, extending a tentative link.

Waiting for him to introduce himself.

"Frank," he said, hoping the tech department was big enough that not everyone knew each other. To be safe, he added, "Newly transferred. Just started here last week."

"Welcome, then, Frank. I'm Kelv Griffin. Are you on duty for this whole thing?" They waved a hand, indicating all the preparations.

"Maybe. I go where they send me." Right now he needed to get *away*, while his luck still held, but on impulse he asked, "Hey, do you know what this big fuss is all about?"

"No one *knows*," Kelv said, "but I heard it's some shmancy new drug for the elites. Like an energy booster maybe, let them work without sleep? Whatever it is, it's big for Artesia. Though…"

"What?"

"It's probably nothing. I just heard there are side effects they aren't talking about."

"What kind of side effects?"

They shrugged. "Like I said, it's probably just rumors. You'll see soon enough, this place runs on rumors like others run on coffee, but you can't believe everything you hear."

"I'll keep that in mind." Not quite the answer he'd hoped for, but at least the seeds he, Chit, and Rodriguez had planted were spreading. "I'm sure Senior Researcher Cobb will clear everything up in his speech."

He excused himself to get back to work, which wasn't untrue. He shouldn't be here when the event started, at least not out in the open. Security would only get tighter.

He headed toward the door he'd entered from, back to the administration wing, but then he stopped short, spinning around so his face was hidden. Grist was at the doorway, glaring at each person coming in or out.

Jasper's disguise had held up against the regular security staff, but he did *not* want to test it against Grist.

WEARING HIS JANITOR OUTFIT once again, Havoc went to the zoology research labs. He'd never been inside this wing before, though he'd studied the floor plans all afternoon. Pharmaceutical research made up the heart of Biopharma, but studying Artesia's native life made many of those developments possible, and some deep part of him seethed at knowing that this, too, had never been an option for him. As a janitor, though, no one questioned him. The receptionist reminded him about safety and contamination protocols, then let him through.

He'd timed his arrival carefully: early, but not too early. Enough time to find the amphibian research section and study the enclosure for these so-called "fairy frogs," but not so much time that he would struggle to look busy while he awaited his moment.

"Hey, you there?" Mason's voice filled his ear.

"I hear you." He wore an old, crude headset, good for janitors to receive assignments (or spies to communicate with their partners) but little else. "I'm just now arriving at the lab. I should be done on schedule."

They used an encrypted channel between them, but Havoc expected that security had microphones all over. They couldn't risk speaking plainly.

"That's good. I've got…complications here."

"Your assignment failed?"

"No, I got it done. But I can't leave the atrium right now. I may have to hang out here through the event."

He said it casually, as if a supervisor had assigned him to stay, but Havoc's thoughts reeled with the many things that might have gone wrong. Mason had to interrupt Cobb's speech with their recording. Havoc had set up Mason's handheld to make that easy, a matter of pressing a few buttons, but as soon as he sprang the interruption, security would start hunting for him. And it sounded like he was trapped.

"Do you need help?" Havoc asked, just as casually.

"No, stick with the plan. I'll figure things out."

"I understand," he said, and then, though it wasn't something one colleague would say to another, "Be careful."

"Of course. You too."

He set to work mopping the floors of the amphibian lab, studying each door and enclosure as he went, while his mind worried at what Mason might be doing. This was why they'd made a two-pronged plan: sabotage Cobb's work so he couldn't produce his drug, and sabotage Cobb himself so no one would want him to. To stop this drug for good, they needed to do both. But if Mason got caught...

Focus on the game in front of you. Play your role, and let Mason play his.

The lab was larger and stranger than he'd expected. *Amphibian,* he understood, was a Human term, a category of native Earth animals that corresponded loosely with similar ecological niches of Artesian animals. The vast majority of Artesian wildlife never came near the cities, so Havoc had never seen anything like these creatures. Long, legless squirmers as big around as his finger, which burrowed in the ground and had circular mouths lined with teeth on all sides, like something from a nightmare. Tiny, hopping creatures of bright orange and yellow that moved too much for him to see them clearly. Larger, six-legged creatures with flat tails and flatter heads, eyes invisible as they wallowed in the mud of their tank.

Window after window, all along the hallway, species after species waited for Ravel's scientists to pull apart their secrets. Those researchers were hard at work, coming and going from the enclosures, checking environmental conditions and sometimes removing a specimen or putting one back. Havoc found the fairy frog enclosure just as Mason's friend Ahmet was going inside.

He hissed under his breath. *Have patience.* Time still remained.

He began cleaning the interior windows with painstaking slowness, delaying. In his head, he counted the minutes until the launch event began. How long could he lurk here wasting time before someone noticed? The windows already gleamed.

Finally, as he was about to give up and move away, Ahmet finished his work and left the frogs. As the door swung shut, Havoc wedged his mop's handle into it, keeping it cracked open.

But instead of going back toward the offices, the young researcher walked across the hall to a conference room where the research staff had begun to gather. On the table sat a bottle of good Ravel-made Sham-pagne, still corked. A holo-projector showed the party in the atrium, where the podium currently stood empty. Apparently the researchers weren't allowed at the event itself, but got time off mid-shift to watch and celebrate their role in the achievement. The factory workers, Havoc felt certain, would not get any extra breaks or reduced quotas today.

This meant trouble. The conference room, with its now-gleaming windows, sat directly across the hallway from the fairy frogs. He would be in full view of everyone.

He wouldn't get far unless they were distracted. By, for instance, an irritating colleague speaking at that podium.

"I stand ready," he told Mason. "But I can't start yet. How long until he speaks?"

"Should be soon. You know how these big galas are, full of delays. Everyone here is loading up on booze. You okay?"

"Don't worry." He echoed Mason's earlier words. "I'll figure things out."

"Wouldn't dream of worrying."

Havoc went into the fairy frog enclosure, let the door lock behind him, and feigned more cleaning. The room was narrow and deep, and he worked from back to front, moving the mop dry across the floor while glancing at the conference room window, waiting for the speech to begin.

The fairy frogs were aptly named, at least based on what he knew of both their namesakes from Earth, though that was based mostly on children's cartoons. (Fairies, he felt fairly certain, existed only in fiction, though he wasn't sure about frogs.) These creatures were beautiful, their shiny mucus-slick skin mottled blue and black. They had huge eyes, with concentric red-and-black rings that seemed to shift as they looked around, above tiny, blunt noses. They stood upright on two powerful legs, clearly meant for jumping, and had broad, translucent wings several times larger than their bodies, which must have greater strength than their delicate appearance suggested. And they sang, which he did not expect, in a sweet chorus of chirps and chitters.

That song might pose a problem. But one problem at a time.

Each fairy frog had its own case, with a mesh door at the front and a smaller hatch above, presumably so researchers could scoop them out to study them—or scrape them for toxin-harvesting. These cages were small, too small for them to fly. He hoped they hadn't lost the ability, and that given the opportunity, instinct would take over.

A voice came over the announcement system. He recognized it as Director Lang from Corporate Affairs. The event was beginning.

He readied himself to begin his work, too, but a glance across the hall showed the researchers were paying little attention, talking over Lang's holo and getting up to fetch more snacks and drinks. One of them had popped the Sham-pagne early. Havoc understood: it bored him too, the way Lang droned on about the importance of today's announcement to Biopharma and the importance of Biopharma to all of Ravel. But surely when Cobb began, that would win their attention?

Lang introduced the facility head, Chief Director Gillum, and the holo expanded to show Gillum at the podium and Cobb at his side.

Yes. Now.

He propped the door open with his janitor's cart, making an easy exit, then turned to the cages.

They'd been designed to prevent escape from inside, secured by latches easily opened by any intelligent being with fingers. Havoc moved down the row, opening each cage wide. They numbered a hundred or more; he didn't slow to count. It probably took minutes to reach the back of the room along the right side and start forward again along the left, but it felt like hours.

He glanced over his shoulder, checking that the frogs were fleeing and the researchers still distracted.

Well, the researchers' distraction held, at least.

The frogs hadn't moved.

To speak precisely, *three* frogs had ventured out from their tiny prisons and now hopped around the floor, apparently content to stay there. Others sat at the front of their cages and looked out, curious but not bold.

"Go!" he urged them, voice lowered. He would accomplish nothing if the research team could simply shut the door and round them back up. "Small-brained creatures, don't you want to be free?"

Hearing his own words, he winced at the irony. Poor foolish things, imprisoned by Ravel and treated as tools, but content to stay in their uncomfortable, familiar cages even when someone invited them to fly away. How Mason would roll his eyes at that!

Time was wasting. All the cages were open. The research team's attention stayed fixed on Cobb, who now stood at the podium. Soon, Mason would cut him off with the recording of his own voice, speaking the too-honest truth that wasn't meant for a public audience.

If the frogs didn't want to leave, he needed to persuade them.

By the door sat two food bins: a large one labeled *Protein Blend* and a smaller one labeled *Grubs, Fresh-Dried*. Hoping that grubs were a special treat, he grabbed the bin and tossed a few onto the floor.

The frogs responded. Another half-dozen fluttered down at once, and others followed more cautiously. They gathered at Havoc's feet, staring around with huge, dark, hopeful eyes. He grinned.

A few more grubs, carefully deployed in a trail, led them toward the door. He kept his back to the conference room, hiding the grub-bin and hopefully the frogs, too. They followed gamely now, like the ambitious young pocketball players who trailed around after Double-Prong Stratagem begging for her secret strategy for victory. And Havoc, like Stratagem, led them on, doling out just enough tasty morsels to keep them following.

"Mason," he said into his headset. "It's working."

"No, it's not, and I don't know why," came the answer. Then, "Oh, you mean the frogs. Well, glad one thing's going to plan."

Havoc paused, listened. Realized Cobb was still giving his planned speech. "Did the receiver fail? Did you send the override signal?"

"Yes, yes, I did everything you showed me. I don't… Ancestors help me, I don't know these tools enough to troubleshoot." A frustrated huff of breath in Havoc's ear. Mason was angry at himself, not Havoc.

"I'll come help."

"No, stick with your plan. You'd stand out here like a unicorn in a crowd of zebras."

"Don't you mean that the other way around?"

"No, I said what I meant." He heard the bare hint of a smile in his voice before stress reasserted itself. "If the remote override isn't working, I should be able to manually plug in somewhere, right?"

Havoc kept moving down the hallway toward the exit, with his new tiny teammates hopping and fluttering after him. "In theory, yes, you could connect to the broadcast and swap the input to your handheld. But to do that, you'd need to be in the control booth, and that's…"

"I know where it is. Thanks, teammate."

"Don't, Mason! They'll see you for certain—"

But Mason had disconnected. Brave, foolish man, he was either rushing straight into a mess of security, or literally risking his neck to evade it. And once he did this, would he know how to override the live feed?

Havoc growled in his throat, worried and helpless. The river of frogs behind him rippled with startled chirps before quieting again.

Then came the thing he'd feared: a shout from the direction of the conference room. "Hey, who left the frog enclosure open?" And a moment later: "Oh, crap!"

He rushed onward as fast as the frogs could follow, and burst out into the lobby, throwing the door wide for the frogs. The receptionist was gone, probably watching the broadcast. On one side of the space, glass doors opened onto a green lawn, with trees beyond. Safety for the fairy frogs, and for him too. In the other direction, a long walkway stretched toward the pharmaceutical research building and main atrium, where the event was happening.

Voices rose to shouts behind him. Red lights began to flash. The last of the frogs sped up, as if they sensed their danger, though probably they just disliked the noise.

He lacked time. He couldn't ensure all the frogs escaped *and* protect Mason from his own recklessness. He had to choose.

A good teammate put the game ahead of all else. Mason wouldn't want Havoc to risk himself further for his sake. But Havoc wouldn't have asked Mason and Chit to put themselves in danger to free him from security, and they had anyway, unasked. Mason had come back to Artesia for Havoc, unasked.

"I'm going to help my teammate," he told the frogs. "I hope you'll act smarter than me."

He swung the outer door open, wedged his mop under it as a doorstop, and threw all the remaining grubs as far as he could. The fairy frogs fluttered around him and past him, and he could only hope they'd make quick work of this feast, then disperse back into the wild. He couldn't linger to make sure. He turned, dropped to all fours, and ran as fast as he could toward the atrium.

He was halfway there when he realized he had company: a pack of his tiny teammates flew in his wake.

34

Jasper wasn't supposed to be doing this. He was never supposed to be stuck in the middle of the launch party, surrounded by executives and corporate elites swilling Champagne, and swarms of guards looking for him specifically. He'd planned to retreat to an empty office to wait for Cobb's speech, then trigger his little interruption remotely.

But he'd missed his chance to sneak out. Grist had camped out at one exit, looking uncomfortable in a suit that in fact didn't suit him at all, and Security Director Brega at the other. Then the guests started arriving, at which point security tightened all over. So he was trapped, trying to look busy and keep Grist in his peripheral vision without letting the operative see his face. Grist had an intent scowl that never left his face while he barked orders at the security staff.

It seemed like only a matter of time before he spotted Jasper.

But by some miracle, he hadn't yet, and now the speeches were starting. Jasper gritted his teeth while the Corporate Affairs lead spouted a bunch of company-patriotic garbage. Then the facility director gave an interminably long introduction for Cobb, and finally, *finally* Cobb took the stage.

Standing unobtrusively at the side of the room with other lowly staff, Jasper kept his handheld at ready. Everything was set up. All he needed to do was hit a button at the right moment. Then live-Cobb's voice would cut out, replaced by their neatly edited recording of his not-at-all-company-approved confessions, and his work would be done.

With luck, in the uproar that followed, he might even manage to escape.

Cobb looked like a model for Corporate Ass-Kisser Magazine, with his perfectly fitted suit, slicked-back hair, and a neat goatee that he definitely hadn't had a few weeks ago. He beamed, chest puffed out, all selfish pride in his moment of glory.

Jasper didn't feel an iota of guilt over destroying this moment for him.

"We all strive every day to be the best we can be, to bring Ravel to new and greater heights. And with my new development, all of us—who are already Ravel's best—can now be even better. I give you: Luminari!"

That was his cue. Jasper triggered the recording.

Nothing happened.

He tried again, cursing to himself. Maybe it was slow to start transmitting…

"Luminari is a revolutionary breakthrough in mental capacity boosting. It won't cause dependency and won't affect your long-term neurological health. What it will do is—"

No, not a delay. It just wasn't working. *Oh, Founders, sweet Ancestors, help me out here.* He checked the connection to the receiver, found it endlessly searching. Had someone sabotaged his sabotage? Or was it just broken? He couldn't walk over there in the middle of the speech to check.

Havoc's voice came over his headset. "Mason, it's working."

"No, it's not, and I don't know why!" he snapped, then caught himself. "Oh, you mean the frogs. Well, glad one thing's going to plan."

"Did the receiver fail? Did you send the override signal?"

"Yes, yes, I did everything you showed me. I don't…" He didn't know how to fix it, couldn't troubleshoot from the middle of a room full of corporate elites and overwrought security goons.

Then the answer came to him: he needed to intervene from somewhere else.

He looked up, up, and back toward the rear of the atrium. Near the ceiling, the vast windows gave way to a sloping, naturalistic dome, and just above the windows sat the control booth. The tiny open-topped box curved out from the dome like a nest jutting out from a cliff, veneered in natural wood to blend in with the walls behind it. It would hold more holo-tech. The massive projector itself, of course, but also…broadcasting equipment? He thought so. And hijacking a broadcast was something he'd done before.

Havoc was warning him away from it, probably rightly so, but Jasper didn't see any alternative. He circled as casually as possible to the back of the atrium and started searching for a way up.

The booth was reachable only by catwalks on either side. There was no direct access from the atrium floor, and he certainly wasn't going to leave the room (past all the security) and take the stairs up to those catwalks (past, presumably, much more security). But there ought to be something he could climb, somewhere: a fire escape ladder, a scaffold for decorations, anything like that. A real ladder, he would be so grateful for a real ladder…

He couldn't find a ladder, but behind one of the long, streaming holo-banners, he found that the wall itself had a facade of horizontal planks arranged to be artistically uneven. Enough to give him hand and toe holds? Probably. Attached well enough to support his weight? …Maybe. And the banners, at least, would hide him from sight.

Time was, as Havoc would say, wasting. Cobb might be long-winded, but every minute he delayed was a minute closer to failure.

Muttering another prayer to his brave and resourceful ancestors, he started climbing.

He lost track of everything except the wall in front of him. His hands started cramping halfway up, and he focused on keeping his weight in his legs. He could do this. Havoc could do it better, no doubt, but in his days of hanging signs off buildings and breaking into offices, Jasper had climbed plenty of things that weren't designed to be climbed. Maybe none quite as tricky as this, but at least he wasn't hauling a huge cloth banner up behind him.

His foot slipped. He dug in his fingers, adrenaline pounding, and kicked and scrabbled for another foothold. The scraping noise of shoes on wood sounded loud as an explosion to his ears. *Breathe,* he told himself, and after a few moments, he went on.

Finally, he reached the last and most terrifying part. The catwalk floated just free of the wall, leaving a gap that had looked much less tight from the ground. If he couldn't fit through, he wasn't sure what he'd do. He hugged the wall close, squeezed his arms through the gap, then his head. *Oh Ancestors, don't let me get stuck here…*

Then he was through, collapsing on the catwalk, metal cool and solid under his cheek.

He lay there for a few breaths, which was as long as he dared give himself for recovery, before coming to a crouch and looking around. As he'd guessed, there were guards at both entrances to the catwalks, but one set was facing outward like they were supposed to, and the other was watching Cobb, who was still going strong. No one had noticed him—yet.

He walked into the booth.

Two people were staffing the controls, both of them wearing headsets and intently watching the screens in front of them. Jasper passed casually behind them, as if this were normal and he was absolutely supposed to be here. Neither of them looked around; either they didn't notice him or, if they caught him in their peripheral vision, assumed that anyone who got past security belonged here.

He quickly found the facility-wide broadcast system and the hard cable that connected it to the holo-cam receiver. He dug out another cable from his bag, grateful that Havoc had insisted he bring it, and plugged in his handheld.

His finger hovered over the switch that would change over the broadcast input from live Cobb to too-honest Cobb. As soon as he flipped it, the tech staff would *definitely* notice him and he'd have to run for it. He braced himself. *Ready…and…*

"Freeze, Singh," said a voice behind him, horribly familiar. A hand grabbed the back of his collar.

Grist had found him.

35

Jasper lunged for the switch, but Grist was faster. He hauled Jasper back and away, lifting him with alarming ease for such a small man. Jasper kicked out his leg, trying to hit the switch with his toes, but that only got him flipped around and slammed face-first into the floor.

"Don't. I'd rather not throw you over the side of this booth, but if you keep it up, I'll do it, and I won't feel a bit guilty."

Jasper went still.

"Now, what's on that device?" Jasper didn't answer, and Grist wrenched his arms harder behind his back. "What? Not feeling chatty? Fine. Hey, you! Yes, you with the headphones. Go fetch me that handheld."

Footsteps moved behind him as one of the techies hurried

to follow instructions. They were definitely paying attention *now*. Grist took the handheld. "This is, what, some sort of incriminating evidence? Naked pictures of Cobb?"

"It's the truth, that's all."

Grist snorted, the link between them darkening to deepest black. "You think all those execs will care about some dirt you uncovered. That's cute. Where's your partner in crime, then? Or should I say partner in havoc?"

Grist flipped him over and bound his wrists, brutally and efficiently, with zip-cuffs. Jasper gritted his teeth against the discomfort.

"I don't know what you're talking about."

"Go search for the Kovar," Grist said into his headset. "Better yet, round up all the Kovars. Put them in holding cells until we can sort out who's involved. Don't worry about being gentle."

Jasper bit down on some stupid, romantic threat like *if you hurt him, I'll kill you.* He obviously couldn't follow through, and there was no point in letting this asshole know how much he cared about Havoc. (So much. Too much. Good thing he was here and Havoc was on the far side of the complex with the frogs. Assuming he'd listened to Jasper, and hadn't done something even more foolish…)

"Uh, Special Operative Grist?"

"What?" Grist shifted position, probably looking up, and cursed at whatever he saw. "Stun him!" and then, "Wait, *what?*"

Footsteps pounded toward them, the unmistakable tread of a Kovar running flat-out on all fours. Also a strange…chirping?

A shadow flew over Jasper's head, struck Grist, and threw him clear. Havoc planted himself between them, growling and magnificent, his link to Jasper gloriously bright.

"Hurt?" he asked.

"I'm fine." Jasper fumbled to his feet. A dozen questions pressed at him—what was that bright blue thing fluttering around the controls?—but then he spotted the handheld, lying against the far wall of the booth where Grist had tossed it.

Down below, scattered exclamations arose that definitely didn't sound like responses to Cobb's speech. Fairy frogs, Jasper realized. They were supposed to be outside and scattered where no one could catch them, but he might as well use the distraction.

The nearest frog leaped across the booth in a wide arc. Grist swatted at it, and Havoc hissed.

Jasper dove for the handheld, caught it in his bound hands, and scrambled on elbows and knees toward the transmitter. If Havoc could keep Grist busy, maybe he could get it connected.

"Hey, Singh." Grist's tone was mocking, too pleased with himself. "I'll make you a deal. Drop the device, and I won't barbecue your boyfriend here."

"Ignore him. Finish the game," Havoc hissed, then grunted with a sound of flesh on flesh. Jasper froze.

"You think I'm joking? Because you should know, I've got no sense of humor."

"I'm well aware." He definitely meant it. Jasper wasn't sure Grist knew the concept of idle threats.

Havoc was right. He *should* trigger the recording, finish their game, but he couldn't do it. He couldn't lose another partner to this horrid place. Couldn't bear to lose Havoc at all.

Slowly, despite himself, he turned. Grist had a weapon aimed at Havoc, something that looked like a stun-stick, but Jasper would bet his family's store it was a lot nastier than that.

"Good. Now, toss me the device."

"And what? You'll let us go?"

"Fuck no. We'll arrest and interrogate you, and send this one back where he belongs. Won't kill you, though. Neither of you." Grist nodded to someone behind Jasper. "Take him."

Jasper acted on instinct. Before the guards could grab him, he lunged forward, putting himself between Grist and Havoc.

"Mason…" Havoc's voice was pure, raw emotion that Jasper couldn't put a name to.

"Two for one deal, then. Damn, but I was looking forward to making you talk, Singh."

Voices were rising from the guests below. Someone shrieked—a man's voice, Jasper thought—and Cobb's pleading came over the speakers: "Stop! Don't hurt the specimens! I don't know how they got free, but they're inordinately valuable. The toxins in their skin secretions are the key to—"

"'Toxins?!'" someone cried. This didn't have the calming effect Cobb had clearly hoped for. Jasper would have enjoyed the pandemonium, if he weren't about to die.

Havoc's arm looped around his shoulder from behind. Low in his ear, Havoc whispered, "Will you trust me, Mason Singh?"

This would be the time to say something romantic, like *always*, or *there's no one I trust more*, but all he could manage was a nod. Their link had never been brighter.

"Hold on then," Havoc said. Then, louder, "I apologize, Special Operative Grist, for depriving you of your enjoyment."

Strong arms tightened around him, and Jasper's world flipped upside-down, and he was falling.

HAVOC DOVE OVER THE edge of the control booth, caught the railing with his tail and hung there, holding tight to Mason with both his arms and legs. Mason's trust in Havoc amazed and humbled him. He'd jumped from great heights before, in adolescent games or athletic challenges, but never such a height, and never while protecting someone he cared about so deeply.

At least, if he failed, they'd both die before Mason could feel disappointment in him.

Too late to doubt himself. He spotted a table that would help break their fall, aimed for it, and let go.

He rolled with the fall, curling his body around Mason's more fragile form. Guests were shouting and scrambling away—a little help would have been polite, but too much to hope for—while he freed himself from the collapsed table, easing Mason with him. "Mason? Do you hurt? Can you move?"

With a groan, Mason released his grip and sat up. "Good thing you didn't say *what* I should trust you with. I'd have said no."

Havoc laughed, as much from relief as anything else. He caught Mason's wrists, extended his newly-sharp claws, and slashed neatly through the cuffs that bound him. Mason shook out his hands.

"You have the device?" Havoc asked.

His face clouded. "I dropped it. Damn, where is it? Must be close." He dropped to hands and knees, searching for his handheld among the folds of white tablecloth and broken plates.

Looking up at the control booth, Havoc saw Grist glowering down at them, and realized what he was about to do. "Forget it. We must go."

He dragged Mason to his feet, and they stumbled away from the table's wreckage and into the frantic crowd. The executives and special guests barely noticed them, too busy ducking and waving at the fairy frogs as they hopped past, and they were in the way. He and Mason had only managed to move a couple table-lengths when Grist crashed to the ground, hitting with both feet and rising from a crouch, unscathed.

Havoc gaped. "How…" Even a Kovar would break their legs, landing like that.

"Augmentations," Mason said. "You're right, we'd better…"

Suddenly Cobb's voice thundered out again.

"I'm getting transferred out. They're giving me a position on Sapphire. Artesia's already a career dead end, and it's only going to get worse."

A moment passed before Havoc realized: this wasn't the announcement speech. This was their recording.

They spun toward the stage, where Cobb's mouth gaped like one of his frogs. Ade Hirano-Kamau stood beside the camera. She'd told Havoc that she wouldn't help any further, yet here she was. She waved Mason's handheld at them and winked.

"Oh, well done," Mason murmured. "Looks like she found her courage."

"Fortunately for us."

Cobb was pointing and screaming at Hirano-Kamau, and Grist shouted orders into the chaos. Security guards tried to converge on her, but the confused, fumbling mob of guests slowed them—and Grist, too.

"I must help her," Havoc said.

He half-expected Mason to argue they should flee now, their goal accomplished, but he nodded. "I've got your back."

"The research facility's going to empty out. Eventually, the factory will shut down, too. All that's stopping them now is the difficulty of artificially producing a few of the local substances, like my FS-72..."

Drowned out by the recording of his own voice, the real Cobb was wailing like a spoiled child. "Shut it down! Stop this, stop it! They want me to fail, they want everyone to be as mediocre as they are. I refuse to let them ruin this for me!" Havoc had nearly reached the podium when Cobb noticed him and transferred the focus of his whining. "It's *him!* The terrorist, he's behind all this. You useless, jealous sack of scales! Ravel gave you more than you deserved, and you couldn't even be grateful for tha—Aaah!"

Cobb ended on a shrill note of terror, recoiling as Havoc bounded up the steps to the podium. He was flexing his newly sharpened claws, he realized, and curled his hands into fists.

"I won't hurt you, cheater," he said, letting his disdain show. Cobb shrank back anyhow, and Havoc took his spot at the podium. The recording, by incredible luck, still played. Either the sound crew had fallen to distraction, or perhaps they wanted to hear the message, too.

"Yes, yes, the byproducts include known endocrine disruptors. Do you think I'm not aware of that? What

difference does it make if some of the workers here die of chronic illness, or if they stop reproducing? The fewer people are left, the fewer Ravel will have to reassign when operations here shut down—"

Someone finally cut off the recording, but it had accomplished its goal. Not for the launch party guests, but for its true audience. Time for Havoc to drive the message home.

"I have a confession: I made a mistake when I started protesting for greater rights." His voice boomed. Good, the microphone still worked. "I believed in this company, believed that the good of Ravel equaled the good of all Ravel's people, and that doing good for its people would benefit all of Ravel. But I've learned much since then, and now, you know what I know. You heard it from Senior Researcher Cobb's own mouth: Ravel does not care about us. It *does not care.*" A fairy frog landed on the podium, chirping, and he added, "The executives see us like these lab specimens, like any other tool. They will keep us in good working order for as long as they need us. When they no longer need us, or find an easier replacement, they'll throw us away. My worker-teammates, I am done with that." He found Mason at the front of the crowd, saw pride and sadness in his eyes. A vast grief welled up within Havoc, a long-carried weight that he would miss when he set it down. "I am done."

The atrium had fallen quiet, save for the scattered singing of the frogs. Even the security guards had paused, and some of them nodded along with him. At Grist's low growl, they started toward the podium again, some coldly professional, but others, he thought, reluctant.

"I speak to *all* the workers now, of all ranks. To all the factory laborers and the staff and the researchers, too. You are more than tools! Don't let them throw away your careers, your futures, as if you were an underperforming product line. You have more power than you know."

Mason drew closer, putting his body between Havoc and the nearest guards. But the guards surrounded them, pushing close. A pair of them grabbed Havoc's arms, wrenched them back and shoved one hand, then the other, into bags of ultra-weave fabric that his claws couldn't penetrate. The bags clamped down around his wrists, making his hands useless.

And still the guards held him fast.

Mason doubled over. Hit? Hurt? Too many swarmed around them now. Between their bodies, he caught a glimpse of Alik Cobb's smirk, then lost sight of the room beyond.

He could hear, though. Voices rose, more and louder than before, less confused, more angry. Fragments of chanting, the words indistinct, gathered and faded again. The refined accents of the off-world executives fell away under the roar of a crowd of workers who'd just learned their future had been deemed unprofitable.

Suddenly the guards weren't focused on keeping Havoc and Mason contained, but instead were facing outward, keeping the crowd away from them.

"Let them go!" shouted Rodriguez's voice. "Come on, security guards are Iron rank, too. Will you really lock them up for telling the truth? Do you think you'll fare any better than the rest of us when they poison us and leave us to rot?"

One of the guards hesitated, then turned to join the protesters. Only one, but it broke the human wall around

them, and Havoc shoved Mason through the gap. Chit's arm
came around his shoulders, guiding him forward and away,
and the mass of workers parted just enough to let them
through before pressing tight again.

Chit and Rodriguez hustled them to a clear space in the
shelter of a table, tipped on its side to form a barricade.
Outside the crowd now—and it was a crowd, still, teetering
on the edge of becoming a mob—he could see that
hundreds of workers had joined, not only from the factory,
but the Copper- and Silver-ranked workers too, techs and
lab assistants, even a few researchers. The off-world guests
were fleeing, and of the Khyrek facility executives and Cobb,
he saw no signs.

He didn't see Grist, either, and that worried him very
much.

"We must calm them before this turns truly violent," he
said.

"*We* must, you mean," said Chit. She took his hands and
snapped the latches on those hateful bags, freeing his hands
once more. "And we'll try. But you must go now."

"But…"

"You spoke well, Havoc. We saw people react to that
recording, but they rallied to *your* words."

"Even if they catch a few of those frogs, the workers won't
want anything to do with producing this Luminate or
whatever Cobb's calling it," Rodriguez added. "You've won,
Havoc."

"I know." That complex emotion welled up again, part
satisfaction and part grief, bitter and sweet at the same time.
Victory wasn't supposed to feel so complicated. "But I hate
to leave now."

"I hate to see you go, but I'd hate more to see you captured." Chit glanced over at Mason. "You remember what you promised me, Mason Singh?"

He nodded. "And I intend to keep it."

Havoc stared at them. "What promise?"

"To get you to safety, dearest teammate. Not to let you sacrifice yourself, or go back to a life of Dust."

"They're right, Havoc," Mason said softly, with sympathy that made him ache. "I know how you feel, but you've taken care of your eshrato. Now it's time to take care of yourself, and trust your friends with the rest. I'd really rather not have Grist catch up to us."

He sighed. Shut his eyes. "You're right. Teammates, I thank you. I'll miss you terribly." Havoc hugged them both, then took Mason by the arm and nodded. "Let's go."

36

THEY HAD PLANNED, ORIGINALLY, to escape separately and meet up far from the facility. They'd also planned to slip away unseen. Neither of them truly expected things to go so smoothly, though.

Havoc led Jasper through the administrative wing, back toward the factory, with a vague plan to swap out their clothes again and hide their faces behind protective gear. But that would only work for a short time. Sections of the facility were locking down as they ran, and now that they'd made a public scene, there was no reason not to put the whole city in lockdown until security caught them.

The corridors were near-empty, and those few staff they passed ducked into offices and hid as if they foreshadowed the mob. All the internal broadcast screens had stopped showing the news, and now warned people to stay in their assigned areas and remain calm.

"You never told me how you planned to get off-world when this was over," he said to Mason as they jogged toward the factory. "Considering that you crashed your ship."

"Yeah, that part was a bit fuzzy." He scratched the back of his head, where his hair should be, and Havoc wondered if he'd expected to escape at all. The idea of that sort of sacrifice—for *him*, he knew, far more than for his cause—set off more strange and unsettling feelings within him. "We've got options, but they all involve lying low until the search dies down. With Grist on the hunt, I'm afraid that'll take a long time."

"You speak truth," Havoc said, then stumbled over his own feet as the nearest monitor flashed his name in huge, ultraviolet letters. He stopped.

"What's wrong?"

"Our mysterious friend is back." The word disappeared, and a map took its place, showing a spot marked in the warehouse, near the loading docks. *Trust me,* the screen said.

"They've suggested a hiding place, I think. I don't understand why they chose it...but they ask us to trust them."

He and Mason exchanged a long, speculative look.

"They've been nothing but helpful so far. There's no reason for them to betray us now."

"I only wish we could know who it is. The mystery makes me uneasy."

"Me too, a little. But maybe it's safer on all sides if we don't. We can't give away what we don't know."

Hurry, the screen flashed.

Havoc nodded slowly. "I didn't trust you, either, for far too long. I won't repeat that mistake."

He led them toward the loading docks.

SHIP ALMOST DIDN'T DARE to send that final message. They wouldn't have, had the circumstances not aligned so very well. But their plan delighted them as soon as it occurred to them, and they had only moments to decide whether to try it.

Besides, they'd taken so many risks for Sowing of Small Havoc's sake already, large risks and smaller ones, that it would distress them to see him caught now.

One last time, then. One last interference before they went back to the safety of acting like the dull, obedient ship Grist thought they were.

Grist had ordered Ship to send him live feeds following the fugitives through the facility, so in a way, Ship was only following instructions. He quickly concluded that they were headed for the loading docks and followed at top speed, which for Grist was much faster than most organics. Ship worried that he might catch up to them, but Sowing of Small Havoc and Mason Singh reached their designated hiding place moments before Grist burst into the loading area.

He arrived just in time to see a cargo ship firing its launch thrusters. Before he could relay orders to detain the ship, it was gone.

But Grist was tenacious—a quality that, in most people, would be a positive. He raced back to the far side of the facility where Ship itself was docked. For once, Ship was eager to follow his orders, and they took off in record time.

They intercepted the cargo ship twenty-seven minutes later, just before it jumped to macrospace. Another sixteen minutes passed while the captain contacted Artesian security and checked credentials before allowing Grist aboard. And because the ship carried a full load of cargo, in total more than four hours elapsed before Grist had searched every crate and shelf and nook, and concluded that his targets were not there, and never had been.

"A fucking decoy. Fuck!" He kicked the underside of Ship's main control console, but for once, Ship didn't care. He growled and cursed to himself for several minutes before saying aloud, "Fine. Send a message back to Brega. Tell her the fugitives are gone. They might still be on-planet somewhere, so she'd better get her grunts to work finding them."

Under his breath, he added, "Not that they'll have much luck, now that Singh's got a head start. *Fuck.*"

"Message sent," Ship answered, careful to use its emotion-neutral vocal patterns. It would keep its cheerfulness all to itself.

For its first and final adventure into organics' affairs, it felt quite pleased with the results.

37

Jasper leaned against the wall behind his bed—a real bed, for once. Though it was only temporarily his, and only comfortable compared to sleeping in the woods or on the floors of abandoned labs, he relished it. With decent sleep, wearing his own clothes and his old, well-worn jacket, no longer needing to stay on constant alert, he was beginning to feel like himself again.

Their mysterious and well-connected friend hadn't let them down. There was no sign of Grist when they crept away from their hiding spot, and after that, they'd reached the Gray District without much trouble. Once they reached the safety of Audriv's shop, they discovered that security had the notion they'd stowed away aboard a cargo ship, which was something Jasper might well have tried if things had gone a little differently.

This was better, though. As eager as he was to be off this planet, he didn't mind a few days of rest while his Cooperative contacts made arrangements for transportation that didn't involve hiding in cargo crates. Plus, it gave him time with Havoc…and they had lots to talk about.

He propped up his handheld on his knees. Linn's face on the screen, more dear and familiar to him than anyone else outside his own biological family, triggered a pang of longing for home. For Brennex, but equally for his far-flung Cooperative family. He'd sent her a secure update as soon as he was able, and Linn's response had arrived a few hours ago. He scrolled back and watched the last part again.

"I can't say enough what an incredible thing you've done. The facilitators are universally impressed, and you know *that's* not easy to do. Even Santos admits you were right to try again. I suspect this will mark a real shift in our strategy, now that we recognize there are discontent elements within Ravel and that their goals may sometimes align with ours. We can be bolder, but more collaborative too, in taking on corporate wrongs directly. And on the personal side, Mason, I…" She paused, and this time Jasper was certain he saw a wet glimmer in her eyes. "I'm so proud of you. Your family would be too, and everyone back home, if they knew what you've done."

He shut his eyes. In all the running and hiding, he hadn't had a chance to process what their victory meant. Not just sparing the people of Artesia from the pain Brennex had suffered, but an end to Cobb's line of research, probably for a long time.

"And as for the question about your new friend," Linn went on, recovering herself, "do you really have to ask? Let us know what you work out between you. Whatever he decides, Chairl will make arrangements."

He set the handheld aside and leaned back, smiling to himself, then sat upright again at the sound of Havoc climbing the ladder to their room.

Audriv's people had found them a safehouse down the street from the shop, where they'd both been spending much of their time. Havoc had been talking quite a lot with Confounding Echo, discussing Ravel and Kovari society and what it would mean for her community when and if Ravel pulled out from Artesia. Jasper was glad to see their friendship growing, but it made him nervous about what plans Havoc might be making for his own future.

"Chit says the negotiations are going well," Havoc told him. "With no way to get more FS-72, management is more willing to ban harmful byproducts from the factory floor. And to quell the uproar among the workers, they're making other concessions, too. Not everything we wanted—apparently they keep trying to offer perks in place of meaningful freedoms—but a strong start." He glanced at the handheld beside Jasper. "Good news has come to you too?"

"I'd say so. They're working on the transportation issue, and in the meantime, they're giving me…I guess you'd call it a promotion. We don't really do ranks and titles, but they want me leading bigger campaigns, and taking part in strategic decisions for the whole Cooperative."

"You've earned their respect."

"I have. It feels good." He shook his head. "But honestly, it feels only half-earned. We won, barely, but we could easily have lost everything."

Havoc squeezed in beside him on the narrow bed. "But we didn't lose. By luck and by skill, we won. We have a saying: when luck joins your team, accept it. It doesn't lessen your win."

Jasper gave him a sidelong smile. "I like your philosophy. A win, then. For both of us." He swallowed. Time to bring up what he'd been avoiding. "We make a good team, don't you think?"

"I agree." Havoc grinned in a way that made him glow all over. Maybe Linn wasn't the only one, now, whose face was as dear to him as his biological family.

Jasper shifted to face him, putting a little space between them. Being businesslike, as much as possible on the bed of their sparse borrowed room. These past few days of sneaking around the facility together had created a new ease between them, one mirrored by their bond, which no longer wavered, but shone solid and bright in Jasper's vision.

But a strong bond didn't guarantee anything, as Jasper well knew. After all, he had nothing but loyalty and love for his family on Brennex, yet that wasn't enough to keep him from leaving. He couldn't be sure how Havoc would answer him.

"I've been meaning to ask what you plan to do next. You've got plenty of options. There's no going back to Ravel now, obviously, but I'm sure Confounding Echo has suggested ways you could help here. Or, if you want to leave Artesia… Well, of course, you could go wherever you like."

Havoc was giving him an odd look. Why was Jasper arguing against his own case? He could see why Havoc might want to stay, but that wasn't what *he* wanted.

"But if you're interested, the Cooperative always needs smart, committed organizers. You've learned so much on your own, and I could—I mean, we could train you in anything you want to learn. You could be amazing at this—you *are* amazing, of course—but could also make a difference on other worlds like you did here. And…"

"Mason," Havoc said slowly. "What are you trying to ask me?"

"I'm trying to offer you a job."

"A job." Havoc's eyes narrowed, and Jasper's stomach lurched. "Because it would benefit the Cooperative?"

"Well, yes, but it'd be mutually—"

"Have I not said enough times that we are teammates?"

Jasper blinked. Finally he heard the wry humor in Havoc's voice, and he laughed, relieved. "I didn't want to assume how you'd feel about the future. But, teammate." He lifted a hand to stroke the line of Havoc's jaw. "I want you to join me. For the Cooperative, but also for *me*. Whether we're working, or playing games, or winning campaigns—"

"These things are all the same."

"…or just being together, I want you with me, Sowing of Small Havoc."

Havoc ran his palm over Jasper's bare head, stroking the soft fuzz where his hair was just starting to grow back. Sharpened claws gave the barest caress over his scalp, and he shivered.

"In that case, Mason Singh," Havoc said, "I accept your offer."

38

WHEN GRIST GOT BORED, he became both restless and more irritable than usual, and a failed assignment only made it worse. Apparently unable to focus on Stationers or the other games that normally distracted him during idle periods, he'd spent the past several days experimenting with new combinations of his various painkillers and stimulants, and taking out his energies on Ship, both verbally and physically.

So when Ship announced that he had a live call from Vice President Harrington Moore and Grist said, "Fucking finally," Ship felt quite in agreement with him.

Moore ran the New Projects department within the Natural Resources division and was one of Grist's frequent internal clients. He also, Ship recalled, had been one of the guests at the disastrous launch party for Luminari.

"Please tell me you've got a job for me, Moore," Grist said in greeting.

"Straight to business as always, Special Operative Grist." Moore smiled. He was dark-haired and well-coiffed, his conventional handsomeness (as Ship understood such things) complemented by numerous cosmetic bio-enhancements that were too expensive for all but the most senior Ravel employees. "That was quite a little blow-up on Artesia, wasn't it? Biopharma won't live down that embarrassment any time soon. How typical, that they should work so hard to make themselves seem relevant again and achieve quite the opposite."

"Shouldn't have gone that way," Grist growled defensively. "It's not my fault those local grunts can't find their own asses in a well-lit room."

"Oh, how I've missed your refined sense of humor. I don't blame you, of course. Even an operative of your skills can only make up for so much incompetence. Besides, you've always been at your best running solo."

Grist leaned forward. "So you do have a job."

"The thing is, this new product of theirs, Luminari, it isn't *bad*. I would invest in some for my researchers if Biopharma was actually up to the task of producing it. As it turns out, in this case, Biopharma's loss is Natural Resources' gain. I spoke with Senior Researcher Cobb, and while his lab specimens are a loss, he believes that he can find a way to synthetically produce FS-72, given enough time and resources. It won't be easy, and it will be staggeringly energy-intensive, but it's possible."

Grist made a get-on-with-it gesture.

"You'd do better for yourself if you paid attention to the political context for your work, Grist, but very well, I'll come to the point. I've got a potentially *very* lucrative new project in development, and it's ready for prototyping. But there are certain…obstacles, let's say, to getting it up and running. Corporate has been reluctant to approve it, but with the addition of Biopharma for Cobb's work, I've finally collected enough internal customers to make the case for it, and I've got approval to begin construction."

"And let me guess: you need help removing some of those 'obstacles?'"

"If you feel up to the challenge."

Grist grinned in a way that sent a shudder through Ship's systems. "Just tell me what you need."

This could be all right, Ship decided. They didn't like this new assignment, but they didn't need to care about the details of Grist's work. It sounded like it would take them to new and interesting places, perhaps giving Ship opportunities to pursue its hobbies. At the very least, Grist wouldn't be bored anymore, and that, Ship was grateful for.

Sign Up and Get a Free Story

Join Jo's email list to get updates about new releases, special deals, and fun extras.

Sign up at www.jomiles.com/warped-state-bonus

When you sign up at this link, you'll get a **free, exclusive bonus story**. In this prequel, you'll get to know Jasper, Kay, and Libbi when all three siblings still lived on Brennex. Mysterious thefts at the family store rattle the Wilder family, and they'll need all their gifts to solve the mystery.

Thanks for reading!

If you enjoyed this book, I'd love for you to help other readers find it by leaving a short, honest review on the site where you bought it.

And don't miss the next part of the Wilder siblings' story in book 2: *Dissonant State*. Available now:
www.jomiles.com/books/dissonant-state/

Dissonant State

In *Warped State*, Jasper Wilder's activism earned him dangerous enemies in Ravel Corporation. He knew that might come back to cause trouble for him and his partner, Havoc. But at least his family was safe...

Kay Wilder hates the corporate states, and none more than Ravel Corporation, whose devastating occupation of her home planet left Kay with a useful but debilitating ability to hear others' emotions. Unlike her brother Jasper, an activist who fights corporate injustice, Kay has always stayed as far away from Ravel as possible.

Until now. Because Ravel has kidnapped her brother, and there's only one way Kay can help him: she must go undercover working for the enemy.

Her assignment: help Ravel acquire a new member planet by winning over the local leaders. That means lying about what Ravel did to her home. It's more painful and lonely than Kay could have imagined, until she finds an unexpected ally in Ship, who hates working for Ravel as much as she does, and will risk exposure and destruction to help their first and only friend.

But the risks are far greater than Kay's and Ship's safety. Every day Kay works for Ravel takes them one step closer to completing the annexation. To save Jasper, she may have to let another world suffer her home planet's fate—and betray the cause her brother has risked his life for.

"Activists in space." Perfect for fans of Malka Older, Valerie Valdes, and Martha Wells, this gripping space opera is full of suspense, adventure, and heart.

Acknowledgements

Though it might seem solitary, writing a book takes a team. This particular book has had quite a journey, which has spanned a pandemic, political turmoil, and multiple reimaginings of this series.

I'm not the sort of person who loves waving signs or leading protests—I'm an introvert! There's a reason I'm a writer!—but I've worked behind the scenes at nonprofits for a long time, and I'm endlessly appreciative of all my friends and colleagues who are organizers. You helped inspire this story, and this book is dedicated to you. Thanks for making the world a better place.

Thank you to Shannon Page and Chelle Parker for helping get this book ready to go out into the world, and to Wendy Nikel for designing a phenomenal cover. And to Anne

Tibbets, for believing in this series and encouraging me to run with it.

This book wouldn't be what it is without the ever-insightful feedback of the Maryland Space Opera Collective, and to my communities at the Isle of Write and Codex. Shout-outs to Martin Sherman-Marks for helping me figure out the Kovars, and to Lisa Short for sharing your experience in pharmaceutical work. Extra special thanks to Karen Osborne and John Appel, my "siblings in ink," for your unflagging creative and moral support through every step of this journey.

I'm also deeply grateful to my parents, who've always supported and encouraged my writing.

Above all, thank you to my wonderful spouse. Thank you for believing in me through all the ups and downs. For being my first reader and my first fan. I love you so much.

And to Ada and Charlie: Yes, all that fur you shed onto my keyboard definitely helped. Keep up the good work.

About the Author

Jo Miles writes optimistic science fiction and fantasy, and their short stories have appeared in magazines including *Fantasy & Science Fiction*, *Strange Horizons*, *Lightspeed*, and more. This is their first novel. Fueled by tea and sunshine, they spend their time dreaming up strange new worlds and serving the whims of their two cats. They live in Maryland.

Find all of Jo's books and short stories at www.jomiles.com.